THE BIRTHDAY
PARTY

THE BIRTHDAY PARTY

Laurent Mauvignier

Translated from the French by
Daniel Levin Becker

**TRANSIT
BOOKS**

Published by Transit Books
2301 Telegraph Avenue, Oakland, California 94612
www.transitbooks.org

First published in France as *Histoires de la nuit* by Éditions de Minuit in 2020
© 2020 Éditions de Minuit
Translation copyright © Daniel Levin Becker, 2022
Originally published in English translation by Fitzcarraldo Editions in the UK in 2023

ISBN: 978-1-945492-65-5 (paperback)

LIBRARY OF CONGRESS CONTROL NUMBER: 2022945968

COVER DESIGN
Anna Morrison

TYPESETTING
Justin Carder

DISTRIBUTED BY
Consortium Book Sales & Distribution
(800) 283-3572 | cbsd.com

Printed in the United States of America

9 8 7 6 5 4 3 2

This project is supported in part by an award from the National
Endowment for the Arts.

There are secrets within secrets, though—always.
David Foster Wallace, *The Pale King*

1

She watches him through the window and what she sees in the parking lot, despite the reflection of the sun that blinds her and prevents her from seeing him as she'd like to, leaning against that old Renault Kangoo he's going to have to get around to trading in one of these days—as though by watching him she can guess what he's thinking, when maybe he's just waiting for her to come out of this police station where he's brought her for the how many times now, two or three in two weeks, she can't remember—what she sees, in any case, elevated slightly over the parking lot which seems to incline somewhat past the grove of trees, standing near the chairs in the waiting room between a scrawny plant and a concrete pillar painted yellow on which she could read appeals for witnesses if she bothered to take an interest, is, because she's slightly above it, overlooking and thus observing a misshapen version of it, a bit more packed down than it really is, the silhouette, compact but large, solid, of this man whom, she now thinks, she's no doubt been too long in the habit of seeing as though he's still a child—not her child, she has none and has never felt the desire to have any—but one of those kids you look after from time to time, like a godchild or one of those nephews you can enjoy selfishly, for the pleasure they bring, taking advantage of their youthfulness without having to bother with all the trouble that it entails, that educating them generates like so much inevitable collateral damage.

In the parking lot, the man has his arms crossed—robust arms extending from stocky shoulders, a thick neck, a prominent chest and a tuft of very straight chestnut hair that always makes him look unkempt or neglected. He's let his beard grow, not too thick a beard, no, but it doesn't suit him at all, she thinks, it only accentuates his air of gruffness, that impression he never fails to make on people who don't know him, also giving him a more peasant-like look—she couldn't say what a peasant-like look actually *is*—the image of a man who doesn't want to leave his farm and stays there, literally *cooped up*, scowling like an exile or a saint or, all told, like her inside her house. But for her it's not so bad, she's sixty-nine and her life is rolling quietly toward its end, while his, he's only forty-seven, still has a long way to go. She also knows that behind his gruff exterior he is in fact sweet and thoughtful, patient—sometimes probably too much so—and has always been obliging with her and with the neighbors in general, at any moment he'll lend a hand, of course, without a second thought, to anyone who asks, even if it's her he readily does the most favors for, like he's doing today by driving her to the police station and waiting to take her back to the hamlet so she doesn't have to ride her bike for something like seven kilometers both ways.

Bergogne, yes.

Even when he was a kid, she called him Bergogne. It happened simply, almost naturally: one day she addressed him by his last name to tease him; this amused the child and it amused her too, all because he often imitated his father, with that serious and furrowed look children sometimes have when they act like responsible adults. He was flattered, even if he didn't really pick up on the hard, ironic edge she took when she called his father by his last name, because often it wasn't so much to compliment him as to unleash a scathing comment his way or treat him the way an old schoolmarm scolds a kid, addressing him as sharply as possible. She and Bergogne senior argued readily, as a matter of habit, as one does among friends or close classmates, but anyway that no longer matters—thirty years, maybe forty? diluted in the fog of time passing—and none of it ever really mattered anyway, because they'd always been close enough to speak their minds candidly to each other, almost like the old couple they'd never become but had nonetheless, in a sense, been—a platonic love story that never found the space to play out, even in their dreams, for either of them—in spite of what the acid-tongued and the jealous might have insinuated.

It had remained after the father died: Bergogne. His last name for speaking to his son, to this particular son and not to the two others. Since then, if it's been without the slightest irony, just force of habit, it would still be with that same tone in her voice, at once harsh and with a hint of superiority or authority of which she wasn't even aware, when she called him to ask him to pick up two or three things for her at the Super U if he was passing through town, or to take her if he was going—a *town*, imagine calling it that, that village with its population of three thousand—but also with the sweetness of childhood he sensed behind her words,

Bergogne, I need a ride,

as though she were murmuring in his ear my little one, my boy, my kitten, my treasure, in a fold hidden within the coarseness of his name or that of her voice, in her way of saying it.

She used to come spend holidays here in a very elegant old house on the riverbank, and everyone looked at her like a grande dame, vaguely aristocratic but above all vaguely mad—a Parisian artist, exuberant and batty—wondering just what kind of peace she expected to find here, in La Bassée, reappearing as she did more and more often, staying longer and longer each time until one day she showed up for good, this time without a husband in tow—what she'd done with her banker husband was anyone's guess—come to settle down with some of his money, no doubt, even if nobody knew why she'd decided to bury herself in a dump like this when she could have settled some place in the sun, at the seaside, in regions that were more hospitable, milder, less ordinary, no, on this point nobody could say, they just kept wondering, because even if they're fond of their region people aren't stupid enough to not see how banal and ordinary it is here, how flat and rainy, with zero tourists to combat the boredom wafting from its trails, its streets, its waterlogged walls—and if not why would they all have dreamed at one point or another of getting the fuck out?

She'd said it was here and nowhere else that she wanted to live and age and die—let the others keep the Tuscan sun, the Mediterranean and Miami, thank you very much. She, crazy to her core, had chosen to settle in La Bassée and hadn't even wanted to buy or visit any of the three handsome houses in the center of town, which looked like surprisingly decent faux manor houses, in the grand style, with turrets, exposed beams, timber frames and dovecotes, outbuildings. No, she had wanted to live in the middle of nowhere, saying repeatedly that for her nothing was better than this nowhere, can you imagine, in the middle of nowhere, in the sticks, a place no one ever talks about and where there's nothing to see or to do but which she loved, she said, to the point that she finally left her old life behind, the Parisian life, the art world and all the frenzy, the hysteria, the money and the parties they imagined around her life, to come and do some real work, she claimed, to grapple at last with her art in a place where she'd be left the hell alone. She was a painter, and the fact that old Bergogne, the father, who sold her eggs and milk, who killed the fatted hog and bled it to its last drop in the yard, who spent his life in rubber boots covered in shit and animal blood, caked with soil in the summer and with mud the other eleven months of the year, that he, who owned the hamlet, should become her friend, this surprised people, and, bizarre as it seemed to those who wanted to suspect an affair, if only to make the whole thing imaginable and comprehensible, no, it had never happened, neither had ever shown the slightest attraction to the other, not the slightest amorous or erotic ambiguity, until one day he sold her one of the houses in the hamlet, making her his neighbor, further fueling the rumors and speculations.

All the same, it wasn't out of friendship or the desire to have her by his side each day that he sold her the semi-detached house; he had simply, after years of refusal, of stubbornly denying the obvious, resigned himself at last to selling the two houses that his last renters had left to go leap into the maw of mass unemployment deep in the housing projects of some midsize city, leaving him faced with this undeniable fact, this idea or rather this observation that tied his stomach and brain in knots, that all the young people were leaving, one after another, abandoning the hamlets, the farms, the houses and the businesses, a veritable hemorrhage to which, from where he stood, everyone was indifferent; of course nobody would stay, there was fuck all to do in La Bassée anyway, true enough, but there was a nuance between having fuck all to do and not giving a fuck at all that no one seemed to see, because no one wanted to see it. Bergogne's father had had to accept that his sons wouldn't stay either, that they wouldn't live with him in any of the houses in the hamlet and maintain the farm, as he would have liked, or else he'd believed until the end that they would, as he had done before them, and his own father before him.

His wife had died long ago, leaving him alone to deal with three sons; Bergogne père had hoped the three of them together would have a better shot at making the farm grow and prosper, but he must have finally understood that only Patrice would stay, the two youngest having quickly chosen to leave him, as one of the two had put it, deep in his own dung. They had both gotten the hell out as soon as they were of leaving age and there was, alas, nothing surprising about this, La Bassée had long been destined to waste away, to disintegrate into shreds, a world—his world— uniquely fated to constrict, to contract, to fade away until it finally vanished from the landscape completely—and they can call it desertification if they want, he brooded, as if to say it's a natural progression we can neither prevent nor reverse, but the truth is they just want us to croak without a word, with spittle on our lips but still standing at attention, good little soldiers to the end; La Bassée will disappear and that's that, it won't be the only nowhere of which there remains nothing but a name—a ghost on an IGN map—except La Bassée is such a banal name that four or five other places have it too, this particular Bassée not even being the one in the North, tucked between Arras and Béthune and Lille, a real city and not a village like this, anyway, all of it will be sucked up, swallowed down, digested and shat out by modern life and maybe it's just as well. It was all going to disappear, Bergogne père raged, not only the farms and all the hamlets with them but also the residential areas from the sixties that had sprouted before shrinking and withering without ever having had time to bloom, and the metalworks, which after many years of death throes had finally shut its doors like all the rest, just as the housing projects that had sprung out of the ground wound up ghost ships, like pustules on unhealthy skin, right when they all thought La Bassée was about to expand, with its brand new factories whose names sounded like Terminators and which were going to show the competition a thing or two, factories they didn't yet know were riddled with asbestos and carried inside them this revolting pestilence that would eventually kill off everyone to whom they once promised the good life.

So Patrice's two brothers followed the advice their mother had left them before she died, fucking off in unison, one going off to sell shoes near Besançon and the other, the one who was no doubt the cleverest of the three but also the most pretentious, going off to work *in finance,* as he said with enough contempt to let the others know he had no intention of living like a hick all his life, becoming a teller or an accountant at the Crédit Agricole of Bumblefuck—so long as it was far away from here he must have felt he was fulfilling a destiny—and no doubt living and working not in a city but in the interminable suburban periphery of one. The three brothers didn't get along and had stopped fighting after Bergogne père died, as though finally reaching the resentful conclusion of everything they'd shared since childhood: first games, then boredom and indifference, then irritation, and finally the desire that each strike out on his own, ideally as far from the others as possible. But he, whether he goes by Pat or Bergogne fils, by his first name, Patrice, or even just his last name, Bergogne, with his characteristic unhurried calm, his serene determination, coarse and unrefined, had said he didn't want to sell, that he would keep the farm and that he'd stay there until the end, come what may, which is to say at the geographical center of the family's history, eliciting their reprobation, their exasperation and their anger, but also their incomprehension—fine, they'd demanded, you find a way to pay us our share. Which he'd done, going into debt until the end of time and probably far beyond what was reasonable—but he had held tight and the farm remained in the hands of a Bergogne, as his father had wanted.

So, of the hamlet, the Bergognes still have the house where they live, some fields, about a dozen cows, and the milk, which Patrice supplies to the dairy that produces butter and cheese—not enough to live on, but enough to not die.

She, it turns out, had bought the house that abutted his, and has lived there for twenty-five years. Patrice has known her for at least forty, she's a face from his childhood, which is surely why he stops by to see her every day, why he's become attached to her, not as if to replace his own mother, who died too early from cancer, but simply because she's there, is a part of his life, having been present through his adolescence and his adult life and becoming, over the years, not a confidante or a simple reassuring presence to lean on but in a way his best friend, because, without having to ask her for anything, just by showing up at whatever moment of the day, by accepting a coffee and the hooch she serves him in a glass no bigger than a thimble or pours directly into the coffee cup, he knows he can trust her and she won't judge him, knows she'll always be there for him.

• • •

She thinks about all this—or rather it crosses her mind, Bergogne's story, as she watches him, observing the puddles in the parking lot still wet from the morning rain, despite the eye-burning light on the cracked, battered asphalt and the reflections of the white and blue-gray clouds in the puddles, the bursts of sunshine on the white body of the Kangoo, a white that turns blinding when the sun pierces through the steel-gray clouds; Bergogne takes a few steps as he waits for her, she keeps watching him and feels a bit guilty for making him waste his time, he has other things to do besides wait for her, she knows it, she's a bit vexed by all this time wasted because of some idiots who don't know what to do with their lives or how not to ruin other people's. But she can't pretend nothing's happening, it's a little different this time, she didn't want it to get more serious, and anyway he was the one who offered to bring her—she doesn't know why, since he was a child he's often made the first move, responding to desires she hasn't had time to articulate. He's always been this way with her, not because he wouldn't dare disappoint her, or because he's so intimidated by her and her appearance, which has always expressed something quite different from all he knows, and maybe something unsettling too, something ferocious, maybe, because with her long hair that she's always dyed orange, her makeup and her sometimes overly color-ful dresses, her thick plastic eyeglasses with a row of shiny baubles covering the frames, she could well have frightened an impres-sionable child in a region where no one ever even dreams of being so visible. No, though she's always been eccentric, he was never frightened or anxious, quite the contrary, he immediately felt a respect for her, a love, which she felt right back; and there, even in an unflattering backlight—he's gained a lot of weight since he got married—she's swept up in a wave of tenderness for him and for his patience; she only hopes she won't have to wait for hours, or rather that she won't make him wait for hours.

But no, no, she knows it won't be long. On the phone they promised her it wouldn't take too much time. And now what do you know, she hears steps, a movement behind her, a door opening and creaking, fingers tapping on a keyboard, a phone ringing, all at once the sound of the police station rises up in her, for her, as though she can finally perceive it, is finally here, as though by hearing the scrape of an office chair on the tile she's returned to the lobby of the police station and can finally feel the slightly warmer air of the radiator near the green plant, the odor of dust wafting from it and suddenly the voice of the officer calling her—she turns around and it's the same graying beanpole in front of her, the one from last time, who gave her his name and rank, which she forgot as soon as she left the police station, before she even got into Bergogne's car. This time she tries to remember his name at least, so much for the rank, a name that sounds Polish or Russian, like Jukievik or Julievitch, but it doesn't come to her right away, no matter, she's just entered his office and the officer invites her to take a seat.

He's extended his arm, hand open wide to indicate the black imitation leather chair that's hardly new—she notes the rips, like very fine flakes of skin, or rather like newspaper ashes flying above a fire in a fireplace—the officer's hand, thick and long, brown hairs mixed in with white, a silver wedding band, and, as she's sitting down, before she even has time to rest her back against the backrest or her buttocks on the base of the chair, just in the time it takes to begin the motion of sitting on the chair's edge, of placing her purse in her lap and starting to open it—fingers seeking the zipper—the officer will have had time to go around his desk and sit down in a firm, resolved motion, wedging his buttocks into the seat, and, without even realizing it anymore because unthinkingly he makes this same motion dozens of times a day, will, with a dry clack of his heels, move the chair closer to the desk by elongating both arms symmetrically, taking hold of the two edges of the desk to pull it toward him in a single gesture, there, hardly a thing, he won't even be aware of himself doing it and what he will see, on the other hand, is this orange-haired woman who, he'll have time to remember thinking the two previous times, must have been pretty, time to notice how obvious it is to him again, she must have been very pretty, which is to say that in spite of her age she still is, giving off a power, an elegance he already noted the two other times she came, yes, rare to see that, such an energy, something so lively and intelligent in the body and in the eyes. Now he looks at these hands that have taken an envelope from this dark red purse, practically black, just long enough to think *blood red,* and there it is, extending her arm toward him across the desk, she holds out the envelope and the anonymous letter she's just received.

Anonymous letters, yes, they can smirk all they like, or tell themselves with a knowing smile that it is perhaps, unfortunately, a French specialty, we'd have to see, all those stories from World War II, a rustic country specialty just like rillettes and foie gras in some regions, a loathsome tradition, quite pathetic and happily often without consequence, but one that all the same they can't take lightly, the officer explains as he explained last time, with fatalism and a touch of weariness or dismay, because, he repeats, behind an anonymous letter there's almost always someone embittered, someone jealous, an envier with nothing better to do than brood on their bile, thinking they can offload it by insulting a more or less fictitious enemy, by railing at them, by threatening them, by spewing warmed-over hatred at them through the intermediary of a sheet of paper; there's nothing we can do, and anyway, reading the letter she's handed him, or rather skimming it—he took out his reading glasses and hasn't even bothered to place them on his nose, just holds them a few inches from his face—while with the other hand he holds the sheet, even though the folds of the letter, the quarters, keep falling in on themselves, as though the letter is reluctant to reveal its contents, these words written on a computer, 16-point, in the most banal font imaginable, Courier New bold or something like it, all of it centered and printed on ordinary 80-

gram paper, he casts a quick glance, a long breath, a light shrug, murmuring,

Certainly it's not very pleasant.

But already he's put his glasses down and, with a sharp motion, as one does with a particularly insignificant object, he lets the letter fall back onto his desk—it rests on the fold for a moment before listing and then lying flat on one side—anyway, yes, we'll have it analyzed, but since that didn't tell us anything about the others I don't see why this one would give us anything more to go on. People are insane, but when it comes to the details they can be quite skillful, I'm sure there'll be no prints, nothing we can use.

He smiles as he says this, marking the end of his sentence with a frown, dubious or fatalistic, apologetic too, and he feels obliged to keep talking because the woman is waiting and because she's leaning on her seat, waiting for him to say something, so yes, he continues,

In general, letting off steam in writing is enough for them, all the energy they put into mailing their letter is tiring enough and they leave it there.

Except this letter wasn't mailed, she says, someone slid it under my door. Someone came all the way to my house for this.

The officer remains silent, he's just stumbled over his certitudes, over the strategies he tried to deploy so this woman would think it's not so serious, since after all they haven't stopped at merely insulting her, calling her a crazy woman, this time they're threatening her. She's noted how the officer stopped talking, watched a shadow of doubt cloud his facial expression, the corner of his mouth, eyes, eyebrows, right, right, right, he finally summarizes, how many residences where you live?

Just the hamlet.

Yes, and how many of you in the hamlet?

Three houses. Bergogne with his wife and daughter. The other house is for sale, and then there's me.

She is silent for a moment and, before he can respond, because she knows he has to respond, he owes her an answer, has to say something reassuring on behalf of the police, of the government and whatever else, he straightens in his chair and maybe makes it pivot, in the time it takes to blink he collects himself, but before he says anything, before he begins to sketch out what he means to tell her, she's the one who speaks,

But I can defend myself just fine you know,

almost raising her voice, responding in advance to what he'll surely say if she doesn't chime in fast enough,

I have my dog you know. I have my dog.

2

This blue, this red, this orangey yellow and these drippings, these green spots of uniform color, of glaze, and these unruly, ebullient shapes, these bodies and faces rising out of a deep dark brown, out of a halo of mauve, almost luminescent, or else conversely brushed, rough, rocky, shadowy, these shapes wrenched from the darkness by colored splashes; landscapes and bodies, bodies that are landscapes, landscapes that are something other than landscapes, that are organic lives, mineral lives, proliferating, invading the space, spreading out across the very large canvases she paints on— most often square formats, two meters, sometimes less, sometimes rectangular, but in that case vertical and almost never horizontal. When she was young she greatly admired Kirkeby and Pincemin, their earthy and colorful paintings, but that was so long ago that she feels that young woman she remembers was never really her.

In La Bassée, the names of contemporary painters mean nothing to anyone. Maybe the kind of painting she loves, or loved, means nothing to anyone and she can't talk about it with anyone, but so much the better, because she doesn't want to talk about what she does, she doesn't like to talk about painting or art, it's always exhausting and false to talk about art, always the same considerations, hollow and repetitive, interchangeable, things a bad painter or a good one could say equally legitimately because both are identically sincere and intelligent, even if only one of them has talent, has power, has form, an intuitive sense of the material and the conceptual, a vision, because to her artists are there to have visions, which is why she once made a series of Cassandras that she painted as though they represented fragility and truth lost in a world ruled by brutality and lies, thinking that artists either tell the truth or say nothing, and say it so much that they don't know they're saying it, even though nobody believes them, *because* nobody believes them. Don't speak, just paint, don't waste your precious strength splitting hairs to arrive at the same banalities as everyone else, just paint those promises words can't keep; have the vision of that which hasn't yet come to be, paint the apple while looking at the apple tree in flower, the bird in place of the egg, turn toward the future and welcome it for its mystery, not to be the one who knows before everyone else does, better than everyone else does, anything but that, not the way she did it for too long, when she was young, philosophizing and palavering about everything she held dear, slathering what she did with more than enough words to suffocate ten generations of artists—so no, not a word more, that'll do, for forty years she's tempered her tongue to open up her vision, to open herself up to her vision, to force her gaze to go deeper, the way one tries to see at night, to get used to the darkness. She has the good fortune of having an art that can speak without having to run its mouth, so she doesn't restrain herself, she found the right place for it when she bought this house that was in no way appropriate for a painting studio. She could have chosen a better house for it but she'd liked this one, having Bergogne's father as a neighbor was reassuring to her, the distance from town too, and anyway she had enough money to tear down the partitions that separated the living room from the dining room, to transform the whole thing into one immense room by straightening out the walls, putting in rails and panels to multiply the surfaces on which to hang canvases, optimize the space, mount special lamps, a whole system to get the perfect light, white and natural, without aggressiveness or distortion of color tones so as to avoid the unhappy surprise of discovering, as soon as she took a canvas out of her studio, a yellow where she thought she'd laid down a white. She didn't much care about destroying her dining room and her living room, clearing away what Bergogne's father had done with the house for the previous tenants; she'd paid for the right to destroy these rooms designed to receive guests, to host dinners and parties or to have a family life, to nurture relationships, everything she no longer had, everything she no longer wanted or had never wanted, and she'd paid dearly for this: for a house that would be her studio, because the whole point was for the studio to be in the house and not next door.

This way she can spend her time in the studio and come back into the entryway and the kitchen by crossing a space the size of a table, barely more; upstairs she's set up her bedroom and kept one of the two guest rooms, because old childhood friends still drop by sometimes, those who haven't forgotten her, who come to see her paintings and ask how she is or tell her how they are, who leave with paintings and sell them for her, even if she doesn't sell much anymore—they tell her she's not accommodating or pliant enough with the market, that she should show her face at art fairs a bit more often, which is to say at least once every now and then because in fact she never goes, she never answers invitations from the gallerists who used to like her work, nor mail from her old buyers or patrons, they tell her it's a shame she doesn't make more of an effort and that she's turning her back on everyone, a shame for her and for her painting but above all a shame for her audience, she has a duty to her audience, she who'd had one and eventually lost it through her negligence, really it's a shame—yes, no doubt, she answers, no doubt, but oh well, she's happy and she doesn't give it any thought, she certainly is a bit rigid and takes her painting too seriously, no question. In reality, it's just that when she paints she forgets that she's also supposed to play the artist who's successful at selling her work—which she could do, because she knows what she's doing, what she's painting, even if she lets herself get swept up and surprised by the images that come to life at her fingertips, she also knows inspiration never comes to anyone by chance and that you have to work, read, look, think, reflect on your work and, once the intellectual work is done, only then do you learn how to forget it, annihilate it, learn how to let go and allow this thoughtful conceptual world to be overrun by something that comes from beneath it, or beside it, that makes the painting surpass what you'd planned for it, when all of a sudden the painting is more intelligent, more alive, and crueler too, much of the time, than the person who painted it.

She knows this, she seeks the moment where it's the painting that sees her, that moment where the encounter occurs between herself and what she's painting, between what she's painting and herself, and of course this is something she doesn't share. She prefers for Bergogne, as he does every day when he comes over for lunch, to tell her about what he's doing in the fields, to tell her about the calves, about his ongoing work or about his wife Marion and about Ida—especially about Ida, whom she spends a great deal of time with, because every day, when she gets out of school, Ida comes over to have a snack and hang out here while she waits for her parents, who often come home late.

Today, Ida will come around five o'clock; she'll talk about what she did at school, and she, in turn, won't tell her that her father drove her this very morning to the police station, just as she'll keep Officer Filipkowski's words to herself—not that she's suddenly remembered his name, Officer Filipkowski's, just that she read it on the piece of cardstock he handed her at the end of their meeting, a card on which his name is printed, under which he'd added, in ballpoint pen, his mobile number, repeating two or three times,

You call me with the slightest concern,

insisting that she should call him if she received another anonymous letter, especially if this one was slid under her door, yes, like the Kraft paper envelope she found last night, late in the evening, which she told Bergogne about in the morning not so much out of fear as out of irritation and a more and more poorly contained anger,

These assholes are starting to piss me off.

Officer Filipkowski had been clear when he said that, even if they were vague, even if they were nutty and barely credible, they were still threats, the whole thing had gone up a notch, and not just because of the words but also because they had come, they had shown they were willing to venture all the way to her door. They were talking about burning orange-haired witches, after all, about cleansing the world of crazy women who'd be better off staying where they came from—were they blaming her for being Parisian, for not being from here? When she's lived here for so long?

She had an inkling that she was really being punished for sleeping with a married man or two—had something been said, noticed, guessed? or even confessed by the husbands themselves?—husbands with whom she'd probably made love a few times without there ever being any question of making them full-time lovers, much less husbands—no thank you, she'd had her fill of that—but maybe a woman wanted to get even or one of the men resented her for refusing to become his "official" mistress? And the police officer had again wanted to make her admit that she maybe did have an idea of who could be behind these letters, these threats, the insults polluting her head, because the words in these most recent letters sometimes kept her from sleeping, but she'd answered that no, she didn't know, and didn't need to lower her eyes or look away when she lied to the officer, she'd looked him right in the eye, what do you want me to say? an old maid like me, I haven't the slightest idea, I don't have any enemies and I don't know anyone. The officer had seemed perplexed, he had let a short skeptical silence linger, as though he understood that she hadn't told him everything and didn't intend to do so, that something in her was resistant to the idea of drawing up a list of potential perpetrators, of making herself an informer, knowing that in any case there was nothing they could prove against anyone.

All of this, of course, she wouldn't tell Ida when she came into her house. The little girl would put her backpack down in the hallway, which is to say the kitchen, and go wash her hands in the sink. She, as she'd done with Bergogne when she left the police station, would look innocuous, put on a quiet smile, speak in a soft voice,

Everything alright, sweetheart?

in the same tone as the one in which she'd agreed to tell Bergogne two or three details, as thanks for the time he'd lost because of her. She owed him at least a summary of what they'd told her, you know, nothing special, cops are like doctors, they make these mournful faces to tell you something serious, and afterwards when you think about what you heard you realize they don't know any more than you do. She'd told him they'd check the letters to make sure they were from the same person, and then she'd added, half exasperated and half amused by the assumption: as if I had enough enemies for it to be a different madman each time—I'm sure it's actually a woman, a madwoman, I just know it, the last time I went to the dance I did spend a lot of time with you know who, right?

Bergogne had just smiled; he had his guess but wouldn't ask her whether he was right. She'd kept talking while the Kangoo cruised toward the hamlet, then eventually they'd fallen silent, and she, just for the sake of changing the subject—because none of this is worth the time it takes to tell, right, don't you think?—had said, Bergogne, my boy, your beard is ridiculous and it looks terrible on you. It makes you look ten years older, do me a favor and shave it off, okay? And if not for me, at least do it for your wife, may I remind you that tomorrow's her birthday and even if that was your only gift to her she'd be grateful until the end of time.

Now she's seated in the middle of her studio and, amid the jumble of all her canvases—those hanging on the walls, those just leaning against something, those piled on the stairs leading up to the bedrooms, those not yet framed and still lying around rolled up like calico—she looks at the one in front of her, right in the middle of the room, resting there, stapled to the wall she prefers to work on, not yet framed: the portrait of the red woman.

She knows it's finished, that it's done—it still needs a bit of blue near the eyes. She hesitates to go any further, tells herself that whatever she does nothing more can fundamentally alter the painting, nothing more can deepen it, that to deepen it would be to risk destroying it; the red woman is naked, her body entirely red—a red that's almost orange, but the shadows are a very pure, vibrant red, vermillion, a shadow that's a colored light and not a dark shade of color, which changes everything, an effect she had great difficulty producing. The red woman pierces, with her stillness, anyone who raises their eyes to her; her portrait looks, perhaps, like the one of that little girl who was the source of her entire desire to paint, because when she began painting, long ago now, it was initially to exorcise a photo by David Seymour that had long obsessed her, a portrait of a little Polish girl drawing her childhood house on a blackboard, in an asylum. The child is tracing, in chalk, a circle of fire, the destruction ravaging the drawing; above all you see the terror in the eyes of the little girl in black—that's what the photographer captures. She had seen this image and the only way she could forget it, or manage to live with it, had been to paint it; this was her first black-and-white painting, a large painting, the little girl lost in the shining white of the canvas, her gaze wild and steady. Now, more than forty years later, the red woman she's just finished, she thinks, has almost the same hallucinatory expression—she carries the fire of a house destroyed, annihilated, her breath as if mimicked by the blasts of the bombs exploding on the city. She thinks about this in front of the red woman, in the middle of her studio, and she doesn't hear her German shepherd, who was asleep next to her not two minutes ago. She waits for something to match what she's watching for, a sign of life, because life must come from the painting.

Now her dog gets up because he's heard someone coming, or not coming yet but he knows it's time, between four forty-five and four fifty-five depending on traffic. At the end of the pebbly path leading from the hamlet to the poorly tarred road where they leave the trash bins, a road that joins the county road they take to go into the town of La Bassée, the school bus will stop, its door will open, and Ida, with two children from the neighboring hamlets, will get off. The door will have barely closed behind them with the creak of its hydraulic suspension when the three children part ways or keep giggling for another few minutes, exchange a few more words, then set off, one toward the west, the other toward the east, the third to the north; Ida will walk and keep her hands on the straps of her backpack, paying no attention to the road in front of her—she knows all too well the moment when the poorly tarred road, worn out and hollowed by successive winters and summers, cold and rain, heat and tractor wheels, turns left and leaves the strip of tar behind to become a white gravel path, blinding in the summer but muddy most of the time, and then almost red, or rather ocher, yellow, as it is now, full of the rain that fell all night and into this morning, cluttered with deep wide brownish puddles that she has to walk around and sometimes likes to jump over, with, at the end, the hamlet and the rooftops of the three houses, the barns and the stable, her house, the rooftops green in places because of the moss and the vegetation that have invaded the walls and spread all the way up to the rooftops; there's the hamlet, like a closed fist in the middle of the cornfields and the pastures where the cows spend their days grazing; there are also the trees lining the river that separates the land into two administrative departments; on the other side, a white tuffeau stone church, and here, on our side, poplars all in a row, like an army standing guard, lining and shading the river. But all of that is still far off, it takes a while to get there on foot, and also to get across that tiny little wild wood, like a square of trees parked in the fields, trees whose leaves and branches you can hear rustling as soon as the wind blows in from the right direction, bringing birdsong too, and where the foxes live who hang around a little too close sometimes—they saw one in the yard, very early one morning, before leaving for school.

But this evening Ida is interested only in the tips of her toes: how, with her yellow sneakers, she can roll the sole on the pebbles and sometimes pass over them, and sometimes on the other hand strike them, launch them, send them rolling into the distance. She knows, Ida does, as she steps over the puddles, as she leaps across the biggest ones, making her backpack bounce on her back, that when she arrives, barely through the big gate that will surely be open, on the left, in the stable, her father will be looking after his cows or fiddling with she never knows what, in the shed or in the yard, always in his oil-blue coveralls; he won't see her and she won't try to bother him. No, she'll go immediately to the right, into the first house, across from the French window with the German shepherd behind it waiting for her, because that's what Rajah does every day.

She'll open the door and take the dog's head in both hands, stroke his ears while he tries to lick her, lifting his face toward her, whining with pleasure, and she'll nuzzle him, repeating,

Hello pup, how's my little pup?

and she'll keep going because the front door opens directly into the kitchen, where she'll drop her backpack without a moment's thought, always in the same place, to the left of the door. She'll go wash her hands in the sink, dry them, cross the kitchen and go immediately to the studio; she won't ask any questions, even if inwardly she'll wonder which painting is waiting for her today, will it still be that horrible old red lady who seems to ogle people, threatening to do who knows what, showing her big breasts and her thighs opening up, obscene, to reveal that sex, laid bare without shame, the red woman exhibiting it insouciantly, without provocation or anything else, just like so, just her body which Ida doesn't like because the woman looks severe, looks above all like she's provoking her, as though she has something against her—why are you painting this old lady, anyway? I like the animals and the landscapes you do and even the other women, but this one, I'm sorry, she scares me—that's what she might say if she dared, but she won't dare and won't say anything.

They'll go into the kitchen, Tatie will give her her snack and drink her tea standing up against the stainless steel sink, listening to what happened at school. Then, after the snack, they'll go draw: Ida has promised to make some drawings as gifts for her mother's birthday, and Tatie has promised to help her.

Ida hopes Tatie will like them, her drawings, because Tatie's opinion counts for her almost as much as her mother's.

3

Are you going to give Mom a present?

asks Ida as her teeth crunch into dried grapes and almonds and rolled oats, eating voraciously, as she does every day, what Tatie has prepared for her even though she claims, as she does almost every afternoon, making a pretense of pushing the cereal bowl aside, that she's not really very hungry, no, not really, although you just have to insist a bit or, conversely, act like you're not insisting at all, to tell her with a shrug that you'll just clear away the cereal bowl then, for her to pull it back immediately and say wait, I'll have a little, already making a show of picking at it, as she does every time, before finally gobbling it all up; but it's true that today is a special day, and even though she's hungry she doesn't want to waste her time eating, no, she's in a hurry this afternoon, she and Tatie are going to make paintings for her mother's birthday, because tomorrow—and this is no small matter, it's even kind of an event—Marion turns forty.

Ida still hasn't prepared anything, having pushed off for weeks the moment she'd have to make something herself because she didn't buy a gift like her father had suggested, which she didn't do for lack of a compelling idea, thus condemning herself to the work before her now. Two days ago Tatie suggested that they make drawings or paintings, and Ida said okay, sure, why not, with more resignation in her voice than excitement. But now that she's turned it over in her head, the idea excites her as though it were her own. Tatie promised to lend her gouache or watercolors, and paper like she uses sometimes, with a special grain that holds in the paint, or even a painting board, or even a canvas on a small frame—square or landscape format. Except Ida thought about it and decided she didn't feel up to painting on a canvas, no, ultimately she prefers to try her hand at a drawing, the kind she's been making since she was little, on humble sheets of A4 paper, the same ones she's always written on, drawn on, colored on, painted on, except for those few times when she was five or six, when she'd indulged in long sessions where she and Tatie would lay out a canvas of several square meters on the ground, bigger than a bedsheet, white, a bit sticky, whose *shlock!* she remembers vividly when she lifted her bare knees off the canvas, just as she remembers how hard they laughed, how they both sloshed around in the acrylic colors they'd used to paint—with their bare hands, their feet too, finally flopping their whole bodies down, rolling in it as though they were swimming in swampy, gluey water.

Now Ida prefers to paint with gouache, adding words written in marker, a different color for each letter. She's impatient to start, which is why she scarfs down her snack quickly, rushing to put the bowl in the sink and run her hands under the water—quickly and poorly dried using the too-damp dishrag hanging from the cupboard underneath the sink, there we go—is Tatie also going to make a painting for her mother, she wonders, just as she wonders sometimes whether she would take offense at hearing herself referred to the way her parents refer to her, by her first name, Christine, thinking that surely Tatie wouldn't be against it, she's almost positive.

It's just that Ida has never been able to change or imitate her parents on this point, she can't hear the name *Christine* in her own mouth, it's as though in her mouth it sounds wrong, as though it applies not to her Tatie but necessarily to someone else, because that name sounds too distant from both of them, from their relationship, from what they share between them, within the secrecy of what they feel for each other. It seems to her that Christine prefers to hear herself called Tatie—by her, in any case—so that's fine, in any case Ida could call her by any name in the world and ultimately it wouldn't do anything to change the mystery whereby, as soon as Ida mentions her mother, Tatie dodges the question or even sometimes pretends she didn't hear it. Ida doesn't dare ask her if she has a reason for avoiding talking about Marion, if it's all just in her head or if there's something amiss between them, if what Tatie thinks of Mom means she can't say it, so as not to hurt Ida's feelings, as though Tatie thinks Ida is too fragile to hear true things or disagreeable thoughts, maybe cruel ones, shameful or undignified thoughts, as though it were possible for Tatie to feel bad thoughts toward anyone at all, in particular toward one of her parents, toward someone she loves, and, beyond that, as though it were possible—conceivable—for her to think something bad about her mother, because Ida doesn't see what bad things anyone could say about her mother.

She's always had the feeling that they keep watch on each other, hold their tongues, see to it that everything goes smoothly even if, well, you can tell they're pretending a little, but Ida doesn't see what Tatie Christine could have against Marion, and even if she can tell something is a source of friction between them—but what?—it can't be anything serious, even if you can sense, inside this peace that both women maintain, something artificial between them, maybe effort or affectation, what else, a form of reticence or restraint, even if Ida really doesn't see what Tatie could think about Mom that's so strange that she can't tell her. And yet, yes, Christine, suddenly sharper, more abrupt when she talks about Marion. Almost cutting. Or on the contrary, she starts asking questions, she acts like someone with a problem to solve who's just thinking out loud, she wants to know what they're saying at the house and doesn't dare ask outright, she wants to satisfy her curiosity and hide it at the same time, to not show she's interested in things that don't concern her, that aren't her business, intimate things Mom and Dad say to each other, or don't say. She asks the strangest questions sometimes, almost lowering her voice, as though asking incidentally, casually, but because she lowers her voice it's as though she's afraid to be heard—by whom?—as though she's about to ask strange, possibly forbidden things that would be best kept to oneself.

For now, as they're setting up the gouache and the paper on the kitchen table, Ida pushes the point a bit, Tatie, are you going to give Mom a present? Christine does eventually answer, but not right away, first she wipes down the table with a sponge, then with the dishrag, looking so focused on what she's doing, or on the answer, which she has to think about, it takes some time, that for a long while the kitchen is silent except for the clock ticking on the wall, is it because she doesn't know how to answer, because she doesn't want to, because she'd rather talk about something else or not talk at all? Ida doesn't know, she can feel Christine holding back, and just as she's about to ask the question once more Christine begins to stutter, drowning in erms that are uncomfortable for both of them, hesitations that are out of character, she doesn't usually speak haltingly, quite the contrary, and so gathering herself up to power through the awkwardness, she finally takes the plunge, yes, a present, of course, I should, I, and then stopping midflight, as though even she's surprised not to have an answer to give, she nods, shrugs her shoulders in a sign of impotence or resignation, you win, well done, it's true, I don't have a present.

But she doesn't say this, and now Ida is already repeating her question, insisting, though not pushily, almost playfully, as though she can't imagine that this question could be awkward, or that the discomfort she's creating in Christine could betray not only the bother of not having thought of a present but also the truth revealed behind the forgetting, the lack of interest it shows in the little girl's mother's birthday, or not only in her birthday but, via her birthday, in Ida's mother herself.

Are you going to give Mom a present?

I don't know. I'd need some time, I don't really have any ideas. And in slightly too quick a motion, Christine goes to pour more tea. Ida sees her turn away and refill her cup; she watches her, from behind, leaned over, and she waits. Christine turns around and says yes, I should, it's true that I didn't think about it, didn't take the time… She watches the little girl with her elbows spread apart on the table, settled firmly on the oilcloth with its old pattern of wildflowers lacerated by knife cuts and blanched by tracks of sponge and scouring powder, her hands up close to her face, her chest leaned down so close to the table and the paper on which she's about to draw, her frail arms and her long thin fingers, her delicate face, her eyes so black and shiny, lively, intelligent, almost combative, and then the hair with its butterflies and hearts holding back the longest locks to leave her forehead and eyes uncovered, her face turned toward Christine—her face waiting for answers, needing to understand why these hesitations and these silences, these prevarications before answering, when it should be so simple, her question is a simple one, it's as simple as answering it, she can't imagine Christine won't answer that of course she's made a present, Ida will discover it tomorrow when her mother does, at the birthday party; she doesn't understand this discomfort and Christine can sense it in the very short silence that follows, Ida almost annoyed, look, I'm giving her a drawing, you could give her a painting, couldn't you?

So Christine launches into an explanation that she means to make simple and clear and that she's muddying without really realizing it, yes, you're right, but I'm not sure she likes my paintings very much. You know… not everyone likes them. Some people don't like them, I mean really, not at all… A lot of times people don't say anything because they don't want to hurt your feelings, or because they don't know how to say it… your mother, I think, after all this time, she must not like my paintings very much… And Christine won't tell Ida how much people's silence, no matter how considerate it's meant to be, is hurtful, how it negates you more surely than if you didn't exist, because you're taking a risk by giving these people something and they should be beholden to you for it, that's what she thinks, Christine, who used to suffer from the indifference, at her openings, of certain so-called friends who preferred to talk to her about the quality of the champagne or about her new haircut than about her paintings, yes, she could have killed them for it, and here, now, Christine can't explain to Ida that that's one of the reasons she finally came to hide out here in this hamlet so long ago, to avoid those little stab wounds of hurtful phrases and condescending smiles, of murderous silences.

Flowers, yes, an English garden full of flowers, a jumble of spots and colors from which a sense of harmony will still emerge, as though the confusion produced not the disorder we tend to associate with it but a surprising order, distinct from the more conventional, banal order of a proactive arrangement; amid the flowers a drawing of a woman, colorful as well, nameless flowers that exist nowhere but on this paper with gouache petals enhanced with marker, detailed with lines that assimilate the contours and articulate this portrait that's meant to look like her mother but whom Ida first drew as a bony and exaggeratedly stretched-out little girl, endlessly rangy, as though to Ida her mother is just an elongated version of a child, as though to her an adult's body is nothing but childhood in a larger format, without body hair or hips or breasts or any of that, none of which she sees, none of which she seems to pay any attention to, because it's herself that she's drawing, projecting herself into an adult life that's something like an exaggerated childhood. Above her mother's face she's written the words "happy birthday mom" in capital letters, a different color for each letter, alternating warm and cool colors. She's taken care to replace the O in "mom" with a drawing of a very red heart, pink inside with a tiny heart at its center, yellow, then an even brighter yellow inside of that, as though it were molten, irradiant, and for the pleasure of continuing to draw and color and paint

with Tatie's doting eye over her shoulder, her suggestions, her en-
couragements, because she likes to know Christine is nearby, sometimes laying a hand on her shoulder, furrowing her brow, pausing to
think before she encourages her to try this or that approach—why
not make a path through your flower garden? And why don't you
put a few warmer touches here, see, they're blue, green, don't you
think a bit of yellow and red would wake the whole thing up?—
Ida has started another painting, with a heart that fills the whole
page and is expanding, growing, seeming ready not only to spill off
the page but to swallow everything, a heart *this big,* that's what she
writes inside, in a spiral,

Mom I love you with all my heart this big.

This one is less colorful than the other but she likes it a lot,
she likes the idea of the words spiraling off toward the heart of the
heart, but she needs her father's opinion, definitely, will Patrice
prefer it to the other one, the drawing with the flower garden
and Mom inside, in the middle, Mom like a queen in her garden,
lulled or even dazed by the thick perfume of the flowers, knowing
that in this kind of garden there will never be bees or wasps, no
mosquitoes either, just beauty—a beauty that doesn't fade, doesn't
get you dirty, doesn't sting, doesn't hurt, that just spreads its perfumes, its lights, its splendor throughout the world, asking nothing
in return but our wonderment—Mom in her dress and especially
in the hoop earrings she likes to wear when she goes out dancing
with her girlfriends some Friday nights.

Ida wonders which of the two drawings Patrice will prefer.
He'll definitely need to choose; she thought she could maybe give
them both as presents but since she's not sure of herself, because
she's always been afraid of doing something wrong, she needs her
father—his permission, almost, to validate what she's done. She
crosses the yard, followed by Rajah, whom she asks

What do you think Rajah?

and since he seems uninterested she tells him you're right, it's
not interesting, I can't draw like Tatie, Tatie knows how to draw

and paint and make up images, she's really good at making things up, she's so good at looking that afterwards it's not hard for her to reproduce all the things she managed to see, it's like it just goes from her head to her fingers without any effort; she's lucky, Tatie, that she knows how to do that. There are people who know, but me, she thinks as she enters the stable, where she's greeted by the cool air and the earthy, grassy odor of cows and hay, by the smell of milk too and of the animals themselves, their excrement and the flies it attracts, with their formidable lowings that seem multiplied by the ceiling and the cinderblock walls, but me, I don't know.

She's always overwhelmed when she comes in here. She knows Patrice doesn't like her to come, he always has lots of work to do with the animals; it's his territory, and no one but him and the veterinarian and these cows is allowed to be here. And anyway it's not a place to talk, no, it's a place where Patrice spends a lot of time milking the cows and looking after them, cajoling them, taking the time to care for them, and if Patrice doesn't want Ida to come here it's because these dairy cows aren't enough to make a living from, and he has to sell off all the calves born throughout the year for their meat. He doesn't want Ida to go near them, he's worried she'll get attached and want him to stop selling them, or that she'll be too sad about it, that it won't take much for her to hold it against him, calling him all kinds of names, getting who knows what kinds of ideas about him when even he has to admit he has a hard time watching them go, these calves with whom he forges a tender, almost paternal sort of bond each year. He feels it but he pushes it down into himself, this stirring that would have him not send the animals to the slaughterhouse, and he pulls himself together, his father did it in even greater numbers, and the pigs wound up there too, so why is he so reluctant about it when it has to be done and he couldn't make ends meet without it, especially since, when he goes hunting on Sundays, he doesn't have the same qualms about the game, the partridges and the hares, the pheasants and all the rest. But it's also that he's sensitive to the fact that intensive farming ruined his father's life and the lives of the farmers in the region—along with others more or less his age and the few young people who still go into this crazy line of work, he wants an agriculture at a human scale, considerate of animals and of men. He's proud of his creamery and of selling to a cheesemonger who doesn't try to haggle too much—his clients are loyal, a good number of them too, even if Patrice also knows that at the slightest incident it'll be a catastrophe; he borrowed a fair amount of money so everything has to stay on track, and so far, even if he has no margin for error and he sometimes lets fear overtake him, he has long spells of insomnia, you could say it's more or less on track, and that if he's lost sleep it's not because of this or not primarily because of this. The real reasons for his insomnia—he knows what they are. He works like a maniac to keep them at bay. He spends time in his fields, what he does doesn't much resemble the agriculture his father practiced, that's true, he has a wife and a little girl to feed, and when he sees Ida running toward him, her eyes shining with mischief, so alive, so joyful, he knows he's right to be wary of pesticides, even if he hates the eco-warrior types who hate him right back—he knows his daughter's future is the only thing that should matter.

Dad, dad, tell me, tell me,

One after the other she unveils the images: the immense heart, colored like a rainbow, with its declaration unfurling in a spiral, and the other, the flower garden. She waits, dances in place,

Okay, which one? Which do you like more?

Patrice hesitates—pretends to hesitate, to prolong the suspense—and he doesn't answer her right away, he purses his lips, ah yes, which one, that's tricky, he doesn't know, he hesitates some more, still pretending to think, looks from one back to the other and finally he says,

Both, I like them both!

No, you have to pick one.

I can't.

You have to pick!

I can't, I'm just a big old bear.

And before she can protest in the slightest, he takes a step toward her, letting out a growl that thunders in a way she'd never have thought him capable of. She loves these moments when he pounces on her, she screams and laughs at once, she backs away at a run, letting out little shouts throughout the yard, shrill as a flight of swallows over the yard of the hamlet, then she takes off with a great laugh that carries all the way to Christine's house.

Crossing the yard, Ida can feel how hard her heart is beating, as though she too lives with a wild beast right in the middle of her chest.

4

Like all localities, the hamlet has its name posted when you arrive: a long horizontal signboard with white italic letters on a black background, like a banner of mourning for some sordid story or maybe the credits of a movie that didn't get filmed, its title more or less promising a sequence of events, a story, except nobody remembers having read or written it, or having ever known anything of its origins, as though it has no actual beginning and has always just been there, Three Lone Girls Stead, floating above the passage of time thanks to a sign tilted slightly over the edge of a ditch, its base stuck into a mildew-covered cinderblock held in place by a stone that someone must have put there one day to root the sign to this spot where the asphalt road gives way to a gravelly path.

Nobody ever stops in front of it or reads it; the sign could disappear without anyone noticing. When she moved here, Christine went to the town hall to inquire about the name—she'd known Rhonne, L'Hospital, The Two Hanged Men, Griefshield, Whitestone, Blackbramble, The White Horse—names with strange, most often poetic sonorities redolent of the bitterness of olden times, rising up like miasmas from the sewer and memories of mass graves, with their witch burnings and religious wars, their unverifiable persistent legends of characters and events that must have been true for long enough that their names were eventually engraved somewhere in reality. Christine did some research and learned that a stead is a kind of hamlet and that people had been living here for a long time, since long before the Bergognes and the three houses, but she never found anything about the three lone girls, no one knew or seemed to have ever known who they might have been, and it occurred to Christine that people must have looked at these women in the past the way she sometimes felt people looked at her, with suspicion and mistrust, using her to fuel their malicious gossip, just as they must have done at one point with these three girls who no longer existed anywhere but in the name of the hamlet that served as their grave, as a memorial, as though by sinking into oblivion, perhaps by seeking it, they had found a refuge in the very name people were only too happy to give them.

Ida left her father to work and crossed the large square yard, this well-trodden, even downtrodden earth where there are still some stunted gray tufts from an old lawn that hadn't withstood the bad weather or the cows' hooves, the weight of the tractors and machine tools and cars, and above all the lack of upkeep, because neither Bergogne's father—whose idea it had been, and who had sown the lawn before forgetting about it and abandoning it entirely—nor Patrice really cared, no one had ever had the time or the desire, no more the women of the house who worked on the farm, in the fields, or anywhere else, some in the factory or cleaning homes for old people, than the kids—Patrice's two brothers, the last to be referred to as *the kids,* with that hint of irony subtly denouncing some real or imagined heedlessness—who wouldn't have thought to lift a finger even if the notion of maintaining the lawn had crossed their mind, which in any case it never did. The yard was also too big, the ground hard as rock, packed down, compressed, compacted by generations of people and animals trampling it.

The yard is surrounded by high walls, not quite two meters, lower than those of a barracks or a fortress, like in all the hamlets in the area, a reprise of feudal sovereignty; the two houses, Christine's and Bergogne's, are set in a row on the right; continuing counter-clockwise there's the shed where Patrice parks his car and the tractor, where Marion parks her car too, because obviously she has one, as everyone does in the countryside, all of them stuck by definition several kilometers from the city where they have to go from time to time and where she, for her part, goes every day. You need your own car if you want to get around freely, which everyone accepts without question except for Christine, who, by taking rides from other people or riding her bike, except when she decides to walk, which she usually does, continues to demonstrate without even trying that she's not like the people from around here, an incurable city dweller stranded among the rurals, and even though she's shared this life with them for so long it's as though she wants everyone to know beyond any doubt that she'll never be completely assimilable, no more than she was back in the heart of her Parisian life, always balking at any suggestion of belonging, as though she presumed, through signs as quiet and desultory as not knowing how to drive, to be able to escape the dominion of a community and the custody of a group.

Past the shed, still going counter-clockwise, there's the stable, next to the shed made of sheet metal and cinder blocks, then to the left of the stable a barn that serves as a dumping ground, whose roof will soon cave in if something isn't done and which is being overtaken by rust because it rains abundantly on it all winter; old farming machines, a tractor—a vintage 1954 Babiole Multi Babi on which you can still see, here and there, cracked and burst, the sky-blue paint that hasn't been devoured by rust yet—an old McCormick riding mower and a ping-pong table, two Peugeot 103s, a broken-down Motobécane 41; then coming back toward the gate and Christine's house, onto which the yard opens, that thick wall, cracked over its entire length. And so, side by side, like twin sisters, Christine's house and the Bergognes', and hiding behind Christine's, more independent, isolated, with its smaller and better-kept yard than the Bergognes'—a real lawn, clumps of perennials, an English-style hodgepodge, a gravel path, trimmed fruit trees, a well that's strictly decorative but whose stone has been cleaned and its ironwork repainted—another house, this one for sale, the former owners having just retired to a house by the sea, practically across from Fort Boyard—better than it looks on TV.

At home, on the orange oilcloth on the kitchen table, Ida is about to do her homework; it's high time, the minutes are rolling by, the hour is getting late, soon it'll be evening. Ida left her two paintings at Christine's house, thinking that in the end her father wasn't wrong, there was no reason she had to choose between the two, her love for her mother was great enough to include a heart *this big* and a colorful flower garden at the same time. Ida has to do her homework, even if today she won't give it the time or attention she should; she made the paintings for her mother's birthday, which took her some time, and of course she messed up, had to start over, ruin three sheets of paper for nothing, then clean Christine's paintbrushes and the table, and finally put everything away before crossing the yard to show her father the two paintings—or drawings, she says painting and drawing interchangeably because to her painting is still just a kind of coloring in of shapes that were drawn first—and then going back to Christine's to put the totally dried sheets, which had started to crinkle, on the kitchen table.

She picked up her backpack and ran back to her house. Ida set her backpack down on the kitchen table. She opened it and the folders slid out along with the school planner and two or three other things—a ruler, a pencil sharpener which she carelessly put back in her bag; she took the folder she needed and the ballpoint pen from her pencil case, she told herself she wouldn't spend too much time on it, she couldn't get it all done, or at least not very well, wouldn't be the first time, nobody's going to check, but at the very moment she was getting down to it, as though everything was arranged so she'd get to school tomorrow without having had time to do any of it—oh well—she doesn't like conjugations anyway, and math even less—that blessed instant, as it were, delaying once more the moment she'd have to get down to it, was the second she heard the telephone ring out in the living room.

Mom, is that you?

Ida already knows her mother is going to tell her she has lots of work at the office that she's behind on and that yes, she probably won't be home before night falls—Ida imagines her speaking as she does when she's on the phone at home, reflexively wandering toward the table after she's pressed the cell phone between her ear and her raised left shoulder, which she lifts as high as she can against her tilted head without even realizing it, already starting to speak, her tone transforming, cheerful all of a sudden, lively, amused or simply reinvigorated as though it's just been roused by a breath of fresh air or a piece of good news, and without even noticing Marion takes her pack of cigarettes and her lighter from the table, she rushes outside as though fleeing this house where her family life is keeping her locked up inside the all-permeating love of Ida and Patrice, both of them too demanding or inquisitive for her, and now Ida imagines herself, as she talks to her, listening to her mother's words and through them her breaths, her restarts, the sound of her sucking on her cigarette, the moment she breathes in and pulls on the filter, the smoke escaping from between her teeth and rising to dissipate in the sky—the motion of her neck when Marion lifts her head and seems to breathe out toward the clouds as if to push them farther away—things she does without realizing it but that Ida knows by heart, like the inflection of her voice when she calls to say she'll have to be home late because of work, always half joyful and half ashamed, not asking permission but waiting to be excused, her voice cheerful like it is every time, and like every time, and like today too, Ida answers her mother in the same cheerful and lively tone; she talks, restarts, recounts with that slight excess that yes, her day was great, yes, everything is good, and she forces that tonality of joy because she knows Marion wants to hear that everything is good, always good; they joke, as though the telephone's primary purpose weren't for Marion to announce that she'll be back late, as though it were worth specifying, it happens so often, she has lots of work at the printing shop so she really has to, that's how it is, like every time Ida knows what her mother is going to say, take your bath sweetie if you want us to have time to eat dinner together, or else you'll have to have dinner all alone, there's chicken in the fridge, or you can ask Tatie but you know how to manage by yourself, and if you prefer then take your bath.

Like every time, Ida will talk about Tatie; this time it'll be about that horrible red woman who strips her bare with those eyes that seem to have seen the end of the world or who knows what, she says, forcing herself to laugh gently at Christine, because she knows that with her mother she can mock Tatie gently, slyly, as if to bring them closer together, not to criticize or badmouth her, it's not out of ill will or nastiness, it's just for fun, Ida believes this without any ulterior motive. She'll talk about the red woman and her mother will put on her offended voice, her scandalized tone— this will make her crack up, to hear her mother get up on her high horse—saying I don't want you looking at such monstrous things at your age, who ever heard of such dreadfulness, making the little girl laugh, starting to laugh herself, knowing that neither one of them believes her anger but they enjoy the lie. This will last a few minutes, and like every time Marion will finally say she has to go, her boss is eavesdropping on her, which Ida knows, of course, if her mother is taking the time to call her it's because she's stepped out of her office, she's in front of the entrance to the print shop with her cigarettes in one hand and her phone in the other, and she imagines that as she talks Marion must be raking the gravel with the tip of the sole of her shoe, tracing semicircles and lowering her eyes, occasionally glancing toward the reception area and the two girls at the front desk.

Marion won't tell Ida that once she hangs up the phone she'll throw away her cigarette—what's left of it, the butt too short, smoked almost to the filter, which she'll grind out with a motion as furious as her smile will be fake when she passes her boss in the hall, offering him—take a good look asshole—a furious smile, knowing perfectly well that he's ogling her—go on, take a good look—and that she'd only have to give him a look for him to feel entitled to cheat on his wife, to whom he swears his fidelity constantly simply because he doesn't have the means or the opportunity to cheat on her. She knows he's only looking at her so scornfully, so smugly, because he doesn't have a chance with her—she knows this feeling, this resignation that rises up from very deep—he'll say to her in the same fake-casual tone, so, Mrs. Bergogne, another cigarette break? to which she'll reply with the same rictus fixed to her lips, not teasing but sarcastic, playing the airhead he wants to see her as, oh you're so sweet to look out for my health, giving him the finger as soon as his back is turned— fucking loser—like almost every day.

Marion needs to get back to her two colleagues quickly; they're behind on a lot of work and will need to buckle down, though in the meantime they'll mess around too, Lydie saying, you know the guy we met at karaoke the other night? She'll use the setup to say she thought he was pretty good-looking but then she realized—what an idiot she was, just terrible, no really, I swear, I realized he works at the same company as my husband. They'll have a good laugh, resolve to go back to karaoke soon or go dancing one of these Friday nights. Maybe Lydie will complain that she can't go out with her girlfriends, Nathalie might envy Marion's freedom,

I mean, how do you do it? He's pretty chill, your man. He looks after the little one, lets you go out dancing with the girls— does he trust you or does he not give a shit?

Marion might answer that she's not going to let a guy make that decision for her, not him or any other, that's all, she's old enough to decide by herself. So yes, next Friday, we'll all go out?

And then, in conclusion,

It's my birthday tomorrow, we could at least treat ourselves to a bottle of champagne among girlfriends, no?

5

Resist,

   Prove that you exist,

   And, as she lets the song carry her away, she can barely make
out the hamlet in the falling night, the sky turning from a pale blue
with pink fringes to a deep midnight blue in which the hamlet is
like a black smudge emerging from the flat gray of the fields; from
her car she sees no lights to pierce the darkness of the hamlet, none
at all, even though at Christine's and at the Bergognes' the lights
were turned on long ago, but Marion isn't paying attention, she's
probably not even looking, she's singing,

   Go on and fight,

   the radio turned all the way up,

   Refuse this world of egoists,

   the bass,

   Resist,

   the car vibrating,

   Resist,

   Marion loves this France Gall song and at the same time Marion is singing it

   Resist,

   as though it's about vacations or about love,

   Resist,

without wondering whether or not she's implicated by what it says, taking advantage of this moment alone in the car, this bubble of air, not very long at all—the distance from the print shop to the house—a few kilometers to herself, the length of two or three songs, no more, and now she's already exiting the county road and turning onto the tiny road that leads to her house. She recognizes the vibrations of the bumpy road under the wheels, the cracked tar, the potholes, the ditches to the sides and the fields that spread out, pushing back the houses, the streets, the rows of trees, and soon there are no homes at all, no more streetlights with their succession of orange halos spreading over the road like sinister paper lanterns, that's all behind her now, nothing but her headlights to illuminate this road she knows by heart, with the river on the left running toward the larger river it will flow into about thirty kilometers farther on, the river behind the trembling row of poplars, and before long the path and the black and white sign announcing the three lone girls who seem to defy this man's world and promise that solitude is not a punishment but a solution.

Like every night, she drives very slowly through the metal gate that's always open. She gets a brief glimpse into Christine's house, because there's a French door in front that looks straight into the kitchen and, even if Christine seems to never be there—still in her studio, no doubt—in the kitchen a light is on, cold and white, almost blue, visible very clearly from the outside; the French door opens up a bright space in which Marion sees only, most often backlit, the silhouette of the German shepherd, his ears perked up, alert, Rajah, who must have heard the car coming from a ways off or who's just in the habit of waiting, like he does in the afternoon when he watches for Ida's arrival. Maybe he's just accustomed to Marion coming home at this hour, passing in front of her neighbor's house without really paying attention, she doesn't imagine Christine is concerned to hear her car coming into the yard, because she recognizes the sound of the engine, she knows the time, and only her dog seems to care about Marion's arrival, because he's also there to keep watch—he barks once or twice, lazy yelps without any particular conviction, just for the sake of it, to signal to his mistress that someone is coming. And maybe Christine, from the studio where she paints, or from the armchair in which she likes to sit, almost asleep, and listen to opera—Puccini and Verdi—but also contemporary music—Dutilleux, Dusapin—pretends not to hear her dog, or orders him to stop yelping and pawing the ground like he's doing, scratching the tiles, slapping his tail against a chair, telling him it's no use bothering her, look at the time, you know who it is. She says it fairly loud because the dog is in the other room, but she issues the order with a kind of gentleness and patience that she certainly wouldn't show a human who dared disturb her for something so trivial.

Marion will enter her house—their house—through the door that opens right into the dining room; she'll hang her jacket on the coatrack and drop her purse, which is hanging from her shoulder by a thin leather strap, onto the couch in the living room, where she'll glance at the television; she'll hear the news, it's already after eight, you haven't had dinner? You haven't eaten, kitten? Did you at least take your bath?

And now she takes her daughter in her arms, Ida having come out to meet her, repeating no, Mom, you don't say "eaten," you say "had dinner," we haven't *had dinner*—Ida is a stickler and her father is so proud when she corrects them, him and Marion, on their mistakes and their imprecisions—Dad and I wanted us to all have dinner together, we were waiting for you. Patrice will come out of the kitchen, everything is ready, he gives her a kiss on the lips—well, not really on the lips—pretending not to notice that tonight again she's turned her face slightly, just barely, he grazed the corner of her lips and then slid over to her cheek, that's something at least; Patrice has made the meal, tonight like almost every night, and while he's cooking—so to speak, mostly he reheats frozen foods—he doesn't think to himself that his wife goes out of her way to come home late, as though trying to avoid the moment where it's the three of them together, no, he pushes away this thought that sometimes tries to force its way past the barrier he's built up against it, a fraction of a second every night, sometimes more than a second, a few seconds, then, when the thought gets loose and spreads across his mind, but each time he rejects this bad, this acid idea that would have Marion go out of her way to come home as late as possible, no, that's not true, or at least only partly, because Bergogne knows she wants to see her daughter—on this point he has no doubt—and anyway doing the cooking doesn't bother him, it's not a burden for him, what's so hard about opening some cans and emptying them into a pot, taking a salt cod puree out of its cellophane and removing its aluminum plate and putting it in an oven-safe dish? On the other hand, it's always Marion who ends up serving at the table. He doesn't like serving, can't seem to bring himself to do it, as though he thinks it's degrading or not a man's job, even though he's the only one in this house who wears an apron from time to time, because only he repeats the gestures of his mother and his grandmother when he roasts meats or game, because he's spent enough time living alone to have had to learn to cook at least the basics, and besides he likes to eat, just as he likes to have friends over to share a nice Charolais beef, a good red wine, even though he doesn't know much about it; so no, no problem cooking every day, even if he finds it impossible to go all the way to serving at the table, which remains something like a reality that doesn't surprise him, that doesn't surprise Marion either, who takes over as though she's the one who prepared the meal, as though she's the one performing, all the way through to the end, the motions that lead from the stove to the trivet on the table.

Every night it falls to her to pretend in this way, to keep up a kind of appearance that means nothing to her, that he believes means nothing to him either, of which in any case neither of them seems to realize they're going out of their way to preserve the most obvious elements, as though they have to make themselves believe the meal was prepared by Marion and not by Patrice, as though their life depends on the maintenance of this illusion that neither of them is entirely conscious of. Marion takes the pots full of vegetables and the hot skillets, she takes plates from the kitchen cabinet and slides the cooked vegetables and meat onto them—knowing they eat too much meat, this too out of habit and laziness—and she seasons them, garnishes them with parsley and piment d'Espelette and meanwhile at the table Patrice and Ida are stuffing their faces with bread, their jaws seeming to dance or seeming to struggle to chew, misshapen by the dough, by the hunger that's already been tormenting them for a good hour of repeating to each other let's wait for Mom, grazing, nibbling, digging into the cornichons and the slices of sausage and the pâté, like every day, this one like any other.

They always wait for Marion to come sit down to start speaking to each other—bits of conversation they don't quite finish, interrupting themselves at any moment because, wait, listen—and they prick their ears up for two minutes at a subject of interest on the news, abandoning what they'd started to say and that they'll pick up again in a moment or tomorrow or some other night, because every night the same conversations come back, sprawl out, stretching from one day to the next, one week to the next, as though it's all just a single conversation repeating, unfolding, shifting each night, made up of identical words or with marginal variations on a detail, a new idea, about their day, yes, Marion says, I don't know, today wasn't very interesting, honestly I think the girls and I did something stupid, well, we made what a client asked for, posters, bookmarks, without asking if he had the rights to the images.

More meat, sweetheart?

Ida doesn't answer and it's as though Marion has been speaking to fill the silence, she doesn't see that Patrice is waiting for her to continue, but no, she forgets, maybe she didn't quite hear

Patrice asking her to continue, because she's already on her daughter's empty plate, her daughter ate so fast,

More meat, sweetheart?

too fast, she must be famished. So what good can it do, this conversation that her heart's not even in, even if she's the one who started it, as though she's already sick of this story about a mistake they might have made at work because after all she and her colleagues exhausted the subject, turning it over and kneading it in every possible direction, she just brought it up like that, just to say something, and she just repeats,

More meat, sweetheart?

because all that matters to her is her daughter's empty plate. Then she starts again, as though there hadn't been any interruption: we didn't ask him if he had the rights, but then a photo agency filed a complaint against the guy and obviously the bastard turned around and blamed us.

What's the risk for you?

Nothing. Honestly, nothing at all. But tomorrow all three of us have to go meet with the project manager and the director.

And then more silence, as though every topic is exhausted, stillborn, doomed to fail, as though nothing they could say can spring up and sustain a conversation, because at the end of the day, with its exhaustion, all three of them have a feeling that the conversations are empty, reflecting discomfort more than a desire to share their days—so they listen to the reporters' voices coming from the living room, the volume up loud enough for them to hear in spite of the dining room separating the living room from the kitchen. It's never really occurred to them to have dinner in the dining room except when they have dinner parties, as they will tomorrow, because the kitchen is where ordinary life happens; they listen to the television as they would the radio, what matters is what's being said, and they give their commentary, Patrice, yes, about politics, grousing, about Europe, grousing, but Marion never takes the bait because she claims she doesn't know anything about politics, or maybe she just doesn't want to hear about it, and she watches her daughter eat, observes her, seeming sometimes to be examining her to see if she's okay, if everything's okay, as though her daughter is in danger or as though this is the only thing in the world that matters to her, seeing her daughter eat, certainly not hearing about politics, or about anything else, maybe especially not if it comes from Patrice's mouth. And yet every night at some point he speaks, he talks about what happened to him today, at the farm, a calf who broke a leg, a problem with the cheesemonger, more rarely about money—he doesn't like to broadcast his problems or his fears about potentially risky investments, about credit rates, payment deadlines, but every night he feels this conviction that they should speak to each other, they must speak to each other, they have to, he doesn't want any of that deathly silence that reigned over his childhood, around this table, with his parents and his brothers.

So he speaks, whatever passes through his head, and tonight— so I took Christine to the police station today, she got another anonymous letter. He knows Marion and Ida will react, even as he remembers that they'd agreed not to bring up this business with the anonymous letters in front of Ida, so as not to scare her, are these things you talk about in front of a little girl? Can you really talk about threats, about all this nastiness, shouldn't you shelter her and let her believe for as long as possible that the world around us isn't full of raving lunatics and people who are bitter and jealous and petty? Or is it the opposite, should you reveal to her now what she'll find out for herself sooner or later? Should you tell her to prepare her to face that world? They've discussed it several times, not that it came to anything, they don't know but they'd said—Marion had said—no, we don't talk about that at the table.

Tonight it's too late. He's breaking what's been decreed as law, crossing a barrier, but what matters most to him in this moment is to not let the silence grow heavy around the motions of the meal, around their thoughts turned inward to the interior of their own lives and resolutely closed to the others, despite the moments of tenderness they share, which bore like shrapnel some place behind the face to reveal a hidden sign of sympathy, of interest in a story they'd like to hear, to understand, an idea, something, but no, it remains airtight and the only thing shared is the voice of the TV reporter or a story on who knows what bullshit topic, and Patrice persists, just like all families at the dinner table, and he speaks, he drove Christine to the police station, she got another anonymous letter—oh?—he can see Marion pause for a fraction of a second, he doesn't know whether it's to tell him to shut up, he's not keeping his word, and Ida, suddenly,

Tatie didn't say anything to me, why didn't she say anything?

Because it's not important, Marion answers in a voice trying to be almost distracted, to defuse what she senses in her daughter's question, Ida furrowing her eyebrows,

But why do people send letters like that?

and it's Patrice who answers, Patrice who senses he shouldn't have spoken, that Marion will blame him for it, or rather he knows she won't do anything in response to what he's said, she'll manifest her discontent as a kind of cold anger, Marion won't say anything, that's clear, he knows after the meal he'll stay in the kitchen by himself, sitting at the table, that he'll feel in all his limbs the weight of a fatigue landing on him, an exhaustion all out of proportion, can it be that old age has come for him with such sudden brutality? He's forty-seven and sometimes he thinks he must be twice that, he has the feeling that everything in him is shriveling up, puckering, he drinks a glass of wine and he'll hear Marion and Ida upstairs and, without quite knowing why, something will wound him, he'll hear them both laughing, something will send him back to a distant feeling, lost in the mists of his childhood, the sense of being excluded, superfluous, maybe already forgotten or useless.

6

In the darkness of the bedroom, the glow-in-the-dark stars dotting the ceiling shine with a pale anise-green radiance; Ida stares at them as she would observe the night sky itself, hearing her mother's steps down the wooden stairs, the wood creaking, each step with its own creak, more or less pronounced, more or less singular, and it's like this at the same time every night, after her mother leaves her waiting for sleep to come, still all jittery, still stirred by what she's just read to her, Ida looks at the ceiling and takes pleasure in dreaming. Ida can read perfectly well, and she likes reading too, but every night Mom tells a story that she finds in the big book with the yellow cover decked in embossed and gilded letters, a crude imitation of the kind of great golden book that opens old Disney films—a book that gathers stories from all over the world, stories and characters you tremble in fear for, all under a single title: *Stories of the Night*.

Tonight's story was about a man who kills his neighbor because he's jealous of a plot of land the neighbor refuses to give him, but the dead neighbor's dog follows the killer everywhere and howls so loud every night that he's finally forced to turn himself in to the sheriff and confess his crime; of course, the dog finds the spot where the neighbor buried his master's body. The story doesn't frighten Ida, who on the contrary is very moved by the love of this dog, by his loyalty to his master's memory, by his insistence on exposing the killer and seeking justice and reparation—a Christian tomb for his master rather than the anonymity of the slurry pit to which his murderer had condemned him—and Ida is blind to the horrible images that underpin the text, because everything revolves around the dog and his devotion, his love for his master—a dog that, though she doesn't even know if it's a specific breed or a mutt, Ida thinks she'd like to have a dog like that, who would follow her everywhere and do anything for her, like a kind of little brother or secret friend.

Eyes glued to the ceiling, Ida watches as the night sky blurs into the sleep enfolding her, curling up in it and letting herself be lulled and carried off by the drowsiness that falls over her just as she lets herself be carried and lulled to sleep by her mother's voice when she tells her one of the *Stories of the Night*—which are a bit scary sometimes, it's true, they're not all meant for a little girl of her age: some are for children but some are also for teenagers, in which vampires and witches have nights unlike anything Ida knows and that her mother reads to her with a laugh, adopting an exaggeratedly earnest tone as though to forestall any risk of fright for her daughter, letting irony and the implausibility of the story she's telling ring in her ears. But she reads them to her anyway, and Ida claims these are the ones she likes best, even though in truth these stories secretly insinuate themselves into her dreams, even though they color her nights with images and sensations that sometimes cause Ida to wake up in the morning trembling, as if absorbed by presences and voices that whispered stories more formidable than the ones her mother read to her, in that voice she so loves to listen to and that's almost lovelier than the story itself, as though the enchantment is caused not by the words of the story, nor by the story itself, or not just that, but by the energy, the motion, the vibration circulating in the intimate space of the breath that bears it.

That's what Ida loves, though she wouldn't know what to call it. Just as she loves the perfectly rehearsed ritual of her mother closing the book and putting it down on the nightstand beside her, and then the moment when she leans over her daughter—their faces so close—that moment when mother and daughter whisper sweet nothings to each other,

I'll call you if I have a problem.

But you won't have any problems.

Right, but what if there's a dragon?

Dragons? Just knock their teeth out.

So, as she lingers over the night sky on her bedroom ceiling, Ida hears her mother's steps on the stairs, then also, but farther away, the voices and the metallic sound of the television; is Patrice in front of the screen or still in the kitchen, finishing his meal alone, prolonging it further, or, on the contrary, having finished, maybe clearing the table, unless he's waiting—no, she knows he isn't. Even without seeing it she knows by heart what's happening: Patrice sitting on the couch, a thick blue or almost turquoise leather, facing the TV, in the living room, the only moment of the day when he allows himself to do nothing: that is, the only moment he allows his body to relax, letting his mind float above the saturated and too-bright colors on the 16:9 screen, to which he's hardly paying any attention, because in truth he doesn't usually stay in front of the television, except sometimes at night, when sleep stubbornly denies him and he finally gives up trying to find it, but that's pretty much it, because as soon as he settles down to a movie with Marion he falls asleep or nods off in such a way that after a moment he sits back up but no longer understands anything, sometimes insisting on staying there next to her, trying not to fall asleep, on being with her and turning in at the same time, even if most of the time it's not worth the trouble, he falls asleep in front of the screen, he stops following along, letting go of the characters, the situations, the story, all of it.

Tonight, like almost every night, he hears steps on the stairs as he nods off in front of commercials, or maybe the weather report, remote control in hand even though it doesn't even occur to him to use it to change the channel or turn off the television, which he could do because he knows what's going to happen, tonight like every night: Marion will come down the stairs and won't make the gesture he's waiting for, hoping for, even though he knows without the slightest doubt that she won't make it for him, as though it's of no importance to her, which is why he tries to tamp down this mild pain he feels, this minor offense, and besides it's so quick, a breath, there, it's already over, she's passed by a few meters away from him and hasn't made that motion of turning around to speak to him or smile at him. This hurts him a bit, a cold sensation running through his body, lining the inside of his chest, but he chases away the feeling by sitting up straighter and letting the remote slip onto the coffee table in front of him and, the way you jump into the water, holding your breath, your whole body involved, gets up—he really is fat now, his breath is short, it surprises him how much, with age, his body is slipping away from him too—he understands all too well why she doesn't turn around toward him, his body too heavy, his flesh like jelly, almost pink, repulsive, this vile flesh that disgusts him too, this body he endures with scorn and dismay, and, when he walks toward the kitchen, the smell of cigarette smoke invades his nostrils, perfuming the whole ground floor of the house with Marion's presence.

This is the only cigarette she allows herself here, opening the French door in the kitchen; Ida is in bed and Marion finds herself in front of the uncleared table—the plates sticky with sauce and remnants of bread, and the crumbs, the stains, the dirty glasses, the forks, knives, spoons, the trash, the residues, empty yogurt jars, uncapped mustard, the wine cork beside the bottle, the corkscrew lying there, all of this he knows exhausts her because she works too, she's tired too, and for God's sake why, instead of sitting on the couch waiting for her to read her daughter her story, why, instead of flopping down in front of the TV, doesn't he help his wife, he who has said so many times that he'd do *anything* for her, so why, without going so far as doing *everything* for her, doesn't he just get up and clear the table, clean it, put the plates and glasses and silverware in the dishwasher instead of waiting for her to get to it, why doesn't he even ask her if she needs help, as though she could possibly fail to appreciate his clearing the table once in a while, rather than staying there like he does without ever asking himself about why he does nothing, as though because the habit has been established it can't be called into question, or as though yet again it's a declaration of allegiance to old relics, to shadows, rituals, customs dragging along their outdated and misogynist codes even though he, Patrice, is convinced that none of that is who he is. No, he doesn't feel he's anything like the old people he knew in his childhood, not even like his parents, or like his mother, who would never have dreamed of working anywhere besides her husband's farm or of asking him to clear the table, to wash the dishes, she also would have thought it was her work, that this work fell to her because she would have considered it demeaning and degrading for a man. No, Patrice doesn't think about any of this. He sits down every night at mealtime, in his childhood kitchen, and even though it's been completely redone it can't be helped, nothing changes in the secrecy of time, you can't just renovate and redecorate and hide under new paint and modernity, these residues will always surface, vestiges of a time you'd prefer to forget. He doesn't think about it, but Bergogne fils takes after Bergogne père, or perpetuates him by sitting there like him, at the head of the table, the way he saw him do his whole life.

Patrice goes now up to the door of the kitchen, where he knows he'll find his wife smoking, yes, maybe also with her headphones over her ears, because she claims she listens to music on headphones while she does the dishes and cleans up the kitchen so she won't bother him while he's watching television, but he doesn't believe her, he knows it's really to cut herself off from his presence, as though to warn him that she doesn't want to be disturbed, as though to find a moment in which she can continue that cherished isolation she finds in her car on the way home from work, and also in sleep, as she'll do in a little while. He knows all of this by heart, this moment when he sees her from behind, loading plates into the dishwasher or washing serving trays by hand, whistling and singing, probably unaware that she's singing almost out loud in the kitchen, and she's off somewhere in her head, taking drags of her cigarette, almost closing her eyes, eyebrows furrowed, still knowing Patrice is behind her but far enough away, not in the same room but standing in the doorframe, and that he's watching her blond hair that she gets touched up with dye once a month at the hairdresser, the hoop earrings, the light sweater that reveals at the base of her neck, like some kind of magical creature, the outline of a tattoo of which he sees, here, only the exposed tip: a length of barbed wire like a braid of thorns, like the crown above the bloodied face of Christ. The sight frightens Patrice each time: how could she, who never speaks of it, have let someone etch such an image on her back, and why this one, when so many other people have tattoos that are so pretty and so original, Māori, flowery, artistic, whereas you can tell hers was done by someone who didn't quite know what they were doing, at a time when women in particular didn't get tattoos.

Almost every night the same motions repeat, the same slow and insignificant actions, almost mechanical, executed one after another without anyone examining or questioning them—why does he have to brush his teeth before putting on his pajamas and not the other way around? Why does he take the time, like every night, to sit down at the computer on the desk in the living room after Marion has finished cleaning the kitchen and he's seen her go upstairs to bed? He knows she's going to get ready, get into bed, and read for a half hour, maybe a bit less, drooping from exhaustion, sometimes not even managing to turn off her bedside lamp and leaving her open book splayed, almost beached, on her chest, as though sleep has caught her by surprise, as though she couldn't fight the drift of sleep just as he can't fight this need he has, each night, to get up and check all his emails, not only the ones he received a while ago—the considerable number he hasn't taken the time to reply to—but the new ones, the ones demanding a meeting to sell him some farming equipment or reminding him that he owes money, that he should remember to vaccinate the animals, to renew the insurance on this or that, because each day pours so many messages into his inbox that he has to check so he won't choke on them in his sleep, and every night the time he spends doing this allows him when he turns off the computer to be alone in the house—in the hallway upstairs he opens Ida's door and finds her fast asleep, arms outstretched, chest mere inches from falling out of bed, legs scissored over the blanket; he takes the time to gather up this body whose every limb seems to want to leave the others behind and run in the opposite direction of its counterpart, and as he approaches his bedroom he can already hear the long, heavy breath, almost a snore, that tells him Marion has fallen asleep—sometimes he hurries, don't turn on the computer, leave everything, the reminder letters from the bank, the retirement fund, the bookkeeping, and he rushes to his bedroom in the hope that she won't be asleep yet.

Sometimes he finds her absorbed in a book, the book resting on her thighs, looking so focused on a detective novel, so engrossed in it that she doesn't see him. Whether she hears him or not he doesn't know, he's just so happy she's not asleep yet. But tonight when he comes into the bedroom, she's sleeping. He knows he took his time coming upstairs, he noticed that calm with which the house itself seems to sink into darkness and silence, slowly, softly letting go, whereas he can't manage to, suddenly anxious at the thought of a message he absolutely must answer to reassure a creditor, because, though he doesn't dare admit it to himself, he fears receiving a message from a bank that will no longer give him an extension, a message from a process server, a summons, a formal demand, so tonight he took too long, he knows that, he came up and he knew right away that his wife and child were asleep, that they were together, even in separate rooms they were in the same temporality, the same shared world of their own lives, excluding him, leaving him alone by his own wayside. And that's when he finds the silence of the night, just like when he was a child and his mother had to reassure him, to tell him the dead don't rise up to eat children, or to play with them either, as she had explained to him one night when that was what he feared, what he believed. This pain, so often renewed, of feeling like he's not there when she looks at him, when all this beauty to which he believed—used to believe—she gave him access, the possibility of contemplating it, of touching it, cast him back even more violently into his loneliness, just because of an open book that he's now closed and placed on the nightstand.

He watches her sleep, she's wearing just a T-shirt, gray and oversized, in which her body seems to float, and yet her breasts seem heavier than they do in a bra. He eyes them freely, without shame, their shape, the curves, their weight; he'd like to take them in his hands, heft them, caress them even just through the fabric, just as he ogles, still without shame, the too-deep neckline and the skin whose few wrinkles trace lines that he follows, and the neck, his wife's face in profile, her beauty so unassuming in repose, when she sleeps, leaving him and him alone the privilege not of possessing her but of contemplating her, still amazed to have the privilege of admiring this woman and seeing her whirl around him, living, laughing, and sleeping; and too bad if there's still this wound that awakens at this hour of the night, whose pain he manages to numb with the doggedness of his work, with all the worries that overwhelm him and in which he's willing to drown himself in order to forget that his wife, with her breath, her mouth—her lips—the shape of her nose, the wrinkles at the corners of her eyes and the scent that belongs to her and nobody else and that the room, the sheets, the house itself seem to radiate, barely lets him touch her anymore, him bursting with the shame it brings him to want her, knowing that maybe once a month she'll let his stocky body, heavy with fat and muscles, pink and pale, pallid as a corpse's, its skin rough and pungent and sour, this body he looks at with disgust, with shame, satisfy itself inside her, letting him heave and thrust, he sees her doing it, closing her eyes and holding her breath, he knows it—waiting for him to finish the task as quickly as possible, as if she owes him at least that.

7

The electric razor vibrates in his hand and makes the sound of a swarm of bees as he thinks to himself that Christine is right, this black and gray bundle of hairs teeming like insects on his cheeks and chin is ugly and it ages him—or rather it betrays something about him, about his uneasiness with himself, with his image, on the occasions when he bothers to take it into account, not because he really cares but because he knows it matters to Marion and that, even if she'll never tell him so, in everything that puts her off about him, at least part of it must be this negligence, the lack of care he gives his appearance, because he often catches her giving him this disconsolate look when they go out and are forced to face the presence of other people.

He knows Christine thinks that Marion looks down on her sometimes, and he knows Christine well enough to know what she thinks of his wife, how she thinks it, in what terms—if only she'd dare say it with the words in her head, which he's sure aren't especially indulgent or tender, but which Christine can only keep to herself, to the point that they must ring out in her mind—who does she think she is, Marion—Marion that slut—that pretentious Marion playing the diva—stupid cunt Marion. But Christine has never said anything, he knows she knows she shouldn't even try, either because she knows the potential reactions of a man in love well enough to know he wouldn't give her the right, wouldn't allow her the space to do it, all the more because Christine can be haughty and disdainful herself, so on what grounds would she attack Marion? He tells himself, when he thinks about it—sometimes for hours at a time, brooding over his irritation at the words that Christine hasn't said to him but that he knows she's thinking—that we certainly do see the mote in our neighbor's eye and none in our own, and he all but thinks it's her own flaws that Christine holds against Marion, even if he then thinks that above all, speaking of the mote in our neighbor's eye, it's he and not Christine who's the worst in all of this, he who claims to love his wife *more than anything* and doesn't even think to give her a hand with the simplest household chores, or in any case only from time to time when there's no other choice and they have to spend their Sunday doing little projects around the house—replacing a joint in the bathroom or finally getting around to fixing the washing machine—and this all the more because Marion has certainly had to learn to fend for herself, she's spent enough time living alone to know how to change a lightbulb. These days she's the one who does almost all the shopping on her way home from work—the Super U is on her route, true, but does that mean he can't think once in a while to unburden her on the weekend, for instance, the same way he has trouble making it to Ida's medical checkups and even more so when the teacher wants to see the parents; it always falls to Marion, though he often has the feeling that, in some indirect or unspoken way, for anything involving their daughter, she insists on being the one to handle it.

Every so often, on the other hand, he tries to pay a little attention to himself, to not wear the perennial ultra-faded and almost threadbare checkered shirt whose colors have practically disappeared from so many washings and so much sun. He tries to do nice things for her, he invites people over, gives her gifts—lots of gifts—and he tries, more in the hope of drawing her attention than to indulge himself, to make an effort in terms of his appearance, even if he doesn't get his hair cut often enough, has gained too much weight, hasn't given up hunting with his friends. He'd let this beard grow in, telling himself she'd like it, even if obviously it didn't work, it was unsuccessful, there was something shambolic about his beard, not completely thick or robust because he didn't go to a barber like all the trendy guys, and, seeing the clumps of black and white hairs in the bowl of the sink, he tells himself again that he's doing the right thing by getting rid of it; tonight, for her birthday, Marion will rediscover him as she used to know him. She'll appreciate that, and anyway Christine was right, it was ridiculous, it doesn't suit him, each time he tries to *spruce himself up* it doesn't look right at all, and he feels the way he felt as a teenager, when he tried to dress nicely and ended up feeling ridiculous and affected, with his single pair of pleated trousers and his coat with the shoulder pads, his leather tie, firm-hold gel in his hair to go out on Saturday nights to dances at the village hall, where the more resourceful guys always scored with the girls who came in packs, around whom you could see the boys whose hair was long in back and short up top and in front—a high trim, the mullet cut—or short with the rat tail dangling down their neck; guys who were workers, masons, apprentices, artisans, all kinds, boys who like him came from their hamlet, from farms, but also from subdivisions and housing projects, from far away sometimes, and who usually left again with their tails between their legs but who, for the hope of a date, were ready to bear a whole evening lingering at the bar, emptying bottles of beer by the case and counting the empty racks stacking up behind the counter, waiting to be drunk enough to try their luck with a girl they'd known since at least primary school.

He'd seen and taken part in all that, but eventually they all got married, the friends from school and the boys he knew by sight; all the ones who were his age had settled down and in their turn the guys younger than him bellied up to village hall bar, took their chances flirting with the girls as soon as they'd had a bit too much to drink, while he still couldn't do so, finding himself alone like pathetic losers whom you took pity on from time to time, those slightly retarded guys like the Mauduit boy who was always in the fields with his goats and who everyone inevitably called Dumbo because of the way his ears stuck out, a kid who hadn't gone to school and had become an adult as if by accident, or like Albert, whom everyone called Einstein, a kid who eventually met God in person and lived in a converted shed on his grandmother's farm, whose walls he plastered with posters taken from the centerfolds of a collection of *Playboy* magazines he'd found God knows where. For a long time Patrice had continued to go to the dances, nursing his beer while a band played approximative imitations of hits from the eighties, admitting one day that it was too late, that for the kids—the younger brothers of the ones he'd started going with—who now came to peacock and hit on fifteen-year-old girls, he must have looked like a retard also, who some would call a peasant even though they worked on farms too; but they labeled him as one of the village idiots you'd laugh with and then laugh at while bumming their corn-paper Gitanes or their Gauloises, all the while flattering them with big claps on the back, the guys everyone liked for that reason but also because they were pathetic and made everyone around them feel big—all these adolescents who lacked self-confidence, playing at being men and dreaming of picking up girls and taking them out in their Golf GTI or customized Renault 17.

Patrice had eventually stopped going to the dances too—he who'd never danced at them and had almost killed himself ten or twenty times driving home, too drunk not to confuse the road with a ditch as he tore along in his old black Fiat Panda, having left his Peugeot 103 to rot in the barn with part of his childhood and his adolescence, he who'd almost gotten into fights so many times and had once been followed by a guy who wanted to smash in his skull with a pickax—a pickax the guy kept in the trunk of his 205—because he'd caught Patrice giving his fiancée a lingering look, he claimed, and, above all, he who'd never done anything more at the dances than look covetously at the teenage girls who just wanted to mill about in their groups, to dance, to get married, and who, surprise surprise, never saw him. It must be said that after having his offer of a dance or a drink declined so many times, or, if they accepted, having to hear them tell him about their lost love with some pretty boy who left them for someone else, feeling he couldn't take advantage of the distress of a girl who for all her complaining never seemed to have eyes for him, as though he wasn't there, always invisible, always petrified to feel how women only sent him deeper into his loneliness, his failure, his self-hatred, he finally stopped going out altogether.

Since then, there had been two women.

A first one, who didn't stay long but who he loved—or thought he loved—because she taught him that, contrary to what he believed, he could be attractive, that it was possible to see in his build not a fat man but a sturdy man, a sort of rural Depardieu or Lino Ventura, that he had peculiar traits, yes, a bit of a scowling face, perhaps, but one on which you could also see the expression of a great modesty, of shyness, which could be pleasing, and for that matter it had pleased this woman whom he'd been in school with and whom he encountered again one day behind the register at the supermarket; and it was he who was surprised to find himself asking her out for a drink.

After a few months she left, saying she needed something else, and he told himself that was what women left for, *something else,* he wasn't so stupid that he couldn't translate that to *someone else.* And then he met, a bit by chance, a woman who managed to give him confidence, to teach him that it was possible to see his face not as ugly, as he'd been telling himself it was since adolescence, because he confused ugliness for coarseness. This woman who'd told him he had an honest look, that you could see it in him—he thought this was idiotic—this woman who wasn't very pretty, he knew, but since he wasn't either and since anyway nobody was in these parts, who cares, people who are attractive, or who seem to be, we watch them live out their great psychodramas on television, in large apartments to which no one here will ever have keys. So he liked this woman. She stayed with him longer, but they didn't have kids, one of them couldn't, and once the hypothesis arose that it might be him he refused to come to the appointment to have his sperm analyzed—he did for once what he hated in himself, give in to his anger, to that violence he spent so much time locking up inside himself, just as he had seen his father do the opposite and give in to it, and often; his father who each day, yes, as much as he could, under all manner of pretexts, smacked his children in the face, open-handed slaps, to all three boys but especially to him, Patrice, because he was the eldest, ferocious wallops that barely drowned out the cries of his mother begging her husband to stop—Stop! Stop! You're going to kill him!—and it's true that they'd been like that in the family for ages, everyone knew Patrice's grandfather had been a violent man, that he'd finished his life in an asylum when for his whole childhood Patrice believed it was a retirement home, but no—He tried to kill your grandmother with a knife, his mother told him one day when he asked her why there was always so much violence in their house, why the men always had dementia, the grandfather, the father, and him, Patrice, who was afraid of being like them, of having it *in his blood*, and who was disgusted by a violence he could feel bubbling up inside him even though it rarely spilled over, in any case almost never since he had become a man, and never again since he'd met Marion—not the way he'd exploded with rage when that woman he should have married insisted that he should get tested to see if he was the sterile one, she who had mocked him, had laughed a bit, finding these masculine apprehensions ridiculous, these proprieties from a bygone era, and he had slammed his fist down on the table, literally, the way he'd seen his father do often, and then surprising himself with his own anger, letting it swell inside him, Patrice took it out on the chairs, and it was very nearly her that he beat and smashed against a wall, the woman he wanted to become the mother of his children, the one he thought was *the one*, imagining he could demand anything of her and she'd take it because all the women of the hamlet had always endured everything, never leaving their husbands or even thinking of doing so, not knowing that everything had changed, that the world had changed, he who took pride in not being like his father and who, surprising himself when he let that wild, mindless, murderous old fury rise again, the one that had lingered in his family history, had had to resign himself to the understanding that he wasn't free of this violence he detested in his father. So the next morning the woman had left, leaving no explanation but the terror and disgust she had felt in seeing him *mad* with rage—you can't live with a man who has the look you had last night. He decided she was right: she'd been smart enough not to put up with the furious madman Patrice kept locked up in his head.

But all of that is over now; he collects all his beard hairs in the palm of his hand, throws them into the trash can under the sink, rinses the basin, looks at himself—his white skin is tired, sleep still under his eyes, in the thick skin puffing up his eyelids. Now he recognizes his face again, the cleft in the chin, too heavy in the cheeks—right, he tells himself, today is a special day, his wife is forty. Getting up, he kissed her. She opened her eyes and smiled when he wished her a happy birthday. She must have murmured something like a thank you that he guessed more than heard, no matter, he gets up earlier than she does every day, he's used to catching her in the fog of sleep.

In an hour he'll have had his coffee, put on his coveralls, visited his cows, while Marion won't even have started preparing Ida's breakfast or brushing her teeth—and he thinks of this image often, coming back to him from their first days together, seeing her from behind in a hotel bathroom, illuminated by a white neon light above the bathroom mirror, with her black lace bra but most of all, on her back, that tattoo with the barbed wire cut off at her neck and underneath it a giant flower, like a rose with its petals surrounded by brambles, pierced by metallic thorns and drops that looked like tears or blood, as though the petals were bleeding tears or crying blood—a violent image that he couldn't imagine how Marion had agreed to have tattooed on her—he wondered if she had ridden motorcycles in a past life, if she had known bikers or rockers, and he'd tried to hang that image on other images that he could recognize, but what stayed with him of the sight of her in that hotel room, after their first night together, was that before she was a promise of love, Marion was a stranger, with the density of a life he knew nothing about. He'd been surprised by that tattoo because it didn't correspond at all to the image she'd given him when he saw her photo, when they spoke, during those first meetings where she showed up and gave him the impression of a woman who was very serious and above all very coquettish and elegant—too much so?—not at all a girl for a man like him. A city girl, for sure, who liked to be taken to restaurants, to the movies, maybe even to the theater, and he who never went to restaurants or the movies and who would have laughed if someone suggested going to see a play—not enough time, not his lifestyle, not enough cash to throw away on such a trifle—because he'd learned very early on one of the criticisms people always leveled at city folk, what his mother said in her caustic tone, with implacable finality: people in the city, always with their wallets out.

He had believed when he met Marion that it would be impossible between them, wondering how she could fail to see they had nothing in common, when, on the contrary, she seemed happy to find him so different, when she was even insistent, sending pictures of herself and explaining, full of hope, that she was getting a degree and might work in a print shop, while he was wary of telling her about the farm, about La Bassée, wondering how she could even think of being interested in him, yes, great, he had dared, let's meet up. They met and that first time she had laughed—a bit too much, as though she were determined to find him funny, knowing too well that he wasn't—and he'd been astounded that she wanted to see him again, that he should spend one night, then two, then three, four, several nights in town, from the restaurant all the way to an evening at a bowling alley, then another at karaoke, and then that gap he perceived between this girl with a tattoo on her back that he eventually disregarded, not to say forgot, because their nights of lovemaking, when he took her in his arms, in the dark of those first rooms, changed everything, and the wounded rose, the metallic thorns, all of that, then, finally faded out with the lights. In the dark there was only the warmth and softness of Marion's skin, her abandon, her hoop earrings on the nightstand, and this gap he had sensed, he finally forgot it altogether or decided not to see it, not trying to understand, because the most important and most extraordinary thing was that a woman of such beauty and such intelligence should be interested in him, not just for a night, but that she should speak to him of life plans, of marriage—she was the one who first brought up the word, who first dared to say it even though it had been burning on Patrice's lips for months. She must have been thirty-two or thirty-three when he met her, and he still remembers Christine's face, her mistrust, her stubborn, suspicious silence, Christine who had told him that all the same it was a hell of a thing, the internet—I know, Patrice had said, I've never been good with the ladies, if that's what you mean.

No, that's not what I'm saying.

But it's true. You seem to think that because I met her on a site—and he'd fumbled to explain, you know, the dating sites, you can meet real people too. Me, anywhere else, I never would've found a woman like her. You could find someone yourself too, you know, why not?

She had shrugged her shoulders and exploded into a ringing, politely condescending laugh,

Ah! Me? Have you seen me? Aren't you a riot, old Bergogne.

8

Well, instead of chitchatting, you'd better hurry up.

It's true, Christine is right, he has to put up the decorations in the living room and set the table, go into town—not exactly next door, because of the risk of traffic on the ring road—it's Bergogne who speaks of the ring road, while Christine, incorrigible Parisienne that she is, calls it the *périph'*, as though the name would change anything about the reality of the fifty-odd kilometers Bergogne has to travel to pick up his wife's gift.

This morning they did what they do every day: Patrice worked in the fields, Marion took Ida to school and then went to work, Christine sat down in front of the painting she thought she'd finished the night before and, in the studio, found herself with this naked red woman perched regally on an immense armchair, like a queen slightly larger than a life-sized woman, waiting for who knows what, like an aging giantess whose years are leading her into old age, but gently, slowly, accompanying her into her prime without tipping her into decrepitude just yet, an age of nuances that's no longer the age of the body's splendor or triumph but isn't yet the age of its collapse, a human age made of slippages, of eras overlapping, contaminating one another not unlike the successive coats of paint that reveal their presence through glazes, as though age has revealed several eras from a single life in a single image. All morning Christine tried to decipher this woman, wondering not why she painted her, nor why this body had been painted in all these shades, these variations of red, a whole color chart she'd taken care to consolidate by working on their superimpositions, the shadows and lights, the thickness or fluidity of the texture, as though the skin were pure color and the flesh, like in those paintings by Rubens that had so impressed her in Antwerp when she was young, her memory of which is halfway between fascination and nausea, like looking at an overly creamy dessert, had itself become painting, but trying to assure herself that the way the woman was sitting was accurate, believable, not realistic but endowed with a real density: would people believe this woman was sitting in the chair she was meant to be sitting in, would they feel the weight of her body, of her forearms on the armrests, would they imagine the strain of her weight on the chair or, on the contrary, was this a body without reality or presence?

Christine knew she'd do better to stop looking at her—when you stare at a painting for too long you eventually stop seeing it. She would have been better off going for a walk, spending her morning somewhere else. It's nice out, she could have gone to stretch her legs, stroll in the countryside under the almost mild blue sky already spilling out of the winter to make a path toward a more clement season; she could have walked along the river with her dog, to think, which is to say to forget to think and let her ideas and thoughts wander, giving free rein to the movements of her mind, without which there is no thought, to let herself go, as she's done for years, walking side by side with her dog, and just that, sometimes for hours, or crossing the woods, the paths, before coming home and then letting the desire to paint or to read overtake her again, but also the desire to drink tea and listen to music. Besides, today she has cakes to bake. Tonight is her neighbor's birthday, whether she likes her or not; things have been planned and she has her role to play: Patrice will have dinner with his wife and daughter and she'll come over around eight thirty with two or three different cakes. Marion will be surprised, perhaps, to see too much cake for just the four of them, maybe she'll have a laugh about it, not knowing that at nine o'clock her two co-workers will show up.

Voilà. An extra surprise. Patrice thought of everything, Christine thought when he told her about his idea, and it wasn't surprising, he's always lavished attention on his wife, even if thankfully he eventually calmed down, he who for years squandered all the money he didn't have on gifts she didn't need and anyway never asked for, Christine conceded, because while she had many things to criticize Marion for she never criticized her for being extravagant or for demanding that her husband break the bank for her, no, on the contrary, Christine had even heard her often urging him to save money, as though Marion was afraid of the prospect of his putting himself in financial peril for her, and it wasn't rare for Christine to wonder if Marion was just anxious about the idea of not having enough—stingy to the point of the most banal pennypinching—or if she was just concerned and foresighted, like someone who, having known poverty, is wary of it as one would be wary of a personal enemy who must be kept at bay. But Bergogne had been in love to a ridiculous degree, often Christine hadn't been able to help but find him childish, sentimental and servile, or frankly dopey, when she was irritated at him, she who wouldn't have wanted a man to behave that way with her, too dependent, too affectionate, almost obsequious, so attentive he seemed to have no life of his own, as though his life were focused entirely on his wife; Christine had found it hard to tolerate, even though of course she'd never dare criticize him for it or comment on it, no more when he met Marion than she would have pointed out to him today, around noon, when he came through the door for lunch, knocking two or three times on the French door and entering without waiting for an answer—the sound of him knocking the mud off his boots on the metal mat outside before coming in— he goes to wash his hands without saying anything, or with a vague

How's it going this morning?

to which she'll respond with an equally vague

Fine, fine, and you?

and at noon they had lunch like they do every day, but today Patrice didn't take the time for a coffee or to chat for too long, he had to go into town,

What are you getting her again?

A computer, but a nice one, hers is too old.

Right... more than six months?

No, it's not that, he concluded, shrugging his shoulders, as though he didn't know he'd often spent money on his wife and daughter that he should have used to pay off his creditors. He knows perfectly well that he's doing something stupid, but all the same it's something stupid he's doing consciously. Christine ribbed him a bit because he claimed not to know much about computers; she still liked to remind him that he met his wife on the internet, teasing him about it as she does every time they discuss it, to the point that he might wonder if she wasn't going out of her way to return to the subject, as though hoping they'd talk about it again because, the better to defend himself, he would eventually encourage her to do what he'd done.

Patrice was quick after lunch—no, not quick: precise but rapid in his movements, but without inexactitude or haste.

He who never puts anything away in his house, who is disorganized and clumsy the moment he steps inside, even while in his work, with the cows, with the cheeses, he's a man of great mastery in his movements and a man of a formidable professionalism, as though he's really two people, as though the man of the house and the man of the farm aren't the same, as though each of them could look at the other without recognizing him, or as though one could be shocked by the other just as the latter, conversely, could be admiring and envious of the man who so skillfully ran his farm, took care of the animals, spent time with them, talking to them, respecting the milk they gave him, as though he knew the art of transforming milk into gold, in the form of cheese; and it was that man, rather than the other, who fortunately took things in hand in the early afternoon, knowing by some miracle where to find everything he needed, that box lingering in the old buffet in the back of the storeroom, taken out once a year for Christmas decorations—a cardboard box that must date from when Marion moved in, containing a jumble of colored pennants and electric lights and simple folded-paper chains, Christmas ornaments, figurines, a snowman in a snow globe—in which Bergogne knew he would find, among the paper chains, one that had nothing to do with Christmas, a chain of golden letters that could extend a *happy birthday* over several meters, which he'd just have to hang in the living room, maybe over the table or a bit farther back, but close enough for Marion to see it as soon as she comes through the door in the dining room—the real front door being next to the kitchen, on the left, but nobody ever goes through it, they enter through the French door that opens directly into the dining room, unlike at Christine's.

What he'd wanted was for Marion to be bowled over when she got home and amazed by the table as soon as she came in— he'd had trouble finding the tablecloths, had above all wasted a great deal of time choosing between them—and for her to marvel at the decorations and the dimmed lights, the string of golden capital letters wishing her a happy birthday but also, and above all, the table set, not just any old way, with the fancy small plates on the big ones he still had from his great grandmother, which they never brought out because they were too precious and fragile to risk exposing them to the slightest danger—porcelain so fine it was practically translucent at the edges, with a golden trim, with hand-painted lyrebirds and peahens whose paint had partly faded over the years—and two bronze candlestick holders that he took out for Christmas and holidays like two talismans that had brought good luck to the family for several generations, or like two totems with pride of place over the holiday spread; the candles he'd bought

behind Marion's back a few days earlier at the drugstore downtown—intertwined candles in mauve—and napkins that matched
the tablecloth, thick linen with orange edges and mustard-colored
patterns, crystal wine glasses with engraved vine leaves and arabesques, thick hand-blown water glasses—the glass pocked with
air bubbles, lovely artisanal objects whose imperfections confirmed
their quality. He hadn't had time to be content with everything
he could have done, because without even looking at the clock he
knew it was ticking, that the afternoon was opening up in front
of him and he had to do what had to be done—as though he was
overwhelmed, as though he'd fallen behind on his own schedule,
only he was well aware that this feverishness wasn't because of the
time he had left, because time is the one thing he does have, time
is in fact opening up in front of him, it's not so late, Bergogne has
plenty of time, what he has to do isn't so awful either, get in the
Kangoo and drive into town, park not too far from the Darty so
he doesn't have to carry the computer on foot, it's a machine he
imagines must weigh as much as a dead donkey, no use burdening
himself and dragging it along the streets he imagines are probably
swarming with people and saturated with noise; anyway he's never
liked strolling in town, nor shopping, window-shopping, no, not
his thing, even if he's done it many times with Marion—at the
beginning, mostly, when she still lived in town.

He'd have to set off again and stop at the bakery, then at
Picard too, because he'd decided, after looking at their website
and changing his mind several times, waffling over a caterer he
knew, that he'd go to Picard, where he'd buy frozen sweetbreads
with pieces of grilled turkey and little morels, all of it seasoned in
a port sauce, with which he'd also maybe make rice, and as an appetizer there would be foie gras with onion confit or black cherry
jam; he'd have to remember to buy champagne, a few bottles, one
for the appetizer but also two or three for dessert, when the co-
workers would be there—the co-workers to whom he had to send
a message to remind them they were expected at nine, as they'd

already agreed, because he was afraid they'd forget or show up too early. Now a knot of anxiety was starting to tighten his stomach, even if, above all, he didn't yet dare admit to himself that it wasn't just for all these very concrete reasons that he was starting to feel this slight anxiety, but also for another that internally he preferred to pretend didn't exist, rejecting it as though it didn't titillate him, as though it played no role at all in his decision to go into town— when in fact he knew it was really because of this that he'd decided to go, that it was this that had made up his mind to go and not this pretext to which he's still clinging to get in his car and drive into town, his wife's birthday present, like he's trying to make himself believe, to cling to this idea and convince himself of it, obstinately and insincerely, even though he knows full well he could have had the computer delivered and that a caterer could have taken care of the meal; even if he'd worried there would be a problem with the delivery, the weak but extant probability had been enough to convince him he had to drive into town to pick up the gift in person, or rather had been enough to give him the alibi he needed to tell himself he was going into town out of necessity. And then there was also the need to stop at Picard to buy some frozen foods, because he wouldn't have been able to cook well enough for a birthday meal, even if there again he could have made do with the frozen foods aisle of the Super U, or he could just as well have asked Christine to cook, which she would have been happy to do for him, he knows that, or even go see a caterer, as he'd considered doing, he knows everyone in the area, butchers, charcutiers, restaurateurs, guys he went to school with or friends he made hunting or somewhere else, at the local café-bar, at dances, yes, there were enough people in La Bassée or in the canton or even a bit farther out who could have made a birthday dinner Marion would have loved, without his having to drive over fifty kilometers for it. But fine, he'd ruled out all those possibilities and arranged with himself to have to drive into town. And now the knot in his stomach had risen, soon tightening his throat, preventing him from breathing, sometimes freezing his mind too, leaving him feeling drugged and apathetic, having to check several times everything he'd already done and everything he still had to do, a list he refused to write down on a piece of paper but that he wrote, black on white, in his brain.

He's gotten everything ready in the living room, now he has to go get changed; you don't just go into town dressed any old way. You have to make an effort, even just a tiny one: a collared shirt and a half-zip sweater, a clean pair of jeans, clothes he won't keep on tonight but that will do for this afternoon. Because tonight, after he and Ida have both bathed or showered, it'll be something else altogether: they'll have to change to greet Marion, get dressed up in clothes they almost never wear.

And so now he decides to go; before long he's getting into his Kangoo and he knows that as he passes in front of Christine's door she'll wave to him, that Rajah will come out and bark or, if he's already outside, run in circles around the car to greet him; he'll pass slowly through the gate—that's it, the car sets off, Patrice accelerates and soon he'll merge onto the road at the end of the path, passing the signboard and leaving the hamlet behind him to grow tiny in his rearview mirror until it disappears from sight, as he wonders why his heart is suddenly beating so hard, why the excitement of organizing this day, the gift, the meal, the preparations, why all of it doesn't just bring him joy and pleasure, but why he also feels such apprehension, such anxiety. He has a slight headache, feels almost feverish now. His mouth is so dry he thinks he should have brought some water. Still driving, before the car reaches the county road, he pats his leather jacket on the passenger seat; he rummages around, tries to find a way in, there it is, his fingers penetrate the inner left side of the jacket, feel the bulge, the wallet is there, for a second he thought he'd forgotten it, that in his rush—there's no rush—in the feeling of urgency, in the inner rumblings of what feels more and more like panic, he might have forgotten to bring his debit card, but no, all is well, he has his wallet, he knows what he's going to do, he knows it, his guilty conscience and this question: how much money will he take out?

9

She knows she should get to work on her cakes, but she just can't help it, she has to keep delaying the moment of getting down to it and, pretending to be strolling past by chance, just passing by, she wanders into her studio as though it's here and not the kitchen where she has work to do, as though it's here that she has to clear some space to get ready for what she needs to focus on this afternoon.

But it's like every time, all it takes is for her to be convinced that a painting is finished for her to discover that it's not, and this almost by accident, a glance that reveals what the throes of painting had hidden from her, it's happened countless times, that she notices it without looking for it, seeing certain canvases again that she'd left upstairs in the guest room—the guests these days not necessarily being the people who still come see her from time to time, because those people are more like vestiges of old friendships—as though Christine reserves the *guest rooms* for her paintings alone, offers them alone a place to rest after the labor of being born that they've undergone at her fingertips. Often, seeing them again, it's blindingly obvious to her that these paintings aren't finished, and all of a sudden it's like an accusation, a reproach—how could she let *that* happen?—she didn't dig deep enough, didn't push them to the edge enough for a full and irreversible form to appear; and like every time she decides to leave a painting because she thinks it can finally stand on its own, because she doesn't see what she could add without destroying it, denaturing it, she ends up deciding to look it over once more, just one last time, but always casually, as if by accident. And she'll come back again and examine it even more attentively, refusing to think the finish line has been crossed—just as you refuse to stand face to face with that which you've desired for too long, realizing that what you loved was the journey and not the destination. This time, what jumps out at her is that this old red woman isn't just looking down on her, towering above the hand that produced her. No. What strikes Christine is that, as usual, she had to paint it, this painting, had to pit herself against it, had to have it in front of her in order to understand what wasn't working in the very nature of her project—suddenly letting the thought give way to despondency and devastation, this painting is not only too big, this imposing woman, but also sententious, explicit, as though she's the one who finds herself naked in front of her paint-ing, and red as well, but from shame, not yet from anger—that will come later, as it does every time, when, having rehashed it over and over, she'll have the desire to ruin what she's done by tossing buckets of paint onto the canvas, to destroy it for good.

But for now she has to let it go; she'll return to her canvas, but not before tomorrow.

Today she has other things to do—the birthday cakes she promised Patrice and Ida, who helped her choose: an apple tart, a triple-chocolate cake, and then another, with nuts. Well, she's still wavering between thoughts, eye still drawn to the gaze of the red woman, who seems to her so grandiloquent and ponderous that she'd be ready to destroy her right now without the slightest remorse, but her head is already turned toward the kitchen and the ingredients she has to take out or find—she doesn't need the recipes, she's known them by heart for so long, but she has to make sure she has everything, in cooking as in painting you have to lay your tools out on the table, prepare everything first, with the mania she's always had for lists; but this wavering between two concerns could go on a long time yet and find her in a few minutes, perhaps, or, why not, even in an hour, in the same position, hands in her pants pockets, planted right in the middle of her studio across from a canvas with which she's pretending to carry on a dialogue when it's really a trench war, each of them on one side of the ditch that separates them. But it stops, she hears her dog stirring in the kitchen, his nails scratching the door, the tiles too. He's pawing the ground, Rajah is impatient, he wants to go out, and this takes her out of her thoughts that aren't really thoughts, more a sort of dream state—this is how I piss away my days without noticing them going by, she has time to think as she rushes into the kitchen.

Yes, boy, I'm coming!

She sees her dog at the door, ears perked up, alert, as he rises, straightens, barks, and without any further thought she goes to open the door for him. The dog shoves her, forces his way past her, yelps again as he crosses the yard at full speed, diagonally, like he knows where he's going. And he does know, that's clear: right for the stable. Christine is surprised, he doesn't usually go in a single direction with such determination. Instead Rajah usually goes toward the exterior of the house and the hamlet, crossing the gate that's always open, he runs to the end of the stony path, sometimes venturing into the surrounding fields but never all that far, returning quickly, not taking too long wandering in the yard or anywhere else, he's too old for that, except this time he doesn't wander—is he hunting something, ears perked up out of curiosity or tracking a target he wants to reach, taking care to not scare it off by arriving too quickly?—Christine watches him slow down as he reaches the stable: he watches, stays still, pointing even though he's not a pointer, what he's doing, what he's waiting for, watching, she can't see. He goes into the stable. She doesn't have time to wonder whether he'll come back right away or take a while longer over there, anyway in a moment she's not thinking at all, she forgets all of that, her attention diverted by the car she sees coming up the path and entering the yard—a car she doesn't recognize pulls in and makes a full turn to park right in front of her, ready to leave again. She has time to think to herself that it's odd that Rajah doesn't come back toward the car, he must have heard the engine, he usually goes crazy as soon as a car shows up here, especially an unfamiliar car like this one, a white car that looks like a Clio—for all Christine knows about such things—whose driver still hasn't turned off the engine even though he's come to a stop, as though he's looking for something on the passenger seat. She barely has time to wonder what time it is, to think that she doesn't like being bothered, before the guy cuts the engine and gets out of the car.

Right away she's suspicious. She knows his kind. She's known men like him, young or not so young. He has very light eyes, shining, crystalline, short brown hair in a thick mop—an actor's beauty—and pleasant, prominent wrinkles around his eyes. He might be older than forty, she couldn't say, he flashes her a candid smile but she doesn't find it warm or sympathetic, it's too perfect, the teeth white and orderly, it would be too easy to say *predatory*, no, his smile isn't predatory but still she trips over that all-purpose word, which she takes some time to muddle out of so she can see more clearly, more precisely, the nature of this smile that seems to be amused with itself—yes, that's right, it's more amused, violently amused, she might say, than predatory. The man is looking all around with his very light eyes, gray or blue, which seem to be laughing too, and emphasized by those crow's feet, as they say, no doubt this man laughs often or else he spends time in the sun, or who knows what else, she has no idea and in any case doesn't want to know, she has cakes to bake and no time to spare for a salesman hawking insurance or electricity contracts or whatever else she doesn't need anyway.

He's marveling at the house, at the yard, very ostentatiously, very jovial, far too effusive when he tries to show admiration and astonishment, letting out his

Good afternoon,

casually. And meanwhile she's trying to guess what he's going to try to sell her: saucepans, insurance, solar panels, one of those guys who wash up on her doorstep from time to time. But maybe he's not here for her and wants to see Patrice? Maybe he just wants to unload some combine harvesters on Patrice, or some manure, or—who knows?—but no, he hasn't made a move. He made a motion, after standing still for a few seconds, maybe hesitating about what tack to take, unsure how he should proceed, of withdrawing toward the car, leaning against it while continuing to pantomime an exaggerated casualness, too eager, in spite of his surprisingly gentle voice, almost childish, trembling, not at all confident. And now that he's leaning against his car, without moving toward Christine or even having tried to approach her, to shake her hand, after this, then, having put his hands behind him, against the top of his buttocks, palms flat against the car door, legs straight and nose up, as though he has plenty of time and Christine does also, as though the question is entirely at his discretion, he takes more time before speaking: the houses around him, the yard, the sky, he nods, seems to agree with a conversation he's having only with himself, then finally he trains his very bright and seductive gaze on Christine,

Good afternoon,

Can I help you?

I'm here to see the house.

The house?

He's not getting by with just a smile, though that's what he's trying to do, and quickly he uses his hands, takes them out from behind his back, raises them to the sky as though apologizing for his insistence,

The house, yes, there's a house for sale, right? I'm waiting for the person from the agency, he continues. He can tell his answer isn't satisfactory, that when she said *the house* Christine colored her question with a reproach, with an accusation, her tone accentuating her irritation, as if to leave no doubt about it, but also to leave him the option of clearing off without protest, gathering himself up, saying he must be mistaken or at least that he didn't mean to intrude, something like that, instead of which he rushes into explanations that his gestures only confuse—sticking his hands by turns in his jacket pockets, in his pants pockets, then suddenly in front of him again, as though dancing independent of his will but trying to be convincing, whirling in circles.

Well, it was the agency in town that sent me. I talked to a lady on the phone, she told me to meet her here, she said she'd be here, I must be a bit early.

But now Christine is raising her eyebrows and starting to smile in her turn, not because the situation amuses or intrigues her but maybe because she's thinking that this time she's found a way to put an end to this charade, that she'll settle it quickly,

What agency do you mean? There's no agency, I'm the one who has the keys to the house. That's how it's set up with the neighbors, they put an ad on the internet and they tell me if someone wants to come see it. You saw the ad? Who are you?

Oh? But I spoke to a woman on the phone.

There's no agency for this house, you must've made a mistake. There is a house for sale here, but not through an agency.

Maybe they changed their mind? Maybe they turned it over to an agency without telling you?

In that case you'll have to come back, I can't let you see it if I'm not sure.

Right, I get it, I get it… it's really a lovely area. Nice and peaceful, huh? Nobody to bother you. Okay, well, have a good one.

Yes, goodbye, she says, leaving the man time to make a hand motion that he must think is elegant or courtly but that instead betrays his discomfort, his awkwardness. He gets back in his car and she watches him without moving, resolved to wait until she sees the car leave, which it soon does; the car heads toward the gate, the driver takes a look at Christine and this time he doesn't smile at all—his face has no clear expression behind the car window—but his gaze is a bit too insistent, as though he's observing her, considering her or about to ask her something, but no. And then the car pulls out of the yard and returns to the path, and soon it disappears, leaving Christine on the threshold of her house, turning now toward the stable with a funny feeling, an unpleasant feeling that it takes her a few seconds to identify: it's just that she didn't believe a word the man said. Even if she understood that he knew the neighbors' house was for sale, she doesn't believe his story about an appointment and an agency, she has the feeling he came just to see, to see *her*, up close. This unpleasant impression takes root in her, nests there for a few minutes, and only after a minute does she realize she hasn't heard her dog, no, Rajah hasn't come back even though there was someone in the yard, and this, yes, this surprises her, just as now the silence surprises her; she hears nothing, and it's a deafening nothing, as though the silence has erased everything— and she calls her dog, once,

Rajah!

twice,

Rajah!

but her voice is lost in the yard, with the particular echo it has in the afternoon when it's empty. She knows this silence well, just as she knows her dog; he'll come back in five minutes, which is why, going back inside, even though she knows she'll return to the studio for a few seconds, she leaves the front door open, Rajah can come back when he's ready—and too bad if the slightly cold air from outside slips into the house.

10

The town spreads out and already Patrice is regaining control of his motions, of his emotions; like every time he has the feeling of having to face hostility, he suddenly feels paradoxically cheered up, as though awakened, straightened out internally, not ready to do battle, just ready, reactive, as though he can take on anything, see anything, hear or feel anything, and it's as though his brain has started working again when, facing the fog in which he felt he was losing himself a few minutes ago, his thoughts start moving again. Good, he's in control now, all he needs to do is pull himself together, keep a cool head and not give into desires that aren't even really desires, more like impulses and fantasies, barely—it's nothing.

He runs through everything he has to do even as he discovers, this afternoon, a town whose streets are relatively smooth, calm, the major streets aren't congested, they're almost empty—and yet it's not a holiday—there are people near the department stores, true, but the sidewalks are thinned out, large spaces open easily before him, he breathes freely and now his mind is clear and calm; the boulevards, the big trees on the median, not yet leafing but budding more than in La Bassée, the trees here are a bit ahead because the temperatures in town are always higher than they are in the country. In the almost warm afternoon light, the town hall appears with its meringue façade, its white columns, its caryatids and its French and European Union flags flying—or rather drooping, because there's barely any wind—over the large stone staircase that leads down into the pools just in front. The rue Nationale, the brasseries and patios, the wicker chairs, the chestnut trees on the square and the pedestrian street leading to the train station, the lindens, the flowerbeds on the lawn, he knows all of it well because he has to come into town from time to time, plus he often came here back when he met Marion, because this was where she lived. Everything seems calm, nothing to worry about, no, no reason, what spreads out before him isn't the agitation of a town overcrowded with patterns—decorations—window displays and neon lights—crowds—no, not at all, it's a kind of calm borne by the fountains of the large pools in front of the courthouse, which matches the town hall, the people, the streets, the storefronts, the almost languid movement of the town, nothing frightening, he regards all of it with a certain curiosity and a pleasure that surprises even him, maybe because the weather is mild and, like yesterday, because of the rain that fell this morning, the sun is making the cobblestones shine, as though everything seems to be cleaned, gleaming, haloing the town with spring light.

He knows as soon as he enters the store that it should be quick: at the reception desk a woman is complaining that a screen was delivered for her home cinema that's not the one she was expecting, and behind the counter a scrawny young man with his store vest and a few hairs under his acned chin is answering her, we'll take a look, he repeats, and he does, he searches his computer, and meanwhile around Patrice people come and go, salesmen, he's amazed at the calm—not at all a big peak-time crowd—and besides a few passersby who've come to check out televisions it's even downright empty. Patrice thinks this is a good start, it's a weekday, he shouldn't have to wait too long. And indeed, he doesn't wait more than ten minutes before leaving with his package, an enormous box that they hand to him along with an immense plastic bag that turns out to be too small, impossible, so two salesmen rig up a system for him to carry the box, strings attached to a plastic handle that allows him to carry the computer, which isn't that heavy after all, it's fine, thank you, and he leaves the store realizing he didn't think to ask them to wrap it, oh well, he'll have to remember to find some wrapping paper at the house, yes, there should be some where he found the string of lights, he wonders if there's anything besides the scraps of Christmas paper that are handy for tiny presents, but no doubt this package will require almost a whole roll; if there isn't any he'll ask Christine, she'll certainly have something somewhere in all her hodgepodge—and thinking of such light and simple things helps him breathe and feel his body relax. He feels relieved, something in him has just come free, that's clear, he has Marion's gift and he can go home, he has to stop at Picard but the store is on his way, all he has to do is get in his car and leave town.

He puts the large computer box on the back seat of the Kangoo—he could have fit it in the trunk, but no, he puts it on the back seat and closes the side door. He gets into the front, sits in front of the steering wheel, and, out of instinct, without knowing why, he looks in the inside rearview mirror, unable to move, just looking at the computer—the large box and this handle they attached for him—insistent, too insistent, much too much, yes, it's taking too long, now he has to take the car key and start it up. He has to get out of here, he knows it, tells himself, orders himself, but his right hand slips into the inside pocket of his leather jacket, yes, feels that it's there and so takes it, there it is, the wallet is in his right hand, Patrice places it in his left, the fingers of his right hand go in and search its side slit, his heart starts beating harder and harder, he has only a twenty-euro bill and two fives, with a quick motion he puts the wallet back in his inside pocket, a sigh courses through Patrice, a breath so long and so deep it's almost as if that's what expels him from the car, all of a sudden he's opening the door without even looking in the rearview to see if anyone might hit him; but luckily no, there's no one on the road, he's not used to checking, back in the country there's never anyone coming behind the doors you open, at worst a dog but that's it, and now Patrice is on the sidewalk with the car key in his hand. He locks the car, he knows perfectly well what he's doing but he needs to breathe hard just to take some time, some time, yes, it's to take some time that he stops in front of a bank; he slides his card into the ATM and is informed that this machine distributes twenties, tens, he takes no notice. He takes out a hundred euros, he knows that's a lot. He takes the money, that'll save some time, time to hesitate, time to torture himself, to let himself believe he might give up or give in—he could take a stroll, walk down the street, go have a coffee on a patio somewhere and let the world pass by in front of him, all these busy people coming and going, like sparks, images, and then disappearing, returning to the mystery of their own lives, with no connection to his; yes, that's what he'll do. He tells himself that's what he'll do. He approaches a brasserie, the people on the patio, two couples, a student reading a book in which three quarters of the words are highlighted in pink, the empty tables with their metal ashtrays, the water dripping from the trees onto the tables, the wet cobblestones still slippery here and there, and the traces of mud at the bottom of the gutter; and then in the end he doesn't stop and keeps walking, going deeper into the town, telling himself he has plenty of time to get some air— what harm could it do, he has time, still a bit of time, he knows where he's going and tells himself he's going somewhere else—or not even, he pretends to lie to himself by telling himself it's just to think about the things he has to do or that he still hasn't done; his heart is beating harder and harder and his throat is dry, horribly dry, his hands on the contrary are moist enough to remind him that he's lying most of all to himself and that out of everything he's doing here that's maybe the most pitiful thing, this lie he's inflicting on himself when he'd do better to admit to himself what he's come for on this bright and dreary afternoon in this neither large nor small town; all he's doing now is buying time from himself to prolong his lie, his hypocrisy. He tries looking at his watch, taking out his phone, stopping on a street corner to see whether he has any messages, and it's no use, he knows he doesn't have any, but stopping means buying more time, a few seconds before setting off again; he puts his phone back in his pocket and in the end yes, he will stop on the patio of a café on one of the main boulevards— and now sitting, drinking a too-bitter coffee that he takes the time to drink slowly, repressing his desire to drink it in a single gulp, he looks at the boulevards opening up in front of him, with their cars near the converted sidewalks on either side of the median, the great masses of leaves on the chestnut trees shading the gravel alley—the leaves that have already started growing here—the alternation of green and red lights, the cars stopping, starting, the pedestrians clustering then crossing and dispersing.

He'll go soon. He shivers, he's a bit cold. He leaves money on the dark red metal table, the coins make a strange noise on the metal, he gets up, looks into the bar to see if he can spot the server to say goodbye but no, he doesn't see him. He leaves, turns onto the boulevard, under the trees, the crunch of the gravel, an immense dejection seizing him, he walks, he could start smoking again right now, it reminds him of when he was young and how afraid he was of women and how attracted he was to them, and suddenly he sees some, some women, very young African women advancing in pairs. He doesn't want his path to meet theirs, so he leaves the median and crosses the street, waits for a few cars to go by, takes the first street he comes to without knowing where it goes, he doesn't know where it leads, no matter, it's a small street, he takes it without paying attention, and he won't know how to describe to himself later in his car how things happen next, even though he'll try to retrace his path, his heart beating hard enough to burst through his temples, the blood, the blood pounding too hard in his veins, his head, he won't be able to explain to himself how all of a sudden he's walking in the company of this young black woman about whom, as they walk side by side, her slightly behind him, he can't stop wondering, *how old is she, how old is she?*

Instead of which words are exchanged, and of course because he knows them in advance he doesn't really hear that for fifty euros she'll do everything; he's almost dismayed at the price and all the same he says yes, he hears only his own voice suggesting—but to whom? to the girl? to himself?—that he's interested in the young girl, and his absurd and trembling voice asks what her name is—Precious—him wanting to answer that's pretty and it doesn't even occur to him that it might not really be her name—Where are you from?—From Ghana, she answers, and now she's leading him into an alley and he can tell she's prudent, she's keeping an eye on what's going on around them, says she's going to walk a few meters ahead of him and he's not even thinking about the police, will he come out of the trance that's making him lose his basic common sense, is he just guided by his desire, thinking that men once did what he's doing now without being ashamed and without feeling the slightest doubt or the slightest guilt, whereas he's tormented and judging himself with a stern eye, when the young girl leads him not into a room as he'd have thought she would, because ordinarily that's what they do—several times he's been here before, and several times it was in rather sordid rooms that stank of ammonia and piss, cologne, soap and standing water—but this is even worse, he doesn't know how he's wound up in the semi-dark of a garbage shed, standing up, pants around his ankles, dick in the mouth of a black girl kneeling before him—and these motions that chilled him, surprised him, when, before taking out the condom, she took a wipe from a little case and cleaned her hands delicately, mechanically, like a surgeon about to operate, just as she put away with the same cautious and studied delicateness, folding them slowly and with an almost childlike, studently deliberation, the two twenty-euro bills and the ten. He steadies himself against a trash can and doesn't know how he's hard, but he's hard, the girl is holding the base of his cock and working diligently at sucking it. He thinks that if she's holding the base of the cock it's not to fondle his balls or to make him come faster, just to hold in place the condom she slid onto him; he has time to think of this, time to see everything, the trash cans, the sorting system, luckily the bins are empty and the smell isn't too strong, a sickly sweet stench, in a corner there are some tools and a stepstool, housekeeping things, suddenly he panics at the idea that someone might come, the girl gets up and lifts her dress and pulls down her tights, her panties, she turns around so he can take her from behind, offers him her ass and he's not hard anymore, this isn't what he wants, does he want this, to see himself doing this, to see himself fucking a girl who's maybe still a minor and whose life he imagines to be monstrous, appalling, the money that she surely won't keep for herself but give to some mafia or other, and it's no use telling himself all this, somewhere deep down something in him doesn't care, now he doesn't care, he takes the girl's buttocks in hand and his dick sinks into her, he comes to life, he can feel his cock getting hard again inside her and now the thoughts skittering around don't concern her at all, he wishes she were naked, wishes he could grab her breasts, he'd like to take her breasts firmly in his hands, suck them, lick her nipples, images overtake him and then, like electric shocks, all the nights of humiliation, for years and years, this anger that forms each night when he comes into his bedroom and his wife refuses him—how long has it been that she's refused him completely, years now, as soon as they got married everything became depleted, he could keep a log of the depletion that's taken root between them, what they don't do anymore, the crudeness and ease of their gestures, the body odors, good god, the bodies becoming so well-behaved, the good behavior becoming so sad, how soon they start deferring to their fatigue, how they've made love less and less often, once a week, then once every two weeks, then once a month and now every now and then he knows Marion allows him a few caresses that she doesn't take seriously, that she doesn't want, he can feel it, how her thighs stiffen, how he has a harder time penetrating her than he used to because she doesn't get wet for him anymore and how without even realizing it she puts her arms over her breasts to keep him from sinking his face into them, or his mouth, his lips, to take them in his hands like he likes to, he knows how she retracts, how tiredness takes up more space in their bed than he does, always those little phrases, murderous—m'exhausted, have to get up early—and these thoughts give him a kind of bitter, morbid momentum against himself, because he's ashamed of himself, he thinks it's pitiful to let himself be led around by his balls, does anyone really need this to live, does anyone really need—

And now he lifts up the dress and tries to stroke this back and soon he's holding onto the girl's shoulders, he thinks he's not going to come, he doesn't want to come but at the same time he's wild with rage against this shame he feels because yes, he's a man and he wants to fuck, to not live frustrated with everything the way he did in his stifled adolescence, when it was bearable because he told himself it wouldn't last, that it was just a stage before he met the woman who would satisfy him from this perspective too, but that's not how it is, and now he resents Marion, and women, he feels angry, why should he be ashamed of his impulses, why should he have to hide them, he always controls them, he almost always controls them, why should he hide himself and live in shame? If he's ashamed it's because he's disappointed with what Marion forces him to do when she just turns her back to him, even if he also knows she has every right to turn her back to him, what kind of creep would oblige his wife, would force his wife, has he thought about it, no, of course not, but he knows that she, in the past, well, he's understood—thinks he's understood—because she never speaks entirely clearly about these things, Marion, no, but he knows she hasn't always been with men who asked her opinion, but he, he loves her, he loves his wife, he's bursting with love for his wife, he thinks it would be easier if he didn't love her so much, he doesn't want to hurt her, women don't belong to us anyway and yet in this moment he's paid for a woman to lift up her dress and spread her legs, and this strange anger doesn't leave him but gives him even more strength, more desire, it drives him, stirs him, excites him even more because the anger is pushing him with each motion of the hips, each thrust, as though he's avenging himself on women, on the distance of his, but not only that, on his youth too, on the *Playboy* photos in Albert's shed, on hicks like him who never had a chance to rank in the love lottery of the girls and boys their own age, and the hatred, the desire to come, the pleasure of the hatred rises to his head as he tells himself that everyone in the world takes him for an idiot, he who stinks of farm and mud, the rubber of his boots, the sudden hatred because he doesn't love himself and because he never really has—and, for as far back as he can remember, if he liked living in the hamlet, on the farm, away from everyone, it's because the animals, for their part, have never looked down on him.

11

Nice, yes. She just needs to be nice, in her own way, otherwise it's going to be difficult for her to start baking, even though the only desire she really feels is to go back to her painting, to take it up again from the place she's already been several times; but that's how it goes, she knows, the moment she approaches the end of a painting is at once the worst and the most exciting; it's the moment promised and refused in the same motion, close and always pushed off just as she thinks she's reached it. It's always necessary to take it up again, until it's finished, because inevitably, at some point, though you never see it coming, the end stops your hand over the painting and leaves it stopped, as if intoxicated, late to the trajectory the canvas has taken, paint still flowing down the brush, its hairs saturated with color, your hand seized by the obvious fact that there's nothing more to add.

But she promised Ida and Patrice she'd bake cakes, and she's going to get to it. She can tell herself all she wants that it's no big deal, but in truth she experiences it like a sacrifice, even a bit too painful a sacrifice for the actual effort it requires, she knows, but she'll do it for Ida and for Bergogne, because he's thoughtful and sweet with her like only the nephew or the son she never had would be, or the ideal friend she's never known except in him, whose role he fills—nephew or son—just as Ida, as it were, fills the role of the ideal granddaughter whom she cherishes more than anything and, for that matter, whose work she was looking at again, earlier, with affection and indulgence, the two paintings the little girl had made for her mother—for whom, on the other hand, Christine certainly wouldn't make the effort she's about to make now, no, because in truth she never remembers Marion's birthdays, an oversight that returns every year like the dot on an *i* to truly show she doesn't care very much, neither about the birthday nor about Marion, not that she feels guilty, because she's not unaware that the converse is also true and Marion doesn't remember Christine's birthday any more than Christine remembers Marion's. They have this in common, that they feel no particular sympathy for each other, without any pretense between them, without going to the trouble of bending hypocritically to the pretext that they should indulge Ida and reassure her father, or respect the pseudo-familial order between the Bergognes and their neighbor. This point unites them with respect to Ida and Patrice, and it's been this way since the day they met, each of them knows it of herself and also of the other, each can see it in the other's eyes, in the reciprocal impatience as soon as they're in the same room—not that they don't like each other, not even that, it's a bit less than that: they share a hamlet, in a certain sense they share Bergogne and Ida too, truth be told they could almost feel close, complicit, knowing they're in such perfect agreement in the way they see each other, and they could almost fraternize—sororize?—around this shared indifference toward one another, both knowing there's no reason to get upset about a forgotten birthday, just as there's no reason to be hurt by a forgotten gift—they've never given each other gifts—and in this way they're in such tight consonance that you could swear they'd eventually come to understand each other perfectly if they'd only make the effort that Bergogne still hopes they will, he hasn't given up completely on seeing them get along as they sometimes manage to do over a drink, when one can find in the other a hint of conspiratorial concord, a knowing air when it comes to laughing about Patrice's flaws and tics, amusing themselves at his expense.

So she'll make the cakes, they'll have their birthday meal, the three of them, like the family of bears from the fable—a papa—a mama—a child. Then Christine will bring over the cakes, still warm, not before eight thirty, no doubt even a bit later so as not to seem like she's in a hurry nor to let them think she's been hiding in wait behind the door. No, certainly not: she'll come calmly after they've had dinner, hoping Marion's two co-workers will have had the same idea, coming fifteen minutes late to show they're in no rush to get there, that they can manage to not be invasive—remains to be seen—and also leaving enough time to stay with the Bergognes and have them to herself, as though the four of them were a family, even if Christine doesn't like to tell herself this kind of lie, she's not a member of the family, she's just a friend, it's normal for her to leave them to their intimacy before she shows up, even if she hopes they'll have a half hour where it's just the four of them, because she really does like those special festive moments, whether it's Christmas or a birthday, that tenderness that flows through the house, a Bergogne sweet as a lamb and an Ida buzzing like a bee, and then even Marion, cuddly as a kitten—the whole bestiary to which Christine likens them, feeling among them like a fish in water.

She'll set the cakes on the dining room table and Marion will offer her a glass of champagne by way of welcome; Christine will say yes, wishing her a happy birthday and smiling at the decorations, the effort made by Patrice—a smile the two women will share to remark upon Bergogne's work,

Looks like the layabout finally got to work!

Christine will quip as she raises her glass or sets down the cakes, while Ida applauds. They'll cut two of them into six slices, Marion will want to know who the surprise guests are, they'll put candles on the chocolate cake but not cut it yet, they'll cut it at the last minute, and put two candles on it, white candles with a red border on one side, with blue and green dots, one in the shape of a four and the other a zero. Christine will recognize the two paintings the little girl made last night, which she'll have come to collect in the afternoon, the party atmosphere, the table set, all of Bergogne's attentions. She'll take a piece of cake and drink a glass of champagne with them, then she'll claim she should get going and she won't wait for Marion's co-workers, she doesn't care much for them, and if she stays a bit longer it will be just so as not to be rude again, yes, maybe she'll make the effort to stay so she can say hello to them, even if in truth she hates the sound of giggling—more misogynistic than a man, more critical of women than anyone, looking down on most of them, judging them worthy of the scorn with which most men treat them—that's how it is, she won't inflict Marion's co-workers on herself, anyway she can imagine the three of them all too well behind their work computers, chattering about their *girls-only* karaoke nights—those grotesque evenings to which they treat themselves the same way they treat their kids to *pajama parties*—and she, Christine, feels nothing but disgust for all that, she's always detested hysterical females who make women look ridiculous, giving them a bad name, excuse her if she doesn't bow down in gratitude, and, trying to hold back the disdain she feels for them so it's not too obvious, she also tries to temper her consternation and her pitying anger toward poor Bergogne, who gives his wife too much freedom, letting her go out at least once a week to go dancing with her girlfriends—what could be more ridiculous than these fifty-year-old women convincing themselves they're still twenty?—but it pains her for Bergogne, pretty Marion going out to dance and sing with her girlfriends and no doubt be hit on by pretty boys ten or fifteen years younger than her, without even getting into how she must enjoy being hit on, how maybe she even hits on some of them herself, and has, for all she knows, one-night stands—poor Bergogne, just a sap, a victim of his own love and naiveté, maybe of the fear of losing his wife.

Christine prefers not to think about it: as soon as they show up she'll go back to her painting.

• • •

For now, she ignores the noises, hasn't even begun to notice them almost everywhere around her, as she will in a few minutes.

For now, she pays no mind to these rustles, these breaths, these steps that she'll begin to perceive only once she's finished setting up the necessary ingredients and utensils on her kitchen table.

For now, then, she pays no attention to the sounds from outside, nor to the fact that her dog still hasn't come back to her. She concentrates on what she has to do: break the eggs, separate the whites, mix the yolks with the sugar and salt and the walnut halves, add flour and baking powder while continuing to mix—could she hear, at this moment, what's happening right next to her house, even though she doesn't know and would have no way of knowing that at this very moment a man's hand has already held out a piece of meat to her dog, in the stable? How could she know without going to see for herself, which she won't do, because she's not thinking about it? She's thinking about the cakes she has to bake and the painting waiting for her, that's all, not about what's happening right next door, about which she can't possibly know anything. She's still mixing, a consistent dough is swelling up, she's beating the eggs into stiff peaks and in the stable it's already been a moment since the hand tossed the piece of meat in front of the dog. The piece of meat made a sound falling on the concrete slab, a moist, flaccid *flop,* the dog has already leapt on it, not to sniff at it or to question what's being offered to him but to sink his teeth in without any further attention to the man's hand that tossed it; the dog attracted or rather excited by the bloody piece of meat and not seeing that, in the hand the man is gripping so tightly around the handle of a knife, the blade shines like the blades of combat knives, to which the dog pays no attention because what he sees and what he smells, which are occupying his brain to the point of rendering him deaf and blind to any danger, is just this meat, the smell of meat that maybe reminds him of the underbrush and of hunting on

Sunday mornings with Bergogne, the smell of game and the blood of freshly dead animals; the meat is making his head spin so much that he's not paying attention to anything and doesn't see the man in a blue tracksuit, the knife in his hand, the hand advancing and, at the same moment, or maybe just a few minutes after, with a fork, Christine is delicately mixing the stiff peaks of the eggs into the batter waiting next to her while, at the moment she pours the whole mixture into a buttered pan and goes to put it in the oven, the dog will have received a first knife-blow to his ribs, which will have wrenched from him a squeal resembling a cry—very sharp—because the man walking along the stable wall will have surprised the dog from behind and the dog won't have seen anything coming, almost asphyxiated as he was by the taste of the meat, his face buried in the meat; while Christine wipes her hands on her apron, as she so often does with paint on her smock, the dog has had time to let out a kind of cry, even sharper than the first, as piercing as the blade that's just ripped through his ribs and which the hand has already withdrawn in a very rapid motion—sharp—feverish—only to plant it again, not leaving the German shepherd time to recover from his surprise, to try to retaliate, to bite, its mouth snapping in the air, not for long, anyway Christine hasn't yet had time to melt the chocolate in a bain-marie with two soupspoons, no, the hand has plunged into the dog's throat and Rajah has finished crumpling on the concrete slab, his strength failing him, he's whimpered again, slowly, softer and softer, like a child crying, moans, then nothing, a few spasms, astonishment, surprise and pain, the bloody mouth covered with the intoxication of the meat and him a mass collapsed because his paws have given out, the slaughtered body on its side, the head banged against the concrete.

Now the man has pushed the dog's body a bit farther toward the back of the stable, as though he doesn't want to leave it somewhere too open, as if its death calls for somewhere dimmer, more discreet, almost restful, over where there's a pile of hay on the concrete. He does this and wipes the blade of his knife on the dog's fur—one side, then the other, like so, several times, back and forth, back and forth, the way they sharpen their blades in butcher shops, with a rapid and confident motion, almost demonstrative, choreographed; he does it with care and then folds the knife and puts it in the pocket of his track pants. He looks at the dog's body, its open mouth letting the tongue hang out and showing yellowing, ivory-colored fangs, and meanwhile, across the hamlet, at a diagonal, Christine is no longer thinking about her painting, no more than she's thinking about Marion or Ida or Bergogne, no, she's thinking she could listen to some Bach sonatas, that Gastinel recording she loves deeply, even if for a few years, for having listened to it so much, she felt a kind of weariness toward it, almost disgust, not because of Gastinel's interpretation, which she likes very much, just because of her overuse of Gastinel; like a convalescent, she can allow herself from time to time without succumbing to the desire that could quickly return to listen several times in a row, on loop, as she used to do to the point of excess, no, to come back to it and listen once, only once, and that's what she's thinking about right now.

So she stops what she's doing and goes into the studio to put on the CD, adjust the volume, loud but not too loud, enough to hear it from the kitchen, which isn't far, a partition but no door—she had almost all the doors removed long ago, it was too complicated with the canvases and the frames—the music, the cello, and the moment she comes back into the kitchen, the moment she looks at her table to make sure nothing is missing before she starts on the second cake, a man who has finished rubbing off, on the hay, the blood he had on his hands, in the stable, has come out of that stable, in keeping with a plan laid some time ago now, he's come out the back, crossed along the right side of the hamlet, passing behind the shed, his feet sinking into the muddy soil of the cornfield bordering the hamlet; walking along the wall of the shed, he's continued against Bergogne's house, walking briskly, without stopping, per the plan—move along the side wall, slip behind

Bergogne's house, land in the yard of the house for sale, the one where you won't risk being disturbed or seen by anyone, and then you'll come back to the neighbor's house—the one they call the neighbor as though it's a name, her name, as though she's nothing but that—and, in the same motion and without a second thought, still moving along the wall of her house, because it serves as a partitioning wall between the houses, you'll go up to her door: there's a door in the back that opens into a small room where she does her laundry. There you go. That door is always open, every time we saw it it was open—how many times could we have entered the house and done what we're going to do now?

But no, it's now that it has to be done. Now everything is ready. The man creeps up to the door, which he opens effortlessly; he barely has time to let out a sigh because he's gotten his tracksuit dirty—the bottoms of the pants all muddy, the sneakers disgusting—he enters, the music, Bach, Gastinel's cello pricks into his ears like an unexpected breath of fresh air. In her kitchen, Christine thinks there's a draft somewhere, she has the feeling she heard footsteps, but no, no, surely her dog has just come back in, what else could it possibly be, there have never been any ghosts in this house.

12

His house, which Bergogne thinks of now as though he hasn't seen it in ages, as though he's been deprived of it the way a prisoner is deprived of everything that makes up his life. In the car, before starting the engine, he tells himself he's been gone too long, that he's spent too much time away from home. If he sees any infidelity in the hour he's just spent here, it's less for the paid sexual encounter than because he's deserted in his own eyes the place that's his, his work, his farm, his animals who need him and whom he's chosen to leave high and dry by wasting precious time doing stupid things, like a kid or an obsessive unable to control his urges, letting himself be devoured by them like a dog in heat or like the creatures he spends his days with, yes, it has nothing to do with love, it's not even frustration about his wife, it's just a thing that has to be done, that he has to do, just as his animals do it.

He reassures himself by repeating that he shouldn't beat himself up too much for this, lend so much importance to something that maybe has none, after all it's just a hormonal thing; he knows it, just as the girl he's just paid knows she can agree to it because she's making money off something that's not her, that ultimately she gives away nothing that says anything about who she is, even if it comes at a cost to her and she doesn't necessarily want to give herself to the first man who comes along; he doesn't want to know whether she's doing it out of necessity or decided to make it her work, whether she thinks of it as a job like any other or it's a nightmare she's trying desperately to escape—the stories of girls forced into prostitution to pay off their debts to smugglers who stole their papers, the things you hear on the news about African women who were sold an image of paradise but for whom Europe is just another hell. He knows nothing about this girl's case, and in this moment he pretends he doesn't have to think about it, letting his mind cover these questions with the foggy veil of a false sense of propriety—what does he think propriety has to do with it, he who set it aside so easily when it was convenient for him to do so?—and he doesn't want to think about her, he wants to reduce this girl to nothing, or rather it's not her he wants to reduce to nothing but the conditions of her life, evading the question of whether by paying her he's perpetuating her hell or helping her escape it. He wants to release all this, like that intimate and mortifying feeling of always needing to be more inconspicuous, as though to even express a desire is always to trample on your fellow man's. What irritates him is the time wasted, even though he knew all along he'd give in, it's seeing himself waste time for *his own* pleasure, which he's always hated, not only because his parents taught him that the first thing a man should work at is forgetting himself, denying himself or canceling himself out, himself and his problems, because he has to put food on the table for others and to do that he must make himself a mere machine and go to work, but also because work is the only means he has of not thinking about seeing himself as someone who overvalues himself at the slightest opportunity and gives in to each frivolous whim that presents itself to him. His parents had repeated this to him for as long as he could remember, just as theirs had repeated it to them and theirs before them, as though those sentences were the echo of time immemorial, a word from the ancients that had passed all the way down to him, strolling down the corridors of the centuries. Yes, he heard it enough when he was a kid: even if he cut himself deep by falling on the rocks or hurt himself by bumping his head, even if he sometimes got humiliated at school because his clothes were too ugly or old-fashioned, you don't bother other people for something so petty.

Before he even puts the key in the ignition, before he starts the car, yes, before any of that, it's this thought that crushes him. The feeling of shame corroding the thought, of having wanted to satisfy a pleasure that benefits only him. Before even the shame or the remorse of objectifying a young woman about whom he'll never know anything. And now he has to hurry and pull himself together, has to pretend he didn't waste this time satisfying those instincts that he doesn't even ultimately see as animal, because at least animals don't tremble when they come; they do it and don't make a fuss about it, they don't pay for it, they don't buy satisfaction and appeasement, don't exploit the miseries of the world and the vulnerability of women.

And yet, in spite of all of this, what comes now, in his car, is also the feeling of relaxation, of repose, and the truth is that if he comes back to these boulevards from time to time, if he needs to come—not so often, he's not what you'd call a regular here—the truth is that, for a few minutes, alone in the passenger compartment of his car, he feels a wave of peace cross his body that almost makes him forget his muscle pains and his tensions, yes, he comes because he needs it, because he needs more than just to fill a sexual need that anguishes him so much, he needs to cast off his impatience and the pressures he inflicts on himself, as though he's on the verge of falling or exploding into a rage he'd be unable to control if he didn't give in now and then to a kind of loophole—which he also sees as an alibi, a pretext to allow himself to go do it—the way he so often saw his father backslide when he let himself get carried away by his fits of rage—his murderous urges that the old folks still brought up when they talked about his father but also his grandfather and their memorable rages, both of them, *like father like son*—the way he needs to go hunting in order to be alone in the forest, walking for hours before ending up in the company of guys like him, whom he's known forever but with whom he never discusses these things—as though he's the only person to ever experience them—guys who also came along with their own fathers when they were children, for hours, and who had the feeling that they were being inducted by them, being entrusted with a secret of which only they were worthy, he remembers, the only moments his father didn't frighten him, in which he opened a space for him where he could be happy and proud to share it. He developed this taste in childhood, and he still likes to take the time to wait, to poke around, to hunt game, and even if he doesn't like to kill he likes the tracking, the hours spent watching for prey, the heat of the freshly killed animal whose body still throbs beneath his fingers, the softness of its feathers, its fur, this time where he thinks about nothing besides breathing and feeling the cold humid country air, this time he shares with Christine's dog, the two of them alone, before they meet the others, with whom Bergogne will stand near their cars drinking mulled wine out of Thermoses, waiting with amusement or compassion to see who'll come back empty-handed. So he relaxes in his car, the nape of his neck against the headrest, head tilted slightly back; his breath comes from deeper and deeper down, a heavier and heavier drowsiness takes hold of him, it lasts a few minutes. He struggles, pushes it off, it'll go on a few minutes more, he has to straighten up in his seat—there, that's enough, now it's time to get going. And it's at this moment that he turns on the cell phone he'd taken care to switch off. The telephone and its messages. A text from Nathalie, one of Marion's co-workers: three words and a dumb emoticon to confirm what she already confirmed last week, that they'll both be there, Nathalie and Lydie, that they'll come tonight around nine, to which Patrice feels obligated to reply, with two clicks,

Thanks, see you tonight.

Why he's thanking this girl he barely knows and doesn't particularly like, he doesn't know. But then he doesn't know either how he could like these two women who Marion goes out with so often, because he often has the feeling that his wife prefers their company to his; if he doesn't dare admit to himself that he's jealous of them, he can still admit to himself that he doesn't much care for them, he thinks or imagines they push Marion to hide things from him that he's never been eager to broach, even if he'd like, in the morning, or late at night, when she comes home and she's drunk, to force Marion to tell him what she did with her evening, make her say who she saw, who she met, if she danced a lot and if she had fun—oh? yeah? with who?—her stinking of cigarettes and alcohol and remaining hazy on Saturday mornings and, above all, silent. Each time, he keeps quiet and has to make a considerable effort not to ask anything, even though she doesn't even make the effort to let him in on a single detail of the evenings he's excluded from—and, what he's most afraid of, the reason he doesn't like Nathalie and Lydie: that her friends and co-workers are a kind of screen for Marion so she can hide more serious things from him, maybe a lover, he thinks about this often, he imagines one day she'll leave him for someone else, which already happened to him once with a woman who wasn't half the woman Marion is, and so, letting himself ramble along the grounds of the fiercest jealousy— the shadow of someone between her and him—he ties his brain in knots by convincing himself she'll leave him for this man who's already living between them, because from the start he's thought Marion would end up taking off, no question, she has no business being with a guy like him. It's as though the two girls are there to remind him that his days are numbered, that it's a favor or an indulgence Marion is granting him—out of what weakness, what passing kindness?—and doesn't he see, when he comes home from hunting, as he's placing his dead animals on the kitchen table, his rifle still smoking, his game bag with its overpowering smell of leather, the disgust he awakens not only in Ida but also in Marion, who stares at him in those moments as though she doesn't know him, wondering who is this man? Maybe that's why he does ev- erything in his power to be pleasant with his wife, why he always gives in, worrying without even knowing about what, except discovering that she could leave on a whim if he ever admitted how much he dreads seeing her go dancing and drinking—knowing that deep down, most of all, something in him gives up a little more each day on trying to make her happy and contents itself more and more often, if it can't make her happy, with being pleasant to her, and, if he can't please her, with indulging her.

That was why he invited Nathalie and Lydie to share Marion's birthday cake, finding a way to get their phone numbers without Marion knowing. If nothing else, this text message he's received forces him to disentangle himself from his contradictions; he has to get moving, let's go, we're off, soon the engine and the vibration it sends through the whole car when it gets going will finish pulling him out of his discomposure. Patrice concentrates—signal—pull out—merge into traffic and wait for the light to turn green, make a U-turn a bit farther down to get back to the road, as though it were possible by doing everything in reverse to turn back time and erase not what you've done, exactly, but at least the memory you have of it, as though you could erase your motions by making the same ones backwards, but no, you have to give up and keep your thoughts tensed, cross town, and, coming back toward the state road, stop at Picard in the shopping district before the ring road. That's what he's going to do, in a length of time that will seem considerable to him, interminable, not just because he'll have to wait in the checkout line and that moment alone will seem so long that he'll consider abandoning it all, knowing he'd gain a few minutes that he'd just lose again right away because he'd still have to figure something else out for the meal—Super U? the butcher?—but also because he's unable to calm down as he waits in line, to grin and bear it, as he'd had to do while wandering the aisles, his basket in hand, to find everything he'd planned to get. Instead he'd wavered, wondering if this was a good idea, if he wouldn't be better off letting chance and the whim of the moment guide him, before ultimately coming back to his first choice: he spent enough time wondering when he looked at the frozen food store's website that he's not going to change everything now, risk everything, at least he knows she likes morels and sweetbreads—and suddenly Marion is back in his mind, as though he's regaining his footing back in reality.

There. That's done. He waited a long time but he's finally out of the store. He puts the bag of frozen foods in the trunk and thinks that in barely an hour he'll be home. He'll find Ida and they'll get ready, take a bath or a shower, get dressed up properly, finish the preparations and wait for Marion to arrive—even if he knows she probably won't be home before seven, maybe later, she did mention that damn meeting with her director and the project manager, which he knows will be another unpleasant moment for her, maybe even a turbulent one, he's always worried she'll tear down in ten seconds everything she took so long to build, this job she wanted so badly and likes so much. But she's so impulsive, and so edgy at the prospect of domination, no, Marion's not the type to let herself submit, she hates being taken for an idiot who can be easily cast aside, everything in her resists and summons the thunderbolts she bursts overhead with her murderous comments, her smiles, her gestures, an attitude whose effects she knows how to mete out perfectly—their acidity, their violence, their provocation blending nonchalance and anger, ironic distance and direct aggression. She knows how to play with all of it, he knows it, sometimes she does with him what he's seen her do—often—with Christine, when Christine makes a dig at the way she dresses or her table manners and when, by way of response, Marion keeps a cigarette in her mouth, as though sulking, without striking back, not a word, just appalled or intrigued by Christine's voice calling her Madame Dietrich will all the sarcasm she can muster in her voice.

Patrice thinks about this, cruising now down the highway. Thirty kilometers until the exit and the state road he'll have to take soon; there, he's off the highway and on the state road, driving past a first little village and then the second, and as the Kangoo picks up speed he thinks he doesn't need to worry, this isn't the first birthday of Marion's they've celebrated, and even if forty is a bit special and has a symbolic dimension perhaps, something a bit more solemn, deep down it's just a birthday, nothing more, Patrice thinks as he turns on the radio, he who practically never listens to it, some crap they're playing on Radio Nostalgie, songs like the ones they used to sing at the dances back then and that maybe they still sing today, he wonders, even if it takes him some time to realize that another noise is accompanying the radio and the sound of the engine, another noise, another vibration besides the ones that ordinarily joggle the car, alongside the bass from the radio and the shaking chassis, wheels on the battered road—or rather no, it's not the road that's battered,

(a tire)

it takes some time before he understands,

(a tire)

it's coming from the wheels, he didn't feel anything, didn't realize, but now he has to stop, shit, it's a tire, a tire, fuck, does he have what he needs to change it? Yes, okay, but now there's no question, he's going to end up making himself really late.

13

For a few seconds Christine thinks she hears her dog breathing, the claws of his feet on the tile, that joyful panting sound animals make without restraint, without embarrassment or false modesty—but no, she quickly realizes she's mistaken, just as she realizes she's been listening to Bach only intermittently, as though disturbed or preoccupied by something other than the music, or as though the time she has for it this afternoon—as though she's not used to cooking while listening to music—has been impaired by interactions that are scrambling her concentration. She wonders why her dog didn't come before, toward the man and his car, still resisting—at the moment the question takes shape—the impulse that holds her for a moment before she rejects it, to go out and cross the yard to the stable to see what's been keeping Rajah, but she collects herself, discarding this temptation like a childish idea of no importance, as though this idea was a whim and nothing more, repeating to herself that it's not fear but rather curiosity, surprise, what could possibly have kept Rajah out there so long, he who normally runs like mad as soon as an engine can be heard on the road, before it even reaches the sign for the Three Lone Girls?

So, kneading the dough, letting the aroma of melted chocolate rise to her nose, she wonders, now lending only a distracted ear to Gastinel's cello, why that guy leaning against his car left such a bad impression, as though the whole time they were talking—can

you even call it talking?—he made every effort to make a fool
of her without her noticing right away, leaving her a cigarette
paper–thin veneer over his gestures, over the tone of his voice,
over his smile, so she'd perceive the playfulness and irony he put
into them, as though he wanted her to know how clever he was
and that they were playing a game only he had mastered, how he
obviously knew more about it than she did—her sensing now that
she shouldn't have answered him the way she did, leaving him too
much room, too much freedom, when he probably knew perfectly
well there was no agency in charge of the house for sale. He played
the fool to take me for a ride and see how far he could go, she
thinks, now remembering the way the man leaned against that car
that looked like a rental, not a private car, no, too clean, and that
casual and confident air he had, in spite of the signs of discomfort,
as though wanting to conceal his presence by overdoing it, with
exaggerated smiles, expressive hand gestures—his fluttering hands
that seemed incapable of settling down, not stopping until he managed to keep them behind his back, jammed between the car and
him, or when he brought them back under his arms, sticking them
there like you do with a newspaper so you don't have to think
about it, holding them there tightly and acting like he wasn't hiding something.

Now she thinks that it's bizarre that a man can evince the
certainty of someone playing a game whose rules only he knows
and at the same time uncertainty, doubt, maybe even worry, as
though he really had two things in his head rather than one, distinct enough from one another for him to simultaneously feel the
satisfaction of control on one hand and fear on the other, Christine
thinks, leaving her cakes for the moment, looking at the kitchen
table, the dishes, the flour covering parts of the oilcloth. She hears
the cello coming from the next room and it seems to be sending
her a message that she can't quite make out, as though her percep-
tive capacity is scrambled by ideas other than the ones that should
be hers, ideas that return and revolve around this man and the

persistent unease attached to him, increasingly persistent and sticky like the cake batter she's sucking off her fingers—and rather than to Bach and Gastinel's cello her attention returns to the man, with his irritating pretty-boy manner, his thick hair, his very light eyes, blue or gray, but piercing, and above all their formidably amused air as they darted all around, toward Christine's house, skimming the facade but also the roof, and then toward Bergogne's, toward the yard, the shed, not turning all the way around so as not to let Christine out of his sight for a single second, leaving her in his field of vision at all times but making a tour of the hamlet as though it already belonged to him. She thinks back to this and it's perfectly clear, not for a second did he let her out of his sight while he spoke to her, playing casual but not calm at all, so without really knowing for what reason, or based on what intuition, she wipes her hands on her apron and walks to the front door. She's not thinking, she closes the door without a second thought, with a confident, decisive motion, but stops in the middle, hesitating or wavering, as though she's changed her mind in the middle of locking the door. Yes, she hesitates, collects herself. Instead, all of a sudden, she opens the door fully and walks out, her gaze turned toward the stable—across from her on the right—a gaze that swings even farther to the right, toward the shed. Bergogne should be getting home soon and yet something in the air, an apprehension, an expectation, this silence she doesn't understand— ordinarily in the afternoon Bergogne works here or in any case he's never very far, usually her dog starts yapping at anything and everything and wanders around the yard looking for God knows what marvelous thing, then falls asleep on the porch to warm up in the sun, if there's any heating the slab of concrete.

But this time it's not like that. Finally she hears herself calling her dog in her gravelly voice—not used to raising it,

Rajah?

listening to the emptiness in which her query rings out, her question stretching over the hamlet for a few seconds that seem to her very long; then, after letting it wash over her first, she can't stand this emptiness anymore, and wanting to keep it from spreading, from proliferating, she insists and this time it no longer sounds like a question,

Rajah! Rajah!

louder and louder,

Rajah!

assertively, almost angrily,

Rajah!

still insisting,

What are you doing? Come!

but her voice is lost in the emptiness, her voice that's risen too high and revealed her anxiety or that form of bewilderment, or of doubt,

Come!

though she stays still on the porch of her house,

Here boy!

not daring to cross the yard to go see what her dog could be doing over by the stable, she finds it curious that he's not reacting, not hearing her voice, when he's ordinarily so quick to respond.

But she doesn't want to cross the yard, something is stopping her from doing so, from going out to him—as though by doing so she would confirm the discomfort and the questions beginning to rise in her, that little expanse of disquiet at the silence of the house; so she goes back in and this time she locks the door behind her, which she almost never does. The dog has gone off to mess around somewhere, he does that sometimes, he's done it before— well, he hasn't done it for a long time now, that was when he was very young, but this, this idea that's coming to her, she wants to send it far back into her brain, to hide it some place shadowy and unrevealed, unspoken, no question of letting herself be overcome by it, no, she doesn't want to give in to this feeling she's never felt in her house. Never has she been afraid here. So she charges right up to the kitchen table and tries, okay, where were we, what do I still need to do, ah yes, the pie, the apples, finish the frosting on the chocolate cake. Her hands try to take control of what's happening in the kitchen, letting them conduct the tempo, the rhythm, because it's up to them to run the show, these very dry hands, peeling from the paint and the turpentine—she's never been very careful and her hands aren't in very good shape, a bit too red, as if burned in some places. She sticks them into the flour, she has to make dough, knead it, roll it, spread it out, what was she supposed to do again—suddenly she can't remember the motions she has to perform, even though she knows them so well, now she's forgotten them, they've escaped her, she doesn't know how to call them back to her because it's as though her body has begun to tell her it's not important, and soon it's refraining from all motion, from all movement, keeping her at the edge of the table, standing up but almost frozen in place because it seems to her, she thinks that, no, of course no, and then the music, the cello starting again and rising up as though to puncture her eardrums and this music she loves so much is no longer coming to greet her ears like an old companion but like a sinister grinding sound she doesn't recognize and, for a fraction of a second, she wants to dash into the studio and turn off her old stereo, changing her mind immediately and restraining herself without entirely knowing why, or because she thinks the silence might be even more deafening than Bach's *Suites,* more dangerous to her, if she gives in to her desire to go turn it off she'll no longer have to hear the music but what it's covering, because yes, in spite of it all, this mounting worry, this feeling of—what? vulnerability?—is it possible that for once she can say to herself that she's worried, here, at home, in the middle of the afternoon, or is it just that out of all the house's noises, among all the creaks she knows by heart, Christine is noticing some she's never heard? She knows that if she goes to turn off the music, it's because she has to admit to herself this confused sense of hearing *something else*; noises, yes, sounds, vibrations too, that aren't the *intimate* movements of the house. If she turns off the music, she imagines herself being sucked into the silence that follows and being forced to reassure herself, as though all of a sudden she'll have to hear—but she has no idea what. And yet this can't go on, can't stay in this gray area any longer, she needs clarity, certainty, so she rubs her hands on her apron and lets out an ah fuck it, as though she's had enough, or as though she forgot a pot on the burner, and quickly she goes not to the studio nor to the stereo but farther, into the little hallway that leads to the back of the house, where she washes her laundry and hangs it up on rainy days.

She tries to not notice how she does this with a certain quickness or nervousness, as though she's taking her time even though she can tell she's going too fast and there's an agitation rising in her, ordering her to go even faster, and when she gets to the slightly dark room she looks at the door on the other side—the door that's open, not closed like it usually is, even if it's never locked. Christine doesn't understand why Rajah would have come through here, he's never in here. Why did she think that, unless, yes, that must be it, unless it was an animal, probably an animal, a weasel or squirrel or badger or whatever else, more likely a cat, yes, it wouldn't be the first time a cat has come to sprawl in her laundry hamper—except the neighbors have moved and the house next door is empty, for sale, walls left to their own devices without any of the neighbors or any of their three cats, with that crazy little one, Caramel, who she liked and who often came into her house and was never afraid of Rajah; the image comes back, but she knows she won't find the cat in her hamper where he used to like to come sprawl out, or like Blue did once, that magnificent Chartreux who gave birth to a litter of kittens in the sheets that were waiting for Christine to wash—this image of the cat and the swarming, shapeless mass of tiny kittens, blind, almost hairless, sticky, in the creased and humid folds of the sheets, the image appears and disappears just as quickly, almost in the same movement, because now she hears, on the stairs leading up to the second floor, a creak, then another, this time she's sure of it, these aren't the house's noises, they're something else.

Her first reflex is to close the door with such a strong motion that a *clack* makes the wall tremble, this wall that provides nothing but a drywall divider that you could break through with a shoulder, even though Christine doesn't think of that. She's closed the door, this has to be the first time she's locked a door here, with such haste, such awareness of doing it for self-protection, and in any case she doesn't have time to think about it, to think about anything, this time she can say a wave of fear is actively rising up in her, she doesn't really know why, maybe because of the man from earlier and the fact that her dog hasn't come back, the worry of not having her dog with her, yes, suddenly that worries her, why isn't he here, and then that weird guy, now these noises and the open door, so without waiting any longer she heads for her studio and doesn't even look at the big red woman enthroned right in the middle of the room, nor at the other paintings; no, she sees nothing and she turns off the stereo without bothering to stop it at a particular moment—because while she usually takes care to not stop in the middle of a piece, as though it would be a brutality she couldn't possibly inflict on the musicians even though they'd never be the wiser, she prefers to pause her motion and remain in front of the stereo for a minute or two, waiting for the piece to end before turning the sound off—this time she turns it off without paying attention.

When the cello stops, it's already been a while since she stopped listening, or stopped hearing. The emptiness it leaves in its wake fills the space of the studio, of the house itself. Christine raises her eyes to the ceiling and notices that she's holding her breath so as not to be disturbed by her own breathing, to be sure she'll hear all the noises that come to her, already preparing to hear a creaking overhead, in the bedrooms upstairs, noises she won't understand even though no, no, it's silence that takes over and nothing else. She stays like this for a minute or two, except these two minutes aren't like one hundred twenty seconds counted out above her head but rather like the weight of a half-hour silence, and so it's only when she hears a knock at the front door—the time it takes to jump, to collect herself, to tell herself everything is fine, to take a fraction of a second to remember that Bergogne still hasn't fixed her doorbell, which hasn't worked for maybe a year or even longer, but what does it matter because no one ever comes to see her, or so few people do, and now she appears in the kitchen and looks through the door that she had glazed long ago because all these old houses have the flaw of being perpetually plunged into darkness.

The image of the police officer passes through her head, the officer whose name she tries to remember—Philowski? She doesn't remember anymore, and then yes she does, it comes back, Filipkowski, yes, even this feels like regaining control, she thinks maybe it's him come to make sure everything is alright, or because he has some news about the letters, and for that matter this whole business with the letters is beginning to fray her nerves, she's beginning to get anxious over nothing when in reality she has no reason at all to be afraid. She goes into the kitchen with this thought, that no doubt it's him, him or another, so she slows down as she approaches the kitchen, as soon as she's there she'll be able to see, above the table and from the other end of the room, through the top of the French window, the face of the man or the woman who's come and who is now insisting, knocking three times in a row, stopping for a few seconds, then three times again, quite loud, the same, exactly, as the previous ones; then again this pause of a few seconds before beginning again, it begins again, she flinches in the hallway when the three knocks sound again, then gets annoyed, who could it be, and as she enters the kitchen she immediately recognizes the man from earlier, the same one smiling at her the way he was before, with that smile meant to be sympathetic and warm but that strangely lacks sympathy and warmth. She pauses for a moment, but pulls herself together, she doesn't hesitate, rushes toward him and opens the door and, without giving him the time to say a word, looks him up and down, stares at him and pins him with an aggressive eye.

What do you want?

Uh… yes, excuse me. I don't want to bother you, but I was wondering…

I told you I don't show the house if the owners haven't confirmed the appointment.

Yes yes, I know, I know. It's not that. I just wanted to know if, uh, if you might be interested in talking. If you wouldn't want to just talk a little?

Sorry, you've got the wrong place for that.

And already she's closing the door—slowly she's gripped the doorknob, begun to push it, but he, still cajoling, almost amused, has put his foot inside the door to block it, he advances a bit and then sighs, almost shrugging his shoulders,

Oh no, no, not me… I don't want to talk, no. I don't have anything to say. But my little brother, I think he'd really like to talk with you.

She barely has time to understand, she thinks it's a joke, she hesitates, then turns around: from inside the house, a young man in an electric blue tracksuit, with blond hair, bleached, almost white. His sneakers are covered in mud with grass sticking to them, one of the shoelaces is untied, bloodstains on his pants. He looks at her and smiles.

14

He couldn't say how he wound up on the side of the road like an idiot, with a flat tire and the radio still playing that Bourvil song—the only records they had at his house when he was a kid were in fact an LP by Bourvil, another by Mireille Mathieu, and a few 45s, one of which was Sylvie Vartan, whom his mother adored and who said love burns your eyes and goes up in smoke like cigarettes.

Now he hears Bourvil's voice as though it were his father's, coming to mock him beneath or through Bourvil's, to make him take a long hard look at himself, using the actor-singer's soft and fragile voice to scratch out the innocence and naiveté and, by contrast, pull him back to his turpitudes and his ridiculous situation—why did he go so far as to use the occasion of his wife's birthday to invent the need to go into town, out of what opportunism, what cynical turn—as though through Bourvil's falsely guileless voice a time more naïve than ours, though no gentler, is judging him, looking down on him, evoking the nostalgia of a forgotten cabaret and the sadness of the postwar years. Bergogne, no more hardened or clever than anyone else, is this close to letting himself get caught up in the song's sweet melancholy, a man lamenting his lost love and echoing his own story, his own life, like in the song, on a heap of rubble. Bergogne lets himself be consumed by his bitter memories of a time when he too could have said *c'était bien,* it was good, because in Marion he believed he'd found peace and plenty, the consummation of his dating life, the promise of an end to that loneliness evoked by Bourvil's voice; but the loneliness has returned and the song's suddenly reminds him of his own—for fuck's sake shut up, Bergogne, that's enough, stop blubbering all over yourself like a little kid and fucking pull yourself together, Patrice tells himself as he leans over the car radio and switches it off in a sharp motion, taking off his seatbelt in the same motion because he knows this isn't the time to wallow in sickly sentimentality, even if without quite knowing why he remains rooted to his seat and looks at the computer in the inside rearview mirror, staring back at him, how could he do this to her, how could he, it's his love for her that he's smearing by going to get his rocks off on the downlow—and that's what it is, lowdown and shameful—how can he claim to love his wife and say she's everything to him, that nothing would exist without her or that he's nothing without her, after what he's just done, how can he believe that waltz of words he tells himself are his, his own thoughts, because what's true is that he experiences his love for Marion with such fever that he thinks he's not worthy of the chance she's granted him by sharing his life, even if the question keeps coming back of how it's possible for a woman like her to be enamored of a guy like him, the question he's asked himself since their first exchanges over the internet, because when he saw the photo she sent him he first thought it was a joke or a form of prostitution or something like that. Then, after their first date, after their first nights together, even after they got married, the question always found a way to bubble back up to the surface, and he knows that one day he'll have to find the courage to admit to her that he can't take this life they lead anymore, the pretenses on which they agree to convince themselves mutually that everything is fine. He'll have to find the courage to tell her that when he goes into town he stops on the boulevards, that he spends time with—how will he put it? what word to use? Will he use that word he never says and that remains for him almost too cautious a word, or do what people do who talk about someone and say he's deceased when they mean he's dead—why don't they say he's dead rather than trying to cram the corpse into that embalmed, falsely modest word, *deceased*? It would be the same in his mouth, that word, *prostitutes*, no less inopportune and hypocritical; or will he have to say it in his own words, I go see whores, you know, this afternoon I went to see the whores because I need a woman to—

He closes his eyes. Cars pass by on the state road. The Kangoo is rocked by the displacement of air from the cars, some of which are going very fast, far exceeding the speed limit. If he wastes too much time, Ida will be home before him and will be surprised not to find him, even though he promised her he'd be home before her and that he'd wait for her so the two of them would still have time to do all kinds of things together: the decorations and the meal, but also and maybe above all making themselves look nice, as they agreed to do several days ago now, both of them plotting out the organization of the evening while reveling in the pleasure of this complicity, already describing to each other the face Marion will make when she comes back from work and finds them in their finery, with the table set and the *happy birthday* banner, even if they already put it up last year—and probably the year before that too—no matter, because the most important thing is for her to discover the party they've made for her, as though they could do no less for her fortieth birthday, because she'd be surprised and disappointed if they just got her a quick little gift to mark the occasion, even if there's no risk of that, because they've been excited for days just imagining the party.

And now here he is at risk of ruining everything, of disappointing or worrying Ida if he wastes any more time. That's why he needs to shake off this torpor that's frozen him in place. Patrice remains captivated by the inside rearview mirror, eyes still riveted on the reflection of Marion's gift, then finally he looks outside. He can get out of the car, walk around the Kangoo to check the four tires—okay, let's do this, rubbing his hands on his pants he thinks he has to hurry, it's the back right that's flat, he could call Christine to say he'll be late but he can already hear the heaviness of his voice over the phone, telling her he has to change a tire—she'll find out soon, anyway—better that he just get down to it as quickly as possible, now that he's opened the trunk and found the jack—oh right, you need the key to release the cradle that holds the spare tire under the car. He tries not to go too fast, to do everything in the right order,

one: the car is parked in a sufficiently flat and out-of-the-way space, he opens the door again, gets back in, checks that he's pulled the emergency brake and put the car in first,

two: the release key is in the glove compartment, okay, so go in the glove compartment and then,

three: take the key out and place it in the trunk, turn it and feel, underneath, the cradle holding the spare tire release and take the tire,

four: set it next to the tire to be changed,

five: and find the jack,

there, he puts down the jack, gets annoyed because he forgot to turn on his hazard lights.

What else is he forgetting? Oh right, empty the trunk and make the car as light as possible, which he does, emptying the trunk of the two toolboxes he'd left in there; take Marion's present out and before anything else put on his neon yellow safety vest, go set up a triangle to signal his presence a few meters farther up. It's a pain but he'll do it all the same, he's more afraid of cops than he is of an accident, or let's say rather that he believes more in the presence of cops than in the risk of an accident—he can't really imagine someone smashing into his car in broad daylight when his car isn't blocking the road at all. He slips on the vest, unfolds the safety triangle and sets it down a few meters up. Then he attaches the anti-theft socket to the key, unscrews the bolts with two turns of the key—he turns counterclockwise. He has to force it a bit, he

gives it a few kicks to help it, it helps, he positions the jack following the notch on the rocker panel, properly, places the handle and
turns, the car lifts up: soon the wheel is turning in the air.

He changes it and, the more he hurries, the more he feels
things getting out of hand, don't lose your cool, it's stupid, it
won't help anything, it's not like him, normally he knows how to
talk himself down, but here, no, a vague floating, a fog in his head
and yet he continues, he changes the tire, puts the screws back on,
tightens them. He goes to put the wheel with its busted tire in
the trunk, carelessly, as though he's angry at it; now he has to let
the jack down with the handle, exactly like before but the other
way, and of course it's at the moment the car is almost back on the
ground, the four tires touching the ground, that he's seized with
a fit of anger at himself, for the love of fucking Christ why did he
have to go get himself into this shit all by himself and mess everything up, he thinks of the time, a considerable amount of time
wasted, he should already be back at home and he's here on all
fours on the side of the road, as traffic is picking up because plenty
of people have left work and are heading back to the surrounding
villages, like they do every day at the same hour, exactly what he'd
wanted to avoid, and it's at this moment that, without noticing
but because he's not concentrating enough on what he's supposed
to be doing, he doesn't know how it happens, he lets go of the
handle, some awkward movement or some negligence, no, he'll
never know, even later when he tries to explain to himself what
happened, running back over it as though trying to understand an
incident that happened to someone else, that he heard about and
wondered what kind of boob that could happen to, the handle
remaining in his left hand, his right hand with the index and the
middle finger jammed in between, the index cut clean through at
the proximal knuckle, blood gushing onto his hand, he can't stifle
a cry when he tries to remove his finger and it remains stuck, the
middle finger miraculously intact, protected by the index which
absorbed everything, the flesh gashed and drenched in blood, the

wave of panic to use the other hand to open the jack, yes, thankfully the car no longer needs the jack, the wheels are securely on the ground and on that front everything is fine, everything except this incredibly strong pain in his finger, he stands up and shakes his hand, gritting his teeth, and suddenly he's seized with a desire to punch everything that passes in front of him, he kicks the body of this fucking Kangoo covered in mud and oil stains, in dust, in pollen, and a few seconds later Bergogne wraps his finger in toilet paper, he doesn't have a first-aid kit in his glove compartment, just some TP in the back. The blood is flowing abundantly, throbbing through his whole hand, Bergogne is mad with rage—first at himself and at his clumsiness, what was he thinking, son of a bitch, what did he possibly have in his head to let himself be distracted like a fucking idiot, because now he's going to have to clean everything up and put it all back in the trunk, the two toolboxes that should have gone back into the shed at least three months ago, Marion's gift—he takes care not to stain it, let him at least not get blood on it. Ida must be getting home and waiting for him, definitely, she'll be waiting for him and it's his fault, your fault alone, Bergogne, it's his daughter he's thinking of now and no longer Marion, it's Ida who's illuminated in the light of his guilty conscience and this shame that he dearly hopes to fight as he decides to get back in the car, telling himself he has to get back on the road now.

Already he's put the keys in the ignition and his left blinker on. He tries to redouble his caution—no more of this bullshit—and he does things almost slowly, circumspectly, repeating in his head the necessary movements and positions even as he performs them. He knows he won't be able to make it home like this: his finger won't stop bleeding, it's throbbing, burning even worse now than it was a few minutes ago. The blood is flowing too fast, it's dripping all over the steering wheel, getting everything sticky, so he stops: blinker, right turn, where the state road bisects a village that isn't really one, splitting it like a fruit. Houses, a Romanesque church in disrepair—gloomy, gray, soiled by millions of trucks and cars spitting their exhaust in its face—a bakery, a newsstand that's closed and whose yellowed old posters, almost erased by the sun, are almost finished burning in place, and, by luck, the neon sign of a pharmacy, alternating between the usual green cross and information about the weather.

Bergogne approaches and the glass doors open automatically to let him pass. He walks in and a gust of heat hits him in the face, a vaguely aromatic odor. The pharmacy isn't big but there are two counters, one of which is empty, while at the other a young woman is attending to a customer hanging onto her walker, reeling, and as it's throbbing in Patrice's hand, the blood throwing off sparks like the sparks they took as kids when they'd close their hands on the electric fences surrounding the fields where indolent and indifferent cows grazed, it's the same peculiar sensation, the same regular, rhythmic flow that radiated up from the hand into the whole arm—he holds his hand in the air, fingers spread apart, as though if he keeps his hand elevated the finger will bleed less, unless it's to show that he needs help without having to shout it out, so that someone will come to him without his having to ask. It works quite well, the young woman lifts her eyes and she's already leaving the old woman without even excusing herself and speaking to Patrice,

Wait here, I'll call my boss.

Patrice tries to smile at her but doesn't quite manage it, he still hasn't said anything, not a word while the young woman goes into the back room, still without a word to the old lady who's trying to turn around, casting a three-quarter look from a reptilian eye at the intruder who's just stolen her pharmacist, assuming maybe that she'll recognize him—she knows everyone here but this man doesn't look familiar at all. They hear the voice of the young woman who's gone into the back to call the pharmacist, and when he emerges the young woman has already explained, there's a gentleman who's injured his hand. The pharmacist comes in, the young woman returns to the old lady. Patrice approaches the counter where the pharmacist has settled in, soon Patrice hears his voice and is surprised to hear it so shaky and weak, so hesitant, when he explains that he did this while changing his tire just now and then,

Don't worry sir, we'll take care of that, just relax, it's going to be okay. We'll disinfect it and I think with some Steri-Strips it'll be fine.

Patrice holds his hand out to the pharmacist, a guy in his fifties who appears totally myopic because behind his tinplate glasses he looks at Patrice with sustained attention, his eyes almost closed, as though making a great effort, and then he begins cleaning the bloody hand, disinfecting the finger, yes, he murmurs, you sure didn't miss. And then he places the bandages, he takes his time, Patrice thinks he's going to be very late indeed, he wonders when he'll find the time to bring his cows in and trembles with anger at himself.

15

It's always the same scene repeating from Monday until the end of the week, with the few variations that distinguish one season from another, the scorching heat of an early summer, the crackle of raindrops on the roof, the smell of the seats when the sun burns through the windows, the almost cold coolness of the air conditioning or the too-dry heat of the heating in the winter, the rain, the wind, more rarely the snow; and always, at the stop, the same groan of the tires and the unmistakable noise of the door opening and letting the three children off in single file, after they've said goodbye to the bus driver, that woman who always wears the same blue cardigan with the sleeves rolled up to reveal her plump forearms and—in contrast to her square head and her overly strong neck—her tiny earrings, round and colorful like Smarties.

Now, as they do every day except for vacations, the three children get off the bus, and this time they're very happy it's not as nasty out as it was the day before yesterday, with that very cold rain that beat down on the road so powerfully the water rose up on the sides until it gave birth to rivulets like mini-rivers on the shoulders and in the ditches. On rainy days it's hard to get home without ending up completely soaked, not least because you have to cross these huge puddles that always get the bottom of your pants all dirty, your shoes and socks black with mud, all of which makes a good pretext for parents, who always use it as an excuse to stick you right in the tub, repeating *this way it'll be done with*.

But today it's the sun that greets them as they get off the bus. Between the grade school where it picks them up and here it's dropped off almost all the children, letting them off in groups of a dozen at first, then in fours and fives, and finally, as they gradually get farther away from downtown La Bassée—the commune spreads out over a fairly large territory and, outside of town, the houses are increasingly isolated and scarce, soon there are fewer and fewer new homes, tract houses, then almost none, soon there's nothing but grain fields, the river, woods, then farms and hamlets down at the end of roads increasingly remote from the school pickup point—the last children getting off the bus either alone or in pairs, usually brothers and sisters, more rarely neighbors, though it does happen, like now, when Ida is about to leave Lucas and Charline, one going off toward the road leading back across the railroad line, not far from the factory that closed—to almost everyone's relief, because yes, it does happen that people are relieved when a factory closes, like this one where for more than forty years they made corrugated sheets of fiber cement siding for farm buildings and pipe fittings but most of all cancer, and, for those who didn't die from it, depression related to the fear of asbestos, of living with that filth inside them. Lucas walks in front of the corpse of the factory as you'd walk in front of a mausoleum or a mass grave, waiting for it to finish being demolished and for time to erase it from memory, while Charline goes just across from her, with her *Frozen* backpack on her shoulders, making a U-turn a few meters wide before vanishing toward Les Brèchetières, where she'll be greeted by her parents' geese and chickens.

And Ida, so excited by the thought of the evening ahead, keeps stopping on the road to shout,

Goodbye, Charline! Goodbye, Lucas!

forcing them

Goodbye, Ida!

both to turn around to answer in unison even though she's already started running again, no longer listening to them, running in the direction opposite their route. Yes, she's running, even if her run looks more like the walk of a little maniac who's overjoyed that she and her father have to prepare for her mother's birthday, who's been thinking since this morning of the whole plan they made together, though she'd set one for herself first: bath, hair, dress, jewelry, the glitter she'll put on her cheeks. And then she'll help her father, and even though she knows he'll already have set the table and done a bit of decorating, if they planned things to do together she also knows he'll need help, definitely, he won't be able to pull it all off without her. That's the plan, she'll clean her room better than ever, not only her books and DVDs but also the inside of her desk and closets. She'll do what can't be seen by the naked eye, which will impress her mother even more than a quick tidying would; it'll be like a present—no, it *will* be a present, definitely—her mother will be so happy that Ida expects she won't inspect her room so closely for at least the next two weeks, and Ida loves evenings like these so much, birthday parties, not just hers but her parents' too, and Christmas, of course, not just for the presents—not that those don't matter—but mostly because something happens that she doesn't get from ordinary days, and even if she doesn't know what to call this *something* that's absent from the everyday, this thing she feels she can just put her finger on those days when they celebrate a more or less significant event, she knows it exists, it's present among them, in the air they breathe, in the house itself, this *something* that she can't name and can't say what it changes in those moments; but it seems to her, indistinctly, in the fog of a child's perception of the adult world, that in those festive moments something in the air gets lighter, releasing the weight that stiffens the whole space in which they live their daily life. Because time has no more hold on them, Marion doesn't keep glancing at the clock above the buffet in the kitchen, hoping nobody will notice; Patrice talks, smiling at everything and nothing, things they could do on vacation, as though for once all three of them could go somewhere and not the way she goes to camp in the summers, all alone, but with her parents, who this time might find the time they never have—how could her father leave the animals, who'd take care of them if we went away?

They tell themselves on those evenings that they'll spend two days at Disneyland, that they'll take a boat to Corsica or else to La Bourboule; Patrice gets excited as he drinks and talks about things that don't matter and make all three of them burst out laughing, he makes up guessing games, awful puns that make them giggle, but above all Ida sees her parents, they laugh together, talk to each other, she sees them as they almost never ordinarily are, drinking together, and sometimes in the end they put on music and dance—all three of them together—but sometimes just the two of them, her parents holding each other, intertwined and turning in place in each other's arms, which Ida loves with a happiness she can't express, one whose effect on her is so powerful she can feel it, so much that she feels borne by a desire to laugh that spills over at the slightest prompting, a desire to join them, to be with them, always, so much does this joy make her feel that nothing can separate them—she dreads one day hearing them tell each other they should separate, she's not stupid, she sees what goes on, the impatience between them sometimes, the anger that doesn't burst, and she's well aware that sometimes Patrice and Marion don't fight only because she's there and they're waiting for her to be in bed, as if she can't hear from her room, their voices in those cases coming up from the kitchen, trembling with anger, the shouting matches and the reproaches that mask other, deeper reproaches, the pitch rising until Patrice shuts up and disappears into his office. She knows all the house's noises by heart; she's well aware that her parents think she doesn't hear them, no doubt they think childhood is a world hermetically sealed off from adult life even though she knows much more about them than they think, maybe even more than they do, because she's not sure Patrice knows she's seen her mother all alone, perched on the edge of the bathtub, tears in her eyes maybe, that she sometimes catches her lost in thoughts that seem so dark and so far away that Ida has to go to considerable effort to bring her mother back and make her lose that trapped look she doesn't ordinarily see on her.

And when she comes back, Marion lights up and says yes sweetie, sorry sweetie, it's okay, I was daydreaming, but Ida understands the way things hide away like little creatures in the boards rotting in the barn, insects that gnaw at the wood without anyone noticing. Sometimes she can see why her mother doesn't answer Patrice, how he seems to be talking to himself and waiting for answers that don't come, and often she sees the way he stares at his wife. If she could read in his eyes, it's possible that she'd read anger, hatred, resentment, sadness, remorse, disappointment, loneliness, an incomprehension equivalent to the one she feels when she sees him staring at her mother who doesn't answer, who probably doesn't even hear him, and how often it's Ida who has to say,

Mom, Dad's talking to you.

because she knows her mother will hear her,

Yes, sorry sweetie.

and then Marion will turn to Patrice.

Ida knows tonight won't be like that. There won't be those floating pauses during which all three of them sit at the table, clearing away everything that really concerns them to talk about work and bits of news they heard on TV, and then about nothing, especially nothing. Tonight Patrice will be heard, and when she daydreams her mother will do it with a smile and won't turn away. Tonight they'll put on music, there will be presents for Marion, and cakes, and then her mother's friends and her dear Tatie Christine will come too.

Ida walks faster and faster, clutching the straps of her *Yo-kai Watch* backpack. She can't wait, she's going so fast that she's already past the hamlet gate and hurrying toward Christine's house—she waits to see Rajah, his ears up, to hear him bark and stamp behind the door before Christine comes to open it. But behind the French door there's neither Rajah nor Christine, so Ida quickens her pace, she comes up and knocks on the door, more a way of announcing that she's coming in than a real way of asking permission, because it's like this house is as much hers as the one where she lives with her parents. If she knocks, it's also out of habit, even if almost every time she shows up she can be certain she'll be welcomed by Rajah barking or by the way he scratches at the door and jumps around to show his pleasure at seeing her, and so sometimes she does enter without knocking, the dog still comes to greet her every day at this hour when, like today, she enters Christine's house—except this time she's surprised to hear neither Rajah nor Christine.

She's alone in the entrance and so already in the kitchen; Ida doesn't understand why this silence, Christine can't be far off, definitely not, maybe she's gone over to their house to get something for the kitchen, because Ida see all the utensils for the cakes lying on the table and there's a smell of something burning in the oven,

Tatie?

she looks in the oven, yes, it smells a bit like burning,

Tatie, your cake?

the cake burning,

Tatie!

and because she gets no response she turns off the oven,

Tatie!

shouting louder this time, but Tatie Christine doesn't answer. Ida hesitates, should she leave the cake in the oven or take it out? Should she close the oven door or leave it open? She doesn't know and decides to do nothing at all, to leave everything as it is. Ida leaves the kitchen, closing the door behind her, no big deal, okay, can't dawdle, she sets off at a run toward her own house, barely noticing that it's not her father's Kangoo in the yard but a white car, something like a Clio, that's parked. She doesn't pay attention, people often come to see her father and stay for hours, she doesn't stop for something so trivial, and anyway today she doesn't have time, she has other things to worry about: she darts toward her house and tries to open the front door that leads straight into the dining room, but the knob won't budge: it's locked. Ida doesn't try to force it, it happens, sometimes her father goes out during the day and locks the house, then forgets to unlock it when he comes back; no big deal, she knows there's always a key hidden under a pot of impatiens, which in this season look more like a pile of black twigs swollen with water than pretty, sharp red flowers.

Under the pot, a flat key. She opens the door, goes in, goes to drop her backpack in the living room on the right, on the couch, but she spends two seconds standing stunned before the *happy birthday* banner and the place settings, the orange-bordered table-cloth, thinking this is neat, it's so pretty what Dad's done, and the backpack slides down her back, straps apart, as though open, leaving her shoulders and sliding down the little girl's body; she lets the backpack land at her feet with a big soft sound and just gives it a careless kick that slides it over to the wall; she thinks of the key, yes, she knows she'll be yelled at if she doesn't put it back under the flowerpot right away. So without waiting she goes back to the door, takes the key, puts it back in its place outside, then comes back to the house and slips into the kitchen—she's hungry and it doesn't occur to her to go back to Christine's for a snack, no, she's not going to wait, she takes a yogurt from the fridge, she's so hungry, she has to eat right away, no use going back to Christine's for now. And anyway she has so much to do, take her bath, change clothes, do her hair and makeup and clean up her room, do her homework, how's she going to do all that in so little time, especially since her father should be here, where is he? She tells herself her mother won't come home late tonight, it's just not possible, even her boss will agree to let her go home, he wouldn't dare keep her late on her birthday, no, she doesn't believe it. For now she eats some applesauce, some cookies, she hurries and tosses the little spoon in the sink, the yogurt container, the applesauce cup, the cookie wrapper, into the trash all at once; she runs her hands quickly under the water, bends down to drink a swig from the faucet—stretching out, lifting her feet and pushing on her toes for just an instant, almost letting herself rest on the edge of the sink and tilt back, supporting herself with her wrist on the faucet, which she turns on and off in the same motion.

There, that's done. She wipes her mouth and right away she goes to the French door in the kitchen and looks out toward the stable; she needs to see her father. At this hour he should be over there. Without really thinking she opens the door and as soon as she gets into the yard it's not her father she thinks of but Rajah, glancing toward Christine's and then right, left, surprised by this silence, she doesn't get it,

Rajah!

she hears her voice rising in the yard and the echo,

Rajah!

her voice whose echo comes back to her with a deeper timbre,

Rajah! Where are you, boy?

She crosses the yard to the stable. Most often at this hour her father is just coming back from bringing the cows in or looking after the feed or a whole bunch of things that she doesn't always know what they involve but that seem to her to recur so often that, even if she can't connect them to anything, she understands the motions he makes because she knows their choreography, and while ordinarily she doesn't dare go right into the stable—she knows her father doesn't like it—she pauses, reconsiders, but yesterday she did it and they both laughed about the question of the paintings so she knows she can do it the same way today, it won't be a problem, he must be waiting for her seeing as they have a lot to do. She wonders how it can even be that he's still in the stable and not waiting for her at home, she won't ask him, she's already starting to call to him, surprised not to hear any noise as she enters the stable—the relative darkness, the silence, then nothing, she asks,

Dad?

her voice weak and hesitant,

Dad, you there?

as though she has to rest after raising her voice in the yard; so now she does the opposite and calls softly, just loud enough to be heard but not much more. And unlike yesterday, unlike what she might have done even ten or twenty minutes ago, she didn't jump, didn't laugh while letting her voice reverberate with a playful tone, a tone of amusement or provocation—

Dad, you there?

Dad?

Just a hint of the doubt that creeps in when she gets no answer; the beginning of irritation, too, when she starts to think he might be trying to scare her for fun, something as stupid and fun as playing hide-and-seek when she really doesn't want to, but no, of course not, he wouldn't do that. She doesn't ask herself why she's going deeper into the stable when to all evidence her father isn't there, no, she just moves forward in the half-darkness and the cool, amid the smells of the cows. She decides to turn back around, to leave this place because her father isn't here, and why is it that she keeps walking, slowing her steps and looking over there, all the way in the back, in that darker and more isolated part where she can see, on the concrete floor, this motionless mass—at first she doesn't know what it is, then bit by bit she recognizes it, but only by moving forward slower and slower—almost as though she can no longer walk—very slowly she still moves forward—there she is, in front of—and she leans down, she bends her knees, reaches out her arm, her hand, she says nothing for the moment because the surprise and the bewilderment keep her from thinking,

Pooch?

Pooch?

Pooch?

What's wrong pooch?

and her hand,

Pooch,

and her entire body still leaning down,

Pooch,

Ida, knees bent, finally touching the dog and the time it takes to understand that the dog

Rajah?

isn't breathing,

My pup,

taking his face in her hands, saying it again, as though he'll

My pup

hear her, she realizes her hands are wet and dirty, or rather she doesn't realize, her breathing catches, the need to flee and the need to run but she doesn't shout, she just needs to leave, a need that crushes her, she has to leave the stable, the cement is hurting her knees, she gets up, stands up straight, backs up still looking at the dog, she backs up farther, very slowly, still facing him, afraid to turn around, but she has to, has to have her back to the dog and the terror at her heels, and as soon as she turns around she starts to run and crosses the yard holding in the shout that's suffocating her, the shock and speechlessness inside her, she enters the house and rushes to the kitchen and turns on the faucet—on the tips of her toes, tensed, trembling, she flings her blood-soaked hands under the very strong stream of cold water, it splashes, so be it, she rinses the blood and the water squirts and the blood flows from her hands, onto her forearms, now she lets out little cries of fright or disgust at the blood escaping down the drain of which soon there will remain only a few stray spatters on the wall above the sink. She turns down the stream but leaves the water running, her hands under the faucet for a few minutes more, she doesn't understand and she's staggered, her whole body shaking, her strength has left her and she feels like she hasn't eaten anything, her legs and arms without strength. She wipes her hands and finally manages to start thinking again, she has to do what she does when she wants to ask her mother when she's coming home, like she did yesterday, yes, she has to go into the living room, to the phone, take it and call her mother: she picks it up; there's no dial tone. She hears a rustle of leather, a movement, a presence in the room with her: she turns around, in her haste she didn't pay attention.

On the couch, a man is sitting. His brown hair is thick, his eyes very bright, his smile a bit exaggerated, Ida doesn't have time to think that she's never seen this man,

Hello, my name is Christophe.

she has just enough strength to hear,

I didn't scare you, I hope?

16

When they finally hear Patrice's Kangoo pull into the yard, they must think he's been gone far too long, that he's gone too far, or, after starting to worry about him and having plenty of time to let macabre ideas cavort in their heads, images of crumpled sheet metal and dismembered bodies, of mangled iron, the emergency room, hospitals, ambulances, firemen racing across town with all sirens blaring, finally managing to stop listening to that little voice murmuring to them that maybe *something* has happened to him, so as not to let in the word *accident*, so as to keep that word at bay like a threatening animal that you keep at a distance, careful not to break into a run so as not to frighten it and to show it you're not afraid of an attack, it's possible, then, that after having thought all of this, hearing the car pull in, they're finally reassured by Bergogne's return, by what his return means for them, but also what it means for him, due to that fear of an accident that enters Christine's mind almost every time Bergogne leaves, for at least a few seconds each time, even if it's often a lightning burst of anxiety that disappears as quickly as it arises.

Christine hasn't told Ida any of this, of course, just as for that matter she's never told anyone, and her thoughts vanish all at once because soon Ida and Christine won't be alone here, it's enough to hear the noise of the engine they know so well to regain confidence and tell themselves something's going to happen, that they'll finally get out of this story they don't understand—it won't last, it can't, these two guys, the younger one with his bleached hair, too blond, almost white, playing with his knife and passing the time by breathing on the window to fog it up—what's he waiting for?—while the older one, on the other hand, has assumed an exaggeratedly attentive air and won't take his eyes off of Ida, astonished, effusing about her size, how big she is! he says as if to himself, as though she can't hear him talking about her in the third person, or he's talking about her in her absence, yes, I mean really, so tall, so pretty, as though he can't believe it or he's just clinging to this to say something and not let the silence and awkwardness gain ground among them, the way he did earlier, at the beginning of the afternoon, with his whirling hands and his meaningless words.

And as the car arrives, as it comes into the yard, as they hear it pulling up the way it does every time, slowly, before parking in front of the shed, yes, during this time the silence suddenly grows heavier, or comes to a halt, as though becoming a solid in the middle of all of them; they listen, as though everyone knows that soon, with Patrice's presence, everything will change, first Ida and Christine are sure of it, they're counting on him without doubting for a second what might happen, they're so sure that they can't stifle a gesture of joy, Christine takes Ida's hand and squeezes it tight, soon Bergogne's mere presence will put a stop to all of this, and even if they don't say it to each other, even though they surely become more fidgety for a second, Ida can't stop herself from saying,

Dad, it's Dad,

both of them are swept up in a reaction that does them so much good they can barely contain it, and though they don't want to appear too confident they still can't hold back this outpouring of liberation, almost of triumph, even if they don't need to say it to one another, a few looks suffice, a very discreet exchange, a certain nod of the chin as though they're answering a question even though no question was asked, as though they want to show their confidence or say yes to a hypothesis even though it hasn't even been articulated; they share this confidence, thinking it'll soon be over, Bergogne will come in and make short work of these two guys who looked so dumb when Christine shouted at them to let the little girl go, that the little girl hadn't done anything to them, the two guys letting Christine continue but not responding, vaguely shocked or taken aback when she brought up their filthy anonymous letters, asking them what they wanted from her, what they want from her, and what she could possibly have done to them.

For now, the only thing that really changes with Bergogne's arrival is that one of the two men, the older one, the one who said his name was Christophe and who wanted to see the house for sale, said he'd have to go down to, he said, *welcome Mister Bergogne.*

That's what he said: *welcome Mister Bergogne.*

Mister Bergogne, and Christine thought just you wait to welcome *Mister Bergogne's* fist to your face, pretending not to be surprised that in saying this the man had above all confessed to her that he wasn't here by chance, that he knew the names of the hamlet's residents; and in spite of her anger, she still can't get over these words that seem so respectful and polite but that are really what, she wonders, these words that beneath their polish barely hide their irony and sarcasm, *Mister Bergogne,*

You must be kidding,

the mockery blooming already,

Mister Bergogne,

What do you want from *Mister* Bergogne?

And she can keep asking all she wants, in this moment she doesn't get an answer. Christophe leaves the upstairs guest room, where Christine and Ida are being held and where they're both waiting, without quite knowing what for, seated on one side of the bed, with the young blond man standing near them playing with his knife and looking out the window, again and again, curious, maybe worried, repeating to them as though trying to convince himself that it must be great to live here, it's so neat here, really just great, leaving Christine and Ida attentive to Christophe's footsteps going down the stairs—the wood cracking, the quick steps, and then nothing, he doesn't go anywhere, barely a few meters, they listen but hear mostly that he's still in the house; they understand this because soon all the noise has stopped and, surely no less than them, the young man is listening to what's happening, on alert also—he's standing at the window, filling the space between the edge of the bedframe and the window, keeping them confined between the wall and the bed. They don't dare move, not yet, so Ida is sitting so close to Christine that Christine doesn't see what she can do but hold her close, wrapping herself around her more to reassure her than to protect her, even though she doesn't think the young man is capable of hurting her, because since she's been watching him, in profile, facing the window, she can see he doesn't look mean, not truly mean in the sense that he seems to *want* to scare them or hurt them, on the contrary, he seems to want to be gentle with them, almost apologizing for the disturbance, even though for the moment they're not speaking to each other and he lowers his eyes very quickly—it almost looks like he's blushing, that's right, he's probably blushing because they're holding his gaze, returning it with a stare full of anger and incomprehension. It's as though the questions he sees in his two hostages' pupils are so oppressive that he has to avert his eyes to avoid having to face them—just as it's surely already difficult to face this silence and find himself alone with this little girl and this woman, both of whom he can tell have noticed the bloodstains on his tracksuit.

Soon, Christine and Ida think, everything will be resolved. As though Patrice's presence has this almost magical power to wipe out what they've just experienced, which has left both of them in an incredulous silence, unable to demand that the two men give them an explanation, an account, unable to insult or threaten them either, Christine spluttering questions about the anonymous letters, trying for a start to understand what they have against her, as though what matters to her above all is clearing up the reasons that would justify or at least explain why they decided to send her anonymous letters, before killing her dog and holding her here, now, with the neighbors' little girl, hostages—because that's what's going on, right?—except the two guys smile when she asks questions, as though they don't understand them, as though the questions are being asked in a foreign language of which they know barely a word, and their answers—we're going to be nice and calm and everything's going to be fine—seem to her as false as the script of a made-for-TV movie or an American series with formulaic translations of formulaic dialogue, and as she asks her questions she suspects they sound just as false, yes, this falling to pieces to hear herself asking them, or rather launching them like a bad actress listening to herself toss off her tirades, feeling like she has to shriek them to make up for the fact that she doesn't believe a word of them, thus accentuating their hopelessness, shouting out their banality, questions like the ones the victims ask in kidnapping movies, and the stupidity of seeing herself reduced to the status of a character when everything that comes to your mind belongs only to a genre bloated with clichés. So Christine hears herself saying these sentences that aren't hers and that belong to no one, as though there's no one behind her words which are only copies of words whose originals have been lost, sentences undone, emptied of their substance by dint of repetition, until they become these shadows of sentences Christine has thrown out, surprised even while saying them that she should find them so inappropriate and so impoverished, so utterly devoid of truth, of flesh, and, as it turns out, simply of relevance,

Who are you? What do you want? We don't have any money. Don't come any closer. Don't touch the girl. Is it you who's been sending me the letters? What are these letters about? What do you want from me?

Now they can almost hear the reverberation, on the walls, in the rooms, in the very air of the hamlet, of the Kangoo's engine as it enters and goes to park. Patrice hasn't thought about Rajah, hasn't noticed that, unlike what usually happens, the dog hasn't barked and hasn't come out to meet him.

Bergogne is still flustered by the wound in his finger; for the whole ride home the bandage bothered him almost as much as the wound—it reminds him of the arm he broke playing soccer in a field when he was a kid, forcing him to wear a cast on the day of his communion, and the photos where he's smiling in his alb, the white of which blends in with that of the plaster—plus he's vexed by all the time wasted, he wants to believe everything's going to be fine now and gets out of the car grabbing the bags of frozen food, which he'll put in the kitchen, no, no point putting the sweetbreads in the freezer, he'll let them take their time thawing in the bag before taking them out to cook them. He comes back to the car to bring in the computer, remembering that he has to wrap the gift—to go find the wrapping paper, the scotch tape, a ribbon or something gold to make it pretty too, well, fine, too bad if there's nothing left—he lets himself be buffeted by his thoughts and, while he's not curious about the absence of his neighbor's dog, he is a bit curious about the Clio in the yard, wondering who could have come to see Christine at this hour, because when you know someone you feel entitled to your say over everything, someone who's showed up—a salesman, a sales rep, some other asshole who wants to palm off on Christine for a euro some piece of crap that will end up costing her ten thousand if she listens to him, but the guy is in the wrong place, that's clear, she doesn't need any help getting rid of that type of creep—he's not going to stop for that, he has so much to do, the wrapping paper, the scotch tape, everything he needs to find, he'll do it all at the kitchen table. He sets down the computer box, makes sure there's no price stuck on it anywhere, any kind of label. No. He won't forget to give Marion the gift receipt, even if he already can't remember where he put it, it's fine, he'll deal with that later. He starts wrapping and can't be bothered to go find the scissors, he calls out to Ida once, twice, louder, then lets it go; Ida must be having her snack at Christine's, it's fine. He looks again through the drawers of the buffet in the kitchen, in the desk in the dining room, no, he grumbles to himself about objects and their magical way of disappearing the minute you're looking for them and that you find as soon as you no longer need them, there we go—shit, I almost forgot to put the champagne in the fridge—and he puts the champagne in the fridge, thinking he's starting too many tasks at once, he'll surely end up forgetting something important, finally he takes a knife and, folding the paper hard enough to mark it, he manages to cut it with the blade of the knife, which takes time, cut, tape a side, crease down another section of paper, make the folds, avoid mistakes, corners too thick; it has to be smooth, nicely folded, symmetrical too.

There, the present's done. Bergogne is pleased, he didn't do so badly. It's a nice gift; the package is enormous, tempting, Bergogne even found some golden curling ribbon that he fiddles with, fine-tunes, now he has to get changed—take a shower before anything else.

And so, for a long time, a crushing succession of minutes, at Christine's house, they wait, not understanding all the time he's taking to show up, desperate to hear his footsteps, to hear this man whose heavy steps Christine and Ida know perfectly walking on the concrete slab that runs alongside the houses; they'll hear, at the moment Bergogne stops in front of the house, silence, then the rubbing of metal on concrete as his soles scrape the doormat, moving it with them—every day the same metallic sound—they'll hear it and hope like they've never hoped before, even though all of a sudden Christine thinks maybe it's better that he not come, that he not come in, that she should shout out to tell him not to come, maybe it's some kind of trap they've set for him; she's seized with a worry that almost turns into panic, which she tries not to show because she doesn't want Ida to understand what she's thinking, because she fears the little girl's reaction, fears passing on her own fear—but no, it won't change anything anyway, and when Patrice comes into the house, having knocked twice first as he always does, she's pulled it together, telling herself it'll all be over soon, it has to stop, these two lunatics will have to explain themselves because any asshole can terrorize an old dingbat and a little girl, but with a man like Bergogne there, that, she thinks, that'll be another story.

But for now Bergogne doesn't come. He's taking a long time in the shower, because of his slightly pathetic need to let the water flow over him, as though it could wash away his shame—and yet he refuses to admit to himself that he's made a mistake, why not a crime while we're at it, a sin, the way his grandmother would have spoken of sin as she furrowed her eyebrows, down on one knee, before crossing herself and screeching that decidedly hell is everywhere around us; she would have asked the forgiveness of the Most High, saying adultery is a sin, and he, this little god-fearing, almost fanatical goody-goody who loved the Wednesday catechism and Sunday mass, the face of the wooden Christ on his olivewood or mahogany cross over the pews of the Église Saint-Pierre, he who finds that folklore so ridiculous today, what does he still have of that which he believed in so strongly and with so much reverent fear when he was a child, besides this bitter taste that it left in his mouth before crumbling, bit by bit, as his faith eventually disintegrated into shreds?

Today, under the shower water, he rediscovers the naive hope of cleansing himself of himself, he thinks again of the girl, of the garbage shed, the girl's face, the trap of guilt closing around him and him struggling against it—you're not going to pretend you're thinking about her, not going to pretend you have compassion for her or for her life, her misery, you're not going to do that, you bastard, make yourself believe you're a good guy and you're think-ing of this girl when really you don't give a shit and it's just a way of justifying yourself in your own eyes, because you want to think of yourself as a little better than you really are, save your bullshit compassion, she doesn't give a shit and she doesn't need it anyway, what she needs is money, yours or someone else's, yes, a better life but not your bullshit compassion.

And it's with infinite care, almost ponderously, that he takes the time to dry himself, to brush his teeth, to comb his hair, to tend to his eyebrow hairs that are wriggling every which way, and then to cut the few hairs in his nose; an infinite seriousness to get dressed in his black pants and a white shirt, even if he hesitates before putting it on—he might get it dirty if he wears it right away—just as he considers putting on a tie, then no, that's too much, that would be grotesque, a jacket would be ridiculous too. Should he wear an undershirt? He considers this; a tank top, if he doesn't wear a jacket, he imagines it would be visible through the shirt. So he stays in front of the armoire looking for the inspiration that surely won't ever come to him for this sort of thing. He'll just have to take the plunge, he's not about to go over to Christine's to ask what he should wear, is he? He decides to try on the pants and the shirt to see if he feels uncomfortable, if he feels restricted in that shirt which he can clearly see won't hide his belly spilling out of his pants—he's put on more weight since last time—shit, he thinks, not great. But should he leave the shirt tucked into the pants or leave it out, play it casual'? After some reflection he leaves it tucked in, too bad if it's a bit tight, it's fine. He undresses so as not to risk getting dirty—in any case, he also has to remember to bring in the cows. He'll get dressed at the last minute, and for now he'll get back into his jeans that are a little too loose, his checkered shirt and his half-zip sweater with the holes in the elbows. He'll have plenty of time to figure it out later, and time to change his mind if it's not right.

17

Night has begun to fall over the yard, the sky tinted with a bluish stretch, almost gray, fringed in the distance by a pinkish halo, very pale, to which Christine soon stops paying attention because she recognizes Patrice's steps in the yard.

He knocks on the door and, as he enters without waiting for an answer, she wants to shout to him to leave and call the police or she doesn't know what else, she has no ideas, nothing inside her but emptiness, anger and this lump in her throat, this cry that wants to come out but doesn't; she stays quiet, eyes fixed on the young man who doesn't even seem to have heard Patrice—or maybe he's just not paying attention—but Ida is squirming and Christine has to hold her still, to show her by putting her index finger over her mouth that they're going to wait, that they shouldn't worry and shouldn't call out or shout so they don't panic Patrice needlessly, she doesn't know how he'll react, could he react violently, which Ida seems to understand because she straightens up and watches the door in silence.

The young man with the bleached hair turns back toward Ida and Christine; without a word he's preventing them from going anywhere, they both understand this and don't try anything funny, they figure that downstairs Patrice must have been surprised not to find Rajah, that's right, he must have wondered at the mess of kitchen utensils and the ingredients on the table. And in fact he does let a moment go by without moving, in the kitchen, not even daring to call out, just troubled, then finally his voice rises in the silence of the house,

Ida?

but without insistence, almost as though afraid to be a nuisance,

Christine?

as you'd wake someone up,

Ida? Christine?

then, perhaps with more assurance or determination, as though amplified by a surge of irritation,

Ida? Christine? Anyone?

but the answer doesn't come, upstairs Christine clenches her jaw and doesn't dare answer, holding Ida's arm tightly, both of their voices frozen, and the young man, with his dye-burned hair and his light gray eyes trained on them, they don't know what to do and lower their eyes, unlike earlier, simply because the anger has left them; now it's as though they can no longer bring themselves to hold his gaze with defiance and provocation, this guy who's just a kid—he's a kid, Christine repeats to herself, how old is he, really how old can he be?—she stares at him in a stupor, incredulous, and truthfully, though she'd be reluctant to admit it, something in him intrigues her, enough that she thinks, almost in spite of herself—just for a second, before she can hold back such an inappropriate idea—that she could, that she'd like to make his portrait, that he himself is the portrait of something else, something other than himself, even if she couldn't say what. They wait, Ida's eyes mostly riveted to the bloodstains at the top of his tracksuit, and the blade of the knife the guy is idly taking out of his pants pocket—what is it? a Laguiole, like her father has, or an Opinel, or who knows what else? She sees him playing with the knife, humming to himself, with the blade he's idly tracing over his skin, not pressing down, testing his resistance and the elasticity of his skin, perhaps, never going so far as to risk hurting himself as he traces lines on his hands, following imaginary routes down his fingers, over the lines on his palms, slowly hugging the contours of his veins as though all of a sudden he's alone and sees nobody around him: Ida watches him, studies him, but for him it's as though he's all alone, in total silence, and he turns toward them as though he has to make sure they're still there, as though he's forgotten them, because mostly he looks out the window at the sky and the countryside, the yard of the hamlet.

Ida has time to take a good look at his hair, short in back, cut with clippers at the top of the neck and on the sides, but almost domed at the top, tumbling back down in a fairly dense, wavelike lock in front, not very long; in profile the nose is slightly twisted at the top, the chin distorts the face because with the lower lip it sticks out a bit too far past the upper lip, he could have a lantern jaw or maybe the bottom just protrudes a bit, as though it's come unhooked near the ears. And yet his face is gentle—is it because he has no facial hair or because his skin is so white, practically pink? It's like a small child's, but it's not so smooth, no, he has bags under his eyes and blackheads on the wings of his nose, his eyes have a lost expression just as he himself has a lost expression, and he keeps looking out the window before reacting—there, he's straightening up—he stops humming that strange tune that seemed to be repeating these

Boom,

explosions of

Boom,

in his mouth, in his head, his neck joining his head in a slight movement,

Boom,

and he stops, standing up straight, as though he's just woken up in front of Christine and Ida, breaking into a broad smile that exposes his yellow, irregular teeth, one of which looks chipped. He approaches them and they instinctively recoil; Christine tries to hold Ida tighter in her arms, as though to tell him he shouldn't come near the girl, as though to tell Ida she'll protect her, that nobody's going to hurt her, but Ida tries to escape Christine's embrace, doesn't want to be touched, she's heard Christophe's voice—a voice that sounds muted or muffled by the floor between them, his voice coming from somewhere downstairs and obviously directed at her father, that's what she thinks, yes, he's here, she heard when he called to them, Christine and her, but there was nothing after that, and at last there's the very clear voice of the other man, addressing her father. Who will soon come into the bedroom and all of this will be over, the two men will leave, that's what she tells herself, repeats to herself, even though for the moment she doesn't hear her father, just Christophe's voice coming from the stairs, maybe from the studio,

Strange people, these artists, don't you think?

that voice feigning surprise, which Christine and Ida hear as they listen for Patrice's answer, surprised that it doesn't come—did he not answer or did his answer not make it up to them, did it get lost on the stairs, too weak to cross the distance between them?

Now they don't move, they're trying to hear what's going on downstairs, yes, this must all be happening in the studio, when Patrice didn't find anyone in the kitchen and saw all the baking ingredients and utensils, he probably figured they were just in the next room, he'll have gone without a second thought to take a look in the studio, yes, almost by reflex he went into the studio where of course he expected to find Christine and Ida but where there were only paintings waiting for him—just the red woman telling him he's standing before a mystery to which he'll never find the answers. Bergogne no longer feels anger or irritation, everything that happened this afternoon fades into a distant fog of memory, he feels almost nothing in his hand, he's not thinking about it anymore, it'll be fine now. He's a bit worried about the silence that greets him in Christine's house, though—and the fact that she hasn't put any music on, yes, that surprises him—he takes the time to stop and consider the look of the red woman, thinking he certainly doesn't much like what he sees, or rather it makes him uncomfortable, for a second he almost thought she was about to speak to him, but no, it's a man's voice that comes from behind him, a honeyed sneer feigning surprise or a winking curiosity,

Strange people, these artists, don't you think?

From upstairs, Christine and Ida aren't sure how he might have answered. They heard his voice as though it was too far away, too muted, as though it hadn't managed to carry up to them, unable to make it past the shock and the element of surprise that Christophe of course knows gives him an advantage in what's happening—but what's happening? Is something happening, Christine is already wondering as she tries to make out how Patrice might have answered. They held each other tighter, Christine felt her strength coming back, anger and indignation, a strength that comes in waves and superimposes itself on the panic and bewilderment, that erases them, that pushes them far enough away that now Christine can stand up and decides to go to the door, to face the young man, because he's stationed himself by the door. He makes a gesture with his head to order her not to move, just long enough for her, facing him, to hear Christophe's voice again,

Artists really are strange… Don't you think?

and this time the answer comes sharply up the stairs,

Who are you? Where's Ida? Where's Christine? What's going on here?

the two voices distorted by the distance separating them from the upper level, the space of the studio and the one where the two men are facing each other, the distance that separates them but also connects them, because from up there they can now make out the exchange, as one asks the other who he is and the other snickers, turning the question around and letting it linger,

I could also ask you who you are, no?

and it's not hard for them to imagine Patrice's reaction, they know him, you can hear the air move as he does, from upstairs you can almost see him barreling forward with all his strength, all his power—this is a man with not just the density of all the muscles underneath the fat, no, but also the density released by all his bottled-up energy, all the untapped power his customary gentleness seems to hold in—and even though she's not afraid of him because she knows how much he loves her, how much his entire being is drawn to protect her, Ida also knows he could snap her in half without even trying, and this is what both of them are thinking, not that Patrice could be in danger, certainly not, but that it's the two others, Christophe and the young blond guy, who might regret having come. For a few seconds, they're daunted by the silence that follows Christophe's provocation when he asked,

I could also ask you who you are, no?

a few seconds of silence that they can't imagine contains nothing, no, on the contrary they imagine this silence filled, saturated, with Patrice's body hurtling toward the other man's, so thin by comparison; they almost felt, heard, detected the furious steps, maybe even Bergogne raising his hand and grabbing the man by the collar, and the man must have recoiled, yes, both of them almost frightened for him and his provocations and his mocking voice that thinks it can do whatever it wants. And now it's him, Christophe, who they hear, this time without irony in his tone, with an urgency and almost a stirring of panic in his voice, something cracking, shaking, a doubt they haven't heard in him before, and the young blond man hears it too, because for once he turns toward the bedroom door, taking a step toward the door because he wants to hear, he's clearly realized his brother's voice has lost its confidence, they've all heard it,

Okay, everything's fine! everything's fine! They're fine, they're upstairs!

and already from up here they hear steps on the stairs, Patrice's strides and behind him Christophe's voice continuing,

They're not in any danger, I'm telling you everything's fine! They're with my brother.

but now the ironic tone is back, imprinting itself in the grain of his words, as though Christophe has enough space around him again to regain not the upper hand but that amused distance with which he likes to give himself confidence or, in his own eyes, strength, maybe the feeling of being in control of what's happening and influencing events, steering them in the direction he chooses, commanding them like the captain of a ship who believes as he shouts at the clouds that he can head off the approaching storm, even though in reality nobody is paying attention to what he's saying, because now Patrice has made it up the stairs in a few steps, his voice very loud,

Ida? Christine?

exploding,

Ida?

and as he bursts into the room he's barely stopped by the young man in the tracksuit, who steps back, takes a beat, steps farther back toward the window, letting Ida pass as she runs to her father and lets all her terror out in a stream of words that sound like shouts broken up by sobs; her father takes her in his arms and covers her face with his big thick hands that make themselves warm and soft for her, protection for Ida who's letting the tears stream down her face, hiccupping the words she's been holding in this whole time, for too long,

They killed Rajah, they killed Rajah and they said they'd hurt Tatie if I didn't come and,

Patrice, incredulous, leaning over her, trying to console her, to protect her, murmuring to her that it's all over now even though he understands nothing, even though for him it's more like it's all just beginning, but now he's here, he repeats mechanically that everything's going to be fine,

It's going to be fine,

and he shoots Christine a look as though she's going to answer him, explain it to him, tell him what exactly, when all of him is asking what's going on here, who is this, who are these guys, does she know them? does she know what they want? what do they want, these guys, as though for a second it's her he wants to blame for their presence, these two guys, what is all this, the death of the dog, the knife, what knife, Ida's fear connecting these presences to the anonymous letters, the threats, as though in some shameful corner of his brain he's reciting to himself those proverbs about how, yes, where there's smoke there's fire, as though she had it coming, both what's happening now and what's *also* happening to his daughter. For this, for a few seconds, he's mad at her. And this idea insinuates itself in him long enough for him to become aware that he has to push it away like a revolting odor—it's brutal, irrational, irrefutable—but without saying it he blames Christine for having her share of responsibility in what's happening, and even if this fades very quickly it's not as quickly as it should be, just quickly enough that he has time to tell himself this reasoning is absurd, of course it's idiotic, she has nothing to do with it, nothing at all, that's why she's not answering even though he's still looking at her, still seeking an explanation from her that won't come.

Instead: only bewilderment and stupor lingering on Christine's face.

Long enough for Patrice to realize that Christine's expression has just changed because the other man has entered the bedroom. Patrice turns around,

Who are you?

but the other cuts in,

I can't tell you how happy we are to be here.

because he doesn't even hear him,

Right, Stutter?

doesn't even see him,

My name is Christophe and that's my little brother, that's Stutter. We call him Stutter. So. Yes. We really are happy to be here, so happy. She's very pretty, your little girl. So pretty. You're a real beauty, you know that?

Patrice grips his daughter tighter, as if to protect her from the man's words, as though the words he's using to talk about her might hurt or harm Ida in one way or another. Bergogne doesn't like this, and he can feel through the heat of her skin that

Ida doesn't like it either. She's fidgeting, almost feverish, her tiny round smooth shoulders, her collarbone, such fine bones, such a fragile body, so vulnerable, Bergogne feels how badly she's trembling and also that she doesn't want to show it—she's a brave little girl and he doesn't know how much she struggles, but she's struggling with all her strength against the images she's seen, against the disgust and also the anger the two guys have awakened in her; she's trying not to cry even though she can't stop seeing the image of the dog and smelling on her fingers the odor and the sticky matter mixed with the fur and the hay, how the weight of his head, its limpness, is imprinted in the memory of her hands, the corpse not yet stiff and her hands covered in blood, sticky, which she washed, the water turning pink in the sink, a very pale pink on the enamel, hands stinking, the smell of dust, of concrete, arms stretched out under the faucet, the blood, the trickle of water and then this man sitting on their couch smiling at her and asking so nicely to come with him to Christine's because they mustn't leave Tatie all alone, and she sees herself obeying without resisting and without trying to do anything, overcome with hiccups which happens to her sometimes while she's waiting for an adult to,

That's a good sign, it means you're growing,

even if this time she's not growing, she's just overcome with a fit of hiccups, the man telling her she should drink a glass of water while plugging her nose, but her refusing, agreeing only to go join Christine without thinking for a second of fleeing, nor that this man maybe killed her dog. And it's only when she sees the younger of the two, in the bedroom upstairs at Christine's house, with her, that she understands: the bloodstains on his electric blue tracksuit, and in his hands a knife he's playing with like he does it all the time, the knife idly twirling from his fingers to his palms, dancing in arabesques like some kind of magician whose magic is enchanting and extraordinary—but dark.

18

Sometimes accounts have to be settled at all costs, and so be it, even if there are days where it would be better not to settle anything at all, Marion thinks, because when it all spins out of control you can do what you will, try to take it all back, try to smooth things over, or even not do anything, just wait in a corner for the clouds to go off and rain down on other heads, other landscapes far away, but nope, it won't do any good, birthday or not, reality doesn't take the day off, you have to settle your scores and so be it, Marion thinks, if I lose my job today.

The truth, she knows, is that even if she wanted to she wouldn't be able to sit quietly and wait for the storm to pass. No, she can't just let it slide in silence, that's just not who she is. She won't let anything slide at this meeting which after all she didn't call; they're trying to force it on her and her co-workers, even if she knows it's mostly to embarrass her and wound her *personally*, so that she'll own up to every mistake she and her co-workers have supposedly made since she started working here, all her doing, obviously, her malign influence on her co-workers and the team's morale; yes, a meeting so she'll finally acknowledge the degree to which she's been turning her co-workers against management and sowing chaos in the company, and too bad if this meeting happens to fall on her fortieth birthday, which makes her wonder whether that dickhead project manager didn't go so far as to schedule it on purpose just to ruin her birthday, as if to herald a year of raining frogs and bad luck and broken mirrors, admonishing her to submit if she wants to cool the ardors of the vengeful gods, contrary to everything she's done for years, having shown from her very first days here, with everyone, a freedom of expression that surprised and delighted them, an independence that didn't take long to get under the project manager's skin, and confuse him too, a joyous and inventive freedom that impressed and exhilarated them, that inspired them to renew and rekindle not just their own relationships with each other but for each of them in their inner lives, in their entire lives for that matter, all these private lives that had been waiting just for this and were supercharged by it, as though her contagious energy, her life force, had awakened the same in the others, as if everything was electrified by Marion's presence, their collective routine cast into a new and faster world—a sexier and more dangerous world too—but also more alive, as if Marion, just by showing up at the print shop, had brought with her the electric friction of a life whose incandescence could only spread, irradiating the beings and even the things around her.

Since she arrived they'd worked better and faster, whether the project manager liked it or not, he who—whether because he envied the enthusiasm she aroused in the director and the favors he granted her as a result, or because he was resentful about the favors he relentlessly asked from her, nothing professional about those, and which she just as relentlessly denied him—had ended up making her life difficult, until she let her temper get the better of her, revealing in her a tenser character than they'd imagined, more fragile than they thought, more unstable. That she should let herself become negligent after that, that she should make errors, be imprecise or sometimes even absent-minded, that she should suddenly seem distant and disengaged, even checked out, that she should second-guess herself, this had been a surprise to everyone, and a disappointment, which her manager had managed to exploit to undermine her credibility with the director, culminating in this blunder that wasn't a blunder, which he had decided to milk as much as he could, demanding apologies and remorse from her lest she be reprimanded. This absurd business of copyrights they'd forgotten to require from a client, with the consequences quick to follow, the image-licensing agencies turning against the printer, this was a boon at which he was already rejoicing, from which he would profit, but let the jackass have his fun, she thought, and it was coolly, deliberately, without even trying to resist it, that Marion had decided not to avoid the trap, even to plunge right in, head first, yes, instead of smoothing things over she'd decided to show up and lay her cards on the table, okay buddy, if that's what you want, because she too has plenty to say about this coward who's always been too underhanded to make a move outright, not openly venturing anything, no direct proposition, no, but pussyfooting his way forward cunningly, larvally, with his looks full of subtext and his insidious words, lingering around her in wait for reactions that he solicited only by showing up in front of her, but without actually asking her anything, or else leaning over her shoulder to see what she was working on, as though he needed to bend over her shoulder and press himself against her, behind her back, to see her 27-inch monitor—unless he's completely blind, which he wasn't when he was ogling ladies' cleavage over on the other end of the hall—he who had reckoned he didn't even need to court her, to pretend to flirt with her, just brushing by to inflict on her the effluvia of his supermarket deodorant in the morning and his sweat in the afternoon, going so far as to force on her the menthol scent he probably sprayed on with a hose to freshen his breath that disclosed a diseased liver—plus his nose, already blooming into a rotten potato, didn't do anything to refute that general impression—leaning over her and talking to her always in a confidential tone, in a very low voice, as though to justify coming so close to her, leaning over her, brushing against her cheek or her ear, you understand, this stays between us.

And now Marion has to reactivate her anger so as not to give in to her weariness, or to the feeling that she's lost the game before it's even begun.

She thinks again about the project manager and about the unease she's felt since nearly the beginning, for years now, and which
she's never told anyone about, and especially not Patrice, because
even though she has no leverage to attack him head-on—no, he's
never propositioned her, has never made an inappropriate move
nor tried to corner her in the office at night, even though it would
have been so easy because she sometimes stays very late—all the
same she's sure of it, he's tried several times, taking advantage of
the slackness of the end of the day, of the flickering evening light,
just looking at her with that rictus men imagine to be powerfully
virile when it really just betrays their lechery and their vulgarity,
making them as unappealing as a shriveled fruit on a windowsill.
She wouldn't have objected if he'd made a genuine effort to flirt
with her, if he'd made advances without that conspiratorial, scav-
engerly air—she's not a prude, she understands if a guy wants to
take his shot, after all she likes to feel wanted like everyone else,
but there are men who desire you and those who covet you, those
who want you and those who take you, those who seek you and
those who think you're lucky to have found them. She didn't like
this way he's had since the beginning of tracing ever-closer circles
around her, with those petty innuendos, the first of which was
that if she didn't come to him herself he might take it badly, might
think she was resisting him at work too, and this is how she knows
perfectly well that he's decided to punish her for not responding
to his eagerness around her, for her resolute way of ignoring him,
turning him down, kindly at first, then more and more firmly,
responding to his advances not with fear or threats, nor even with
that scandalized anger she could have met this behavior with, but
with a casualness that made him even crazier, as though not only
did he not impress her—and indeed he did not impress her—but
to show him that she found him childish, *harmless,* which for him
was the worst thing, the most humiliating, this way she had of
turning everything around with the feigned innocence of a smile,
putting him in his place without lifting a finger, which brought

out in him the exasperation of desire and the desire for revenge, which was what this meeting was for, to give him the satisfaction and make Marion bend so that, one way or another, she'll finally *lie down.*

Because he was gunning for her.

So he'd go as far as this farce they were forcing on Marion, demanding that she respond to accusations that were merely pretexts, she knew it, just as she knew how much she'd done for the print shop, how much she'd changed the lives of everyone here, first Lydie's and Nathalie's, then those of the whole office, and not just the way she'd done with Patrice, at home, but with all the people she'd met, because to all of them she was an urbanite, a modern girl, not that there aren't any modern girls here, but not like this, not this outspoken and this free, not with the nerve and the inspiration she brought them; yes, Marion had been that breath of strangeness and fantasy, of dreams and rejuvenation in all of their lives. And now, she thought, if, as her director and the project manager wanted, she let them belittle her without talking back, without flinching, she would definitively lose this aura she'd acquired among all of them when she arrived here; she would sink into mediocrity, effaced and insignificant. She'd been flattered by this recognition life had never given her before, this existence in the eyes of others, and she knew she'd sooner lose her job than lose that flicker of desire she awakened in them.

And so, no question, she'd tell them everything that was on her mind without mincing her words—for this she has faith in herself, she knows what she's doing—and all morning she hoped the day would go by without aggression or tension, the better to strike her ax blows into the conformism of the meeting, catching them off guard with her own violence, which would short-circuit the hushed, civilized violence they thought they were using against her, because she knew they'd do everything they could to make her quit without getting their hands dirty by firing her. They'd respect proper form, protocol, a veneer of politeness, embarrassed faces, as though it had nothing to do with them, contrite, reluctant to do what her own mistakes had forced them to do. This was the kind of idiocy she might have spent part of the afternoon thinking about: the day is going by without incident, everything is fine, so far it's neither malicious nor aggressive, they only know they're waiting for a meeting where the three co-workers will be chastised by a director and a project manager just waiting to come at them guns blazing—she feels a wave of anger as she thinks of this creep trying to make her sit through fifteen minutes of hell just to avenge all the fifteen-minute frustrations he thinks she's caused him, but it's nothing, she's been thinking for days now that she's ready to tell him, in front of their director, face to face, that just because she refused to lick his balls doesn't mean he can take it out on her, knock down all her suggestions, diminish everything she says, sabotage her at every turn; just because I don't want to lick your balls, she'd say it just like that, something vulgar to catch them off guard, words like ax blows—bloody, crass, uncompromising—with just the right amount of acerbity to still the ripostes of even the toughest adversaries, so much would they be taken by surprise, and if they wanted clichés she could give them an earful, she'd grab the bull by the horns or, less chastely, more directly, rub their noses in their own shit—they don't know it, they had no chance of even suspecting it, but Marion comes from a world where words work to warp themselves into things as ugly and trivial as the reality in which they swim, or rather splash about; she's not easily intimidated, no, she can get into it because she knows what she's done for this place and what it's taken from her. They could admit that she's changed the office's atmosphere, everyone knew that when Marion came something loosened, that her presence had breathed some extra energy into the entire company, so if they didn't see how things could have deteriorated this far—deteriorated and not just, as might have been expected over time, with normal wear and tear and force of habit, that the fever that had risen with Marion's arrival simply eventually fell back down—

if they didn't see that, she had a few truths she could remind them of, she could expect the two girls to support her for all the freshness and freedom she's brought, and even the project manager would have to admit that for years he got to fantasize about her, that at least she'd never stopped him from thinking of her when he fucked his wife—and here she imagined scandalized shouts, stupefaction, *you go too far,* outraged looks, prideful preening, *how dare you,* the director speechless, flabbergasted by her nerve, *hey now you watch your language, Marion,* by her vulgarity, how could she say such things without flinching, looking the project manager dead in the eyes, his face probably white as the sheet he could hang himself with from shame, his jaw set as tight as the spot in which he'd stay stuck.

When she enters the conference room, the director is already perched on the edge of the table and glancing out the window, into the gray of the coming night, or at his smartphone, looking a bit serious, perhaps, lips pursed, while the project manager, standing pale behind a desk, pacing in place, is fussing over piles of open files, papers everywhere, like a prosecutor in a movie who's going to hog the spotlight until a small-time lawyer wipes that smug look off his face—that's what the whole movie turns on, how will the pathetic little lawyer beat the prosecutor who claims to have a damning file in his hands. Marion tells herself that in an hour or two it'll be over, she'll go home and when she gets there her husband and her daughter will be waiting, they'll drink champagne to toast her termination or her triumph, in the end it doesn't matter, they'll listen to music, she thinks that right now they must be decorating the house, getting the dining room ready and cooking, that they must feel like they're putting on disguises by dressing up. For the moment, she thinks that she can't wait to join them, just as she imagines they're also eager to see her car pull into the yard of the hamlet.

19

The hamlet which remains stock-still because Christine, Ida, and Patrice know now, all three of them, that already there's nothing left of the party, nor of that joy to which all the preparations should have contributed. It's over, already reduced to ashes, even if Ida refuses to believe it and still thinks she's going to wake up, that all of this is maybe nothing but a product of her imagination, even though of course she doesn't intellectualize it—neither her age nor the situation gives her the means—but she feels that confusion that comes from living in reality as though it were an altered or distorted version of itself, a bit as though it's life that's begun to imitate television and not the other way around, those shows she watches on TV on Saturdays and Sundays in which she's already seen people get kidnapped plenty of times, even though her father says she's too young to watch that sort of thing and he thinks at her age you can't tell the difference between what's fake and what's real, never agreeing with Marion when he brings it up, because then Marion says children still have to learn that the wolves in books aren't wolves but men, crueler than any beast would ever think to be in real life. She says: TV is harmless if you talk to children about what they're seeing, you have to explain to them the world in which they live and in which they're going to live, it's not like they'll get another one.

To which Patrice responds, furrowing his brow, that there's no hurry, that you can give kids a few years of grace, not ruin their childhood, and, shrugging his shoulders, he reminds her that she's the one who doesn't want them to talk about the anonymous letters Christine's been getting, on which point he does agree with her, she's just not being consistent, why try to protect her from that if it's only to put a big heap of macabre images in her head, no, no need to stuff Ida's mind with the dangers we face, Marion, to live is to be in constant danger of death and she'll know it soon enough—Marion then getting angry and refusing to talk any more about it, as if to say she herself understood too young what she shouldn't have understood, but above all that she understood the violence of learning it for herself, without anyone to help her name and face the reality of it, and each time she finally goes quiet, as though no one will ever understand her on this issue.

So now, yes, Ida is surprised to see reality changing shape before her eyes, resembling images from those shows while not altogether matching them, and somewhere in her head she can see herself tomorrow, telling Charline and Lucas on the bus to school that her mother's birthday party didn't go at all as planned, that there was no party because the whole hamlet was taken hostage by these two weird guys, and then, talking about this, she'll derive a kind of pride from it, forgetting the anxiety, almost disregarding Rajah's death, and then maybe it will come back to her along with the image of the guy with the almost white hair, and maybe in the end she'll go quiet, overwhelmed or caught up in the reality of it, as if underneath her feet a bottomless pit has opened up, threatening to swallow her, because now there really are two men who are mean and who look like villains and if she can't believe in their villainy it's because it's too much like the image she already has of it, it can't be *this* true, there's something she doesn't want to resign herself to believing, as though everything is about to evaporate all at once, to dissolve, as though a voice—Tatie's? Patrice's?—is going to reach her and she'll finally hear the words she knows by heart from having heard them dozens of times,

You off in dreamland, my love?

even if that voice doesn't come, if nothing comes at all. To-night it's like a bad dream is taking over and, because it's taking over in real time and lingering, luxuriating, she can see it's not a dream, not a movie, not a story she might have read with her mother; she thinks that unlike the stories her mother tells her, this one won't necessarily end the way she wants it to, the way it should, and the anxiety rises, by stages, stronger and stronger, turning into sensations throughout her whole body, pins and nee-dles invading her hands, her heartbeat accelerating, her breath as though she's been running—is that blood she thinks she hears in her ears, the flow, the heartbeats thumping in her head? She's start-ing to get a headache and her eyes blur, something hardens in her stomach, freezes in her chest. She wondered why the one called Christophe smiled at her so much, as though he was proud of her or as though this was all just a joke, what joke, why a joke, and if she hadn't seen her father's face, and Christine's, their looks go-ing from bewilderment to disbelief, from disbelief to anger, their worry also, maybe she would have believed it really was a game that everyone would stop playing soon, before starting to laugh, Christophe repeating how pleased they are to be there, he and his brother, talking his smooth talk while raising his hands in front of him, regaining confidence—his smile wider and wider—his or-derly white teeth—and his look going from one to the other to the other as though mindful not to forget anyone, to speak to ev-eryone, even to his brother, who'd stepped back to move closer to Christine, placing himself between her and the window.

At some point Patrice stood up and decided to go on the offensive with more questions than he'd asked so far, leaving behind the bewilderment that had left him in silence, almost snuffed out, and threw out a salvo of questions, or rather threats, orders jumbling together—you're going to get the fuck out of here, what the fuck are you doing here, what do you want, what is it you want, what do you want from us—almost exclusively addressing Christophe, who let him finish and responded without getting upset, without showing the slightest sign of irritation or impatience,

Right, here's what we're going to do,

simply placing his hands in front of him, the way Ida has often seen her teacher do when she wants calm in the classroom, miming something like the foot on the brake pedal in a car, palms seeming to press down on the air, in little repetitive, delicate motions,

Let's calm down, let's calm down,

and, like Ida's teacher,

Right, here's what we're going to do,

his voice almost consoling, Christophe speaking first to his brother,

You, you're going to stay here with the lady,

turning to Christine,

All you have to do is show him your paintings, he'll be happy.

and as his brother nods to say yes, everyone has noticed that he's holding the knife toward Christine, the point of the blade against her right side. Christine has stiffened, her breath at once panting and weak, as if restrained, suspended as she holds herself very straight with her eyes trained on Patrice, expecting him to obey, to not try anything funny, or telling him all her disbelief, how she can't get over what's happening, as though the man is pressing the point of the blade strong enough to show that with a single motion he could sink it into her flesh with the same in-difference as he was breathing on the window before, looking at nothing in the yard, resting his eyes on the landscape but sliding over it as though that's not what's imprinting on his retina—now, similarly, the blade is pivoting on its edge against the fabric, dig-ging into the skin, already hurting her, for the moment just a drop of blood, forcing Christine to recoil in a movement she makes without even realizing it, the way you instinctively shy away from a source of heat.

Now, as for us, we're going to go set up the little party and wait nicely, okay?

Christophe's voice continues, this time addressing Patrice and Ida, as though Patrice and Ida are going to respond that yes of course they agree with him, that they'll listen without making any trouble, even though he must see that maybe they aren't even listening, standing there holding each other tightly, Patrice gripping Ida by the shoulders, no longer quite knowing whether he's protecting his daughter and comforting her with the gesture or if he's the one taking comfort in it, a reassurance he needs because he no longer understands what's happening to them, just as Ida, staring, can no longer see anything but the blade of the knife and Christine's body, the way she's holding herself straight, her face ashen in a way Ida has never seen, her pallor going so well with the young blond man's pallor—Ida doesn't see how, with his other hand, the left, the young man is pulling at Christine's back, keeping her close, preventing her from making an attempt to dodge the point of the knife, no, it's impossible, he could do nothing and not pull on her blouse and it still wouldn't change anything, she wouldn't try anything, she can't believe it, she remains speechless and stares at Patrice and Ida, suddenly so fragile, just as the other man

I can't tell you how happy we are to be here!

circles around them, bustling, still smiling, almost apologizing for the disturbance,

We don't want to bother anyone but you'll see, in a little bit you'll see, as soon as he gets here he'll explain that we couldn't do it any other way, isn't that right, Stutter?

Yeah, of course.

And of course Patrice refuses to leave. Out of the question to leave Christine alone with this guy. Out of the question and yet, for the few seconds he believes he can refuse, resist, Patrice doesn't try to negotiate or parley, nor even to struggle to make the two guys let Christine go. No. He doesn't even try to find out who Christophe is talking about while he continues to explain that they have nothing to do with it, that they've only, shall we say, obeyed orders, that they went along because that's how it goes. And Patrice, instead of asking questions, instead of trying to take advantage of this door cracked open just enough for a glimpse of some answers—who, why, for what purpose?—didn't try to find out more when Christophe said that this person, and only this person, would explain everything, because of course it wasn't up to him or his younger brother to give any explanations, Christophe seeking his brother's eyes,

Isn't that right, brother?

and the other answering with the same amused, childish complicity, a motion of the chin, a nod of the head, the same fake-embarrassed laugh that spreads through the room and isolates Christine and Ida even more, Patrice not knowing what to do, how to act, he doesn't ask anything about this person who's supposed to arrive, not even whether it's a man or a woman, he just wants this to end, Christine terrorized—the point has sunk a little deeper into her skin and her eyes have started shining with a wild gleam, anger concentrated in this look along with this worry spilling over and mingling with panic, which Patrice sees when she looks at him and asks him wordlessly to obey the man, yes, to do what they say,

Do what they say,

Christophe accompanying his thought with a motion toward the door, he's getting ready to exit but, as Ida and Patrice aren't moving, he takes a step toward them and, full of false courtesy, of knowing sweetness,

Come come,

and neither Patrice nor Ida can feel their legs anymore, their arms, one and the other incapable of thinking, of wanting, feeling caught in a trap and unable to get over the feeling of being caught in a trap—Patrice letting the same physical sensation rise in him, this limpness, that particular aphasia he felt this afternoon when, beneath the moving shadows and the rustle of the leaves of the trees on the boulevard Balzac, he followed the young woman, answered her with that feeling of being led, of letting himself fall into the guilty inertia of subjugation, as though he couldn't resist or even just refuse and go on his way. Now something comes back of this sensation—the dry mouth, the clammy hands, the heart beating too fast in his chest while in the brain nothing seems to be giving orders anymore, nothing even seems to be able to imagine escaping, finding an exit from a situation in which you've let yourself get mired in a kind of limp pleasure—yes, something pleasant in the impossibility of deciding, of fighting, in abandoning yourself to inertia.

It's Ida who understands first that they shouldn't resist, helped by Christine giving her a sign with her head to say it's going to be okay, they should go, she'll be just fine by herself. So Ida takes her father's hand and with a simple movement—she pivots toward the door—helps Patrice emerge from his lethargy; he takes his daughter's hand, a slow, indecisive, resigned motion, a look a bit too long and evasive, like a request for permission from Christine, who answers with a sharp, almost brittle voice,

It's okay, it'll be fine, everything's fine.

So at last he acquiesces, he has the passing image of his cows, who'll have to spend the night outside, he murmurs something nobody hears, and finally they exit.

20

When they found themselves alone in the upstairs bedroom, Christine and Stutter no doubt both very quickly felt the same sense of unseemliness, of embarrassment, as though a shadow of obscenity had slid between them, not a discomfort they felt for one another but the idea, still below the surface, that they should find themselves here, two strangers, a man and a woman in a bedroom, beside a bed, even if there's nothing around them but paintings turned to face the wall and the main wall separating them is their difference in age.

And then this padded silence of the room encloses them further, this silence they were able to deny or reject at least while they could turn away from it by listening to the steps of the others as they went down the stairs to the first floor, then a bit longer, the same steps getting quieter and quieter as they left the house—Christine recognizing the friction of the draft stopper Patrice changed a few months ago, with its disagreeable steel-wool screech—then, with an effect like that of a carillon, the friction of the metal doormat, the burst of cool air entering the house and rising to the bedroom, the door closing and the reverberations floating back up the walls, still the sound of steps but now dulled because they're coming from outside, moving away toward Bergogne's house and soon leaving nothing in their wake but an almost imperceptible sound to which they both nonetheless stay riveted, knowing they'd hear the slightest word if there were any, if a single word were spoken it would travel to them, coming up from the yard to the window and from the window to the bedroom, knowing that in that case they could embroider something to say around it or that, even if they didn't say anything, it would be enough to make the space between them a bit more habitable. Maybe they hoped or waited for this word that didn't come, that phrase that, even saying nothing of importance, would have served as a buffer, dampening the violence of this silence that kept them mute in the bedroom, and would somehow have given an indication of the tone—the behavior, the words to say or not say, the gestures—to maintain here, in the bedroom, where, having taken a big step back so as not to stay pressed to her, as though the real inappropriate gesture wasn't his hand holding a knife against her, the young man feared she would interpret this false proximity as an advance or an inappropriate gesture. As soon as she felt him loosen his pressure, without a word, Christine had moved away immediately, then gone to the window and stuck both of her palms against the glass, almost at shoulder height, leaning her forehead forward until it rested on the glass, leaning over the yard to see if she could catch a glimpse of the three others, knowing full well that this was impossible—she knows the noises of the hamlet better than anyone.

So she wonders why she's doing it, if not just because it allows her a brief escape from the pressure that's slowly growing heavier as the presence of the three others fades, a pressure caused not only by not knowing what's going to happen now that they're no longer here and she still is, alone with this young boy whose bad cologne, tart and peppery, is mingling with the smell of sweat and something else, perhaps something to do with excitement, adrenaline, she doesn't know, but maybe what bothers her too is the young man's gaze on her—its steadiness, as though he's expecting something of her—but also and above all the pressure of the questions she's holding in and about to launch at him, because she can't hold them in anymore, she knows it, though she wants to keep them to herself a bit longer, the better to control them, to not squander them, a salvo of questions like weapons with which, at the right moment, you strike an adversary you know is stronger than you, yes, weapons that must be used at the perfect moment because they can be used only once and they have to do more than just help her understand what these guys want, what they're doing here, why their anonymous letters, why this aggression against her, them claiming not to know her, what do they want from her if they don't know her? And who's this person they were talking about who's coming, is it someone she knows? Someone they're working for who has a score to settle with her? And why did they leave like that to go to Bergogne's house—they mentioned the party, so do they know about the birthday and the evening's plans? And, behind this tide of questions, the even larger tide of words to scream at them to get the fuck out—if it's still possible to get anything from them—or to compel them to talk, to make them talk, to drag out of them why they're here, what they want, because they obviously want something.

And now Christine has just turned around again and has her back to the window. The young man is walking toward the door with quick steps and turns around as he closes his knife; he almost looks like he's marching from one foot to the other, as though he's dancing. He's folded his knife, holding it tight in his fist, then he smiles—at his fist, at his knife, she doesn't know—long enough for her to notice how solemnly he's doing it, how he slides his hand enclosing the knife into the right pants pocket of his tracksuit, pushing it down so deep that it bulges out the top of the leg—you can see his knuckles and the shape of his fingers hugging the electric blue fabric—and, watching this, she hasn't yet noticed that he's observing her, long enough to break the magnetism created by the sight of the hand in the pocket of the tracksuit, in her turn she raises her eyes toward him and it's as though for the first time they're looking at each other: one facing the other, not talking.

He's chewing his bottom lip and exposing his bad teeth, his lips, which are very thin and pale, almost bloodless, but go well with the tone he has from his very milky skin. She thinks he's of Nordic stock, maybe English or Belgian or even German, from the Netherlands, why not, his skin is very white, is it dotted with freckles or maybe not, she doesn't know, just as she's not sure but it seems to her all the same, yes, that this skin is growing pink as she stares at it, and it's as though her gaze has the power of those magnifying glasses you place between the sun and some substance that's just asking to catch fire—dry grass, twigs, newspaper—as though the fire is igniting inside him at this very moment, as though the heating of his cheeks, his forehead, is the sign of a greater fire taking hold, to which the young man doesn't yet know how to react, whether he should react, and for a moment that seems long to both of them they remain face to face, not moving and not saying anything, him just letting the red rise to his cheeks and finding nothing but that childish, resigned gesture that consists in lowering his eyes and tilting his head slightly as if to admit that he doesn't know what to say, that he's ashamed, that he feels filthy with these bloodstains on his trackpants, his knife in his pocket; and in fact he takes his hand from his pocket and rubs his two hands together—the rough friction of too-dry palms, a sigh, but this time he has to lift his head up when Christine,

What's the story with those letters?

…

The letters, is that fun for you and your brother?

The letters?

Yeah the letters.

Letters? What letters?

Why are you sending me letters? what's the point? what did I do to you, anyway?

I have no idea what letters you're talking about.

Ah, you have no idea.

We don't do crazy stuff like that.

Oh really?

No.

You don't call this crazy stuff, keeping me here? You kill my dog and what did my dog ever do to you that you had to kill him?

I didn't want to.

You didn't want to?

No.

Are you fucking with me?

No I didn't want to.

But it was you who did it, though?

…

Nothing to say?

…

It wasn't you?

…

You dare tell me it wasn't you?

…

Look at me when I'm talking to you.

…

Look at me.

…

It wasn't you?

Don't think I don't like dogs. It's just—

It's just what?

Nothing, it's just…

Why did you kill him?

I didn't want to.

So why did you?

Would've attacked.

You like that, killing animals? you enjoy it?

No.

You enjoy it?

I said no.

So why did you do it? were you scared of him?

No.

Did your brother make you?

That's not your business.

Who is your brother anyway and what does he want from me? I mean, what do you all want from me, really? I don't have any money, I don't have anything, I have nothing for you, you hear me?

…

It's been months now that you've been pissing me off with those letters.

That's not us, the letters.

Who is it then?

I have no idea.

You have no idea… You expect me to believe that?

You think I give a shit about your letters? My brothers need me here so I'm here, that's it.

Ah yes, that's it… You think that's it?

If my brothers do something they have their reasons.

And you say yes to everything, is that it?

…

Nothing to say?

…

I'm Christine. And you?

…

I'm talking to you. You must have a name.

Stutter.

What?

Stutter.

Stutter?

Yes. Stutter.

That's not a name.

…

What's your real name?

I didn't want to kill the dog.

So why?

It was the plan.

The plan?

The plan.

What does that mean, "the plan"? Huh?

I said I didn't want to.

Did your brother make the plan?

Okay. We should stop talking.

What's his plan?

I said we should stop talking.

What does your brother want?

I said be quiet, we have to stop talking.

What does he want here?

...

Who is your brother and what does he want from me?

Shut up I said.

I'll shut up when I want to.

I said shut your fucking mouth,

and now it's as though his whole body is on fire, as though he can't survive without spreading these flames burning him, and all of a sudden he charges at Christine and stops so close to her that for a moment she stumbles backward and almost falls. She stays there, dumbstruck by the violence of the gesture, stopping just a few centimeters from her—long enough for her to stare at the young man's face, and this time it's no longer a skin turned pink by shyness or embarrassment but a skin turned crimson by anger staring back at her with eyes wide open, shining and furious, but whose rage is as feverish as it is uncertain and trembling; a funny kind of child's anger that trembles all by itself, that's taken aback by itself too, as though it's about to overflow and the young man is himself stunned by it, not only surprised but maybe frightened too, as though it's someone else overflowing from inside of him. In the time it takes her to understand this, Christine is able to decide that he's the only one here who should give in to fear, even though he's the one holding the knife, even though he's the one who could strike. Or in fact not *even though* he's the one, but *because* he's the one. She decides to not be afraid, it's her only option, the certainty takes over her mind, it's barely an idea, a fact that rises inside her and that her whole body enforces before she's even really aware of it because, before she can even articulate it, she who stumbled backward has stood back up, her body has rooted itself solidly, upright, chest tilted slightly forward, the way someone who's about to leave the house on a very windy day prepares mentally to take on the squall; she stands before this flushed face, its eyes too shiny, and for an instant nothing remains but the breath of their bodies and maybe Christine murmured a light

oh,

or even nothing—maybe he just imagined she murmured something—soon his face loses all the blood that had rushed in and becomes pink again, then white, then pale, almost ashen, like his voice, in a moment, colorless too,

Well anyway, let's not stay here. I want you to show me your paintings. You know, I used to do tons of paintings, at the center. You should've seen them, I mean by the end I felt like it was all I could think about.

21

What if I refuse?

Patrice lets this question buzz in his head and doesn't dare let his lips repeat it the way he managed to throw it out earlier, and this time he doesn't start again, he doesn't want to hear

If you what?

because he's seen how the guy might counter if he decided to insist, as though he could adopt that saddened or dismayed look again in the face of Patrice's obstinacy or stupidity or denial, remaining incredulous the way he was the first time, when Bergogne said, with as much threat in his voice as defiance, in response to this forced plan,

What if I refuse?

not expecting to see Christophe adopt that saddened look,

If you what?

looking sincerely surprised and almost dismayed to have to answer him,

If you what?

before saying something with a sigh to cut him down to size, to put a choice to him that isn't really a choice, continuing the same pattern but twisting it, if you say no, ah yes, if you, arranging it in his ironic and cloying manner, yes, if you refuse, not needing to go any further, letting the ellipsis linger there without having to place it, just accompanying the end of his phrase with a fatalistic, resigned motion of the shoulders, as though he doesn't want to belabor the fact that refusal will have consequences, and that as of the moment Patrice knows this he'll have only himself to blame. Christophe didn't need to say any of this, of course, which is why he's set aside those threatening airs, just shrugging his shoulders, saving himself the trouble of answering or trying to explain—what's the point of making the effort to say it, why say it?—if it goes badly with your neighbor you'll have only yourself to blame, it'd be too easy to let yourself off the hook and blame someone else but everyone has to accept his share of the responsibility, you're an adult, aren't you, just have to know how to grin and bear it and good things come to those who wait, my friend.

And all Christophe can say to Patrice, when they enter the house, in a tone that's meant to be sympathetic and kind, he says without playing a game that not he even he believes in, as though he's heard, whistling in his ears, this mad question gnawing away at Bergogne,

What if I refuse?

and everything that comes with it, the temptation simmering in the air, palpable in the presence of bodies, in the way Bergogne is building up, through restraint, all the brutality of his motions— opening the door, turning to Christophe, coming up very close to him, too close, but without saying it, simply because he doesn't know how to react, stuck on the image of Christine in the upstairs bedroom and the man in his electric blue tracksuit, the knife—the blade—he tightens his fist—the wound in his finger awakens—he says nothing but his whole body is shouting it, what if I grab you by the collar and smash your smug fucking face into this fucking wall, what if I break your nose, what if I bust your face and explode your skull—

What if I refuse?

If I refuse?

If you refuse, Christophe seems to answer calmly even though he's saying nothing, smiling, looking enchanted by the table settings, the golden banner and its *happy birthday* that seems to dance over their heads as soon as the door opens, flung around by a light breeze, yes, if you refuse, Christophe seems to answer, even though he's just raising his eyebrows in a show of admiration and amusement—mockery?—if you don't want to do what you're being asked again to do, then you know perfectly well what will happen, or, if you don't know it's because you claim not to have any imagination whatsoever, unless the fate of your neighbor seems more insignificant or anecdotal to you than her dog's? or because you care so little that you're capable of leaving her alone, without trying to do anything to be of service to her? You can't believe what's happening, of course, a guy like you, even a catastrophe couldn't possibly happen to you, it just couldn't, right, not here, nothing ever happens here, it always stops at your door, maybe that's what you're thinking even now, and you can stay there with your arms dangling like that, refusing to watch the show, but that doesn't mean you're not part of it.

Not only, of course, has Christophe said none of this, but in fact he's wasted no time creating movement, spreading a falsely festive, joyful ambiance, playing the host interrupted by the early arrival of guests he wouldn't dare ask to come back in an hour, or to whom he might just go so far as to suggest, timidly, with a contrite expression, that they make themselves at home over on the living room sofa with an orangeade or a glass of sparkling water while he gets everything ready. Christophe gives the impression of having always lived here, of knowing the house better than Patrice and Ida, pressed to one another, fused not only to each other but to the tiles in front of the table covered with the orange-bordered tablecloth, as though Ida and Patrice have just entered someone else's house and, by some strange and ridiculous reversal, they're the ones who have shown up at the home of people they know nothing about; or perhaps, more likely, both of them dazed by

Christophe's speed, by his casual whirling way of running from the dining room into the kitchen, rummaging and rooting around in it—opening and closing the refrigerator, cupboards, drawers, buffet, china cabinet—and coming back into the dining room to ask them questions,

Did you remember to buy bread? Yes, sorry, I know I'm being awfully familiar with you, I hope you don't mind? No, you don't mind—giving the questions and the answers, speaking to himself, punctuating it all with commentary for an audience known to him alone, or from time to time, raising his voice, to Patrice, to compliment him on his planning, hey, this looks great, what you bought, do you have an account at Picard? is that right? … it's true, there's never time to cook… never time for anything, really. Should take the time, but we never do. Me, I like to cook but I just don't make the time. Food's my thing, though, I love red meats, dishes in sauce, all of it, it's not super healthy but who cares, we're not going to the beach, right? Our mom, she used to make us these casseroles, braised beef, blanquette, buddy, I'm telling you, it's… You know the type. And booze too, and red wine and beer, beer especially, well, that was mostly our old man's department, he always did enjoy his libations. Speaking of which, I see you got some champers, great, and some red. What is it, a Bordeaux, a Bourgogne? I don't know much about wine. Anyway, we'll make short work of them, the bottles. I mean, hey, no expense spared here, right? You really do spoil her, your little *esposa*.

What?

You didn't take Spanish? Your little wife.

What?

Patrice heard himself repeat, finally emerging from this torpor that still paralyzes his mouth—the pins and needles on his lips and in his fingertips too, the shooting pain of the wound that's come back—as though he's finally going to manage to move back into his body, to inhabit it again, because finally the anger is rising inside him, just as the questions are taking him over again, invading him, and this certainty too that he's not going to let himself be led around—why at this very moment does his mind turn to his mother and that expression she snapped at him so often when he was young, trotting it out in front of his aunts, who chuckled, hearing him talk, that he was a nice boy and his niceness would be his undoing, look at him, the minute he finds his better half she'll be leading him around by the nose; which his mother repeated, washing the dishes or hanging up the laundry or filling mazagrans with coffee reheated in a battered old pot, indifferent to his docile, see-through presence, blushing behind his acne-burned skin, as though a woman, beginning with her, would always have the better of him, using his niceness as a chain to leash him to her, to lock up any attempt at backtalk, of which she was sure he was utterly incapable. And maybe his mother, if her spirit or her diaphanous dead-old-woman aura is still wandering this house, visiting on it the slightly rancid effluvia of maternal tenderness, of sweet cajoleries, maybe, then, she's whispering in his ear to not let himself be led around by his nose in his own house and in any case not in front of his little girl, appalled to have to tell to him that a man has to defend his family, his home, and that she's very disappointed—though not surprised—to see him put up with the swaggering of this guy he could shatter with a fist if he could just be bothered to, except Bergogne, instead of his mother's, which he now lets disappear into a far corner of his brain, hears the real and resonant voice of his daughter,

Dad?

and her tiny hot hand,

Dad? Dad?

almost burning, moist too,

They're not going to do anything to Tatie, right, Dad?

clinging to the rough skin of his hand, his daughter's voice, pale and trembling in a way he's never heard before.

As though Ida has to make a great effort to even talk to her father, to tell him that suddenly she's distraught at the thought of having left Tatie Christine alone with the boy with the knife. She clings to her father and the tears flow without her realizing she's crying. The tears stream down her cheeks and she sniffles; she holds firmly to her father who drops to his knees and wipes away her tears with his big dark fingers, earth-colored or sunburned, almost brown. She wants to speak but she's having trouble, her chest is heaving so hard, it's like the panting of a little animal caught in a trap, exhausted from running. It's good, yes, this comfort, when her father takes her in his arms and holds her very close to him, as though he's transmitting to her his strength and above all his love, his ability to face up to anything and to know how it's all going to end, obviously well, definitely, because he's here and soon Mom will come too. The guys will finally leave, also definitely, but now and then the image of Rajah pierces through her and turns her stomach, a torrent of tears cuts through her chest and she has to let out a very long, tearful breath, she knows it, her dog, his head still soft and heavy in her hands and his mouth open, the slobber on his pinkish gums and the eyes already glassy, narrowed, the blood and the treacly odor that come back and everything comes back in a spasm of terror and hatred, like the smiling face and the too-blond forelock of the young man, his slight lantern jaw.

But already her father is drying her tears and standing up, taking her by the hand,

Come on, sweetie.

and they both go into the living room. Bergogne takes his daughter in his arms, strokes her hair and sits her down on the sofa. She watches him and they both glance into the kitchen where they hear the man bustling around; he's cutting bread, whistling as though he's a friend, as though he's truly happy to be here. Is it possible that he's *truly* happy? father and daughter seem to be asking each other, not daring to speak about him, just asking questions with their eyes and letting those questions circulate, then Patrice murmurs that everything's going to be okay, nothing's going to happen, see, this guy doesn't look dangerous.

Mom, I want Mom.

She'll be here soon. In the meantime you're going to watch cartoons, okay?

She's barely nodded before he's gotten up, taken the remote, found a cartoon show—let Ida at least be in a world she knows, where she can feel at ease, until her mother comes.

Now Patrice sees the man rummaging in the cupboards and Bergogne rushes to the kitchen, a returning momentum pushing him, carrying him,

What do you want from us? What are you looking for?

Right now I'm looking for a dish that goes in the oven.

How long is this nonsense going to take? What do you want? money? you want money? Is that it? Are you the ones harassing Christine? I'm warning you, we've gone to the police and they could show up at any moment, they said they'd stop by whenever, she's being watched, your stupid letters, what the hell's that all for?

Letters? What letters? What are you talking about?

As much as the two men might believe they're alone, face to face, they haven't forgotten that Ida is watching them. Because the living room is separated from the dining room by nothing more than a gap where there must have been a French door once, like the ones in the houses in a subdivision. Patrice took down the doors between living room and dining room, and from the living room you could see the dining room table and, on the other side, the entrance to the kitchen. And it's over there, from the living room, that Ida, distracted only intermittently by a cartoon whose animation is choppy and violent, slapdash, simplistic, a thing for boys that wouldn't really interest her under normal circumstances and now seems incomprehensible to her, looks into the kitchen, a look that's at once worried and furtive but very probing too, and tries to make out what she can. She's waiting for the moment when her father leaps at the man who's taken off his jacket and is now standing up in a white shirt. Soon she lowers her eyes, she can tell Christophe has seen her and shot her a look that's meant to be conspiratorial—she thinks it's for her benefit that he says, delivering it in such a loud voice that she's certain it's meant for her, hey, listen, now we can finally move on to something else, you hear that?

    he says,

    A car,

    he smiles,

    That's a car we're hearing, no?

22

In her car, Marion can turn the volume all the way up on the old Nirvana hit she used to spend entire nights dancing to, years ago; she can breathe and even laugh if she wants, nobody is there to point out that if she's laughing so hard tonight it's maybe just because her laughter allows her to stave off her own anxiety, to keep it at bay, just as she could also keep it at bay by starting to cry or shout in order to let go and unwind this tension she's accumulated and that it seems impossible to get rid of.

If she's able to burst out laughing in her car, she doesn't want to admit to herself that it's not out of joy or the feeling of having triumphed over adversity, of having succeeded in flipping the trap that had been laid for her and, with humor, candor, turning around a situation that didn't look good in the least. No, this isn't the joy she's feeling—and the pride that goes with it—and what's really making her laugh is a victory not over others nor over a situation but over herself. Though she doesn't articulate it to herself, the truth is that she's laughing at having surmounted her fear, having been able to keep it in check, to bend it to her will. She also succeeded in taming this terror that she'd feared more than any real danger, yes, because when she walked into the conference room she first had to master her fear of succumbing to her own fear, because more than anything she had feared letting herself be submerged by it, paralyzed by it, stifled by it to the point of not knowing how to answer when they started to put her on the spot—in the hot seat—asking her questions about this regrettable incident that has put us all in a delicate situation, don't you think, Marion, with a trial to handle that we're going to lose anyway, at least on procedure, because we know full well that an error was committed on our side and that, as the director said, we'll all pay for it because we're all in the same boat.

Around five o'clock, accompanied by the suggestive silence of the girls at reception, who would shoot each other no end of knowing looks as soon as the door closed behind them, Lydie, Nathalie, and Marion went into the meeting room. Two of them thought they'd get off at best with a sharp dressing down and that would be that, while Marion had decided she refused to be dressed down or read the riot act or given an earful or simply yelled at—call it whatever you want, I'm too old for it—no question of their trying to teach her a lesson, of their infantilizing her, scorning her, no, out of the question, she'd repeated to her co-workers, I'm forty years old to-day and goddammit it's out of the question for them to moralize at me or talk to me like a teacher disappointed by my worthlessness, as though we're idiotic little things who can't handle ourselves, who can't own up to our mistakes or take responsibility, plus, if we did something dumb, it's also because everyone else didn't know how to or didn't want to do their job, okay?

It was clear to her two co-workers that she wouldn't give in and that, unlike them, Marion had no intention of taking any abuse unless the project manager accepted his share of the blame, acknowledged his role in the mistake, no way they were going to be patsies or scapegoats or punching bags; and when Marion had sensed that her two co-workers were ready to cave, she repeated to them, Lydie, Nathalie, come on, I mean, are you with me or what? We all agree, right? It was his job to make sure, not ours, shit, I'm not making this up, am I? And if Lydie and Nathalie ad-mitted they agreed with her, that they knew she was right, they couldn't hide that they also thought that, even if it was unfair and all of this was just a pathetic excuse to give them shit, fine, all of this, they finally said it, is a trap to catch us out—suddenly throwing a veil of modesty over this truth that all three of them knew, namely that if the project manager actually wanted to make someone pay it wasn't the three of them but Marion alone, of course, none of them daring to say it, afraid to put a crack in the wall behind which they'd always managed to defend their shared positions; but Lydie and Nathalie would prefer that they drop it, even with the truth on their side they could still wind up with all of the blame falling on them, and no use being right if you wind up saddled with reprimands and penalties, if you lose the year-end bonus with which you were planning to go away—no, you can't imagine the look on the kids' faces if at the end of the year you have to go back on your promise to take them somewhere because you didn't get your bonus, all of it for reasons that maybe weren't worth it and which aren't the kids' fault anyway. The order of things is an order, pure and simple: nothing to be done. Hunker down and wait for it to pass. So neither one of them wanted to pay for Marion, even if they both knew Marion was wrong only in acknowledging that which they didn't want to face, Marion who obstinately refused to understand that they're employees, just employees, that there are managers and bosses above them, and that sometimes, even if it's unfair, yes, that's the way the cookie crumbles, because you do have to pay for others, even if it's a travesty, so be it, at this point it's time to say it could be worse, much worse, all the factories have closed and there's only this print shop left, that's the main thing, we still have our jobs and nothing's more important than that. That's what they'd have liked to make Marion see, because they were afraid she'd draw them into a confrontation in which they had everything to lose. And it's true that Marion had listened to them with a kind of disgust she'd barely managed to conceal, dismayed to hear them backpedaling. She'd listened to them with her eyes wide open, attentive and dubious, because she couldn't believe that in order to not rock the boat her two co-workers were prepared to take responsibility for a mistake that wasn't theirs, or not completely, or only marginally; and if Marion was willing to accept that she had no doubt been careless, admitting that she should have made sure the project manager had done his work properly, namely vetting the photos, finding out about the rights, yes, she was sure, nonetheless, that she didn't have to pay for mistakes that weren't hers.

As a result, she'd gone into the meeting as determined and calm as it was possible to be, resolved because she knew there was nothing else to do, this has been going on for too long, she repeated to herself, placing the incident that served as pretext for this meeting on par with everything that had, for months now, evasive and malign, seeping into her working relationships, fomented enough resentment, mistrust, and vengefulness to justify finally, as they say, laying her cards on the table.

Deep down, even though she maybe wasn't even aware of it, or if so then so hazily that it manifested only as a vague trembling in her voice, a slight change in her breathing, her pupils narrowed, her neck a little stiff, but almost nothing, the only thing she feared, the only thing she worried could stand in the way of her resolve, and the only one that could rise up before her like an impassable obstacle, that could nail her to her spot and make her accept everything without trying to argue, without any hope of getting back up, was that fear—a terror as old as childhood, or time immemorial—would pry into her with such force that it finally petrified her, rendering both speech and action impossible. So, when she entered the conference room, she panicked for a few seconds at the thought of lacking the guts, of not having the courage to hold her own against the weakness of her two co-workers—even as she understood them and didn't judge them, asking them if not to support her openly then at least to refuse to turn on her as soon as she reached the front lines, because Marion wasn't entirely sure they wouldn't turn tail, uniting against a common adversary, giving in to the threat of reprisals, to intimidations. She expected at least a well-meaning silence, one that didn't implicate them any more than it would condemn her. So, as she came in, she feared for a few seconds that she wouldn't be able to bear the preordained judgment of the two men waiting for them: the director, sitting on the edge of the table and refocusing after spending too long daydreaming at the window, with maybe something of a grave or distant expression, lips pursed, and the other, the project manager, pale and standing behind a desk, pacing in place, revealing files in front of him, loose pages, all of it stacked in piles on either side of the table, him in the middle, seated now and squirming on a plastic chair in his oversized prosecutor's suit.

When she plays back the scene in the car that brings her home, already trying, as she starts the engine, to move on to something else, to leave behind the oppressive, overserious atmosphere of the print shop, turning the music all the way up and singing along as loud as she can, in fake English, to grunge from the nineties, driving a bit too fast because she's eager to get home but also because, on the heels of her knockout win, she lets herself be carried away by the joy of relief and even self-satisfaction, yes, she doesn't tell herself that she needs to shake off this anxiety that's been weighing on her for two days, that she's been repressing the whole time she's been anticipating this meeting, no, only that she's happy with her victory over the project manager. She has every right to be, she knows. She's also pleased and proud that Lydie and Nathalie, when the three of them reconvened in the print shop's parking lot after the meeting and its sensational, unexpected conclusion, surprised more than anything else that night had almost completely fallen, the streetlights already casting their sinister orange tint on the concrete and gravel in front of the office entrance, all three relieved to finally be able to move on to something else, had both embraced her at length, thanking her as though what she'd said was also what every girl working here carried in her but couldn't express. She'd felt their gratitude, sincere, simple, and she'd answered with a provocative, amused air, lightly boastful,

Come on now, girls, I'm not going to let that asshole ruin my birthday!

Then they'd taken the time for a cigarette—Marion, that is, the other two having stopped smoking long ago—one or the other of them repeating,

I can't believe that turnabout—yes, this reversal, after suffering through a good half hour of presentation by the director about the purpose of the meeting, a monotonous and tedious presentation of a situation with which everyone was familiar, everyone having to brood over their own frustration at these precious minutes lost, irretrievably wasted listening to what they all already knew, but at a crawling, indecisive pace, with an inability to add anything new in the way the facts were laid out, any simple texture that could have created any sort of interest. It had been flat and soporific, which was maybe the intent: the voice, the tone, the indolence or fatigue, the distress the director wanted to emphasize by way of showing that the matter was serious, as painful for him as it would surely be in the decisions necessary to resolve it. Then there had been another fifteen or twenty minutes led by the project manager, minutes that now overflowed with information, that swarmed with increasingly direct, ad hominem attacks leveled almost exclusively at the three co-workers, and eventually at Marion, then at Marion exclusively, all of it in an exaggeratedly melodramatic register, a real trial, or rather a simulation, a trial reenactment, before, without leaving them any respite, the director and the project manager launched into a series of questions, each more pernicious than the last, until Marion couldn't take it, couldn't bear it any longer,

My goodness, a real fact-finding committee!

and, while the two men remained silent for a moment in the face of her insolence, waiting for an apology or an acknowledgment from Marion, stunned by her temerity, she had not responded and had started to laugh; at first to herself, a quiet laugh, reedy, restrained, not seeking anyone's approval, as though complicit with what she'd been brooding on in her mind without having said it yet, waiting for someone to give her a reason—which didn't take long. The project manager, mad with rage and gasping with contempt or anger as he ordered her to say what she had to say when, to everyone's surprise, the director started to smile too, then to laugh—hardly an uproarious laugh, of course, rather a laugh like a veil ripping, a light fog that suddenly changes the atmosphere as it dissipates, casting a new light on it, lively and warm, as if accompanied by a welcoming gust of air. This movement had surprised everyone, encouraging Marion to launch into it, but without the violence of the words she'd expected to resort to. She'd been able to let the truth of what she thought come out almost gently, without the need for anger or aggression, explaining without blaming anyone for it that, frankly, everything about this meeting was absurd and grotesque, medieval, calling everyone in their turn as a witness or taking them to task, honestly, do you see us here, is this the Kommandantur or what? are we in Soviet Russia? what century is this? Honestly, is this how we speak to each other, among people who work in the same company, for the same things, we all like working here, don't we?

And the project manager could repeat his accusations all he liked, she flipped them with such facility that even he was stunned—no, I'm not checked out, I'm just discouraged that I'm not taken seriously, that people pretend not to listen if I bring up an idea, or that it gets ignored only to be brought up two hours later by someone else, and no, no, it's not that I'd rather go home to my sweet little family, as you put it with the contempt you have for women, that's it, right?—and the project manager, flailing, what kind of unfounded accusation is this, I have nothing against women—oh no, of course not, you love them so much, shall we talk about that, about your love for women? Lydie and Nathalie started to laugh, an uncomfortable laugh at first, then to agree discreetly, then with conviction, force, to finally say yes, it's the truth and this time it was the director himself who took the floor, turning to the project manager, I told you if I heard one more time that—leaving the other one pallid, mumbling, they don't like me, that's all, they're out for blood, and Marion picking it up, oh, no thank you, no thank you, we don't want any, you can keep your blood and all the rest. We just want to work like normal and that's it.

And now, on the road, the houses are already getting sparse. Marion left Lydie and Nathalie in the parking lot in front of the entrance to the print shop. Tonight she has to hurry, she's spending time with her "sweet little family," she repeated, emphasizing the expression with little finger quotes in the sky. She said good-bye to her co-workers with a mark of affection maybe a bit more pronounced than usual, proud of a battle won and still under the sway of her emotions, not quite able to believe it, as though none of them was entirely sure what had just happened. As she does every night, she has to drive straight ahead before turning off at the branching junction marked by that horrible wayside cross with its silvery Christ who looks like a botched Silver Surfer. Every night she has a word to share with him, not that she's ever believed in him but she tells him about her mood, her thoughts that aren't really thoughts, like tonight, rolling up without signaling to turn left and disappearing into the countryside, she let out a thanks buddy full of irony and joy, as though the blessing of a Christ on the cross could really be granted her, she who's never set foot in a church.

And now Nathalie and Lydie are alone, wondering what they're going to do with the evening before going to Marion's,

You brought the gift?

Yep, yep, I have it here.

A drink at Chez Marcel and then the pizzeria?

Sounds perfect.

Oh, did he confirm?

This afternoon. I didn't tell you? He sent me a text.

What time?

Around nine, nine fifteen. You know, for the cake.

23

It is indeed a car pulling in. Like every night at the same time, this time or sometimes much later, but Ida always hears it, whatever the time, even when she's in bed and she can't get up because she's not allowed to, even if the prohibition maybe only excites her and she's itching to throw off the covers and run barefoot into the hall, to run down the stairs four at a time and cross the dining room to leap into her mother's arms, and so be it if her father yells, ordering her to go back to bed, because even if she loves her father with all her might the love she feels for her mother is greater than the idea, even the possibility of her might; it's a certainty she's had forever, an attachment to her mother stronger than the one she feels for her father or for anyone else, an attachment that unfurls to the point of overflowing when, from her room, she hears Marion's car, the nights she comes home late, even if that doesn't happen that much anymore, it seems to her, except obviously those Fridays when she meets her co-workers and friends to have dinner and go dancing.

In that case, it's Ida who'll go find her early the next morning, to curl up against her, and in spite of her need for sleep—she remains bleary with fatigue, her breath dense with alcohol and tobacco—Marion lets her daughter snuggle up in her arms, opens them to her almost without realizing it, and Ida is happy to take advantage, neither of them surprised that Patrice already left a long time ago, he never stays in bed in the morning and goes out very early they're not sure where, to the fields, to see his animals, maybe to the market already or, why not, hunting, depending on the day of the week and the season, with guys he's known forever and still sees from time to time.

Each night it's with the same feeling, the same overflowing emotion, that Ida hears this engine that she'd recognize out of a thousand, because of the long time, interminable to her, it takes her mother sometimes to make it to the house, as though her mother is trying to find a way not to come home right away, to preserve a bubble for herself, alone, for just a few more seconds, long enough to extend her solitude by parking her car, by turning off the engine, by reaching for two or three things on the seat next to her—her handbag, her lighter, her Winston slims which she smokes with a bulimic appetite that makes her look like she's thinking about things that are none of anyone's business—Ida seeing this as an additional reason to curse those cigarettes, she who would so love for her mother to stop smoking and who asks her every Christmas, or for her birthday, what would really make me happy is if you stopped smoking, even if deep down she doesn't know if it's really for her mother that she wants it or, more selfishly, to control the images she conjures of her mother's death or of her suffering, pitiless images like the ones she sees on the black cigarette packets with their terrifying warnings. But Ida knows full well that her mother won't change a thing for her, because each night when she comes home Marion has just very recently snuffed out her last butt, either in her car as she pulls into the yard or just before entering the house, on the patio, in that old terracotta pot that no longer serves any other purpose since nobody uses "table-top trash bins" anymore. Ida understands that she can't believe her mother, and each night she resigns herself to the fact that Marion simply can't quit smoking, not even to make her happy, because what her mother needs most is to be alone for a moment before joining them, her father and her, and that for this solitude only cigarettes give her the pretext.

• • •

On the television, teenagers with huge round eyes, with exaggeratedly prominent muscles, with blue hair sculpted into flinty blocks, are pitching shouts and kicks and punches at each other, they're leaping around and firing lightning bolts, the sky is catching fire around them—these fighters frozen in contorted and frankly ridiculous poses—all of this too fast for the landscape behind them, which disappears, vanishes, but already Ida has stopped seeing it, she's leaving the manga behind and darting out even though her father is telling her not to move, but, maybe because she doesn't hear him or because she can't hear him, she's crossing the living room and the dining room, she wants to leap into her mother's arms and shout to her that she's scared, yes, she wants to shout to her that this is beyond even the idea of what she thought fear could be and to let out this shout she's stifling and,

Mom,

in a breath,

Mom Mom Mom,

tell her, yes, everything she's seen, what's happened, the two men, the one whose hair is so yellow it's almost white, his knife, he killed Rajah—screaming to her mother that she saw her dog in the stable and that he's dead, that she saw her dog dead and it's horrible, the feeling of death on her sticky fingers, the smell of blood, and the other one, now, who's with Tatie, and all the words and images threatening to explode the moment she sees her mother, Ida wants to keep them inside, she can feel them so close to escaping that she's afraid she won't be able to hold them back and won't say them the way she should. But all of this is very brief. Why didn't she hear. Didn't pay attention. Didn't pay attention like she normally would have. Why not normally, but what does normal even mean, normal nothing, no more normal, what is *normal*?

She hasn't heard that the car that's pulling in isn't the engine of her mother's car.

It's not the same way of coming into the yard and stopping the car.

Ida has to be facing the dining room door to understand, in the yard, yes, a blue car that has nothing to do with her mother's—she wouldn't be able to tell the difference, to name one make or another, but this car isn't her mother's, and that freezes her where she stands. She stays facing the door, long enough to feel her father's hand on her shoulder, not knowing whether it's to hold her back in her flight or to console her for the disappointment that this car that's just arrived isn't the one she was waiting for, unless it means he's as surprised as she is, and in fact he grips her shoulder without even realizing he could hurt her. She hears her father grinding words between his teeth that she doesn't understand right away, because her first thought is that he's speaking those words to her, but no, she realizes that no, she looks at him but he's not even paying attention to her,

Fuck's sake who are these guys,

he stares at the car and continues, through gritted teeth,

What's going on, what is this?

it's short, not even a moment that belongs to them: Patrice and Ida are now alone with the labored metallic shouts of the manga coming from the living room.

Christophe has just gone out the kitchen door and soon they see him, yes, inhabiting the role of host, on the patio just outside the kitchen, showing his satisfaction—a satisfaction he accompanies with effusive and delighted gestures—at the car that's parking while, behind the French door, Ida and her father watch the scene in a daze that paralyzes them for long enough that, without reacting, they see the other man appear, the car door has opened—Ida now clutching her father's hands with both of hers, winding her fingers into Bergogne's big strong fingers even though he's just loosened his grip on her shoulder. He too is discovering this man who's getting out of the car and already walking toward the patio, greeted by Christophe, who they hear saying he's so happy to see him, so happy, nodding when the other asks him questions that they don't understand, that they don't perceive the way they perceive, by contrast,

Yes,

a motion of the head,

Yes,

then another and then, to an inaudible question,

Yes, yes,

very clearly Christophe's voice,

Like clockwork,

he says: like clockwork, that old expression Patrice hasn't heard since his childhood, which troubles him enough—as if he's dealing with two children come back from another time—that he doesn't even think to himself that he should take advantage of this moment to call the police or warn Marion, to tell her not to come, yes, just tell her not to come or to try—what? try what? a coup? to grab a knife, a weapon? But he can't figure out what to do—Christine's face—the blade of the young man's knife. No. It's not because of that, not even, just that he's almost hypnotized, and on the other side of the door the two men are exchanging pleasantries, patting each other on the back, Christophe complimenting the stranger on his outfit and the stranger who,

Nothing less would do.

Patrice recording this bit of phrase that will roll around his head for a spell, leaving behind a strange taste, as though they've just sharpened his desire to understand. And perhaps it's to know, just to *know,* that he's incapable of acting or disrupting the course things are taking, this shift he can't quite make up his mind to believe in, it's too much like something he recognizes, a decisive event but one altered by this remoteness in time that blurs it, takes away its sharpness and the precision of its details. And that's why everything seems fake to him and he has such a hard time reminding himself that just a few meters separate his house from Christine's, and that just a few minutes too are keeping him away from what he saw there—are the young man and Christine still frozen in that wait, the way they left them? or, more likely, did they finally leave the bedroom? Patrice can feel panic rising, worry, as though the image of the hand dancing with the knife near Christine's body is finally becoming real, finally possible, as though it's finally emerged from this mist that causes disbelief and haloes the whole scene until it finally appears to him in its violence and its reality: the blade of the knife, Christine's petrified look, his own disbelief and nothing else, not even Ida's terror as he could feel it in the way she held his hands, begged him to do something to make it all stop, as though he could have spoken words the way in childhood you believe they can work, sharp and unstoppable, magical and powerful, efficient as weapons.

And now, at this precise moment, Christophe and the stranger go to enter the house, not through the entrance in the kitchen but directly through the French door in the dining room, exactly across from Patrice and Ida, who no longer know quite how they should behave, nor what role they're playing in a game that doesn't seem made for them—they're just here, as powerless as actors milling about backstage awaiting instructions, for as long as it takes for the director to decide to give them an action, some lines, a pose to hold, even a silent and motionless one. And so now that the two men are approaching the French door in the dining room, Patrice is seized with so acute an awareness of the danger Christine is in that he realizes as though he's waking up, as though he can finally *see*, and for an instant the panic is so strong that he's ready to open the door at a run and grab one of these guys by the throat, to threaten him until the other man, through a window or a door at Christine's, finally hears him and lets Christine go. But something holds him back, a single thing: he knows, yes, maybe because of the death of the dog—as though this were just a threat, a way of giving Bergogne time to determine the potential cost of some initiative on his part—that he can't take the risk of paying such a high price, he won't take this risk, deep down he's known it this whole time, because what they would do—yes, what they're capable of—he doesn't doubt, without knowing why he doesn't doubt it, for even a second, the guys seem believable even though he wonders what exactly that means, *believable*, crazy enough or motivated enough or dangerous enough to dare to kill a woman they don't know anything about and probably don't even know. They're here. They were capable of coming this far. Of killing the dog—and for a second, barely a second, it's his daughter that he doubts: did Ida see right? Did the guy really stab the dog? But why doubt his daughter when the only enemies are here, in front of him, three men he knows nothing about and who are threatening his family, can Patrice really question his daughter's word, or at least the way reality appeared to her, perhaps distorted by her age, by her fear? Doesn't a child interpret what she sees? Can you be sure of what she sees, of what she says she saw, he wonders even as he himself doesn't doubt the bloodstains on the young man's tracksuit nor the knife in his hands? Yes, the two men were capable of coming here and threatening them, they planned what they're doing, that's a fact: so Patrice wonders whether he could take the risk of acting, as though in their preparation they didn't have the advantage over him of having anticipated his reaction. And, in this moment where it would still be possible, could he grab a weapon, even though he knows full well that, even though he has a knife and his rifle at hand—and what would prevent him from going into the living room and grabbing, from where it's mounted on the wall, with the cartridges on the shelf next to it, the hunting rifle he inherited from his father, with which he likes to hunt pheasant and partridge in the woods with Rajah on Sundays, or, from the kitchen, one of the knives he uses to prepare meat?—in any case he would be incapable of stabbing anyone, much less of pulling the trigger on the rifle while deliberately aiming at a man.

In the time it takes to think all this it's already too late; there's no longer any question of any of it, neither acting nor even having

any idea, just taking a good step back when the two men open the
door and enter, the stranger first, followed by Christophe

Come on, come in,

and his laughing voice,

you could say we've been waiting for you.

24

Who are you? What do you want?

Patrice's question brings an even sweeter smile to the stranger's face—an odd kind of face, Patrice thinks. The man is maybe in his fifties and, scattered sparsely on the top of his head, he still has some chestnut hair that the gray has yet to replace completely. His face is so pale that his eyes pop out like two feverish and sickly marbles, even though the man is handsome—Patrice notices this right away—with a capricious beauty, not a harmonious and homogenous mix of symmetrical traits, deep and expressive, but an angular and hard beauty, unbalanced, a face too narrow but handsome, *assertive*—you can read something decisive in it, something categorical, almost peremptory, but also positive and engaging—that Patrice could find charismatic and seductive, almost peaceful, kindly, maybe because the man is tired and the bags under his eyes are swollen folds that make him milder, as though weariness has erased his traits and with them any tendency toward aggressiveness, revealing only a sweet and affable face.

The man isn't tall, he's thin, gathered into himself, lean, muscled and skinny, or rather dried out, as though he's exhausted himself by working out and monitoring every gram of his food intake, forbidding himself any kind of fat or sugar. You can see from the prominent muscles in his neck that his body is vigorous, but Bergogne doesn't linger on this, what strikes him now is his voice, this voice that troubles him because it trembles with a softness that scatters into space like some volatile, fragile perfume, the voice of someone whose youthfulness has borne the brunt of the deep lines on his face, the brutal reality of time's passage.

Who are you?

Bergogne doesn't get an answer and his question hollows out a place inside him from which it won't be dislodged, or only once the man has responded. But for now it's like the man barely seems to have noticed him,

Oh, and you must be...

he's leaned over Ida,

Ida?

smiled at her,

You're Ida? My name is Denis. I'm the big brother of these two jokers... I hope they didn't frighten you?

It was after this moment, at last, that he finally managed to meet Patrice's eyes, that he smiled without any apparent ulterior motive, even daring to make the impossible or senseless gesture, in Bergogne's mind, of extending his hand, as though wanting to shake in as friendly a way as possible, waiting, reflexively, for the other to do the same and reach out an open palm toward his, imagining—or not doubting—that Bergogne would shake his hand just as two strangers would do before sitting down at the same table to negotiate a contract over a drink. Did he believe something so stupid, or is this stupidity feigned, does it demonstrate his contempt for Bergogne, or does he think the man in front of him, staring him down with hostility and suspicion, will soften simply because someone offered him a hand, that Bergogne will be so naïve as to let himself be lulled into submission just because a guy in a suit, vaguely gentlemanly, shows up as though what he's been put through, him and his family, and their neighbor, this whole time, is just a trifling little inconvenience?

I hope they didn't frighten you too much? My name is Denis, I'm their brother.

He straightens up completely and faces Patrice. He tries to smile at him, or rather he smiles but fails to give it the inflection it would need to carry out his intent, fails to pair it with the lasting, joyous eye contact it would need for the smile to become a site of faith, of exchange, in the absence of which it remains just a facade, a sketch. The man—Denis, then—collecting himself while raising his hand and striking his index finger against his forehead, letting out this unexpected noise from his mouth, almost burlesque, a click of the tongue against the palate,

Ah! I forgot the most important thing, I'll be right back.

and without anything further he leaves, spinning around at full speed without leaving Ida or her father time to react, to understand, because he's already out of the house and running to his car, a few seconds in which Bergogne and his daughter, but also Christophe, watch him look in the trunk of his car—all three of them silent but not altogether inert, Christophe has already opened the door and run toward his brother to ask him if he needs help, and from the house Bergogne and his daughter hear them, with their voices seemingly stretched by the space of the yard, by the coming night, their voices distant and thunderous, saying things that resound with a strange banality, yes, go put the champagne in the fridge, Denis answers, as Ida and Patrice hear before seeing Christophe reappear with a bottle of champagne, facing them, chipper as a kid waiting for his Christmas presents, hopping inwardly with a happiness that only he knows how impatient he is to make come true, while Denis comes back from his car and with a very quick movement, there we go, he's facing Patrice, two wrapped gifts in his hands—a box with a pink ribbon and a package Bergogne knows very well, the kind he and Marion give Ida whenever they go into town to get her a birthday or Christmas present, and the simple yellow logo, the blue paper, yes, all at once it's enough to drive Patrice Bergogne mad with anger, a rage so strong he almost raises his hand to the guy and restrains himself just in time, he has to, he knows he has to, it lasts barely a second but there's no question of not saying anything, of not doing anything, no, he follows the man who places the pink-ribboned package on the table, among the plates and silverware, Denis then leaning down to Ida,

Here, this is for you.

handing her the other package,

I hope you don't have it already?

sweetly,

I think, for a big girl like you,

murmuring,

It should be just right.

And while Ida has this man in front of her who she's never seen, whose gesture of handing her a present, in the same way one would set a trap, she perceives as a kind of aggression, this gesture she associates with the love people have for her, she can't believe it—two arms reaching out toward hers to give her a gift—she remains motionless, unable to understand how she should react, how she should receive what's happening, or how to read it, to decode it, because she knows what they've always told her about how children are supposed to be suspicious of people they don't know, you must never accept anything from people you don't know, their gifts are never free; and yet, without even realizing it, she takes a step forward, she gives in too quickly to her curiosity, the man presses the point and comes forward with the package in front of him, now he's almost at her height, his face across from hers, she can smell his scent and see how he's waiting for something, there's hope shining in the man's eyes, intense, feverish, just as the gift is maybe burning his hands from holding it too long between his fingers, just as her fingertips are also burning to take it and open it, because until today she's never had to turn down a present from anybody. She wonders, can you really refuse a gift, would it be possible to turn it down if you say—

Who are you? What do you want from us?

This time Patrice has risen with all his force, with all his anger, and his voice carried so loudly that Ida almost felt it was her who her father wanted to reach, forbidding her to touch the package, ordering her to fall back; and already she's making this very slight movement backward, the feeling of having done something dumb and, above all, having been caught committing an error that her father will punish her for, definitely, she knows it, just as she knows it wouldn't be so serious if she didn't already have the punishment she's inflicting on herself for having displeased her father, by making him angry and giving him the impression that she can be won over so easily. But the man, the one who said his name was Denis, doesn't seem bothered by Patrice's voice, even quite the opposite, and, imperturbable and calm,

It's a video game, don't you like video games?

in the same soft and tranquil voice, unconcerned about Patrice, he's trying to tame Ida, just as you'd try to subdue an animal with food while dreading a peck or a bite at your fingertips; but in reality it's not this that Denis might fear, but that Ida could pull back and refuse to take the present, because what is he trying to prove with this game besides his strength, his control not only over her, of course, but over Bergogne's house itself, on everything related to Bergogne?

This lasts a few seconds that stretch out, drag on, a few seconds in which Ida approaches and starts, hesitant at first, then more and more attracted, tempted, resisting less and less and soon not at all, she starts to reach out her arm toward the gift—she's almost stopped seeing the fingers holding the package, or the pallid face smiling a smile at her that means to give her confidence and courage, asking her to take it, here, it's for you, but without trying to rush her, without ordering her to do anything, without forcing her to make it quick, but insisting in such a way that she feels oppressed and unable to decide, casting quick looks toward her father, expecting him to acquiesce, to give the permission that deep down she's hoping for with a simple motion of the head, yes, it would be so easy, but it doesn't come, of course it doesn't come and instead she sees him lose patience, suddenly it's all going very fast, too fast, Patrice comes over to her and soon her father's hands are taking the present and pulling it from the hands of the man who seems momentarily overcome by Patrice's strength, as though for a second Denis and Ida have been immobilized, turned into statues, as though time has stopped for them but sped up for Patrice, allowing him to wrench the package from the man's hands without the man having time to react, keeping his hands closed for a few seconds around a present that's just been wrested from them, the hands holding the emptiness in front of Ida who hasn't had time to react and remains as if wrenched from a hallucination until her father's voice makes everything in her shake as soon as she hears her name—Ida—her father's voice calling her—Ida—ordering her not to move—Ida—ordering her to obey only him—Ida—to look at him—Look at me when I'm talking to you—and her, bruised, wounded, doesn't dare take any risks and lets the tears stream down her cheeks that are soon crimson with shame and agitation, fear of her father, yes, of that voice she dreads hearing, sometimes, from her room, because that thick and rough voice vibrates through the walls of the house when he's mad; Patrice—his motion is so violent, so surprising, that for two seconds he seems to be the only one able to move. Christophe comes from the kitchen into the dining room, in his hands are the bowls he's taken it upon himself to fill with peanuts and pistachios, he doesn't understand anything, a stupid look frozen on his lips, and in front of him Patrice, the gift in his hands, needs only three steps, three strides to go out through the French door and throw the gift which smashes in the distance, with a motion whose violence stuns Ida and the two brothers. Patrice retraces his steps and now he walks up to Denis and stands over him with all his strength,

What do you want, who are you? you think we're going to sit here doing nothing and you can just take us for a ride like idiots—

I get it… I get it. Calm down.

I'll calm down if I want to, this is my house and nobody tells me what to do, so you can shut your mouth and stop treating me like a fucking idiot.

And it's Christophe, from the threshold of the kitchen, who answers,

Not very nice to make the little one cry. Not so clever, you know, making her cry like that.

but though Patrice doesn't see him, doesn't hear him, it's at this moment that he realizes he's frightened his daughter, and something in him turns over, a regret, the shame of his violence, Ida's terrified eyes, the reproaches they're perhaps articulating to him. Ida has drawn back, now she's at the edge of the room, alone, she lets the tears flow and represses her fear or her anger. Denis, now, sympathetic,

Hey now, Ida,

sickeningly sweet,

That wasn't very nice of him, was it?

then he turns to Patrice,

Don't you think?

and slowly, with an apologetic and contrite air, as though pained,

You know, I don't want anything to happen to your neighbor, I don't want anything bad to happen to anyone, that's not why we're here. But what's the use of making the little one cry, you know? Honestly, what difference is it to you if I give her a present?

Patrice doesn't answer, or rather the only answer he can manage is to keep silent, to go join his daughter at the edge of the room, pretending not to see the way she recoils as he approaches her. And then no, she lets her father wrap her in his arms, lets him hold her tight—his heat and his strength like a refuge—he's right, he's right, she shouldn't have accepted that gift and he's the one who's right, yes, a thousand times, she wants to say sorry, sorry Dad, but she can't because she's mad at him for not knowing how to say things in any way other than his outbursts of anger, and now that he's taken her in his arms, now that he's holding her so tight against him, she knows that, even if in the same room, a few meters away, there's this guy in a suit watching them, curious in his turn or amused, yes, she sees him as she opens her eyes, behind the curtain of tears, a silhouette melting into the half-light of the dining room while the other one, Christophe, is no longer speaking, just putting the bowls on the table, yes, she knows everything is going to be okay.

Nothing is audible but the kitchen clock; the television releases, the volume very low, the canned laughter of an American series.

It will be dark soon, night is falling over the hamlet. Ida nestles tight against her father—she thinks of her mother, she needs her mother so much—but why, why does Marion always have to take such a long time to get home?

25

And while Marion is getting there—she's on the county road and, at this hour, surely won't pass anyone—the joy of the victory she's just had, and with it everything that so recently seemed to her an inexhaustible source of satisfaction, is already giving way to the even stronger, and also more impatient, joy of going home.

Marion feels liberated and she's singing like a madwoman, *take your time, hurry up,* the music at full blast, she loves karaoke so much and here, in her car, she's doing karaoke for herself alone, just her and these songs she's always loved, thinking all the same that she won't be able to tell Patrice everything about the reason for her joy, because how could she explain to him what she's always refused to talk to him about, haul out the story of the project manager when she's never even mentioned it in front of him, the kind of fear and exasperation her boss awakened in her, which could go as far as anger, sometimes as far as the urge to vomit, which she'd ascribe to all the causes that weren't its cause at all—her period, indigestion, a stomach bug, a meeting with Ida's teacher—telling herself nothing could justify talking about it or complaining about it, yes, it was just an anxiety, and, like her co-workers with their husbands, loved ones, friends, families, she'd never opened up about it to anyone, and certainly not to Patrice, without quite knowing why, out of embarrassment, maybe, or shame at pressing the point.

Marion won't say anything about it: as though the project manager has at least won the intimacy of sharing a secret with her.

In any case, what matters now is the joy to come; what matters is feeling free-spirited, and for this she wants to banish the image of the office and the print shop, to stay the course toward the reason she accelerated, and now here she is turning off the county road; very soon she'll come to that narrow road pocked with potholes, cracks, a road whose shoulders are frayed and crumbling, there, she's turning left onto the gravelly road, with the rustling under the wheels that she knows by heart and no longer hears, out of habit but also because most of the time she leaves the music all the way up when she pulls into the yard. She passes the sign announcing the Three Lone Girls Stead and she turns off the music, she's opened the window to get rid of the smell of tobacco—this time she won't light a cigarette as she gets out of the car, right at the moment when, having parked, she takes her bag. No, this time she'll be quick, her bag is ready next to her, no knickknacks or cigarette packs to pick up, it'll be enough to roll up the window and hurry home for the party to get started.

When she pulls into the yard, her car going at a walking pace, Marion is surprised to see the white Clio parked in front of Christine's, and more so at the blue car stopped next to her house—a Seat—almost facing the French door leading into the dining room. She drives very slowly, has time to wonder about the two cars, to imagine that maybe Patrice invited some friends—but what friends? Does she know anyone with blue Seats and white Clios? She can't think of any, but maybe she's mistaken. Maybe he invited François and Sylvie?—no, they're in Brittany. Jacques and Fabrice? The Gains? The Thourots? The Tertipis? Dom, Flo, Charlotte and her big family of travelers? No, they're too far. She wonders, searches, goes through all the friends he could have invited, her curiosity highly aroused and of course she wonders and really can't think of anyone, since she's been here she hasn't met anyone who drives cars like these, she's really not sure who he could have invited, whose company they both enjoy enough to think it would be a good idea to gather them here.

Like every night, Marion will reflexively turn her head toward the light from the house, she'll glance into the lit-up rectangle of the French door into the dining room; she'll also see, though less clearly, on the left, smaller squares of light that look into the kitchen, and the same for the living room on the right. But tonight it will also be to try to see who these guests could be that she wasn't expecting, and just in the space of a glance through the French door into the dining room and the passenger window of her car she can make out two men's silhouettes, but it's too quick for her to identify them, plus that warm yellow light that looks like the heat of a fire in a fireplace irradiates everything—all that appears is the flamboyance of the table and the decorations—even from far away, even so quickly—she's already parking her car in the shed and can now see only by the light on the patio and the one through the French door, which dilute into the darkness across from her, but the image has imprinted itself on her eyes, two silhouettes, the orangey yellow of dimmed lighting and the banner with that golden *happy birthday* that Patrice insists on hanging above the table to make her happy, her or Ida—these party rituals among them that bring the three of them together—and she finds this childishness touching, the gesture of a kid hidden deep down inside a man so far from childhood that she can't help but smile.

She gets out, tonight not wasting time on any of the delays she usually strings together. She's out of the car right away, goes around it, walks across the yard, is already letting the light from the house blind her. She has to make it to the patio to begin to see, all the way at the back, Patrice comforting Ida—Ida is crying, this she can see immediately. In fact she no longer sees anything but this. Patrice is trying to console her, drying her tears, he's talking to her, that's evident, Ida and Patrice don't seem to see her, they who two minutes ago would have raced out to meet her, they're not moving, don't even really know she's going to enter the dining room and, when they see her, it's first because they heard the door open and felt the evening air rush in, because they heard Marion's voice crash against an invisible wall when she tried to ask

What's going on?

and wasn't able to say it, couldn't ask that question, breaking it off in the middle, remaining suddenly silent,

What's—

Patrice and Ida seeing Marion standing a few meters away, on the other side of the room, her back to the door, frozen, and the two men looking at her, Christophe near the doorframe of the kitchen and Denis near the dining room table. And what happens now happens very fast—or maybe it would be better to say it happens in two distinct times that occupy the same space, at the same hour, but that don't come together in a single temporality and instead slide over one another, not meeting, or if so then only for Patrice, who in a flash sees the intensity of his daughter's reaction and his wife's inertia, the speed with which Ida slips out from between his arms to run to her mother's, how she crosses

Mom, Mom,

the dining room, shouting,

Mom, Mom,

for that fraction of a second in which Patrice doesn't know what his daughter is going to shout and almost fears he'll be the one she accuses of having thrown away the gift they gave her and not the three men who took Christine hostage, who threatened her, killed the dog, the three men who are forcing their presence and want to make us believe they're happy to be here, with us, as though he can already hear,

Mom, Mom,

Marion's body frozen, Marion's collapse, Marion's death in her expression, her movements, as though everything has stopped—and everything stops for her for a fraction of a second, her face locked on Denis's, Christophe's, long enough for the strap of her purse to slide off her shoulder and for the bag to not fall only because she's holding her arm against her hip, all of this very fast, Ida's speed toward her mother, Marion staying frozen seeing the two men and the way they come toward her, stand in front of her, just a few meters away; Patrice sees all of this and it's as though he understands everything, everything is resisting him but he understands, through Marion's face and the collapse, so fast, that he read in it—the smile and the gaiety erased like makeup wiped away at the stroke of a rag, leaving a gray and featureless face, without texture or life, as though the blood has withdrawn and with it all the years branded in the folds of skin, leaving a page not blank but translucent on which nothing can be written, too fragile, too thin, it's like the sea receding far away before surging back in a tsunami, pallor sets in, and yet, luckily for Marion—because this is lucky for her—Ida clutches her, clings to her,

Mom,

Marion letting her purse fall to her feet without even noticing, without anyone noticing or caring, what counts is the flat and broken voice,

Mom, Mom,

the tears choking her, Ida who doesn't know how to dry her tears, so happy and relieved to see her mother, as though she's certain that everything will be fine now and it will be enough for Marion to speak for everything to go back to a point before any of these strangers has ever crossed the threshold of the house, has ever come, where Rajah is still barking in the yard or scratching at Christine's door and Christine is cursing herself for not having started her cakes earlier; Ida can hope once more for something— what?—but Marion holds her very tight, Patrice doesn't know if it's for Ida or for herself, to hide herself from the men who are here and, attentive and patient, not saying anything, not doing anything, just standing there, Christophe sometimes looking at his big brother Denis who's staring at mother and daughter with the hint of a dazed sort of smile that doesn't mean anything, or maybe it does, it means something, it wants to show that it means something, that it wants them to understand that he's savoring this moment, and how much he's savoring it, even if they don't know what it is, there, painted on his face, between his lips, neither joy nor pleasure, nor curiosity or tenderness, it's as indecipherable as it is unwholesome, yes, this wrinkle of the lip that betrays bitterness and violence—how can they be sure, they can't, but there it is—and Patrice understands that Marion is holding her daughter so tight because she's as overwhelmed as Ida, who hasn't said anything yet besides

Mom, Mom,

which she repeats as though it's her breath itself, as though she's releasing it not to speak but so as to not collapse, because the child can feel that what she thought was the happiness of seeing her mother is metamorphosing into an emotion that just might drown her completely.

Now it seems that, for Marion, what remains to be done is to console Ida and embrace her, given that for the moment all she can do is show her astonishment and she doesn't want to do that, not at any cost: she remains silent, as though all possibility of speech has been drained from her, as though she's suddenly been cast far, far back into silence—that old intimate silence of her childhood, like when, as a little girl, she preferred to close her eyes and not hear the foster families who substituted for her mother's absence as soon as her mother disappeared on the arm of a brand new husband for whom she'd remake a life in which her daughter had no place, casting her off then to the status of little gray ghost, nonexistent, insignificant, like a perforation in her mother's life or leftovers in pink packaging, a cumbersome and pretty bit of waste that her mother no longer wanted to hear about, this little girl-shaped shadow that would be found later at the homes of the people who took her in, doing what they could, saddling her sometimes with brothers and sisters for a few months and sometimes for a year or two, never more, children the little girl never thought of loving or even of hating, whose presence and names she chased from her memory as soon as they tried to make their mark there, keeping nothing of them but the jealous memory of a doll, a smell, a toy and then nothing else, no, because very young she decided to keep quiet and not have any memory for people, to remember only moments shared with her mother, like that, in bits and pieces, a few months out of her four years, one year from seven to eight, then at eleven, twelve, thirteen, in fits and starts, her mother more damaged each time, decrepit, or on the contrary seemingly smoothed out, rejuvenated, blonde or redheaded, rolling in it— and then it would be a party for a few months, loving words, promises to never leave each other again, tendernesses, cajoleries, escapes to seaside hotels with beach views for a few days or a few hours, the money blown and slipping through fingers maybe covered in rings, like a princess's or a mafioso's, it lasted as long as it lasted, until her mother turned back into someone somber and ugly, exhausted, dulled by a strange lethargy, a daze that returned, permeated her, and, as though resigned, she waited prostrate for the monster to rise up in her again, for the shadow to claim her completely, always with this look of reproach in which it first showed itself and that Marion had learned to recognize, her mother's intense exasperation, a scorching insult, a laugh bursting out and falling away with the words

You, slut,

hurtful and humiliating and the same refrain,

Always trying to push me into the grave,

spitting a bile she could no longer contain, alcohol, dirty whis-key-soaked sheets, locks busted open with hammers to find an old bottle hidden behind the bleach and the mop; it would last until a man showed up and everything wound up worse than the last time, a man wanting to save Mom, wanting to love Mom, wanting all of a sudden to touch Marion who knew not to tell Mom, to keep quiet in front of Mom, who wouldn't say anything to Mom, to protect her, thinking sorry, sorry, even though it's too much, all of this, of course it's too much, even while living through it she thought it was impossible to live through—she's always known how to forget things like that, how you bury them inside yourself so you don't suffer them anymore, how you barricade yourself from the inside and how childhood invents hiding places locked up tighter than closets, and now, here, an adult life later, even though everything has changed and she doesn't even remember much from this child-hood that she's denied the way one denies a shameful relative, she chooses this stubborn silence that gags her as much as it protects her.

For now, even if she knows very well where he is and what he's doing, how he's keeping watch for her slightest movement, she seeks Patrice; she wants to know what he knows about the men who are here, have they been here long, did they talk to him? She makes up her mind, gets up, or rather wrenches herself from the ground, as though from now on there will be no deciding, just wrenching: gets up, strokes her daughter's hair and runs her hand over her neck—will Ida feel the clamminess of her palm and that sickly, ferrous odor of fear?—brings her to Patrice without a word for these two men whose insistent attention she can feel on her every movement, and this triumphant irony of Denis's—is it a triumphant smile or else, behind it, a meaner and more curious grimace, amused and enjoying, without false modesty, the effect of the bewilderment he can read on Marion's face, in Marion's movements, in Marion's reaction?

Denis turns to his brother, the two men exchange a look, De-nis nods to show that he's impressed and, in return, Christophe just shrugs his shoulders in a way that's no doubt meant to reply that he doesn't understand this pantomime of family life either, and they start to laugh, while now Patrice and Marion are connected by the pres-ence of their daughter, there, between them, Ida clutching her par-ents who aren't saying anything to each other, only questioning each other, holding each other with this look in which Marion can already read her husband's incomprehension and in which he must read hers, even if it's not the same kind, because both of them know that if the question for him is who these two men are, for Marion it's maybe only what they're doing there, how they got here. And Denis's voice,

No kiss for us?

followed by Christophe's, lighter, less bitter and more provocative, in his excited, jovial way,

Aren't you happy to see us?

plunges everyone into a flurry of motion that springs to life, soon everything will spring to life, the television will continue spewing its hiccups of advertisements and cartoons that no one will think to turn off, until the moment Denis gets going with surprising suppleness and fluidity, a sort of reptilian movement, swung or danced, not effeminate or precious, not even eccentric, but strangely devious, in the way the body bends, moving forward with the fluidity of the great predator making a circular arc around its prey, tacking to better defy expectations, going to one side before starting back in the other direction, smoothly, sleekly, moving toward the French door in the dining room only to come back to the kitchen door and skirt around his brother, who just pivots to follow Denis's movements, gone off this time toward the edge of the room, taking time to show how interested he is in the house, in the décor, in the china cabinet and those porcelain plates with their lyrebird figures painted in verdigris, in the pearl trim, in the wallpaper with its straw-colored patterns embossed in the shapes of cherries, and then he stops to look at the fawn tiling imitating ancient terra cotta—Denis lets out a sigh, stops so everyone can hear him, understand him, and he resumes walking, his head nodding gently, and him lingering, drifting from object to object without ever stopping, scrutinizing the trinkets and the table to which he keeps returning, picking up a plate and examining it like a goldsmith verifying the quality of a piece of gold, a jeweler that of a diamond, of a stone, turning over the plate, turning it over again and setting it back down, biting his lip as though dubious about its real value, and then, suddenly, very abruptly, turning to Marion,

Aren't you happy to see us?

but not waiting for an answer, because he knows she won't answer, holding tight to her daughter and her husband, who for his part isn't hearing any of the words crossing the room, Patrice in whom everything seems to be reiterating, in the same exasperation, his rage, his disbelief, his incomprehension too, as though it's against Marion that he wants to release this tension bearing down on his trapezii and smothering him, who is this, Marion, who are these guys? but without saying anything, without a word, and yet Marion can't avoid this interrogation leveled at her, stuck as she is between his gaze and Denis's—and Christophe's, maybe, but as a distant, less intense echo of what's playing out—caught in the crossed beam of the two men. For now, all that's possible is, puckering her lips, setting her jaw, to send her husband all her distress with a sigh, a raise of the eyebrows that's almost imperceptible but that he'll recognize, a movement that imprints on her face a sign of helplessness, and to say without a word, through the steadiness of her eyes, the pupil dilated, that she's capsizing, that she's panicking; he'll understand perfectly well that she's begging him not to ask anything and that she's beseeching him, in her silent and urgent way, to hold onto all the questions she knows are overflowing in him, but what can she do, huh, what can she say, what can she stammer, murmur, or project, like little spat-out bones, disjointed syllables,

I don't know why they're here, I swear to you I don't know.

but she doesn't say anything, and it's as though Patrice has heard what she can't even make audible for herself.

Denis continues his nagging, obsequious walk in the other direction, beginning now to circle the table, no longer interested in Marion or Ida. He speaks as he looks over the plates, the flatware; he stops to pick up a knife, acting as though he wants to examine the details, its line, then he does the same with the glasses, as though inspecting their cleanness, and, with an almost dampened, exhausted softness,

Happy birthday, Marion. I brought you a gift… just a little something. I know you like these.

He takes the box with the pink ribbon and turns to Marion, holding it out, but without waiting he puts it back down. Because nobody is speaking, someone has to, and from the back of the room it's Christophe who reappears,

You don't want us to wish you a happy birthday?

…

Well, Denis? Did you ever imagine she wouldn't even want our B-day wishes?

Denis just making, by way of response, a laconic and vaguely disappointed gesture, or playacting disappointment and disillusion, resting his eyes on the box of chocolates and then picking it up again, toying gently with the pink knot of the package,

Maybe she doesn't like chocolates anymore?

Then, from far off, dull, Marion's voice,

What about the other one? The other one, where is he? Where's the other one?

With Christine, says Patrice.

If we're not careful, you're going to ask us to leave or you'll kick us out, am I right? says Denis.

I don't want you to leave her alone with him. Bring them over here. Go get them.

Hear that, brother? Marion doesn't want that. She doesn't want that. No, listen to me, Marion, here's what we're going to do—and he speaks softly, his voice slower and slower, murmured, as though sucked up by the noise from the television. He leans down toward Marion,

I brought a bottle of champagne. You still like champagne, right? We're all going to have dinner here, together. And then afterward you're going to be so gracious as to offer us one of these little chocolates and a cup of coffee, okay? See, Marion, that's what we're going to do first—that's it.

26

Colors, at night, when they are exposed to artificial lights, are drowned in a world where they lose all the depth and power they naturally accommodate in the light of day.

What a sentence. And it doesn't mean anything. Or does it? Sure...? Don't give up painting for a writing career, he'd have liked to tell her.

He closed the notebook and tossed it back onto the work table carelessly. Or maybe just in a manner showing the disdain the notes inspire in him, without even saying what he thinks of them, just repeating in his head that this lady had to be pretty damn pretentious to write things about what she did, as though you could both do and watch yourself doing, say and watch yourself saying, like a traveler taking notes on the way his feet sink into the snow as he climbs the Himalayas without taking the time to look up at the mountain rising before him. But for the kind of stationary travel that is painting, in a remote old house out in the middle of nowhere, where each chair, each piece of clothing, each room reeks of dog and dust and is permeated with the smells of paints and chemicals, of turpentine, what point could there be in taking notes on what she does? Is it like a diary, a log book? Do you learn things by reading it that you're not supposed to know about her life, or about her neighbors' life?

The idea barely crossed his mind before his fingers flipped through the notebook and found on its pages nothing but the same black handwriting, quick but also precise and orderly, rigorous, industrious and fine, almost obsessive in the way it follows imaginary lines, respects the unmarked margins, and obsessive too in the stubbornness with which it speaks only of painting, that of the masters she'd have liked to see again, that of new painters she'd have liked to discover in some other way than on the internet or in books, reflections, quotations, like this one on the first page: *Culture is what is done to us; art is what we do.*

This surprises him, this kind of sentence. He doesn't get it. This kind of quotation. *Yves Klein.* Not knowing who that is, that name. Not getting it hurts him, it's like an insult meant for him, a wall placed in front of him to show him his powerlessness to climb it, to put him face to face with his stupidity. For a moment he raises his head to watch her carefully; is this really the old lady who writes down this kind of stuff? Where does she find sentences like that? He shrugs his shoulders, tossing the notebook back onto the board that serves as a table—a huge plank of plywood set on trestles, covered in a heap of loose papers, tin boxes crammed full of pens, markers, others with colored pencils, charcoals. He wonders whether he could have written things about the paintings he made, a long time ago, but then he never tried, the idea never even occurred to him; no, the truth is that he's never known how to note anything down and that even if he'd have liked to be able to he wasn't capable, like when they asked him at the center to talk about what he was painting and the drawings he was making and he couldn't do anything but lower his head and just show the doctors, who were expecting words, his smooth brow, and, above it, a shaved head that kept, as though inside a shell, all the secrets that were going moldy or, on the contrary, bubbling in his brain, although one time he was able to say that to him painting was not a game but something very serious. And now, in Christine's studio, he can see she doesn't treat this like a game either, he can at least give her that, that even though she makes bizarre things, landscapes and sometimes abstract forms that look like rocks, drippings, rips and tears, or something like interwoven brushstrokes, and leaves, stems, flowers—all of it requiring a lot of work, sure—for her it's not a game either, even if, instead of seeing in this a point that could bring them closer together, he sees the complete opposite: confirmation of this arrogance in the way she stands up straight, in the way she shut up and gave him the cold shoulder—like when they came from upstairs down to the studio, her passing in front of him with such scorn, such brazenness, almost brushing against him, leaving a trail of her scent behind her—because as idiotic as it seems to him she's wearing perfume, yes, here, in a little backwater where the only people she interacts with all day are a little kid, cows, and a farmer, she's wearing perfume!—and everything that might have brought them closer together would only distance them, only close her off in a bubble of scorn and self-importance, and him in a bubble of suspicion or defiance, of resentment and humiliation, not yet anger but already, just under his skin, the desire to fight.

In the studio she'd turned on the lights—tracks of bulbs whose white and natural light rubbed out the shadows—and he'd been as confused and uncomfortable as if he'd been in front of a couple making love, as though he was witness to a scene he wasn't supposed to see, or as though it was Christine herself who had shown her naked body in front of him, exhibiting herself to provoke him, so raw was this stream of light, showing him *everything*, as though the woman was challenging him to go up to her canvases and stare at them, as though she knew he'd lower his eyes before her paintings, because her painting asserted itself so forcefully that he would experience that assertion and that vitality not as a sign of the power of her expression but as his own crushing defeat, as though Christine's painting was a death sentence to whoever dared lay an eye on it.

And so, from near the light switch, where she was watching him, she saw him head toward the paintings and then turn back to her, staring at her for a few seconds, letting his shoulders shrug in a way she didn't understand—did her paintings seem ridiculous to him?—and then swerve toward the work table and pick up the first notebook on the pile of books she hadn't yet put away. She stayed there watching the young man finger and flip through its pages, handling them without excessive care but with a kind of attentiveness all the same, with his singular face, his pallor and his beauty thwarted by fate, his hair burned by dye, and Christine saw him and wondered what he could be thinking about, not even thinking that she was letting him do what she wouldn't allow anyone to do, just as she wasn't surprised at the space between them, leaving her so close to the kitchen that she could have tried to run away, to take the key to the house for sale and go hide out there, or escape through the fields and head for the woods or the road. But no. She just watched him, and when he tossed the last notebook on the table she didn't say anything, not even that he didn't have to touch her things. He let his eyes linger on the desk, paused over two sheets of paper that he picked up—quickly, like a source of amazement, joy, and curiosity all in one—and it was only at that moment that she walked toward him, approaching at a rapid, almost aggressive pace to tell him

No, those you don't touch.

But before she spoke, he'd already turned to her and she came to a halt, Christine suddenly paralyzed by the sweetness of his face, by the sadness—or rather than sadness, she saw the overflow of a melancholy and an infinite sweetness, a sort of ravaged tenderness, and that movement of the lips that accompanies it; he is here, in his hands he's holding the drawings Ida made for her mother's birthday, and he seems touched to see them, as though at this precise instant she could say to him now you see this whole business is ridiculous. But Christine doesn't seize this moment. He puts the two drawings down and this time he's made up his mind to confront Christine's painting, to go see it up close and face it. But he can't do this in silence, which is why he starts speaking in a very loud voice, tossing out things as they come to him but above all letting them take up all the space, words darting around, bumping into each other, so that she can't say or do anything under the whirlwind he's creating around her, so that he too is numbed by his own voice, so as not to have to endure Christine's painting, because other people's paintings are threatening, they always know more about you than you do about them.

And this is how he starts, fists deep in the pockets of his track pants, already starting by saying it's been a long time since he's touched a paintbrush, because when he got out of the center, where he stayed for close to two or maybe even three, four years, he stopped painting overnight, he didn't have money to buy paints and brushes, and even if he had he probably wouldn't have thought to buy materials, you don't buy that kind of stuff where we're from. He started to say this with a laugh, opening his mouth wide only to regret having opened it, almost thrustinwg his long thin hands in front of it to hide his teeth and the pink of his tongue, the mucous membrane of his mouth, as though he regretted not having laughed but having thought he could keep painting after what he calls the center—a hospital?—and she learns how for him, in his life, the center was the place where he did a lot of painting, always gouache and acrylic on poster-sized sheets, and if he wanted bigger he had to staple the sheets together, and it was like pulling teeth to get a fucking stapler because the nurses would get annoyed and I was always bothering them when a TV show was on or right when they'd cleared off to the patio to smoke and sit down, cheeks glued to their fucking phones.

He explains all of this too loudly, rattling it off and walking toward Christine's canvases, approaching them, and it's as though he's going to sniff them, touch them: but no, he doesn't dare. Just as he doesn't dare say he's struck by what he sees. He'd like to ask her why he's never known how to paint, why the color always refused to come clear for him, why whenever he tried to handle it it always ended up clouding over, muddying, coming apart under his fingers, why it became sludge and earth, why it was only drawing, sometimes, that was gracious enough to open a horizon to him. And even though he's talking too loud and he stops to chuckle and sometimes he turns around as though to demand apologies rather than explanations from her, he continues to approach the canvases, he brushes against the walls they're hanging on, sometimes leans or stands up straighter the better to dive into a detail, stands on the tips of his toes, comes close enough to stick his nose into a single centimeter of painting as though he wants to penetrate its substance, understand its texture. He observes and stays quiet for a few seconds, as though he's forgotten that Christine is behind his back, a few meters away, that she's watching, not thinking of trying to escape, more occupied with trying to decipher his behavior than with listening to the stream of words he's rambling, no doubt for his own benefit, she thinks, because not only does she not understand everything he's saying—not that he's really stuttering, though sometimes, in chunks, pieces of phrase come loose and startle themselves and then return to where they started—but she has to admit he's only doing with his words what she does with painting, call them pentimenti, restarts, superimpositions that confuse any comprehension she might draw from it, but it's not important if she doesn't understand his lurches and skids, she understands that he's talking only to himself, and now she's stopped caring, it's as though she's just a spectator who wants to leave the theater but doesn't dare to, wondering when it's going to end, when he's going to stop, but above all at what point he and his brothers are going to get around to leaving; but in the meantime Stutter is talking, almost palpating the paintings, with a demanding and curious eye, and he continues talking to himself, his voice sometimes so low that Christine can't hear anything anyway—it's softer than her heartbeat in her chest, softer than her urge to look at what time it is without him seeing her do it—but she doesn't care to be heard or even to strike up a conversation, he's not interested in her and it's just as well, she'd rather all his attention be focused on her painting rather than on her, and even though she's not really listening to him she's seeing something that holds her back, something she's letting herself be drawn into and may get bogged down in, because there's *something* there, she doesn't know what it is but it troubles her, this young man, too blond, speaking to himself and repeating, adding misaligned modulations, outsized swerves, variations like ricochets in the opposite direction, negations, deviations—his story almost at a shout when he blurts out, with a snicker, oh, I remember it when I was crazy and the night they arrested me, when the police showed up—then, in a whisper, yeah, the police and the van in the night, the face of the blue siren sending Morse codes into space—and then finally, almost stammered, I was so sure it was Morse code being sent into space, I remember, I knew the little green men were gonna show up on Earth and I knew we call them "little green men" because that's the best way the people who saw them can describe them, I knew where they were gonna land and I was the only one who knew... You can't imagine how hard it is being the only one who knows... but it was clear, it was such a clear night, so I went to greet them because somebody obviously had to, in a farm I knew and I started emptying out the barn in the middle of the night, carting logs into the yard where their spaceship was gonna land, and I fucking torched some cords of wood—a huge blaze that made the night tremble with its thick yellow and orange light and its smell of oil burning on the bottom of a mess tin—I danced, best I could, total lunatic, it's true, I was completely out of it and I took off all my clothes because all the work made me sweat and pant like a mangy old donkey, with the flies pissing him off, and also to feel the heat from the fire because even though it was summer I stripped down to the bone waiting for them to arrive. Except instead of them it was the police who the farmer had called and they showed up and stuck handcuffs on me in the van, with the plastic smell of the seats, the cold of the handcuffs and the iron digs into your bones, before the boys came to get me—the smell of the hospital and the always ironed white coats on their breath—remember the farmer's son was at his bedroom window watching me with this crazy face while I was drumming the cops with kicks, they took some in the balls, the cops, they didn't take me so easy—my shouts, my bleeding gums and the teeth coming loose swimming in this disgusting liquid, I remember that too, you think you're dreaming when you look back but no, the police and the night falling back down like a stiff blanket over the fire, it was true, it was all true, horribly true—like your dog dying—real as a punch in the face.

Suddenly he stops talking; it's as though the paintings are peering at him, as though they've heard him too and are now taking it upon themselves to judge him. Now he turns around: he's afraid she's escaped. But no, Christine is there, not far from the wall. You crazy? That it? What's it they say to you, these faces? Huh? Faces, I think, is the only place where there's people. Behind the faces. Never in the arms or the chest... nothing... bodies, that's just the meat of the dead; but a face, a face, that's something else, right? Don't you think? it's like a body trying to escape... No? I'm fine now you see. I'm out. My brother, I mean Christophe,

The one I know?

The other, yeah, that's Denis.

There's still time to stop.

To stop what?

All this nonsense, what you're all doing here.

It's not nonsense.

Oh no?

No.

Why do you listen to them, your brothers?

...

You don't think they're using you?

...

Why are they the ones over there, having a party?

And you, what good's it do you, all this painting shit?

This? none, I guess, I don't know... It's true... I can't say...

We can go out there, if you want, both of us. We'll tell them to stop. You all have to leave and—

And then silence. He doesn't respond. Christine knows what she has in front of her, what she recognizes in his features, behind his features, as if hidden behind the blond banality: a wounded young man, the story you can glimpse as it allows this mixture to surface, in spots here and there, as if by forced entry, this mixture of anger and helplessness, of violence, of lostness, of submission to his brothers.

For a moment she sees all of this on the young man's face—but in a few seconds she wonders if he'd really dare to catch her if she tried something. Yes, he probably wouldn't hesitate to pounce. And it takes Christine only a second more to understand this fascination she feels as she stares at him, which is to say as she begins to dismantle each of his features to record them, because in this young man's face what attracts her more and more, what troubles her to the point that she can no longer bring herself to take her eyes off him, it's—she doesn't know quite what word would be the right one, if there's a single one that could hold them all, express them all, to hold the fascination and the interest she feels for this face—that she has a very sharp awareness that if she wants to see it, this face, if as a result she almost wants to paint it, maybe it's because it's the face of the man who's going to kill her.

For a fraction of a second, she sees nothing but this ending. If these guys have any savvy at all, what else can they do? If they're here for something—money? what money? there's no money here. No. They'd have finished a while ago—will they spare Ida? Will they dare lay a hand on Ida? She thinks it more and more resolutely in her mind: they're going to kill us. They're going to kill me. And to chase away this thought,

I'm sick of hearing your bullshit.

while moving very quickly into the kitchen, she throws out the first thing that crosses her mind,

I'm sick of hearing your bullshit. I'm going to eat something.

but he's already on her—the raised fist rearing up, and threatening, right in front of her face, stopping just short of striking her.

Her. The fist. The speed with which it all happens. She closes her eyes, can't believe it—nor can he.

And when finally she dares to open them again—after how long?—she sees his face, behind his face, that he's as scared of her as she is frightened of him: fear, now, is their only common ground.

27

Yes, he's always been scared; even when he was little, even for nothing. He had a BB gun and we called him the little hunter when he shot at chickens and rats, cats and dogs too, but that was only to annoy the neighbors. We thought it was hilarious to hear them call their little beasties from across the subdivision and at the crossing, on the yellow field. It's true, he really was always petrified, the little hunter—afraid of everything. But now there's nothing to be scared of, Christophe continued, he's not dangerous, wouldn't hurt a fly... a dog, maybe. But we're past the days when he'd see aliens everywhere and all that nonsense—Denis, remember the time he shaved himself? Not just his head but also his eyebrows and his legs, his arms, his armpits, everywhere, he shaved off all his hair and put it in an envelope and sent to his middle school principal—shit, the face that guy must have made when he saw that!

But listening to Christophe, who has started talking about their little brother, nobody wants to react, no more the Bergognes than Denis, who has no desire to hear Christophe go into it again; Denis stays quiet, closed, this doesn't make him laugh the way it amuses Christophe, it's too regular a topic among them, the story of the little brother, the day their family life fell apart and they realized these *strange things* weren't just *strange things,* and that it would be on Denis to deal with them because he was the eldest and had always carried a sort of duty, the way in all sets of siblings the roles are assigned from the beginning, no one knowing how or by whom, but with such force and clarity that everyone accepts what will follow at his heels for the rest of his life, as was the case for Denis, who had to make up for his parents' negligence and take care of everything because nobody else would have, certainly not Christophe, at least for the first two years, when it was Denis, then, who supported their rundown parents, who'd fled reality through their TV screen, who'd been so afraid of the hospital—as though setting a single fucking foot in one one day would doom them to never come out again—while Christophe shrugged his shoulders because Denis kept telling him yes, the stuttering is nothing, having a stutter is no big deal, we have to see what they say about him at the hospital, Jesus, Christophe, come on, why don't you want to hear this?

And after the diagnosis came down upon them Christophe hadn't known how to cope with his brother's sickness, other than with a rageful incomprehension, as though they'd been told they themselves were infected, in their flesh, in their bodies, that a part of them was also sick and raving mad, which had sent him into an anger so great that for a long time he was unable to hear the word Denis repeated to him, looking him in the eye, implacable, enunciating each syllable as though that retard Christophe would finally hear it—Stutter has an acute form of—and the word he refused to hear morphed between them into a shared sickness, gangrening them both, Christophe letting his anger put up a screen in front of him so he wouldn't see it, and letting it destroy everything in its path, spilling over everything that moved, until, exhausted by his own fury, he shut himself up in a silence that would have kept him from going to visit Stutter for all four years of his confinement if he hadn't had to go to the hospital and take over for Denis—But let's not spend the whole evening talking about Stutter, Christophe finally concluded, leaving a strange weight in the wake of what he didn't say, just as for anyone who met him between the moment Stutter entered the hospital and today this reversal was strange, Christophe turning from the angry mute obstinately denying his brother's sickness to this sardonic chatterbox, amused by everything and inclined to connect everything back to the same sickness.

Anyway, that's enough. That's enough of that.

Then, after the silence that followed, the sound of everyone taking their seats around the table, the chairs crunching like bones or vertebrae between teeth, and eventually everyone sat down: Patrice and Marion, Ida next to her mother, on the living room side. To Patrice's right, with his back to the kitchen door, Christophe almost naturally improvising the role of chef and waiter, while Denis settled in with his back to the French door, not afraid of what might come from outside but resolved to keep these three in his field of vision, these three he wanted to possess completely, as though he was the lone spectator for whose benefit the Bergogne family had come together and sat down like this: the father on the left, his wife in the middle, and her daughter next to her, on the right.

Marion opposite him, then.

Marion not saying a word and remaining so stiff you might think she's tied to her chair—but no, she just refuses to lower her guard, as though she has the means to stand up to Denis, there, just across from her, on the other side of the table with, between them, taking pride of place above it all like a perverse and malevolent touch of irony, the golden letters wishing her a happy birthday. Now she's sitting, and Patrice has also finally sat down. Soon the three Bergognes are settled in, huddled together, their elbows almost touching, brushing against each other, forming a fragile sort of chain and not exchanging a word among themselves, even if Patrice seems on the verge of speaking, his lip fluttering sometimes, his Adam's apple twitching in his throat as though a fist-sized animal is thrashing around inside, plus he has this way of running his fingers over his mouth that comes back every twenty seconds, as if trying to wake up his lips—yes, you might think he's about to speak, but he's unable to, he can't do anything but look at his wife because he wants to hear her, hear her voice, as though he's about to hear the voice of a stranger, because as soon as she came in and he had to accept this idea that did not, alas, altogether surprise him—not that he was really expecting it or ever thought for a moment that this would happen someday—he realized this idea didn't shock him so much, yes, his wife knew these two men, and probably the third too—which it didn't take long to confirm—and, even if he was unable to explain to himself why this idea didn't surprise him, it had made its mark as soon as Marion entered the house, while thirty seconds earlier, before she arrived, when she'd already gotten out of her car and was making her way to the patio, he wouldn't even have thought of it, still thinking these were just some lunatics, three nutjobs, remembering that for quite a few years now people had been saying the countryside was the new hunting ground for thieves and dealers, who were safer here than in cities— stories of people being tied up, scores settled, guys slaughtered in the open country and found weeks later in the undergrowth half eaten by foxes—and as soon as she came in, as soon as Marion's face fell to pieces before his eyes and he saw her pass from one state to another with a speed that left no room for doubt, as though her face had been captured by ghosts or had suddenly remembered that it was a ghost too, Patrice had dropped the idea of gangs settling some score between the combine harvester and the tractor, and this time he'd thought: yes, Marion knows these guys.

And from this, now, he feels an unpleasant acid sensation rise in him, the vague impression of a betrayal, a negative feeling against his wife; for a few seconds he's angry at her, indignant, resentful, even if the resentment is tempered by the uncertainty of not really knowing what he resents her for—maybe just for having had a life before him, obviously a bad one because he wasn't part of it. Or maybe he resents her for thinking badly of her, maybe he blames her for having to think badly of her, as though it's her fault that he's forced to have negative thoughts toward her, yes, she's the one who's forced him to do this, and he could almost shout at her that she's an absolute bitch, not for making him suffer almost every night by turning her back to him, no, but for destroying the whole story he'd made up about her, constructed around her, everything he wanted to see in her, everything he'd built, loved, his love, and he sees Ida watching all of this, wondering how he sees her mother, and he wonders what a child like Ida must think—she's always observed everything, just as she's observing him now and also observing the two brothers, with their satisfaction so flagrant—Ida struck most of all by this air of joy overflowing from Denis, as though everything in him is radiant, even if this radiance doesn't warm anybody, doesn't illuminate any joy or any face but his, even if it's not joy emanating from him but rather a kind of excitement mixed with triumph, an expression Ida has never encountered; she sees this air of triumph in Denis, this self-satisfied grimace, and even if she can't name it, it seems to her that she recognizes it.

But that's not it, something else is going on, in his restless hands as he serves everyone champagne, in the way he speaks with a kind of confidence she doesn't really believe, a fragility that makes it so nothing looks exactly like it should, behind the confidence and the act, a slightly exaggerated way of standing straight, of raising his flute of champagne and addressing Marion with something somehow forced, something smacking of effort and application, as though not even he believes what he's doing, as though he's doing it only to materialize what he'd resolved to do one day, but is exhausted in advance by the thought of bending himself to the images he must have been visualizing for so long that they seem borrowed from someone else's imagination. She sees this, Ida does, but in her mind these aren't logical and articulate sequences of thought—Ida is smart and very observant, but she's not so gifted that she's lost her childhood to an obsession with the arrangement and interpretation of signs, just as she's not yet able to submerge herself in a labyrinth of connections, and, from the swarm of details skittering around before her, she's not even capable of drawing any conclusions or establishing relations between cause and effect. No, everything is there, suffusing her ignorance, but the suffusion is deep and returns sensations to her that she feels as she stares at this man with the tired face, as though that shine in his eyes is the characteristic glint of fever and she can recognize it just as she recognizes, behind the cheerful voice and the too ostensibly joyful, even grandiloquent gestures, the violence hiding or the unease trying to pass for a simple expression of modesty and shyness. But Ida doesn't know any of this yet. She doesn't understand what she perceives in the man who, behind his smile, his glass raised in front of his eyes as if to conceal them, is saying very clearly, his voice barely wavering,

Marion, I wish you a happy birthday.

low-pitched, solemn, waiting for what exactly, for everyone to answer thank you? bravo? as though there isn't, in the house next door, a woman being threatened by his lunatic brother? Because his brother is a lunatic. He's a lunatic, and it's Marion who thinks this; not what Christophe tried to convince them, that Stutter has been cured of an evil he had as much trouble recovering from as Christophe did accepting its name, but crazy with a lunacy that you can't understand, that you just have to try to get away from. This is why Marion is waiting for something to happen, wondering if Christophe really believed what he said when he claimed Stutter wasn't a danger to anyone, is he really so harmless, this man who's capable of stabbing a dog to death, of holding a blade to a woman who could be his mother? How could Christophe think anyone would give the slightest credence to what he says, no, Stutter is a lunatic and Marion is still wondering whether Christophe really thinks his brother won't do anything stupid or, on the contrary, if he was making fun of her, of her credulity, was it to destabilize her and worry her even more, yes, a game to make her understand the risks and jam them deep in her skull, just in case the idea occurs to her to not obey?

Mom? Mom?

And Ida's voice brings Marion out of her thoughts,

Can I have an apple juice?

Yes, sweetie,

Marion starts to get up,

Hey! don't you move, Marion, it's your birthday, says Denis. You shouldn't move. Tonight you don't do anything.

she needs time to put her glass down and forget the pressure Denis is maintaining on her, his provocation, because unlike her daughter Marion doesn't see anything wavering in Denis's look, no fragility or doubt in his intentions but,

Christophe? Bring an apple juice for the little one!

on the contrary, a total confidence saturated with the hardness of pupils on their target, waiting for its reactions, its attempts to escape.

Denis shoots Patrice a look, Marion hasn't yet had time to sit back down before Christophe pops out of the kitchen, the apple juice in his hands, which he extends toward the table, taking the time to come around to be as close as possible to the little one— Ida drawing back on her chair and not taking her eyes off Christophe, regretting having called attention to herself and, for that reason, once she's been served, taking the glass in two hands, with a kind of fear legible in the smile she shows nobody in particular, or rather only her mother, while saying a practically silent *thank you* to Christophe, no longer daring to venture a look that would have been, if not hypocritical and perfunctory, call it timorous, or prudent, Ida, then, will beg her mother with an insistent eye to tell her if she has to say thank you, if she can, if she should, or if she should just bow her head over her apple juice and drink it, without a word to anyone.

28

For a moment he plays back the film in his head, he tries to see it all again, to picture a beginning, a middle, an end; yes, that's how things happened: after she said she refused to listen to his bullshit, she provoked him by leaving the studio and announcing that she was going to have dinner, as though she were free in her actions and movements—which he couldn't stand—and too bad if afterward he regretted losing his cool, because even if he blamed himself for that fist raised to her it was her fault, she didn't have to do what she did, with that haughty way of passing in front of him, yes, that way she'd addressed him, that scornful tone, that's what he repeated to himself, and if he'd been wrong to raise a hand to her he'd been right to put her in her place, because it was up to him alone to decide whether she could move from here and go from one room to another, up to him alone—tonight he's the one who decides, no one else—not that he has any desire to feel the force this power gives him over this woman, whom he means no harm, but he wants to feel the reality of this omnipotence, just out of curiosity, as though by wandering around inside an outsized freedom he could measure his own ability to impose his will, letting the idea cross his mind that Bergogne's neighbor couldn't do anything to object no matter what he decided, no matter what he wanted, even if ultimately he was surprised to find he didn't really want anything, didn't have any hateful or perverse impulse to satisfy, feeling suddenly empty and disconcerted to find himself with a power in his hands that he maybe didn't care about at all.

But he couldn't tolerate her trying to escape his grasp, because his grasp cost her nothing and presented no danger to her. He hadn't imagined she would be capable of so unreasonable a gesture as leaving the room while speaking to him so disdainfully, no, he had no idea she would dare face up to him so boldly, because he was certain the dog's death had demonstrated that he and his brothers could do whatever the hell they wanted, that nothing could stop them and they'd go all the way if they had to, no matter the price and the disagreements it cost them, the prevarications and the hours of discussion and scrapping over the details or sometimes over more important decisions—this he remembers quite well, because the conversations about the fate they planned for the dog had been spirited, him balking all the more because it would be up to him, after having lured it away with a piece of meat, to stick in the blade that killed it, arguing to his brothers that it's not so easy to kill an animal, a dog especially, with that look of theirs in which you can see the reflection of your own sadness at killing them, or the expression of their own regret at being pointlessly sacrificed. He didn't want to do it, and even if he'd been able to get out of doing it, if Christophe or Denis had decided to take care of it, he found it pointless—since when do we kill dogs for nothing?

No, not for nothing.

Denis had decided: they would kill the dog as Christophe had suggested, first to eliminate a risk—dogs are unpredictable and always present a danger—but above all to intimidate Bergogne and his neighbor, to force them to keep their actions reasonable.

After the long face-to-face that followed, her no longer daring to move, mute, he'd started to bound about and shout, starting to laugh stupidly, nodding his head, whirling around her, red with shame and stammering that he hadn't wanted to hit her and that of course, of course, yes, Jesus, obviously he hadn't wanted what happened but that's how he was, impulsive, jittery, the type who's easily provoked. And if he'd been even more ashamed thinking about it later, because his attitude wasn't what it should have been, he was also ashamed of the zeal he'd shown when she came back with her beers—yes, because at first Stutter had been surprised to see Christine come back from the kitchen with the two bottles. He'd stayed silent for a long while, not knowing what to say or what to do in response to her and this unexpected gesture, just as he'd been unable to tell whether or not he should accept the bottle she was holding out to him. After a moment he started to snicker and cracked a huge smile like a little kid's, open and guileless, to see her succumb so quickly to a Stockholm syndrome he didn't think really existed besides in the fantasies of a screenwriter or a shrink or a journalist, and, if she understood what he was thinking as she handed him the bottle, she'd smiled in turn,

Well, let's not stand around doing nothing like idiots, right?

and then, drinking the beer, Stutter had talked—is it just an old memory lingering in his head, or even a fabrication, someone else's story?—about the time long ago when he and his brothers lived in a suburban area wedged between the country and the city, where they had turtledoves, racing into the story of how they took them out of their cage—the heat of the turtledoves in their hands, their hearts no bigger than marbles and beating so hard through their warm bodies that it felt like their hearts were going to explode—and how they kept them in their hands, and how they stroked them on the head very gently, very slowly, patiently, with a kindness that was almost a kind of prayer, the voice accompanying the motion which eventually loosened, the hand relaxing, the fingers slackening, and the turtledove stayed groggy and tender in their hand, then, totally docile, submissive, it no longer tried to escape, and if it got the idea to fly away it was, after a few spins in the air, only to come back and land on their shoulder, their arm, their head, whichever of the three brothers had tamed it.

But I'm not a turtledove, definitely not a dove and even less a pigeon, Christine had smiled.

Yes, but still you came back with a beer and you didn't try to escape.

Just so you can beat me up? I'm too old for that.

He'd made a faint movement of the eyebrows, as if to say no, no, and it was so visible that she answered, as simply as if he'd spoken: I know how old I am, my joints remind me every day. I can't run, but that doesn't stop me from having a beer.

He'd been surprised, thinking to himself that she was trying to lull him to sleep, yet he let it happen, he wanted things to go well—was it being marooned here with an old eccentric in some godforsaken town in the middle of nowhere that he liked? Or was it just that he'd never met anyone like her? Does he like her because he has the feeling that she's funny, interesting, engaging, or—could it be that word, that idea, that sensation traveling between the rustlings of the air, the movements of their bodies: troubling? He'd thought to himself that she could be his mother; he thought this brought him closer to her and he also hoped it would bring her closer to him; that was probably why he'd let her entrance him with a story he'd never have thought would interest him, but that interested him almost in spite of himself, the daily life of a lonely woman who paints and listens to music and drinks herbal tea at night, maybe a beer from time to time when it's too hot.

She headed to the old stereo and put on a CD, the one that plays *Le Miroir de Jésus* by André Caplet, and he could almost have thanked her for sparing him the hypocrisy of pretending he had any chance of knowing who that was. She came and sat on a stool at her work table, and he resumed his route around the paintings, which he pored over as though he hadn't seen them before, this time listening to the music and holding his beer. It was as though the music gave the paintings a new meaning, a singular depth, wresting them from the banality and the crudeness he'd thought he saw in them, they were no longer so crazy, or it was as though the craziness was inhabited by something besides itself, or that it seemed moving and vibrant, new, reanimated, and Stutter felt like he was seeing the paintings but just as much being looked at by them, as though they had something to teach him, something that, far from excluding him, demanded his intelligence and his ability to be moved. As for the rest, even after this, then, he couldn't have said he regretted raising his hand to her, and if he had a regret it was having let violence take the upper hand even though for years he's been crammed full of medicine to channel or lock up everything inside of him. If Stutter had come so close to hitting her, to giving in to his violence, it was only because his brothers had given him a mission so important that the success of the whole evening depended on him alone, on his ability to keep a woman at bay who was a bit crazy and very solitary, who would try to resist by provoking him, by attacking him in the sly manner of a cantankerous old woman, which she was, just as he had imagined a few weeks earlier, before coming to stay in that minuscule town a few kilometers from La Bassée.

Because while they hadn't come to stay right here, to limit the risk of being recognized, they'd chosen to stay close by, to observe everyone's habits, to get to know the way they lived. The three brothers had already been on the scene for almost two weeks. They'd rented a very modest house in the middle of the country, a little gray one-story cube between the state road and the highway, a short walk from the town where Bergogne stopped at a pharmacy this afternoon. From there they'd followed Marion, they'd hatched plans, put together strategies: mostly they'd waited for Denis, who came back several days after disappearing without a word, showing up even more somber, somber to a fault, melodramatic and taciturn, in a mood he'd never shown before the experience of prison. And determined, that too to a fault, without brooking any argument, without any conviction to put forth to his brothers besides his need for them to settle the scores he had to settle.

End of discussion. That's how it is. Next.

That's what he'd repeat when one of the other two tried to express doubts, to ask questions, that's how it is, end of discussion, and neither had honestly imagined he could say no; the *end of discussion* dispatched any such inclination, even the one that would have consisted in trying to avoid descending with the eldest into his desire for vengeance, for retaliation, *next*, there it was again, returning to shut down the discussion, as though all three of them were in the same boat and it was destined to sink, it was irrevocable, all they could do was close their eyes and wait. So they'd waited for the eldest brother to decide everything about how things would happen and when they would happen. He had rented the house and they had come, had left behind anything at home they might have had to do—basically nothing, or so little that it amounted to the same thing—and they'd scrupulously followed Denis's ideas, these plans that were by turns ingenious and convoluted, sly and wily, or, conversely, after he'd thrown those out without hesitation, plans he scrawled on loose sheets of paper or on the backs of kraft paper envelopes, plans simple and direct, brutal and quick, that at least had the advantage of not taking forever.

And then finally Denis had decided on his idea of how to proceed, and things stopped moving after that.

They required time, patience, observation, and moderation before acting. Which was done. Each played his role with precision. After prowling around enough, they'd realized that one of the three houses in the hamlet was for sale, and Christophe had gone to all the agencies to make sure none of them was offering that particular item; he'd found the house only on a peer-to-peer marketplace site. Christophe had rented a car and bought a suit that wasn't too bad for less than eighty euros at a stock clearance store in town. He was the one tasked with understanding the day-to-day of the hamlet, who staked out the life of everyone there, the schedule of Ida's school bus route, the presence of the dog, the strange neighbor with the orange hair who Bergogne sometimes drove into town in his old Kangoo that was always covered in mud and bird droppings. At night they talked about how they'd do it, they took the car and drove, sometimes they got close to the hamlet of the Three Lone Girls to get a better idea of what they'd have to do on the big day. They'd park the car near the school bus stop, they'd continue on foot to the hamlet, keeping quiet, their mouths burned by alcohol and mustard and the spice of merguez sausages, eyes already sleepy or burning from drinking too much, red from smoking too much, their breath heavy with it each time, but never before two or three in the morning because taking the slightest risk was out of the question. Once, in the middle of the night, they'd even walked into the yard to get their bearings, which was easy because the Bergognes never closed the gate, even if that precaution would have been useless anyway because it was easy to climb the outer walls. They'd found the back door through which Stutter would enter Christine's house, but also they'd inspected the shed where Patrice and Marion parked their cars, but also the stable, how to get in without passing through the yard, so Stutter could lure the dog there—the dog who, that night, had indeed barked a bit and scratched at the door but even so, if Christine heard him, which wasn't certain, nobody got up, no lights in the houses came on.

The rest of the time the days stretched out, they drank red wine and Grand'Mère coffee that none of them liked but they kept buying; they barbecued in the little courtyard, even when it was cold, because nothing beats meat grilled over a wood fire with fries; they stared at the TV for hours on end or played Uno, rummy, crapette at the kitchen table with that old grayish oilcloth that must have looked like something—repeating patterns of sailboats, rowboats, gondolas?—long ago; they read the local newspaper, in which they paid attention to the back pages, to notices of birthdays in retirement homes, to soccer teams from the canton or the department; they put up with the stale odor of the house or, conversely but no less sickening, the throat-seizing smell in the bathroom, a mix of bleach and lavender air freshener, after the strange cleaning lady came to scour everything on the owner's behalf without their having asked, and with whom they liked to chat, casually, about people, about the police; they had shouting matches and reconciliations over nothing, a turn to do the dishes or the laundry that someone or other hadn't respected; Christophe and Stutter talked about women who didn't exist—but never with Denis—pretending not to hear their older brother sneering, murmuring to them to stop jacking off to their fantasies, that'd make them less dumb, he'd say as if to himself, because at just that moment he always lowered his voice, and from the other room it seemed not to try to make it through the walls. The others didn't say anything in response, not even that they wondered how he'd relieved himself in the absence of women in prison, certainly not; they watched TV shows, they went quiet again, they locked themselves in their heads, dreaming little dreams of the future with blond women and green bills, just to kill the time separating us from the big day for which we'd put up with anything: Marion's birthday.

Stutter, for those three weeks, had been responsible for following Christine, because after all he was the one who'd be spending time with her—this had been decided quickly and without discussion, it couldn't have been otherwise, Stutter himself not mentioning—not even thinking for a second—that the choices they were making without discussing them could in fact have been discussed, that Christophe, for instance, could have taken his place and, why not, he Christophe's. But it was in the natural order of things, each one stuck to his role in the brotherhood like a uniform to a soldier, never questioning what came from Denis, because what he said they didn't need to believe in or agree with, no, because before he said it, without imagining why or how, Christophe and Stutter knew he was going to say it.

They had bought Stutter, for almost nothing, on Leboncoin, an old Peugeot 103, a blue beast from the Jurassic era or that of the first pirate radio stations, that backfired more often than it moved forward but that drove, in spite of the spots of rust, the defective brakes, the bald tires, and that sufficed for the seven or eight kilometers he had to drive two or three times a week. Stutter went to the two markets in La Bassée, where, on the pretext of three or four errands to run, he was supposed to follow Christine to take the time to observe her. He'd spied on her this way several times, taking care to not show himself, to stay in the shade enough to not be spotted by anyone, on the sidewalk, repeating sidelong glances or pretending to listen to his phone, reading messages on it with a conscientious look, all the while watching Christine walking, not suspecting anything—of this he was sure, and, frankly, proud— her way not only of dressing, doing her hair, moving around, but also her manner of inspecting others, and life taking shape around her, like a play she didn't seem to want to understand at all and that even seemed, sometimes, to irritate her. He'd been sure of this right away, just by watching her in the crowd of people at the Sunday morning market: she wasn't capable of seeing herself except through the prism of that which set her apart from these country folk whom she was decidedly nothing like, neither in her extravagance, which contrasted sharply with the banality of others, of their erasure foretold by their common clothes and even more conformist attitudes, nor in what she bought at the market and the way she bought it, weighing vegetables in her hand with an exaggerated attentiveness or manifesting her bemusement, look-ing for the best, lingering longer than necessary in front of a stall, as though she suspected shady dealings, haggling over prices and questioning the quality of the products, if not the honesty of the merchant—a pain in the ass, yes, he'd thought, a real caricature of a Parisian.

He had followed all this three weeks in a row, at the Sun-day market on the rue du Commerce, and Thursdays at the place de l'Église Saint-Pierre, off the avenue François-Mitterrand. He'd seen which stores she stopped at, and, by dint of having prepared for this evening and drawing up his portrait of her, he believed he almost knew her, because after they'd decided on the strategy they would deploy the whole day, with all the spectacle they'd set up out of an excess of caution, out of necessity real or assumed—was it essential for Christophe to show up in a rental car in the afternoon to distract Christine's attention while Stutter lured the dog into the stable? Did he have to introduce himself as a potential buyer of the house for sale?—and made up their minds to stick to it, though after a few days they no longer really knew why, clinging to it just because Denis had decided that way and so that's the way it was, Stutter had done nothing but think of her, nothing but think back to the few times he'd followed her in the street on market days, when he'd taken the time to follow her all the way to her bicycle, which she locked up on the plaza in front of city hall but above all he had returned to the few images of her he'd found on the internet, because as soon as he knew what his role would be he'd become attached to knowing Christine, had become attached, if not to her, then to the character he wanted to see in her, the one he'd invented for himself, seeking elements to feed an avid imagination, not that he fantasized about her or desired her in one way or another, but simply to respond to his need to calm the anxiety fed by this woman's life and her image and the idea of spending so much time alone with her, a way for him to reassure this fear that had grown with each day that brought them closer to the day of Marion's birthday.

He had visited and revisited the internet and typed in her name: Christine De Haas. He'd found a few old photos in which she was hard to recognize, a woman with chestnut hair and very fair skin, someone very thin who gave the impression of being not fragile but nervous, agile, sparkling and surely formidably intelligent and free—with all that word contained, for Stutter, of irreverence, of scandalous sexuality and haughtiness, in spite of the Peter Pan collar she wore in the pictures where she must not have been older than seventeen—and rich, which meant unaware of everything, or rather heedless and frivolous, lavish and immoderate, yes, because in the photos where she's a young adult, in an evening gown, with a glass of champagne in her hand, at dinners with a Swiss banker who the captions informed us had been her husband and had given her this Flemish-sounding name that she kept after

her divorce, as though it were inseparable from the compensa-
tory allowance paid her by this ex-husband whom she no longer
heard from anyway, you could see perfectly well that she was rich
and above all that she possessed a facility of movement through
life related to the way money tampers with bodies and postures,
liberating them from that which hinders them, a strange kind of
affected coldness, a stiffness, a feigned distance he'd observed in the
photos, just as he'd also been sensitive, perhaps, to a form of dis-
tinction he'd noticed even more in the street as soon as he started
following her. And then nothing else on the internet. Or almost
nothing. The stub of a Wikipedia page that was skeptical about
its sources, which turned out to be hardly trustworthy; there was
almost nothing to be found in them about her personal or professional life, not a word about where she'd learned to paint or how
she'd developed the taste for it.

Stutter had the feeling that he knew her, that he knew how
she would react before she even realized it, even if he'd been surprised because she reacted—well before he did—by passing in
front of him as she darted into the kitchen, before returning almost
immediately, two cold bottles of beer in her hands.

29

In concrete terms, very little is happening: a table, a woman, three men and a child drinking apple juice. The woman sitting back down, the man who gave the child the apple juice still standing in front of her, smiling at her or smiling into space, not waiting for her to thank him but lingering over her delectable face bent over her glass—and the others doing the same for a moment, even if suddenly something springs back into motion, noisily, because Patrice stands up, the four feet of his chair scraping the tile, moving without paying attention to anyone else but drawing all the attention to himself, because it's his body that demands it, this mass that seems immense in the enclosed space of the dining room, the silence suddenly broken by this motion of getting up from the table, as though he's just broken an agreement that was never articulated but that everyone was obeying, as though this motion is abrupt enough for everyone to understand how angry Patrice is—that's why it went on so long, and also why what they saw, when Patrice stood up, was the violence of the restraint he tried to impose on it, yes, on the gesture he meant to be harmless, that of a man who gets up from the table to go to the living room, to a white wooden cabinet, and get a glass and a bottle of whiskey.

He poured himself a glass halfway up, drained it in one swig, not expecting anything from the others, just the benefit of the alcohol burning the palate and fogging the brain—does Patrice think that by moving he's changed the rules, that by rushing to the bottle of whiskey he's destabilized some laws he wasn't aware had been established over them all? No, he just lets the burn of the alcohol take effect, which leaves him time to think of nothing but the almost painful pleasure he takes in it, then he tries to summon a calm that doesn't come, that's fine, he hopes to feel capable of seeing things clearly again, of simply understanding what's happening, if he can, because this whole time everything has been beyond him, as though reality has begun sending him signals in an enigmatic foreign language, a language unknown to him but that holds no secrets for the others. Bergogne needs time, silence, but it's too late, the relative silence of moments ago has now given way to a salvo of questions from Christophe and Denis, who are drinking, bustling about, talking to each other, exchanging words that nobody else hears or understands, then they turn to Marion, firing off questions that are almost harmless at first,

How you doing?

the kind you ask out of habit or politeness,

You happy here?

not necessarily waiting for an answer,

Nice here, isn't it?

questions followed by commentary that the two brothers aren't exchanging between themselves but each to himself, not hoping to be heard by anyone in particular, no, just because they're letting slip out what they're thinking,

Yeah, you sure do seem happy here,

sentences murmured, barely projected outward, much less directed toward Marion, who in any case is acting as though she doesn't hear them, isn't receiving them, which is maybe why the questions are addressed more directly to her, not asked by voices trying to pull her in by raising the volume, by confronting her, by forcing her to face them, no, it's not that, for now they come out and out again at the same volume but are accompanied by increasingly precise glances, almost ardent, inevitable, soon Marion will be forced to turn her face away, to lower her head, to close her eyes to avoid them while they,

It's not right, refusing to answer when people ask you questions,

as if suspended in the void, one or the other picking up where his brother left off, one always echoing the other, as though pretending to be having this conversation for the first time,

Have to admit, you really seem to be doing well here, guess you can't think of everyone, you know, out of sight, out of mind...

Denis lets Christophe talk, sometimes he even smiles at Marion, as though it's just the two of them in the dining room and together they're going to appreciate and enjoy his brother's witticisms, coming from the kitchen where they can hear him moving dishes around and starting to heat them up on the stove, Denis taking all the time in the world and then, in a calm and poised voice, almost amused too, backed by Christophe's echoing his,

You know you weren't easy to find?

Oh my, no, not easy.

You've always been that way, haven't you? You really thought we'd forget you?

Is that true, Marion?

Marion, no?

Seriously?

Seriously, Marion, that's what you thought?

The two brothers let their laughter ring out and turn back to Patrice, who this time no longer has the slightest feeling of anger toward his wife but instead feels moved by a swelling of love for her—his wife with her face blank and hard, closed, expressing nothing but annoyance and impatience, anger too, maybe, but that seems stricken, yes, as though Marion is collapsing within herself and all of her struggle now is in the hopes of remaining impassive, of walling herself off, of being a wall of silence.

What he sees, Bergogne, is this struggle, this pain, and his wife's strength, her capacity for resistance. Though he doesn't know what she's hiding nor who these men she knows are, he knows she needs him, needs his love, he wants to go to her, and there's this momentum rising in him that he wants to let blossom, even if this momentum is above all his need to answer orders as old as his father's life, his grandfather's, ancestors whose names are long forgotten in the fog of the past, as though he's rising to the challenge of the unspoken that binds the generations together; and this momentum that's his alone guides him now, along with the warmth of the glass of whiskey, along with the wound in his finger pricking through the bandage, toward the table—in reality the momentum of love is diluted in a momentum that's bigger than him, the same push Bergogne would have had to defend anyone when they were in need of help, a momentum that was drilled into his head until it became his own thought, and it's so unthought in him that he stands up before the two brothers without even realizing that the pose he's striking is grotesque—a nice guy, clumsy and naïve, who's never stepped in the ring, suddenly puffing out his chest and pantomiming the daring footwork of a boxer.

But she doesn't need him to defend herself. Marion knows how to take care of herself and it's not impossible that she might look unkindly upon his desire to intervene, to do what he's doing by appearing before them and forcing them, with the presence of his body, to get up, to fight, to do battle. But for the moment they don't even look at him, or they don't believe he really wants to intervene. They're completely absorbed in what they're doing and saying, one bustling between the kitchen and the dining room and the other, seated, chest forward, gently setting down his glass of champagne now that it's empty, repeating again, his voice bearing not a bitter string of accusations but a sort of sadness and disgust, a sort of mournful fatalism,

How is it possible? What you did?

all of it in a breath that exhausts itself before it even really forms a series of questions, more something crumbling, disintegrating, porous,

How is it possible... to... this...

• • •

And whereas Bergogne, standing so close to them, seems invisible to them, it's Ida's voice that draws them—draws Denis, at least, because Christophe is now standing with his hand on the fridge door and lingering over the magnets.

What's gotten into Ida? Did she see her father preparing himself? Did she guess what he intends to do, and it's only to interrupt him and stall the disastrous momentum into which he's trying to leap that she asks her mother if she can leave the table and go watch a movie? Ida repeats her question, she takes her mother's arm and begins to squeeze the fabric between her fingers, she pulls, she pinches,

Mom,

she insists,

Mom, can I watch a movie?

and as Marion still isn't answering, Patrice is surprised at his daughter's presence, surprised that her mother doesn't hear her, and it's as though all his aggression has just fallen away, abandoned him; he just wants Marion to hear her daughter and answer her, the necessary measure of reproach in Ida's voice for her to understand that her daughter is talking to her, that she has to answer her, yes, and Marion reacts suddenly, the time it takes for her to become aware that Patrice is so close to them that she's almost surprised not to have realized he's back from the living room already and that he's pointing to her daughter, for Ida's voice to finally reach her brain. But it's Denis who speaks, addressing Ida:

We scared you, didn't we?

And rather than answer, rather than speak to the man whose name she doesn't remember, Ida blushes, Ida swallows, Ida reiterates her question to her mother who takes some time to react, as though her daughter's voice hasn't really made it all the way to her, or if it has then only muted, distant. But it doesn't last. She sees how Denis is watching, decoding—intolerable to Marion, this image, and she turns to her daughter and takes her in both hands, both of her arms, so small that her fingers encircle them completely, and her voice becomes firm, as though her voice is also taking her by the arm, but to give her an order, even though she just answers yes, of course, kitten, of course, you'll have dinner later. But it's to Denis that the firmness in her voice is addressed. The little girl leaves the table, doing everything she can to ignore the man whose eyes she can still feel following her, the whole time it takes to leave the dining room, pass through the entrance to the living room, and take the few steps separating her from the television and the DVD player, sensing something behind her like the negative energy of adults, something like a single monster with many heads, risen from the underground kingdom of the night.

Once she has the headphones over her ears, of course she'll keep the sound down as low as possible—a trickle right on the line that isolates, in the dining room, the reality next door. And even though a simple sideways movement allows her to see through the frame of where the double French door used to be—she never knew it, but she can still see its outline and traces on the ground—Ida has a very good view of her mother and her father and, across from them, the man with the gift and the other one who's finally come back from the kitchen, yes, with another bottle in hand, who's burst in and sat down to his brother's right, which is to say across from the spot she occupied a few minutes ago. Her father has finally sat back down, which is something reassuring; knowing him, she'd been afraid his violence would spill over. They poured him some champagne and he lingers over his flute and the straw-colored liquid, the bubbles rising in a straight line up the glass and bursting on contact with the air, as though this spectacle fascinates him to the point of cutting him off from everything else.

For a few minutes more, Ida feigns indifference and interest in the screen, even though what's holding her back and forcing her to listen, to be on the alert for any too-sudden movement, is fear. Ida can make out sounds, voices—she'll know if something takes a different direction, even if for now not only is nothing deviating, but her parents' silence is settling in, as the two men talk, their voices almost gentle and calm, Christophe and Denis communicating without raising their tone, just letting a snicker escape from time to time, one louder than the other, a way of exaggerating their astonishment, their disbelief, but that's it. This is enough for Ida to tell herself it's going to be okay; her muscles relax, her body sinks lightly into the sofa, her breathing slows and deepens, her eyes concentrate and focus on the television. She lets herself be hypnotized, carried off by the image. She still hears what's being said in the next room, but everything eventually dissolves into a strange and almost homogenous language, seamless, distant too, throwing off distinctive sonorities, tones that finish running together and drift away from her, meaningless in their musicality—background music that soon she'll stop hearing, only distantly perceiving its melodic line, and most of all the two voices that she pushes far from her own space, in the closed space of an adult universe that this time she wants nothing to do with.

But while she refuses to take an interest, her father is doing the opposite.

He who was prepared to fight just to put an end to all of this, and because he couldn't endure the two strangers' voices nor, through them, the familiar tone the two brothers proudly adopted toward Marion, the arrogance they put into it intended—he was sure of this right away—for him, to belittle him and show him he was nothing in Marion's life, now he's the one who's silent: he listens. And even in the way he raises his eyes to them, moving slowly and precisely from one to the other, as though photographing them inwardly and memorizing their every fold, every movement of their features—as though trying to make a portrait of them distinct from the one they chose to assert of themselves—now, then, eyes fixed stubbornly, frowning, he seems to observe them no longer with anger but with stupefaction, still not really interest, still not yet that unbecoming, unhealthy curiosity mixed with a strange feeling of disgust at his own voyeurism, as though, hearing them, he feels like he's rummaging through his wife's things, checking her datebook against her supposed appointments or secretly reading her emails and text messages. No, it's not that yet. But he can't help pricking his ears up when Denis says to Marion,

So I hear you're working? You have a real job, huh? You went to school, I hear? For... what was it now, ah yes, wait, shit, I can't remember, it's not knitting, the word is

Printing.

Thanks, bro. Printing. That's it, printing. What do you do exactly?

You must earn a good living, no?

continues Christophe, as if to encourage Denis, not because he expects a response from Marion, because he knows Marion has no intention of responding to him, Marion has always taken him for an idiot, no reason that would have changed, she takes him for an idiot and he's burning to say to her, here, right now,

You answer me when I talk to you. I know what you do in your little fucking print shop, I did my research. I might be an idiot but I did my research.

But instead of that Christophe just shoots her a broad smile that reveals all his hatred for her, all the resentment and bitterness gathered up in him like a little pile of ash, the old core of hatred he keeps carefully shut up in a corner of his head for the moment he can at last throw in her face everything he didn't say or do before, knowing he'd never have dared, nor been able to, but no matter. What's important is that she knows how to read his eyes, the curl of his lip, that she understands without hearing them the verminous words he's keeping to himself, shining in his transparent, empty gaze, too bright, almost gray.

His eyes—it's not really his eyes that Patrice sees. But in their intensity he registers the resentment Christophe feels toward Marion. He can read the number of years inscribed there, the length of time separating this moment from another one, etched into a story he knows nothing about, one he almost fears will come all the way back to them tonight, even though at the same time he knows now that everything in him is telling him to let the doors of the past open so he can steal a look in and discover a Marion he's not sure is the same as the one he loves. And what's supposed to hold him back finally gets the better of him; the two men are no longer just intruders or enemies, not even rivals who've come to boast of having had a more intimate life than his in his wife's company, no, but witnesses he wants to hear out, as though it's he who's interrogating them and not they who've come to spill out their stream of resentments and rancors. He reverses the roles and for a moment you can almost see a hint of excitement floating over his face, a smile barely visible on his lips but nonetheless very present, as clear as the keenness of his curiosity, even if he knows nothing good will come of it. But the interest seizes him by the throat, as betrayed by the way he holds his glass of champagne and drains it almost too quickly, the nervous and jerky way he approaches the table, puts his elbows on it and moves toward the two others without defending his wife even though he can clearly see her sending him the signals of someone drowning, suddenly lost, frightened by what the two others are beginning to say,

That's right, my little Marion, a real career?

and as he starts to stare at her with an expression that wants to know, that asks, that almost demands to know, it's she who blushes and lowers her eyes, long enough for her to hear Denis's voice again,

If I understand correctly,

in a murmur, almost cajoling, conspiratorial,

No more little side jobs at highway rest stops?

Denis starting to smile, almost to laugh—but not an open laugh, more a laugh corresponding to a memory of a moment that still surprises him, and one he hides almost shyly behind his fist closed in front of his mouth. Then he lets the words' echo float, something hollow that his phrases make reverberate in space. He feels his phrases circle around them, over their heads, over the table, then come slowly back down toward Marion, an opaque and corrosive smoke falling in a thick layer like dust after an explosion has launched it into the air; he feels the silence that lingers just afterward is an effect not of his imagination but of his words themselves, of the sugared sweetness they leave hanging in the air, unlike that kindly or conciliatory tone they wear too conspicuously and that nobody believes, whose effect is not reciprocal good will or conciliation but an electrification of gestures—so meager all the same, so ordinary, Patrice taking a pistachio and tossing the shell without seeing it land next to the bowl, Marion hastening to pick it up with her fingertips, before tossing it into the bowl, as though everything depends on this gesture that everyone surely notices without seeing that it allows her to hide that she can't bring herself to turn her eyes to her husband's, which don't leave her, which are waiting for something. But she still can't bear it, this steadiness, as though Patrice's eyes are too inquisitive for her to take this face-to-face—as though she's unable to expect anything from it but a confrontation or even already a condemnation, a sort of accusation she fears she won't be able to bear in this moment, imagining she won't be able to even though she wants to find his eyes, yes, with all her heart, she wants to find in him an answer to her anguish, understanding, love, she's sure he'd understand, sure he'd see she wants to apologize because already it's as though everyone has agreed to say that what's happening tonight is partly her fault and, although she wants to apologize for this evening, now she wants Patrice to forgive her for everything she's put him through for years, which she knows he endures almost without a word, getting angry sometimes because he's had too much to drink or because his patience has run out; she knows, as clearly as she knows she's never wanted to truly know, that it's because of what she doesn't give him, and not just sex, but also all the tenderness and all the time she refuses him. He would be astonished—if she had the strength for a face-to-face—by what he saw, because he would see, then, that she's asking his forgiveness for all those years playing the idea of a couple rather than being a couple, and he'd be so surprised too to realize that she's ready to explain to him what for all these years she's so stubbornly closed off to discourage him from asking anything; everything he wants to ask her about herself, about them, about all she swore never to tell anyone, much less, in the secrecy of her memory, herself, this time she's ready to tell him, just as she'd be ready to rush over to her neighbor's house to ask her forgiveness—Christine, everything that's happening has nothing to do with you, this is all me, me and only me, you've been suspicious since the day I showed up here and tonight you'll know you were right when you took Patrice for a sap I was going to fleece, who I was taking advantage of like a whore, I wasn't a whore but I was still a slut who took advantage of him, it's true, you could tell, you wanted to protect him and you were right, yes, for a second she wants to run to Christine's and take back everything that's never been said between them but that both of them have always had their opinions about.

Marion feels the pressure of Patrice on her, his crushing expectation, this accusation in her husband's eyes—she can feel it vividly, it's present like a wave of cold on her skin, these eyes riveted on her that she can tell are unblinking, disturbed by nothing, holding tight to this demand that he points like an accusing finger; she understands what he's feeling, his anger and this discomfort separating them, but she wants him to see hers too, the element of surprise that impedes her still, that she's barely recovered from and that keeps her there with her eyes fixed on the table, her cheeks too pink, as though she's intimidated even though she's not, she's just on the defensive, she wants him to be able to understand, to turn his face away to show he's giving up on knowing, doesn't want to know anything—as though he's capable of forgiving her and ignoring everything—yes, that's what she'd like, what she's hoping for, what she feels as a desire that's already disappointed because he keeps staring at her without moving. And him, he stays rooted to his chair, inspecting her and listening to Denis's voice. She knows—as he knows—that what he's going to hear is everything she never wanted to tell him, but also that it's not what she would have told him, or how she would have told him; if he's going to listen so complacently, maybe it's to punish her for all those years she didn't know how to or didn't want to speak to him. If she could tell him everything now, if only she could, yes, she who for so long didn't want to tell him what her life had been made of, now there's no doubt that she'd rush to tell him, to unburden herself of it too, to lighten her load, perhaps, giving him the gift of a story she didn't want, yes, she wants to tell him everything, so long as it's with her own words.

If she doesn't look him in the face now, she thinks, he'll think exactly what the others want him to think. He'll think it with their words, with the cruelty and the bitter irony they'll mix in, mocking and merciless, not just to hurt her, to be finished with her, but also to destroy everything she's managed to build with her husband—she knows she needs to look at him to keep them in check, or at least at bay, just as she knows Patrice is waiting for it, this request she could send him without a word, to not believe what they say but to believe what he sees in her eyes, in the silent promise she'd make to tell him everything, if everything has to be said, but she doesn't dare, she can't, she can feel how he's staring at her, her husband, the weight of all the questions, no longer like it was earlier when he just wanted her to explain who these bastards were, when they could still worry about the two brothers together and not like now, his eyes shooting darts at her as though she's already been convicted before the others have even recounted what she's done everything in her power to forget. But now they're here. Now Patrice is asking something else. Now he wants to know. And meanwhile,

I don't know if you remember little Barzac?

Denis launching in,

You know, the one with kind of a strange face, with his mouth all puckered?... I ran into him at the market maybe... how long ago was it? I don't know, doesn't matter. Life's funny like that, right? You know where he was coming from? No? You don't know? Not even a guess? No... This guy who's never set foot more than ten kilometers from Les Grivaux, the one time he leaves his little backwater, where does he go? He comes here. You hear that? He comes here on vacation, this moron. More than five hundred kilometers from home. No kidding. Funny, right? He gets out for once in his life, and it's to come to this shithole... Crazy, don't you think? You believe that? And Denis rattles off his story with his voice still very soft, just expressing his amazement at a coincidence that only reality could come up with—A cousin owed him some money or something, I don't remember; anyway, some bullshit. And barely has he shrugged his shoulders, run his hand through his hair, eaten two or three potato chips, leaving his hand in front of his mouth while he chews, he's still smiling to think of this guy who found Marion—I mean what do you call that? Chance, luck? And luck for who, if that's what it is? You know? But hold on, there's more to the story. Because it's not enough for him to show up here. He could've passed you by ten times before he saw you, or not even, just not even run into you at all... He doesn't just have to show up in this shithole, it's not enough for him to just come this far, no, there have to be circumstances, occasions, and as it happens he has to go on a Friday night—not a Saturday, no, which would make more sense, but a Friday, yeah, that struck me—about fifteen kilometers from here, to a club that's not even in this shithole but farther away, an even shittier shithole, a nightclub for hicks, with his cousin who's trying to pick up some chick who... anyway, a club that's probably called Le Maximum or some bullshit like that, with a disco ball and a stupid strobe light, like when we used to go... and who does he come across? Can you guess? Who's still getting all dolled up and swanning around with her girlfriends... it's you, Marion, it's you. It took hours before he even realized it was a possibility. He watched you all night, he said, it was a real hallucination, a ghost, it's a ghost, he said, she hasn't changed, you looked so much like yourself that he even thought it couldn't be you. And yet it was, it's her, he said, it's her. The tattoo on the neck, on the nape, you're not afraid to show it, are you… Always makes an impression, I'm sure, even if these days everyone has one, there weren't so many when you had yours done, girls who would do that… Right, Marion? Still doing the gin and grapefruit at the bar and the little bumps of coke in the pisser? that must keep you fit, no? help you get through the daily grind? No? No… I'm kidding, I'm just messing around. Don't get upset, I know you're not into that anymore… No? Right, Christophe?

Christophe nods, but Denis doesn't even give him a look. He turns away from Marion and lets his eyes wander across the ceiling for a few seconds, like a smoker brooding over the curls of smoke from his cigarette as they rise and spread in ever wider swathes, then he lets his eyes slide over the walls, not pausing to contemplate, idling slowly, showing no interest in anyone and not caring whether or not his brother is planning to answer him, or what he thinks, if he thinks anything—Seedy little Barzac, I never thought he could be so clever… because instead of bothering you, he went and hit on one of your girlfriends, just long enough to find out your name, to make sure. That's what he told me, but that's it, he didn't do anything else. And this time Denis adopts a pained expression to explain, suddenly addressing Patrice too— that little shithead Barzac, seeing him strut like a rooster, just broke my heart… I didn't know whether to kiss him or wipe that little faggot smile off his face… of course he was pleased with himself… he knew I'd be pleased, he could have tried to get some money out of it but no, too stupid, I'm sure he didn't even think of it, he was just so happy to come show off… We had a good laugh at the time… and we drank. Not champagne like tonight, no, the good old plonk, but it was a pleasure… the first good news in how long? Do you know? Say, Marion, you know how long it'd been since I'd had any good news?

He could stop talking and not tell the rest, which ultimately interests only him: how they arranged to come here, his brothers and him, how by great effort, thanks to Barzac's cousin, they waited patiently for Marion to come back to the club one night, on a Friday because they have a karaoke machine and she came with her girlfriends. Oh yeah, they go to karaoke, the cousin said, we know those girls, they're no spring chickens, you can spot them right away. We sort of make fun of their husbands who dote on them, who stay at home with the kiddies, they flirt but really they're teases, they don't do anything, they laugh, they drink, they shimmy around singing to nonsense from the nineties and that's it. And it's Christophe's turn now to explain how they managed to track her down. He says: One time I went to that club, on a Friday. I came back empty-handed. The second time too. But not the third. There you were, with your girlfriends. I stayed in the corner, you didn't see me, but your girlfriends, yeah, they noticed me—well, one of them did, the redhead. She's not bad-looking, the redhead… I cleared off because I didn't want you to notice me… But I waited in the parking lot, until two in the morning, and I followed you… Fuck, Marion, when you're wasted I swear you can't drive for shit.

30

Usually at this hour I come and drink herbal tea in my old arm-chair. That one right there. It's in pretty bad shape now but I've had it with me since I sold my first painting—one of the first gifts I gave myself—I smoke two or three cigarettes, never more, which I always snuff out in that little bowl there, on the floor. Since the chair is turned to face the canvas in the middle of the room, I take my time, I look at it carefully, I go over every detail. Do you like it? You don't seem sure. That's alright. You think I just painted an old naked lady, but at first, if it's red, this portrait, it's because she was wearing a dress I had in my head, something I thought of, I mean, not her, the woman, no, she didn't exist. At first there was no woman, just a dress. Several months ago I woke up one morning with the image of a red dress on a hanger, standing there with nothing around it. I started to draw the dress, and very quickly I had the shape I thought I'd seen in my dream. After that I painted different reds to try to find the right one, but I couldn't do it, not at all, so I thought to myself, I have to put the dress on a woman, and I went looking on the internet. I cut up photos, I combined portraits. I thought the dress would pop out if I showed it being worn. I put an old lady in the dress, but at first she was standing up, like a model from La Redoute, you know? It was ridiculous. I made her sit down, I didn't know why, she had to be sitting... is this interesting to you, what I'm saying?

This time Christine had understood that yes, it was interesting to him. It had even seemed to maybe fascinate him a bit, because he'd stayed there without saying a word, mouth open, nodding his head as if to say he'd just understood that what you see doesn't come like that, thinking that's why he'd never be an artist—because of his impatience, his need to trust in certainties, to not grope around in the dark—and he'd told her, yeah, that's crazy, it's like, like, I don't know, she has folds in her skin, not like wrinkles, no, just that...

Yes, the more I painted the dress, the more she came into her flesh. The more she disappeared into the folds of her skin, the more she became herself. But in any case you always start a painting to find out what you want to paint, you can't know beforehand, or anyway I can't... I didn't want a naked woman, and in the end she's what I'm left with—but the dress, I'll never see it.

He had kept looking at the paintings while she spoke, and he'd been struck by how all of it was transformed by its contact with music; as though the music came into the flesh of a painting to re-veal it, as though the studio itself was transformed, rejecting every-thing else, the past and the last few hours. And that's why suddenly he blurts out, why he feels he has to blurt out, he wants to say how he doesn't listen to music, he doesn't know music, he never really knew this kind of music existed. He likes music, music or what they say is music, but he doesn't understand anything and his voice is going too fast for his thoughts, it trips, falls into the void of a thought that won't come or maybe it's the opposite, the thought precedes it, it's freewheeling and nothing, in his mouth, on his tongue, can hold it or express it, he hears his voice break, repeat, restart, run out of steam—he wants to talk about music and how he could have liked it, he feels like he could have if his life had been different, but look, he doesn't give a shit, he's not complain-ing about his life, it could have been worse, he knew guys at the center—they must still be there, they'll never leave, or if so then feet first. That's how it is, next, end of discussion.

And he doesn't hear that it's only when he says these words that aren't his but his older brother's that he manages to come unstuck from his rut, only

Next, end of discussion,

when he takes Denis's words and maybe even his intonation that he manages to speak.

But though he takes Denis's words, it's Christophe that he's closest to now, because nobody knows him better than Christophe. Not even Denis, who believes he knows both of them better than anyone but who's wrong on this point because, for the last ten years that rose up between them like a wall or an immense thicket of brambles, Denis wasn't there to guide them in their lives, to understand them and support them, to help them or chew them out. For ten years his role as protective and dictatorial big brother lay fallow, and, though neither Stutter nor Christophe had sought to release themselves from a wardship in which they took the greatest pleasure, they'd acquired a knowledge and a closeness between them that nobody could have suspected, not even Denis—especially not Denis—because in his absence Christophe had become Stutter's older brother, the older brother he'd always been in real life because he was the second of the siblings but had never had the chance to truly be in practice—the man in the middle who'd never gained the confidence that he was anything more than a transmission piece that allowed the two others to exist on top of him. He'd become the eldest by elimination, but the eldest nonetheless, closer and more available, a brother, yes, where Denis had all the authority and inflexibility of a traditional father, one you don't dare to contradict and dare even less to confide in or ask for affection, understanding, to say nothing of love. And it's because they found themselves almost alone, with the feeling of being alone, at once abandoned by Denis and liberated from him, that they were able to realize they didn't know each other, had never really given themselves the opportunity to meet.

When that happened, Stutter had discovered a brother more

loving than Denis, and though he had less charisma Christophe had the authority Stutter needed to feel confident. Denis knew it, he hadn't shown any signs of jealousy, maybe he hadn't felt any, didn't feel any at all since his release from prison, no more than he felt the sense of having been left by the wayside, as though he was indifferent to the fact that other bonds had been forged between his brothers, a new fraternity propped up on his absence, a complicity he hadn't wanted to see or that didn't interest him, or that maybe even relieved him of a weight he'd never wanted to carry.

Denis, in any case, didn't have time to care about his brothers' feelings, and, even if he felt obligations toward them, today's Denis feels obligations toward himself first and foremost, and he's absolutely certain his brothers won't have anything to say about it.

For those ten years Denis had remained behind bars, Christophe had most often spent his time with his younger brother at their parents' house, late into the night, leaving behind the subdivision, his house, his wife and their two little girls, preferring to stay in the kitchen of his parents' apartment talking with his brother about Denis and the wrong he'd suffered, about childhood, about the parents who certainly gave us a hell of a time when we were kids, all the while throwing back little glasses of prune liqueur or pear liqueur but also wine—lots of it—and beer, in five-liter casks they polished off in barely two days, while behind the television or in their room the parents waited for the evening to finish, pretending not to hear the bursts of laughter coming from the kitchen, the endless banter of the two brothers who no longer even knew what they were talking about but poured themselves another round, just refraining from saying they were waiting for the return of the eldest, that they were prisoners of his absence, stuck to it like night bugs smashing and burning themselves against a lightbulb. They opened the windows because of the cigarette smoke and, though they savored the freedom of being just the two of them, discovering the joy of a conversation free of surveillance by their parents but also, no less suffocatingly, by the eldest, they didn't realize that deep down they were speaking only of him, the eldest, who contaminated everything.

Those long nights at their parents' house, while Denis was in prison and Stutter couldn't seem to recover his footing in life, as though the hospital had made him permanently incapable of fending for himself, floating like a shipwreck in the middle of a great nowhere that seemed to frighten him, Christophe made promises about the nights of passion they'd soon know because there was no doubt that before long, as soon as the three brothers could reunite, they'd meet girls and among them would be one who'd take care of Stutter, a nice girl with a good figure, not stupid because he needed a girl who was bright but also clever, and it was with those fantasies, and with the others, the first of them being Denis's return, that they invented and drew entire evenings in an alcoholic fog. Christophe promised a great deal, and it has to be said that he'd taken things in hand since Denis's incarceration, because Christophe had certainly needed to look after *the last one*—as Denis, the firstborn, had done—initially by going to the hospital in which he'd never wanted to set foot, then by agreeing to spend time with him. Of everything he'd done for ten years in Denis's place, though with his consent, of course the decision to move *the last one* back in with their parents upon his release from the hospital had been the most spectacular.

Christophe had demanded that they agree to his return even though they didn't want to, not for anything in the world, repeating with a shudder that to them, tiny retirees calcified in implausibly cream-colored fake-leather armchairs, unable to float anywhere besides around their television—for her—or the kitchen window, behind the imitation-lace curtain, to spy on whoever passed by on the street—for him—that to them it was out of the question for that other lunatic to return to their house—which hadn't been a house for a long time, because after Denis's sentencing they'd had to give up the lease on that house which had become much too big for the two of them anyway, the parents had had to flee the neighbors, the old friends who avoided them in the street, had to flee the shame and disgrace of the outcast. They'd wound up in the suburbs without quite knowing how, a real suburb this time, in a high-rise public housing block called B2.

Out of the question, they'd shouted, then they'd panted it, then they'd given in, keeping stuck in their throat what the last one had done to his mother, the father repeated, less and less loudly, with less and less conviction as he saw Christophe, intransigent, force on him the presence of Stutter, the one who'd broken his mother's heart the night they found him at a farm fifteen kilometers from the subdivision, stark naked and torching the firewood, no, this son who had destroyed his mother, to think that he'd once thrown all his papers, his ID, his health insurance card and bank card and movie pass and all the rest into the mailbox at the post office, this for no reason besides being totally insane, and his wickedness, yes, because since childhood he'd been wicked, a child who was never touching or sweet, threatening them like a dog about to bite them, honestly, a kid like that, how many times, because the two older boys had left—they were both almost the same age and him much younger—his parents, finding themselves alone with him in the house, had been terrorized by this young man who'd become big and brutal, *the last*, the one they'd always called *the last*, his parents not realizing that with a nickname like that they'd set themselves up very early on for a hell of a backlash, which had followed, the kids having grown up too fast, the father and the mother aging even faster; the father had been thunderstruck by the speed of his deterioration, as soon as he retired, withering at an exemplary speed—the muscles melting away and soon leaving nothing visible under the skin but a bone structure made of angles and projections, cracks, a man who still had to haul around his tired and fading body for years, though he felt it would soon be no help to him in the face of his sons, especially when, after the hospital, he'd had to take that lunatic Stutter back in—this *last* of the three that he decidedly loved the least—because Christophe had demanded it, he who took himself for a boss now that Denis, the only intelligent son they'd had and who they'd hoped would turn out better in life than the others and better than themselves, had gone away over some business in which he was only a victim, shut away for almost ten years because a woman always comes and brings misery to men who should have made something of themselves.

Even so, no point in painting too gloomy a picture, the three brothers hadn't had an unhappy childhood. It had been quite the opposite, even, a simple life where the parents let you to go outside when you want and don't make you do too much homework. They were left in peace, in any case the parents always had other things to think about than looking after them, as they'd had to explain several times to school principals taken aback by their indifferent reaction upon being told their kids had to be transferred to a different school due to behavior that was, the administration said, inappropriate. Their lives as children had been made up of games and fresh air, hours riding bikes with their cousins and then, later, in their teenage years, riding scooters, then riding motorcycles even if they didn't have a license, and very soon the parties, at barely fourteen, their first beers, their first real scrapes and shady situations, drug deals, schemes, stolen goods. From earlier in their childhood, from the haze of memory, there could also emerge peaceful images of waiting up late for Santa Claus, shivering with excitement under the covers, jumping on the bed dressed like Indians and Zorro, the parents joking with people who came over for an aperitif and with whom they forgot the kids, who from then on raised hell in their room to the general and happy indifference of a family that knew how to disregard its problems and put them out of sight.

31

A smoke—she needs a smoke—and it's not even a thought she has,
nor even a jolt that sends her away from the table to find the purse
she dropped at her feet by the door and that nobody has touched,
as though it's invisible or has blended in with the décor, but yet
another way for her to flee, to buy a few seconds without showing
that she's fleeing; she's simply escaping, for the time it takes to go
to her purse, lean over it and open it to take out her pack of cigarettes and find her lighter, obviously nowhere to be found—the
lighter that's slipped between two things but for fuck's sake what
do I keep in my purse that I can never find anything in it?

But it's true that this purse is too small and deep, that it has
no inside pocket and always, in a jumble at the bottom, house
and office keys, three USB drives, who knows what they're doing there, same for two packets of tissues that she's never opened
and that have been with her for months, a datebook she almost
never opens, a phone charger she uses two or three times a day—as
though she couldn't leave one at the office—a compact smiling at
her from the bottom of the bag with Audrey Hepburn's impish
eyes, some Bic pens whose caps don't match the color of their ink,
a renewal prescription for her birth control pill and an anti-anxiety
drug, some scraps of paper with phone numbers scrawled on them,
she doesn't remember whose they are, a pack of honey candies,
and finally she lays a hand on the lighter, pulls it from the purse

which she goes to set on the sofa in the living room next to her daughter, alarmed by her mother's arrival which pulls her for a second out of the enclosed space of her movie; then Marion quickly turns away, takes a cigarette and sticks it between her lips, lights it and grips the pack in her hand as though she's about to crush it, for the time it takes her to return to the dining room, without even thinking of smoking outside as she'd do under ordinary circumstances; and neither Ida nor Patrice is about to criticize her for it, nor even to be surprised, she lights her cigarette and breathes in the smoke, closing her eyes, her chest swells, you can hear her deep breathing, it lasts a very short time because Marion hasn't stopped moving, no, on the contrary, she's already come back to the table and, after setting the pack and the lighter down next to her, as though she needs her refills, as though she'll barely finish the cigarette burning between her lips before starting in on another, yes, she's sat down, pulling her chair as close to the table as possible, pressing herself very firmly against the backrest, arm folded, holding her elbow in the palm of her right hand while the fingers of her left seem to cling to the cigarette she's about to smoke, as if to tell the two brothers—and maybe Patrice too—that she'll stay planted there, that she won't flee, that she won't dodge anything, that she can face them to the bitter end and that of course she won't give them the gift of showing that she could ever tremble before them, before what they have to say, not even before the way they're going to say it, because what she also knows perfectly well is how they're going to tell it, distilling it slowly and lavishly, not coldly but no doubt cynically, the better to measure the effect each word has on her, ringing out like a revelation or a knife slash or, more simply, an insult.

And now that she's seated and smoking, not paying attention to her cigarette, disregarding the ash that finally falls in front of her, Christophe steals one from her without even asking her permission,

Go ahead, Marion, tell me to fuck off,

then he takes her lighter, lights the cigarette, and

Tell me you didn't give me permission to bum a smoke,

he just stares at Marion, venturing suddenly that she wouldn't believe it but nonetheless it's true, yes, it's true, we were happy to see you were doing well… You were always more clever than the average. At the same time, nobody was surprised, you were always in it for yourself, isn't that right? Doesn't she look out for herself? It's to Patrice that he's directed the question, Bergogne who's stung because he knows the answer all too well, the question that isn't a question and that he wasn't expecting, an affirmation both amused and insidious that's not meant to be answered; Christophe isn't waiting for anything, that's clear, in any case he's already turned away from Patrice—You were like that with the girls. You know they didn't care for the way you ditched them all, your old sisters… They knew you only cared about yourself, but still, to turn your back on them like that after all you'd been through… ride or die, right? wasn't it you who used to say that all the time?

Marion doesn't flinch. She grinds out her cigarette and chooses not to respond; she can feel Bergogne's presence and it's maybe the only thing she's clinging to, the only one that really hurts her: how he must be hearing what the other is tossing out. She broods over all kinds of words that she swells up, that she's ready to toss back, go ahead, asshole, keep going, you shitty little creep you don't scare me and I'm not ashamed, no, I've been through what I've been through—her lips burn to say it, she turns it over for a moment in her mouth, on her tongue, it whistles through her teeth and all of a sudden it comes out just as clearly and powerfully as she'd imagined it. She says it while staring at Christophe, her eyes shining—with what? tears, anger?—separating each word, each syllable, so precisely and so slowly that even she's surprised, go ahead, no really, go ahead, feel free, you can keep going all you want, I've been through what I've been through and I'm not ashamed of that. But she doesn't call him an asshole or any other name, she doesn't need to insult him, her voice holds the scorn she feels for him, no need to sully herself by adding more, no, she deals the blows with a voice that's not cold but blank, direct, unembellished—go ahead, old friend, don't let me stop you, go ahead, you seem to know everything, tell us what it is to be a whore, if that's what you're talking about, and to be pregnant at fourteen too, if you know go ahead, tell us, you can tell us too… And him, with his smile on his lips, jubilant—vaguely triumphant to be shocking who here? Bergogne?—he listens to her and takes pleasure in seeing her anticipate everything he was going to say, when she spits at him that he can also tell them how she and her friends emptied out the bourgeois lady's house where one of them worked, how they set it on fire to cover up that they'd stolen the clothes, the jewels, the precious objects which they resold,

Go ahead, old friend, don't let me stop you,

and tell them how she blackmailed family men by convincing them she had a baby on the way that they were going to have to acknowledge, because she liked the power it gave her over them, she savored this vengeance on the power of men, the violent and ferocious rebellion that gloated in the defeated faces of these bourgeois sloshing around in their certitudes and their comfort, no, no regrets about that, she can say it without blushing and she feels able to repeat it in front of her daughter and in front of Bergogne, without shame but without any particular pride either, it was her youth, her anger, her rage, she's not ashamed of the anger and the rage that saved her life; and her,

Go ahead, call me a whore in front of my husband,

thinking,

little shit, you think I'm a whore because you never fucked me, there's the truth; all the guys I stole from and cheated on at least they did, they fucked me as many times as you dreamed of it, some of them so well I could've stayed with them and believed they were the men for me, yes, there were some among them who deserved to be loved and not betrayed like I did to them—the violence, then, of that bygone time that she presses down so deep that now she feels neither the disgust nor the dread, unlike the way it's happened for years, when that dead world jumps out at her in the middle of the night, it happens, yes, it comes back, leaving her as lonely and terrified when it does as a little kid who confuses imagination and reality, kneading and grinding them both into a heavy new kind of cruelty that belongs to both worlds.

And then there's Bergogne's voice coming toward her,

Marion, I don't care about any of that. I don't give a shit.

She turns to him, they're side by side but turned toward each other, facing each other. She realizes that she's never seen her husband's face so close, nor his eyes with such clarity, such truth. She can't believe how bright and soft she finds them, with that trust they show her and this near absence of aggressiveness, how full of—what is it, is it still love? She doesn't know. But what she's certain of is that Patrice feels no pity or scornful sentiment toward her, he's incapable of scorn or condescension, and in this moment she thinks there's something precious and rare in him, like—yes, as silly an idea, perhaps, as the one that ascribes purity to children, as though their supposed innocence isn't an invention by adults exhausted by their own turpitude. But she sees no turpitude or duplicity in Bergogne's gaze; she can barely make out the brutality of anger and incomprehension, and not for a minute does she imagine what happens in him, sometimes, when he gets lost in the morass of his desires and he's unable to control his impulses, when he lets himself spill over with the resentment and almost the hatred he has toward her out of loneliness. This she doesn't realize, not to this extent, just as he doesn't realize what his wife went through before meeting him, what she needs to unburden herself of and recover from. So what if he doesn't understand his wife any more today than he would have understood the young girl she clearly used to be, yes, he feels it at his core, everything has told him so since he's known her, from her silence to the way she's always evaded explanations or stories about her youth, about her childhood, about her parents or her friends, places from childhood, things she'd studied.

At first, back when they saw each other not in La Bassée but in town, about fifty kilometers from here, at restaurants where nobody knew them, where they were both taking a chance on an encounter that neither of them really believed in, him not daring to dream of her love or even her attraction, her not daring to hope to remake her life with a man who'd offer to relieve her of her name, guaranteeing her a place to take a rest from her life—not even realizing that, like her mother, she was claiming her independence and in the same motion falling under the protection of a man she would despise for the very security he claimed to offer her—so at first she evaded any question, any incursion into her life story, and just once, after she'd taken him dancing, after they'd drunk too much wine and Armagnac, had she laughed to recall her mother and the way she used to hide bottles of alcohol in the cabinets under the sink, her despair and her tragic and above all tragically predictable end—veins open in the bathtub filled with foamy water in a hotel room she couldn't afford.

And now he hears the way she answers Christophe, with her scandalized resolve, that tone that's hers alone when she's looking down on the person she's addressing, yes, this tone Bergogne knows,

Go ahead, you can keep going, I'm not scared, I'm not ashamed, I've been through what I've been through.

with that way she has of turning toward Bergogne as though she can no longer stand his staring at her, as though she feels he's ordering her to explain herself and her life,

I've been through what I've been through,

the same words cracking and trembling with a pain or rather a fragility that vibrates, a faltering that doesn't ask for forgiveness or anything else, only that note be taken,

I've been through what I've been through,

suggesting that none of this is worth the trouble—who can really believe he is the sum of his actions, that he is forever all he has done?—she doesn't want forgiveness, she wants to let this part of her life die, none of which she feels living in her, none of which survives in her, she knows, no images, no echo, nothing but the obstinacy she remembers and that's branded inside of her, yes, to flee, to tear herself from the nothingness that was her life, and her voice shakes so hard that for the first time in ages, neither of them knowing how it happens, Marion and Patrice Bergogne see their hands find each other under the table, their fingers joining together, him amazed at how transported he feels by an upheaval stronger than anything, rocked to the point of anger and hatred against these three guys, letting his concern for Christine flicker into a possible oblivion, as though all of that is fading, dispersing into the depths of abstract possibility, as though on some level Christine has never been anything but a dream, an illusion, as though there's only this bolt of lightning in the middle of the night—Marion has just enough time to notice the bandage on Patrice's finger, she knits her brow, maybe she lets a word escape, shoots Patrice a questioning look, but he just pulls his hand away, and then Denis's voice, sweet, syrupy,

Well, we should eat something, no?

turning to Christophe,

Don't forget the two others, go bring them something, I don't know if they'll have remembered to eat, our two artists.

And it's Christophe's voice, even as he gets up and goes into the kitchen to bring out the meal, that takes over—your name is Patrice, is that right? Tell me, it must not be so much fun to work in farming right now, with the suicides and everything, seems like there's tons of guys who've committed suicide, dropping like flies is what it sounds like—you know any, any suicides? How about you, do you sometimes think about...? Denis shrugs,

You kidding? This is a solid guy. Can you imagine Marion marrying a guy who isn't? You think our Marion would marry the first schmuck who came along? No, Marion made the right choice, that's for sure... Right? We can... I mean, well, you two had no choice but to meet each other, even if... you're so different. Patrice, don't take this the wrong way, but you're not exactly... You don't mind if I'm frank with you, if we're frank with each other... well, you see... you're not exactly Marion's type.

And the voice continues to spread its cloud of poison and Bergogne's hand trembles, stirs, Bergogne letting his fingers run along the table to his knife—a knife with a long tapered blade, perfect for meat, no question, whose handle he takes, around which his hand closes. Denis lowers his eyes and watches him do it, Marion watches him do it; now she puts her hand on his—a protective, gentle gesture, as though she wants, with her hand so much smaller than her husband's, to take it, to protect it—he loosens his grip and lets the knife slip from his fingers, and under the bandage the pain starts to flare again, it's he who no longer dares look at Marion: her hand on his is a comfort so great he wishes the whole universe could boil down to this image and this feeling.

32

But neither the image nor the comfort nor the universe will last any longer than it takes for a champagne bubble to rise to the surface of a crystal flute and burst on contact with the air—and Denis doesn't allow the silence to take root, soon it's his turn to raise his voice to make sure he'll be heard, because from the kitchen, where he's gone, Christophe is shouting to Marion—who isn't answering—to find out if she has a dish or a Tupperware to bring some food next door, and the hinges, the creaking of the cupboard doors, the doors that slam when they close, the utensils Christophe is moving around in a racket that covers Denis's voice, all force him to speak so loudly that after a few seconds he gives up and decides to keep quiet, he who'd started his sentence and has to keep it to himself, and who, when Christophe has finished, can finally address Bergogne, because now it's to him that he wants to speak, not to explain to him the why of their presence, but

I get it, you see these guys show up at your home,

with a sympathetic air,

I can tell you're not happy, that's only natural,

to tell him how sorry he is, almost aggrieved, by everything that's happening,

What do you expect, it's not like we came from just down the street, we couldn't allow ourselves to stop by like this without knowing we'd be welcomed…

Now he turns to Marion, shooting her a look meant to be at once complicit and sorry to have gone through all that's happening, yes, they had no choice, as though they've had to do all of this because of her mistake, forced by Marion, and, turning away from Patrice completely now, he continues, laying into Marion more firmly than before, abandoning all formality so that something of a reproach rings out in his voice,

That's how it is, you see.

but without the unctuousness or the sweetness he's preferred to affect until now,

Ten years, Marion, that's not enough to forget the birthdays and the dates that matter.

showing himself to be inflexible,

There are some dates in life that matter,

almost blunt,

You know that?

And while he leaves his questions hanging in space, he pours himself a glass of champagne as though having spoken has exhausted him or made him disgusted with himself, forcing him to be silent, while Christophe reappears so that there's no pause, just as a partner would pop up in a performance that two duettists have gone to great trouble to perfect over long months, so that the speed, the effects, are synchronized and almost choreographed, one always taking over right when the other stops talking. He's holding a pot in which he's put some sweetbreads and mushrooms, well, he laments, I couldn't find anything better, as though he wants to apologize, even if nobody is paying attention to him, barely disrupted by the odor that might have awakened everyone's hunger if only they were aware of being hungry. But no, and Christophe, picking out a peanut, still standing, as though he's about to leave in a moment, to Patrice,

You know, it's not like we came from next door.

his voice muffled and overtaken by Marion's, which doesn't let him finish, Marion raising her voice to hurl words in his face that not even she saw coming, surprised by the force with which she launches them, where do you think you are, what are you doing here, all three of you, always hanging around all three of you, like kids, you're too old to be hanging out with each other all the time, what is it you really want, you're not gonna get anything, nothing at all—Marion who hasn't heard her voice go up a notch, her anger bursting out in accents that are almost shrill, ragged, as though this time her shock is well behind her and there's no more question of letting herself be bullied, no, nothing doing, that's enough, Patrice looks at her and the anger comes back to him too, in his hands, in his face, he feels the strength and the right to speak for both of them, to say, where he thinks *I,* a *we* that unites them and draws them up in the same anger, you're going to get the hell out of here and leave us alone, now you're going to leave us alone and get the fuck out of here you have no—

But Christophe has slowly put the pot on the table and shrugs his shoulders, as though he doesn't understand the words being said to him, as though he's shocked by what he's hearing, or hurt, perhaps disappointed by the tone in which wife and husband have spoken to them. All the same, he doesn't seem to be asking himself any questions. He continues and, imperturbable and theatrical, takes his jacket from the back of the chair, just smiles at Marion and Patrice—I'll take my jacket, mustn't catch a cold. You know, Marion, he continues as he picks up the pot, we know you didn't ask us to come, we know that. But we... that's how we are, we don't like this, such manners, these ways of... the way you left, see. When you had problems, we... well, I mean, Denis, he came, he helped you out, how many times did he help you out? You can't say he didn't. Can you? And, turning toward Patrice,

When you think back on tonight, remember that we're not necessarily the assholes here. Appearances, for what it's worth...

He stays like this for a few seconds, maybe waiting for a response, but neither Marion nor Patrice says anything, letting him believe he's just had the last word, the one to deliver a truth they'll be stuck with, except he didn't plan on the silence, which he intended to be long and sepulchral, not lasting long enough to produce the desired effect, because from the living room bursts Ida's voice, calling her mother, the way children call when they have some need to satisfy or problem to solve, with a loud and bossy voice that doesn't bother with politeness or moderation, almost a shout,

Mom!

leaving everyone frozen for a few seconds, long enough for Ida to get the feeling of not having been heard,

Mom! my movie isn't working!

but instead of answering her daughter, Marion doesn't release Christophe and Denis, she takes another cigarette, lights it, tosses her lighter nervously and the three men stare at her as though they don't believe she hasn't heard her daughter, and yet she really seems not to have heard, she remains tensed toward the two men whom she attacks more directly this time—what are you hoping for, what do you expect? how long have you been spying on me? how long have you been watching us?

Marion, your daughter's calling you.

It's Christophe who says this.

And Patrice who gets up—leave it, he says, I'll go.

He gets up, without Marion really noticing. Now it's just his anger keeping him upright, and while Bergogne heads toward the living room and approaches his daughter he hears Marion's questions behind him, still the same ones returning, attacking and demanding to know when they knew she was here, how long they've been following her, when they decided on this day and this way of showing up, when they had the idea and made the plan for this commando mission; Bergogne isn't even surprised that she asks neither why they've been tracking her nor what they have against her—as though, of course, she knows—just the details, how they did it rather than why, just as it doesn't surprise him that he no longer cares at all, suddenly certain that he doesn't want to know more, he who just a few minutes ago felt a desire open up inside of him to know everything, as though, because it was within reach, he had to fill the void he'd so often imagined, invented, filled in out of the affectionate madness that had tortured him for years with the pain of not knowing, not what Marion had been through but who she was, and that clearly lived in the folds of what she hid from him.

And now he doesn't care. The present matters more than a past that doesn't exist any more than a cinder in the eye alters reality: it's the vision that changes, the eye that burns, that fills up with tears, but that's it, the world itself hasn't changed. Marion is the way she is, the past doesn't change anything—yes, these guys could disappear now and he could hold himself to this decision to not ask his wife anything, and resume his life and his ignorance with the same blind and loving faith, here, right now—because he too had his share of stories to keep quiet. So suddenly these questions needle him much less than the wound in his finger, they're all the more distant and bustling only in the background, as the breaking waves wash away the rocks of a cliff, working tirelessly, though unnoticed in daily life, at its erosion; Bergogne acts as though this persistent buzz doesn't exist in his thoughts, he focuses on Ida, whom he finds in the living room, not sitting on the sofa but crouched in front of the television and the DVD player, which she's opened, closed again and restarted—he has time to see that she's left the headphones on the sofa and that you can still make out the shape of her body in the folds of the leather. He crouches next to her and takes the remote. They don't say anything at first, then okay, it's not working, what's wrong with the DVD, is it dirty? And without thinking he blows on the DVD, cleans it with his handkerchief—like his father before him Bergogne still keeps broad cloth handkerchiefs deep in his pants pockets, and it hasn't occurred to him that cloth squares deep in pockets are hotbeds of germs, he doesn't care, his practicality tells him he's right and here's the proof, here he is wiping the DVD, putting it back in the player and restarting it, but it still doesn't work, the player won't play the movie anymore,

Dad, who is that?

Bergogne pretends not to have heard. He turns over the DVD and turns it over again as if to try to find a scratch or whatever else might allow him to understand why the playback has stopped right in the middle of the movie, but in reality, without his even really knowing it, he's determined to check the DVD on both sides so he doesn't hear his daughter's voice insisting, though without speaking loudly because she doesn't want to be heard in the next room,

Dad, who is that?

and, since he doesn't answer and starts rummaging through the DVD cases to find the one for this movie, she stays quiet for a few seconds, doesn't help, surprised only to see him act as though he hasn't heard and doesn't want to answer her, which worries her greatly, maybe also makes her angry,

Dad?

while he, by way of answer, takes another DVD from Ida's video library, under the player, turning the case over and over again as though the only solution is to put on another movie, there we go, *Beauty and the Beast*, that's a good one.

No, it's black-and-white.

You don't like it? I thought you liked it. It was a gift from Tatie Christine.

It scares me.

Yet Bergogne isn't listening to his daughter, he puts the DVD in the player and prepares to press play,

Dad, who is that?

Nobody.

Why does Mom know them?

It's nobody.

I don't want them to hurt Tatie.

They won't.

So why are they angry at Mom?

They're not angry at Mom. Watch your movie.

I don't want this one.

It's this or nothing, Ida.

Why are you mad at me?

I'm not mad at you.

Do they want to hurt Mom?

No. They won't hurt anybody.

and once he's started the movie and the opening credits crackle weakly in the headphones, but maybe also for himself, to find a comfort in it that he needs too, as much as she does, he holds his daughter tight in his arms, so tight he can feel her shoulders fold into his chest. He doesn't know why he says it, but he can't help it, words murmured into her ear, this little girl who wasn't expecting it—he who never says anything, here he is trying to reassure her; he who never says anything, here he is trying to explain to her that he'll protect her; he who never says anything, here he is trying to explain that her mother isn't afraid of anything, that they're not afraid of anything, that the men are going to leave, that Christine will come join them. He holds her tight in his arms to tell her that Dad will always be here, that they'll always be together, that he loves her—yes, that word trembling in his mouth—but he doesn't even know whether he says these loving words, so sweet, so rare for him, so comforting, so that his daughter will hear them as words of love and reassurance or if, by saying them, he's only hoping she won't hear how the tone has risen in the next room, because Bergogne is speaking to his daughter to hide from himself that he wants to hear and refuses to hear what's happening in the dining room, that he'd like to understand and that everything in him refuses to understand, and over his own voice he lets Denis's and Marion's words fly, their sentences, her answering him toe to toe and not ceding an inch to the bursts of phrase that ring out and burn the air in the house, passing from one room to another, what could you possibly want now, what do you want, what do you want, and the words rain down and Bergogne wants to protect his daughter from them, as though he wants to shelter them, him and her, from the bombs being dropped above their heads with the

intention of striking them, with words that don't even concern
them, slicing into the anonymity of their life that asks nothing but
to take place far away from this outburst of which they understand
neither the meaning nor the violence, Denis spitting his hatred and
his rancor without worrying about making a shameless or disturb-
ing spectacle of himself, sending out crackling bursts, louder and
louder, his voice rising to reveal contemptuous inflections and almost saturated with his certitude—Marion, ten years behind bars,
ten years with nobody to tell me where you were, don't you want
to know what I went through in there, what it's like in there, no,
of course not, you don't care what it's like, like everyone else, you
don't care, nobody cares if it makes you feel any better, you're not
the only one, you've heard about the state of the prisons and even
if you thought about me from time to time I'm sure you found
it funny to know there are rats in jail, fleas, crabs, filth that eats
your body all day long, Marion, you think I didn't think about
your birthday and about you, you really thought I was going to
let it go—and Bergogne finally loosens the embrace, he strokes his
daughter's hair, tells her to go sit and watch her movie and that
in a little bit these guys will leave, definitely, it's going to be fine,
they've come to say some things but after that they're going to go,
and, as he says it, he feels his heart beating very hard in his chest,
until it feels like his legs are about to give out, like he's going to
end up falling and his breath is going to just stop.

He's on the verge of choking and yet he repeats to his daughter
that everything is fine—choked, maybe, to see that she seems to
believe him, that she's settling down on the sofa—and choked
too by that which, turning around, he glances at the facing wall,
where it meets the other door, the one that goes through the living
room to the patio, choked for a very short moment—yes, he stops
and turns pale—the idea is there immediately—against the wall,
on its pegs, the cartridges and the game bag that should be in the
cabinet just underneath, and he sees the hunting rifle on the wall,

with its leather shoulder strap describing an arc from the barrel to the butt—the time he spends oiling it, caring for it on Sunday afternoons after coming home from hunting—and he has to hear Marion's voice starting to yell in the next room to emerge from this torpor, frightened at what he thinks he has to do, at what he tells himself he's going to do, seeing no other solution, but no, he shouldn't, for now Marion is trying not to shout but it's still something like a shout breaking through beneath her voice, and that's why he returns to the dining room, she's insulting Denis and telling him this is just like him, to wait for the day of her birthday to show up and ruin her again, to ruin her like he always does—how long is this going to last, how long are you going to come like this?

And when he comes back to the dining room, Patrice sees how mad Marion is this time, how wild with anger. She doesn't even see him, her eyes are trained on Denis, staring him down. But Denis takes the time to see him; Denis turns to him, confident, calm, leaving Marion alone with her anger. And there's Christophe, standing by the table with his pot in both hands, waiting for who knows what and no doubt thinking it's no longer time to linger over the spectacle of a salvo between Marion and Denis, as though all the interest he found in it has just dried up and he knows he won't find any more. So he makes up his mind to finally go to the house next door, to give the two others this damn slop that's going cold in the pot, opening the French door suddenly and letting in a great gust of cold air from outside, which shocks them, perhaps, but does everyone some good.

33

In the house next door, Christophe is surprised to be greeted by music. An atmosphere nothing like the one at Marion's, to be sure. The music sounds like something more or less classical, let's say that at first it hits his ear as classical but he can hear there's something different, not clashing and not unpleasant, but as though the melody has started down a totally unpredictable path.

Before entering he knocked on the door, not the way he did this afternoon but with a slight hesitation, as though he was intimidated or hesitant about what he was doing, as though he was afraid to disturb or felt somehow loath to impose, which his next action contradicts immediately, since without waiting for an answer he opens the door and enters the house. He puts the pot on the kitchen table, amid all the utensils and cake ingredients, and as he hears the music he doesn't know if it's this that he's listening to, that's keeping him ramrod-straight in the middle of the kitchen, or if he's waiting to make out the voices of his brother and the neighbor, more likely his brother's, because he wonders how he's managed to keep the other under his control, unless he's just listening in the hopes of overhearing words that aren't meant for him, as though he suspects this woman and his brother of having conversations he can't even imagine, or else maybe he doesn't know if he's really waiting for something or staying there out of stupefaction, fatigue, out of a need to be alone, to take a few seconds for himself to do nothing.

But the music will guide his steps, it's coming from the studio, just like that white light that shines all the way into the kitchen.

Christophe advances and is surprised to find his brother and the Bergognes' neighbor so calm, chatting like two old friends, her sitting on a stool next to a desk covered in notebooks and pencils, and his brother standing in front of the paintings with a bottle of beer, already almost empty, in his hand. She's drinking a beer too, but she's only drunk half—he recognizes the brown glass bottle of an amber brand he likes. He's as surprised as they are to see him arrive, he can tell he's just interrupted them, he doesn't quite know what to say so he just says he's brought some sweetbreads, not much, the quantities weren't planned for so many people, but anyway, just to say,

I left a pot on the kitchen table, you'll probably have to reheat it a bit.

and then he stays there without adding anything or moving, planted there, and it's Stutter who takes over,

Yeah, great,

before going silent in his turn because he has nothing to add.

After a moment, still too long, as though all of a sudden Christophe is almost intimidated or surprised without quite knowing what by, he takes a step toward the paintings, takes a look at the tables with the notebooks and drawing sheets, sees the cans of acrylic paint on the floor, products he doesn't know, oils, varnishes, bottles, bags of pure pigment. He does this quickly, and quickly he gives a hint of a smile,

We were worried about you, we thought, the two of you alone over here without anything to nibble on… But you're doing just fine, I see, with a nice little beer, some nice little classical music in the background, life's pretty good, eh?

He goes to the stereo, finds the CD and reads the booklet and turns the case over as if to locate some explanation he didn't find the first time; he murmurs, Caplet, don't know him, and then,

This is what we're listening to?

Yes.

Stutter… if you don't mind… I wanted to talk to you in the kitchen, just a word… Do you mind?

He smiles at Christine, approaches his brother and takes him by the arm, leading him with a quick strong movement, which catches the younger of the two off guard. It's not that he resists, but he recoils very slightly, looks almost questioningly at Christine, who can't believe it—are they going to leave her alone, are they so insane that they'd risk letting her, why not, make a phone call? She could, couldn't she? Even if she doesn't know how to capitalize on such a short time, because she knows very well, just as they do, that this risk isn't really a risk at all, just as she knows she could or could not attempt it, not yet aware that in a few seconds she'll go searching in the mess of her desk, between the notebooks, among the pencils and the tin boxes; and already she's moving toward the table, not hesitating, or maybe she's even pretending to hesitate, glancing toward the kitchen, then no, quickly she picks up the box cutter, keeping it in her hand a few seconds, too many, an eternity, she grips it tight in her palm then slips it into her pants pocket— her blue box cutter whose rusty blade is still sharp enough to hurt anyone who might attack her.

She stays still for a moment, almost chilled by what she's just dared to do; then she decides to join them in the kitchen, because she doesn't like knowing they're here, wondering what they might be talking about, not understanding what Christophe is talking about, he who's just explaining, murmuring so she doesn't hear, how Marion and her husband are wallowing in an epic sulk—he's like an idiot, doesn't understand anything, and her, if you saw her, she was basically shitting kittens because she'd never have thought we were capable of doing this, that's for sure, we thought she was gonna start crying and asking for forgiveness but no, you know her, she's always thought we were idiots, me for sure, she's always taken me for an idiot, but she played Denis for an idiot too, she thought we weren't clever enough to get a bead on her. Stutter might ask for details about Marion's reaction, obviously he'd have liked to be there for the moment she came through the door and found herself face to face with Christophe and Denis, yes, with Denis especially, of course, how she reacted when she saw Denis, that he'd have loved to know, and they laughed, both of them, Christophe and him, Stutter, who put on their mother's voice to say ah yes I would have loved to be a little fly on the wall to see the face she made. Did she talk right away? did she wait for Denis to speak? was he the one to say hello first? did he get to say hello to her? or else,

We meet again,

or maybe,

How's it going, Marion?

or even,

Weren't expecting to see me?

And her response. Did she stay there with her trap shut, as they say, crucified to her door, coat still on her back, flabbergasted at the set table, the pretty tablecloth, the presents and the two men whom she didn't think for an instant she'd be seeing tonight? He'd have liked to see, to hear for himself whether she'd managed to respond right away, to not let herself be overcome by the surprise. Did she get angry when she realized they were detaining the neighbor? or what, what did she do? give herself the luxury of acting snooty?

He asks all the questions jockeying in his head, he talks fast and doesn't hear the answers. He thinks of questions, asks them, knowing his brother won't necessarily answer, but he comes back to them, he wants to know how Marion reacted and especially how he, Denis, mastered this moment he's been waiting for for so long—yeah, I mean, to wait so long for this and not crack when it finally happens, did he crack, did he get angry or did he manage to keep his cool instead, with that patient hate-filled smile he gets when he's really pissed off, tell me, what?

Because after all these years he'd had to spend constructing all kinds of possible reunions, each crazier than the last, almost delirious, futile, vexing, nonetheless always bringing him something like comfort or even compensation for the fact that in reality he knew he had almost no chance of laying his hands on her again, for years Denis had let his mind wander to fill up that impossible wait, carrying it out rapturously, imagining a whole raft of more or less plausible occasions, and improbable ones too; but it didn't matter, from his prison, the day they told him she'd run off, Denis had had to imagine Marion would do everything she could to make sure he never found her, it'd be just like her to get married in order to hide behind a brand new name, to move on from the one he knew her under, which he'd surely use to try to track her down in all the phone books he could get his hands on, knowing it was useless to look because if she didn't leave France she'd still make sure to get herself out of harm's way, to find somewhere safe, some place so remote nobody would dream of finding her there. Except that with chance, a bit of luck, you never know. And good old chance had smiled upon him, had risen to the challenge. That good old stroke of fate had served up on a silver platter the chance for him to track Marion all the way to a karaoke stage, the kind she'd always liked and that he'd forbidden her to frequent a few months after they met because he was sick of seeing her strut around like a slut for all the guys who came to rub up on her as if he didn't exist.

So it had taken a place like that for him to finally find her, irony of fate, twist of fate, hell of a good show by chance, doing things so nicely after so nicely undoing them.

But Christophe has to stop talking: Christine has just come into the kitchen.

She observes them, silent, inquisitive. A vague glance at the pot, as though she's tossing all her scorn for them into it, as though that scorn, shown by the curl of her lip, mingled with the smell of sweetbreads and mushrooms, of the sauce, might just make her vomit. As if all the calm Stutter thought he felt between them, the lull he thought would settle between them, has just disappeared all at once, because Christine turns up now with the hardness she displayed all afternoon, the same haughty distrust with which she addressed them; she's taken up her brusque voice again, or rather it's that unwavering voice that's taken her up, letting nothing through besides, perhaps, in a bass line beneath the surface, exasperation tinged with cold anger:

Is this going to be much longer?

As long as it takes, says Christophe.

What do you want with Marion?

…

What do you want with her?

There's… food. Then you'll go to bed. Tomorrow you'll wake up and it'll be like you just had a dream. You'll forget our faces, even Stutter's. You'll forget everything and it'll be just fine.

Answer me. What do you want with Marion? What did she do to you?

You're that interested in your neighbor?

No answer. And yet in this moment Christine lets her anger circle around Marion, as though this idea is coming back to her that it's not really the three brothers who are guiltiest of their being here but above all Marion; as though Christine wants to find some attenuating circumstance for the three men, because she imagines in the back of her mind that you don't go in for this kind of adventure—detaining a whole hamlet, not to even mention the death of the dog—without having reasons that are necessarily a bit *valid* for doing so, not legally or morally speaking, of course, because nothing could justify the threat, the terror, nothing, not in anyone's eyes, but maybe it's possible to see them, these reasons, not so far from thinking that where there's smoke there's fire and not so far from trying to understand them, these reasons, or to imagine understanding why these three guys decided to show up here one night with their bizarre look, wavering between agitation and conviction, awkwardness and determination, at once violent and fragile, at once erratic and unconvincing in their actions even as they follow to the letter a plan mapped out by the eldest brother with a method, a strategy, a goal; yes, in spite of it all, one could try to put oneself in their place, insofar as it would be possible—would it be possible to put oneself in their place? could Christine try for a few minutes to understand them, to follow the course of their reasoning, not to excuse them but to make the mystery of their presence, or of the violence of that presence, tolerable, as though it's a matter of defusing the anxiety in which she's being held by the incomprehension of having to endure an episode in which she feels increasingly as though she's merely an incidental element, all the more thrown by the absurdity of the situation, sometimes letting panic overtake her, wondering only if these men will go so far as to kill her over a story that's not even hers.

And it's because it's as though she feels they're reading into her thoughts that Christine closes her eyes. But it's just a blink, she doesn't really close her eyes, or rather she doesn't keep her eyelids closed long enough. She opens them again immediately, a reaction to the flood of light that suddenly enters the kitchen—already the two brothers are no longer interested in her, they've turned their eyes toward the French door, all three of them were mesmerized when the very white light coming from outside lit them up, as if stripping them bare, sweeping its beams over the house; they felt the impression of a flash—but it's not so blinding: just the headlights of a car.

Two cars entering the yard.

The two brothers understood better than Christine what's happening, that's clear, because it takes her an extra fraction of a second. But it also takes the brothers a bit of time to find the means to react, forgetting Christine and her scorn, relegating her to the background of their concerns, erasing her, forgetting her, the only thing commanding them and absorbing them entirely is that the kitchen has been irradiated by lights invading the space, Christophe and Stutter, Stutter,

What the fuck, what is that, what the fuck is that?

along with this shout that's almost smothered itself in his throat a double movement, first running to the door to go see what's going on and, at the same time, throwing his hand into the pocket of his tracksuit to take out the knife—which he does, the knife is out but Stutter's fist is closed over it, as though restraining himself, he turns back to his brother and most of all to Christine,

Who is that?

accusing her,

Who the fuck is that?

pointing at her nose but not yet brandishing his fist or his knife,

Fucking who is that?

getting angry but no longer having the strength to come back to the two others, even less to Christine at whom he starts screaming, she knows something, it's obvious, and to him it's as though she betrayed them by not warning them that someone else was coming, leaving aside the idea that she can't betray them because she's never been on their side, never been their accomplice. Christophe has taken his brother by the forearm and is holding him tightly,

Calm down, calm down,

continuing,

Calm down and put that away, okay?

Who is that?

Stutter facing his brother,

Who is that?

insisting, as though he feels betrayed by his brother too—as though his brother obviously knew better than he did who might show up even though they weren't expecting anyone—but were they not expecting anyone? were they so sure nobody was coming? why did they tell themselves nobody was coming and that it'd be just the family tonight, why did they take it as a given that there wouldn't be guests? what do they know? why, when they talked about it as they had for hours and hours around a table, had Denis and Christophe, usually the only ones to take up those questions, been so quick to dismiss the possibility that guests might join the party—why? You want to know why? How about because it's a weeknight and people have work the next day, because the kid has school, and it can't go on all night, that's why. That's what Christophe wants to yell, so Stutter understands they haven't betrayed anyone and they had their reasons to believe nobody would come bother them, yes, serious reasons, but obviously they couldn't be sure of anything, how did you expect us to be sure nobody would turn up at this hour, tell me, how?

Very quickly Christophe regains control. His voice hardens when he begins to give his brother orders.

I'll go see who it is, I'll welcome them, you be careful.

And, turning to Christine,

Who is it?

Christine doesn't answer.

If you know, say it.

Christine looking Christophe up and down before turning her head away, walking over to the table and taking the pot by the handle,

Who is it?

she takes the pot and raises it to her face, leans over it slightly, breathes it in and goes to put it on the stove; Christine acts as though they're not there and soon the two brothers hear car doors slamming. Christophe's hands are very moist and he rubs them together, palms flat, fingers spread apart on the tails of his jacket, he's uneasy in front of Christine, okay, I'm going, you,

Yes, answers Stutter.

So Christophe exits the house, taking one last look at Christine who doesn't even bother to pretend to notice. No, she's not paying attention, she refuses to, she's staring at the pot on the burner—the bluish flame lighting up Christine's arms and giving them a strange, cold, undefinable tint—but just as quickly she has to turn toward the door, the cold rushes in, a burst of humid air that comes all the way to her and permeates the whole kitchen, the little blue flame dancing more animatedly under the pot, as if excited by the entrance of the air that goes toward the studio and rises at the end of the hall toward the rooms upstairs. Christine knows this, out of instinct she goes to close the door, which is wide open. Only at this moment does she realize that she's all alone: Stutter has gone out behind his brother. She tells herself this is her moment, the only one she'll get, maybe, to run to the telephone, grab it and call the police. This time she's certain that something will happen if she doesn't do anything, how could it not, this idea overwhelms her, the door open, Christophe's voice from outside shrieking at Stutter,

Go! Go the fuck back in!

Stutter begins to go back in but he can't help himself, he has to know, has to see who these people are who are just arriving. He has time to see that it's two women, each in her own car. For now both are nothing but silhouettes in the night but hearing his brother's voice, his haste, he's shot through with the idea that the two women are attractive, he can hear the seductive inflections he knows by heart in his brother's voice, his brother practically running toward the two women, almost cooing already, letting out a good evening,

Good evening,

venomous and wheedling,

I'm Christophe,

and Stutter can't stay on the doorstep and can't see anything more,

An old friend of Marion's,

he knows he should go in and already he's retracing his steps,

We were just waiting for you.

but he has to take a last look at his brother, who he sees walking toward the two women and reaching his hand out. Stutter hears the two girls introduce themselves and he can make out the murderous glance his brother darts at him, without a word,

(Go back in! go back in for the love of god!)

and Stutter finally goes back into Christine's and she's not in the kitchen, and it's as though it grabs him by the throat—where is she? fuck fuck fuck where is she and he doesn't hear the music, doesn't hear anything, his ears are buzzing and he can't hear a single noise, barely the whistle of the flame under the pot and the sweetbreads starting to gurgle over the heat, he barely hears this and thinks to himself that he's fucked up, that's what he's most afraid of, more than the woman fleeing, yes, of having been negligent, of having given his brothers the opportunity to remind him that they can't trust him and that he's clearly not worthy of any respect, of anything at all, and he's so afraid of this that he begins to run and

Hey! hey!

still trying not to ask where are you? where are you? and he runs through the kitchen yelling

Hey!

back to the studio that opens up in front of him, empty, absolutely empty and bathed in its too-white light, atrocious, throwing the colors and shapes of the paintings in his face, the face of the red woman who seems to be appraising him and dismissing him with contempt—but no, he hears in the next room, it's a few meters away, he's not so dumb, very clearly, a breath in one of the adjacent rooms, he knows it, there, there's a bathroom and he sees the door is closed, is it locked, yes, no, he approaches, turns the handle, the woman is inside, he can feel it, it's not complicated,

Hey!

she hasn't had time to go far and he says,

Open the door right now, you have to open the door and come out right now... I don't want to hurt you, I don't want to, open up, open up!

He listens at the door, ear pressed against the wood, he hears the woman's trembling and tear-soaked voice—is it possible she's crying? her? and above all,

Hello,

her voice repeating the same

Hello…

as though on the other end nobody has picked up yet. Now the anger rises in him as soon as he thinks oh fuck fucking bitch what is she doing? fuck fuck she's not calling the cops, she's not calling the cops, I know she's not calling the fucking pigs fuck fuck fuck and he starts yelling through the door and hitting the door, with the flat of his hand, for god's sake, for god's sake what do you want? what do you want? for them to shoot everyone like animals is that what you want? what do you think they'll do if you call the cops huh fuck's sake what do you think they'll do?

34

Living arms coming out of the walls, holding chandeliers; the slow-motion run of the young woman down the corridor, her arms held away from her body as though she's fleeing a film even older than the one in which she's stuck forever; yes, like a lost little red riding hood she crosses the corridor lit by the chandeliers from which arises the flickering fire that will guide her; powerful arms follow the course of her slow, almost impeded run, caught in the soft and sticky cotton of the slow motion, paralyzed by her own astonishment to be crossing, awake, a dream that isn't a dream; and all these arms holding these chandeliers are like fingers pointing at her as much as they point the way; and then, farther on, in a corridor whose too-high ceiling returns her to child size against high walls and immense, immemorial secrets, the open windows and their great drapes whose whiteness is almost phosphorescent, ghostly, dancing in the night wind, and she, dressed so ordinarily—gray, subdued—whose modesty will bring forth her beauty and her humility like a jewel that surpasses all the marvels she'll find here, she moves forward, now, floating above the ground as if demurely, gently levitating, carried by a calm wind coming from who knows where, advancing a few centimeters off the ground and not surprised to be, as though she's being irresistibly carried above herself and above the materiality of her body by a mysterious force or a waking dream—and it must be because it's a dream that, in front of the black wooden door, a man's deep voice murmurs to her in a sweet breath of air: *Belle, I am the door to your room*—all of this in the thickness of an inky black that has swallowed up the screen and out of which voluptuous grays and pure, ample whites sometimes appear by magic, just as the singing that accompanies the film appears in its turn—and it's true, this mystery, its rhythm, the depth of its black and white, Ida didn't want to see them.

But this movie, tonight, she's not afraid of it. On the contrary, it's like a refuge, and Ida thinks to herself that her father was right to make her watch it, because it was a gift from Christine, and so now it's her Tatie that Ida is thinking of, as though Tatie is asking her to be like Belle in the movie, to feel her fear all the way to the end, because they'll have to make it through the night and a world of which they know nothing. Ida feels that what frightens her tonight has a force of attraction that she doesn't know how she could name, nor whether it even has a name, if the curiosity she feels is normal or if she shouldn't find something suspect about it, something dubious, maybe even indecent, rather than this sly attraction that forces her to divert her eyes toward the dining room, which she does without thinking, out of sheer worry or vigilance, out of simple nervousness too; she just glances over from time to time, she hasn't set the volume too loud in her ears because she wants to be ready, alert, the way she imagines the animals in the woods are when her father goes hunting with Christine's dog on Sunday mornings—tonight, she knows a sadness tinted with that disgust she's always felt when her father lays down still-warm pheasants or hares on the sideboard of the kitchen sink—as though in her chest she can hear the beating heart of a hare tracked by the hunting rifle, as though she can make out the sound of rubber boots trampling over dead branches and leaves with an icy crackle, and Rajah's nose moist and very warm, perked up by blood.

But the truth most of all, the only truth now, is that she doesn't like the men who are here, that she's afraid of them, that she knows she should be afraid of them. She's so sure of this that she has to check from time to time that they're still here, she wants to see, she needs to see what they're doing to her parents and to see also how her parents are resisting, because she notes with surprise that all of this is taking too long. She had thought that when her parents were together again they'd find a solution together where words—undeniable, as decisive as weapons—would force these two men to leave, and the other one, at Christine's, to clear off with them, without a word, as though they'd never come. But Ida's too old to believe that her parents can fix everything by mere force of will, she's old enough to know that, like all adults and like children themselves, parents have only a limited power over reality. Yes, she knows that events happen to parents like they do to anyone else, and that their almightiness is a delusion she only pretends to still believe in, out of habit, maybe also out of laziness. She knows her parents are as helpless as she is at this point, but she wants to believe in something, as though her father alone or her mother alone can't do anything but together, with their powers combined, they can, they will, why not, prevail over reality, to make the three men disappear by the simple magic of their union, even though deep down she knows they can't, because after Christophe left she wondered how the one who wanted to give her gifts could stay here by himself for so long without their knowing whether he was dangerous—maybe armed but also quite possibly not—by what power play he was able to remain alone in front of Marion and Patrice, who would have been more than able to subdue him and reverse the roles. But no, the game isn't evenly matched. Even alone with the three of them, Denis is stronger than them, who will never dare hurt him; that's why the others are stronger, it's obvious that they won't hesitate, it's obvious to everyone, the Bergognes, Christine, and especially the three men, who can have their fun with this reality, stretch it in all directions, like a soft dough they can amuse themselves by forming into whatever shape they want.

Ida could spend a long time thinking about this but

Hey there everybody!

she starts, as though she's suddenly been pulled from a kind of reverie, a somnolence, a voice ringing out—a new voice, a woman's—this voice not shaking and so sure of itself, this high voice, amused, altering everything in its path with its strident good cheer,

Hey there everybody!

as though nothing has happened until now, a voice shunting Patrice's and Marion's to the side, of course they didn't dare do anything when it burst into their ears—Ida saw them just get up and exchange a panicked and dismayed look, alarmed, Ida barely saw her mother rub her mouth with her hand and shake her head as though this can't be happening, waiting for Patrice to answer a question she forgot to ask him,

What are they doing here? Why are they here? Did you—

this voice crushing everything in its path,

Hey there everybody, the co-workers are here!

Ida, now, taking the headphones from her ears, losing interest in the movie altogether and leaning over for a better view, from the sofa, of the two women entering like gusts of wind that leave Marion and Patrice frantic for a second, without time to react or figure out what they should do, now watching, with arms dangling, the rapid and almost casual manner, so disconcerting, with which the two brothers have already shifted gears to accommodate a situation they weren't expecting but that they seem instantly able to deal with, with an ease as natural as a magic trick, a game, voilà, change of mask, of rider, they do it so quickly and so fluidly that Marion and Patrice study them with bewilderment and fascination—yes, for a moment it's almost with a kind of mute admiration for this unscrupulous audacity, all this joyous and playful chicanery, this simulation so quickly arranged into fun and games, into a semblance of joy, Christophe continuing,

Quick! Come in quick! it's cold out here in your neck of the woods!

rubbing his hands together to emphasize his ridiculous and stupid phrases that nobody is really listening to, but whose purpose, for him, isn't to make them heard, he knows perfectly well these phrases are stupid, but through them he can shake off that layer of stupor that Marion and her husband can't manage to hide and right away

Good evening, my name is Denis, I'm telling you because it won't be Marion making the introductions—right, Marion? You wouldn't know it but she's awfully shy, our Marion.

the other one continues and Ida doesn't want to hear, just as she doesn't want to hear how Lydie and Nathalie will reply, because she knows them a little, Mom's co-workers, Marion talks about them often, every night or almost. Just as Ida talks about her friends, Mom has to talk about work and the two girls—she says *the two girls* but these are women, not *girls*, because for Ida girls are children or teenagers, but these, these are two women, even two women older than Mom—they're maybe fifty or fifty-five—and to Ida it's as though they've already reached the shore of old age or they'll be there before long, it doesn't matter, Ida can see that Nathalie and Lydie look much older than her mother and that there's also something more banal in their way of being, like all her friends' mothers, who often strike her as banal or rather ordinary, rather short, not very pretty but not ugly either, all dressed basically the same, not badly but not well either, whereas it's obvious, here, between an orange-haired eccentric and her mother, she has another idea of women, a hell of an idea of women, because she knows you can see her mother right away when she arrives somewhere, or rather you can see right away how the air changes and electrifies as soon as she shows up—Ida remembers this with a kind of pride that she had trouble controlling and suppressing in front of everyone, during a school party, when she saw not her mother entering the room where they were rehearsing the end-of-year play, but the men, her friends' fathers, married men whose wives she knew, men who mostly knew her father, who were in the room and who got up without realizing it, staring, blissful, concupiscent, admiring and respectful, in the doorframe, at her mother who had just come in.

It's something she knows, something so singular, almost violent, in people's attention—is her mother that beautiful?

Yes, she's sure of it, but a bizarre kind of beauty that she recognizes not just for the feeling of rapture she gets in front of her, not just for the desire she has to look like her or because she thinks she'll never be that pretty, but by what she feels from what happens when other people lay their eyes on her mother—that little moment's pause they always have the first time they discover her, and that repeats every time, as though each time her beauty explodes in your face, as though you have no chance of getting used to it. And it's maybe because of this that her two co-workers have to make a lot of noise and overdo it when they show up at Marion's, to hold their own in comparison, to keep up appearances, because it's also a fact that you don't necessarily see them when they enter a place, not only because they're older or more banal, it's that they don't dress as well, Ida thinks; and it's no doubt because of this that they exaggerate when they're together, *the two girls,* and if Ida judges her mother harshly sometimes it's because all three of them play at being ditzes, Ida blaming them most of all, the two girls, for forcing her to change her image of her mother, making her into a kind of delayed adolescent who starts to giggle the way the three of them do, with their knowing looks that leave them, Patrice and her, when they come see Marion at home, totally off to the side, as though they don't know this Marion laughing with her girlfriends—voices speaking a bit too loud, laughs ringing out a bit too high, their ways of approaching Ida with excessive gushing, declarations of love, marveling at anything and everything, as they're already getting ready to do, as they're already doing now, doesn't matter which one of them,

My my, look at that spread!

echoed by the other,

This isn't a birthday party he made for you, it's a wedding!

before breaking into a big noisy burst that makes Ida turn off the television and quickly go back to the dining room, because this time she has an idea, or maybe it's barely an idea—more of an impulse—an urge that pops up from somewhere, she doesn't know where, to which she abandons herself completely, breathing deeply, yes, here she goes, she knows what she's going to do, run and cross the dining room as fast as she can with her head down, not only avoiding the people and the words but taking advantage of the general disorder to run to the two women who've just arrived, thinking that if she hurries she can force one of them to hear what she's going to shout, because she's going to shout, she has to, pounce on whichever one is closest to the door and who maybe won't have come into the house yet, or who will maybe still have her hand on the doorknob, the door not closed behind her, to tell her to not close it, to leave, to get back in her car, to scream at her that they shouldn't be here because the men here aren't friends, they took Tatie, they killed Rajah, we're not doing anything because we're terrified of them and they're laughing at us, at the time they're taking to torment us because we're scared of them, of what they want, we don't know what they want or why they decided to stay here like this for the whole party and then afterwards, afterwards what are they gonna do to us, we don't know what they're gonna do to us—no, she doesn't even have the time to think that in any case neither of the two women would believe her if she tried to put her idea into action, she realizes she won't have time, and not just because everything is in her way, her parents themselves, terrified to see her rushing in the way she does and almost trying to restrain her,

Ida,

her mother coming toward her,

Ida,

her mother turned to her, her mother's voice saying,

Ida,

repeating with that cajoling sweetness mixed with anxiety that begs her not to move, not to try anything,

Ida my kitten,

(Ida my kitten doesn't hear anything, Ida my kitten doesn't want to hear anything)

Ida my kitten come here,

and Ida wants to close her eyes and charge and shout,

Ida my kitten,

not listening to her mother who's stammering and trying to hold her back,

Ida my kitten,

Ida brushing aside the thought that her mother preventing her from doing what has to be done, her mother cheating, lying, acting natural, and her father too, both of them, it's all to protect Tatie, but if not then why would they protect these two guys who seem to find this funny and who are bustling around and getting all excited? Ida finds it ridiculous, literally unbelievable, that these two guys could be her mother's friends—could anyone believe that, even Lydie and Nathalie, who aren't bothering to listen to them, so busy are they both playing their role as *super-cool-and-down-for-anything girls,* perky, ditzy, the anger rising, Ida tightening her fists, all this noise, this excitement, too late, the door is closed and the two women are here, soon everyone is assembled, huddled around one another and Ida, alone, as though nobody has seen her, as though she's not here, as though—

Ida? you okay?

for a second she stares at the door and thinks she could just walk in a straight line and cross the dining room without anyone seeing her, and she watches her defeat, she sees Denis and Christophe circling the two women and hurrying to welcome them,

Yes, your coat, thanks, we'll find a place to put this,

and the two others smiling and laughing now, rushing to their friend who no longer sees her daughter, Marion turning away from Ida, Patrice turning away from Ida, and both of them look so frightened, so flustered that Ida doesn't recognize them, for an instant she thinks she sees something she's never seen, what's it called, what she's seeing, their stiffness, their lips forcing themselves into a grimacing smile, the stiff necks, the bodies so rigid they both move as if by jolts, without flexibility, she's the only one seeing this, recognizing that strange posture of bodies and of souls—the lying gaze, the rigid falseness of a voice shattering like a broken ceramic object being swept over the tile, and soon, like tornados of excessive good cheer, the two women pounce on her astonishment—Ida isn't moving now, has almost stopped breathing, knowing everything is calcifying already and she won't be able to say anything, she sees that even her father seems to be playing the game of not saying anything, he's letting Nathalie and Lydie · kiss him hello,

Thanks, sweet of you to invite us,

and responding only with a dead-fish smile that Ida hates seeing on his face, her father clinging to it as they repeat in the same voice,

So sweet to surprise her!

with just a smile that doesn't look like a smile, or in any case not his, no, not exactly, rather a dead smile, he doesn't even hear Denis's voice asking him several times where the glasses are, the champagne flutes,

They usually come in sets of at least six, don't tell me Marion's already smashed two?

and Lydie,

You obviously know her well.

Nathalie rallying, smiling at Denis,

Bit of a scatterbrain, our Marion.

Ida waits, are they going to stay quiet, her parents, or are they waiting a moment before they tell the girls not to stay, they can't see them after all, no, they're not doing it, won't do it, Christophe has even gone to fetch chairs from the kitchen, nobody says anything to him, Marion and Patrice don't say anything. The other one sets up the two chairs at the table and they, like the others, for now, remain standing right in the middle of the dining room;

they're there, that's all, not saying anything but shooting looks at each other as though they're waiting for the other to respond, to say something—and Ida can't take it anymore because Nathalie is already leaning over her,

My little birdie, how are you gorgeous?

and of course she doesn't notice the little girl stiffening or how she begins to move backward,

You've gotten even bigger since last time, my goodness!

how she tries to turn to her mother to ask her to do something,

What's wrong my little birdie you're all pale?

Ida staring, stubbornly, at the doorknob, over there on the other side of the world, not even hearing Lydie's voice—is it Lydie who's talking to her or is it Nathalie now?

You're sure you're okay my lovely?

Ida staring, hearing the voice as if high up in a tree,

You look strange sweetie,

Marion, have you seen your daughter, she's all pale?

Ida staring, finding the strength

Yes, yes, I'm okay,

to smile and say,

I'm going to bed I'm sleepy,

understanding how alone she is, the doorknob too far, everything now too far, the adults, the two women gave her a kiss, one smells like vanilla and the other has lips greasy like the skin of a duck confit and pale as fromage blanc; Ida staring, letting feelings rise up in her head that are too strong and the voices rising,

Mom I'm going—

while everyone worries over her, examines her, Ida rearing back enough to recoil and get away from the two women's cajoleries,

You're all pale sweetie,

Are you feverish sweetie?

Are you sick what's come over you you're all—

. . .

And Bergogne, pale as she is, wanting to pick up his daughter and take her far away, because yes in fact she has seen a ghost and so leave her the hell alone, but reality breaks like a mirror smashing into how many pieces that remain stuck to the same flat surface, thousands of times, the same crushed, blurry reflections—and the voices coming,

Marion?

Marion kissing her daughter and letting her go toward the stairs, everyone worried about her, alarmed for her as she runs with her head down, eyes fixed on an obscure point somewhere between her feet or just in front of her but nobody has time to see it, to grasp it, Bergogne wants to catch her as she races past and tell her everything's okay, it'll be fine, everything's going to work out, but he doesn't dare make a move toward her because he sees above all how badly she wants to get out of here and that's what she does, not turning around, not listening to her mother's voice already explaining to the others,

She's tired,

and one of the women,

Have to be rested for school,

Yes school,

and jaw set Ida charges toward the stairs, for a moment everyone is surprised without saying anything—a few seconds' hesitation and a few

Good night, beautiful,

as Ida climbs the stairs and leaves the women's voices behind her. Bergogne follows with his eyes as Ida staring climbs the wooden stairs that surely crack under his daughter's steps, but he doesn't hear this time because Ida goes up faster than usual, almost running. She disappears and when he can no longer see her Bergogne returns to the dining room and everyone who has resumed—except Denis, who's smiling at him with a quiet, almost trusting smile, almost friendly, as though he wants to tell him that in another life the two of them might have been friends or even that they still could be, yes, why not, or that the two of them aren't so different after all or that they could understand each other, yes, quite well, on certain topics, in spite of appearances and in spite of the silences, because there's this kind of twinship between them, imposed on them by this woman, separating them and uniting them at once. But it's not as though Denis seems to be thanking Bergogne for this passive complicity, more forced than instinctive, no, plus this feeling doesn't last so long; it's just underlined by Christophe's voice, pressing Nathalie and Lydie to find out so what's this achievement of Marion's that one of the two of them has already brought up, may I ask, we'd love to, and as he's insisting,

More secrets, eh, Marion ?

he hands out the flutes, some peanuts,

No thanks, we had dinner,

Thank you, no, very kind of you,

We're here to see her blow out the candles,

And for the little gift too,

Ah yes, you have a little gift?

Should we give it to her now?

After she tells us about her great feat, of course,

Christophe resumes, laughing as he raises his flute

(good lord I'm going to be hammered)

and he can't help but smile at Nathalie and Lydie, the women explaining how they were summoned by the big boss himself and the project manager, and they explain, one adding details, the other shading them in, how this meeting was a trap laid by the project manager because see in this company it's like everywhere else it's only the girls who do any work and it just so happens the company is run only by men go figure. Both of them pitch in their commentary—meanwhile without anyone noticing Christophe and Denis have pulled out the chairs to invite them to sit at the table, which they do obediently, without paying attention, continuing to talk, to tell stories, pausing only to raise the flute of champagne and wet their lips, very lightly at first, then swallowing a mouthful of fine bubbles that sparkle in their mouth, bursting under the palate, on the tongue,

Happy birthday, girl!

Happy birthday!

Yes happy birthday,

Nathalie and Lydie raising their glasses and Denis and Christophe raising theirs, everyone putting into it all the enthusiasm they know Marion and Patrice will lack, both of them reluctant to raise theirs, their glasses that weigh a ton each of hatred and anger, like this difficulty smiling, saying

Thank you,

in a voice crushed and almost toneless in Marion's throat, which the women will take as a sign of shyness—a sudden shyness they don't recognize in Marion and that each will wonder at to herself, still not understanding that behind the pallor of her voice is the indecision of not knowing how she should react. And it's only when all of this is over that Marion's co-workers will understand the meaning of this shyness, how when the two brothers raised their glasses Marion and Patrice were both nearly unable to imitate them, bad actors, and them, thinking suddenly that the couple didn't want to see them after all, telling themselves they were surely two guests too many, that he'd invited them but now he regretted it, that he could tell the idea didn't please his wife, Marion wasn't happy to see them, maybe because she'd seen enough of them for today. This thought had cooled them off, even vexed them, they'd wondered if they wouldn't leave right after their drink, almost forgetting they had a present for their friend, Nathalie keeping it in her purse, both of them hurt and asking each other with their glances,

A welcome like this,

but not daring confess it to Marion, because mostly it was a feeling of surprise or rather of disbelief at the way Marion and her husband turned their eyes away as soon as they looked right at them, the way they shrunk away, letting the two men take up all the space, oh yes, happy birthday Marion, forty years but it's like time rolls right off you, no? Don't you think Marion doesn't seem to age?

And now the two women, rather than let themselves give in to discomfort, dive headlong into the description of this afternoon when Marion was such a star, where were we, oh yes, a trap set by the project manager because he wanted to make us pay for some mistake he'd made, though we should have checked before rushing and acting like he'd confirmed,

We'll spare you the details,

and sparing the details they continue, both of them, their voices overlapping sometimes, one letting the other take up all the space and then cutting her off suddenly, an octave higher,

I should say that the,

We forgot to tell you that she,

spreading out their story without even seeing that Marion is listening to them and that she's remaining silent, shrinking away, making herself smaller and smaller as the other two study her with their eyes shining from admiration and alcohol; they had a bit to drink at the pizzeria where they went for dinner, and they give off a mix of odors, residue of wood fire, ash, pizza dough but also beer, light smells that mingle with the ambient air, too heavy and sticky from the warmth of the heating but also from bodies, as if burning with fever—is it fever that's burning in Marion's eyes?—Patrice watching her no longer secretly, as he had done while the two women started talking about this famous accomplishment they still can't get over, letting their amazement and admiration ring out in front of everyone, paying no attention to the discomfort in which they were placing the object of all they were saying, as though they were talking about someone who wasn't there, as though Marion their co-worker was still at the office, was always there, as though she had no life but the one in which the two of them kept her shut up under the lid of their day-to-day, belonging to them like an object they'd decided to love, to admire irrespective of her will, like a doll they'd dress and undress to their liking without any concern for her own desire, indifferent to her shyness, and spreading out unashamedly and for their own pleasure alone, in front of her loved ones or in front of those they think are Marion's loved ones, all the unwavering admiration and affection they feel for her.

35

She opened the door; yes, she'd been crying. She's all pale, and
for a moment he almost doesn't recognize her. She's holding the
telephone in her hand. He takes it from her without a word, she
doesn't resist. He feels the trembling heat of her fingers—her hand
in his, warm and submissive, trembling like a turtledove. He takes
the handset and throws it in the sink—the wireless handset seems
to sled down the basin, then comes to a stop. Stutter looks at it,
but not her. She, voice very low, trembling, aware of her failure,

 They didn't answer,

 as though he could understand her disappointment and her
dismay. But he's not sure it's him she's speaking to, maybe like all
people who live alone she's speaking mostly to herself. Then finally she sees him, yes, mad with rage, maybe, but above all frightened and disoriented that he might be blamed for not managing to
accomplish the task he was given, or maybe he's just disappointed
by her naïve and utterly poor attempt to cross him, but no matter, now he has to act as though nothing's happened, as though
everything that's happened didn't happen, as though they can erase
it like a detail or as though it's enough to close the bathroom
door, with the telephone handset stranded in the sink, and let her
rush out, contrite, pale, coming back half tripping, holding onto
the wall as if on the open sea, heart and stomach at the tip of her
lips, fragile, too old, but coming back bit by bit, gathering herself

while repeating it's nothing, it's nothing at all, nobody was there, nobody answered so it's nothing, they're already in bed because nothing ever happens here, the cops go to bed early or they stay in front of the TV and don't hear the phone.

As if that were enough, then, for everything to fade away, for nothing to have ever happened, besides her coming back toward the kitchen teetering as though she'd had too much to drink or the house was reeling, and him behind her, without a word, following her before they both took a seat as though it were their assigned place—Christine in front of the pot on the stove, trying to concentrate, to recenter herself—clearing the table, putting down place settings—while the other sat down as though all he had to do was plop down on a chair and wait to be served, he who's never known anything but his mother's cooking, frozen pizzas, quiche Lorraine, and, for four years, the hospital tray with the paper boats of macaroni, pasteurized cheese pallid under its cellophane and boiled vegetables, faded like they'd been soaked in bleach.

And now: flour, the remains of the eggs, the rolling pin for the dough, the utensils, the smell of chocolate, the insistent burning smell coming from the oven, a still warm and sweet odor of cake. To Christine all of these are like relics of a world disappeared centuries ago that she's suddenly taken the time to unearth, a difficult vision to bear, like learning of the death of someone who's just left your house and whose glass you find on your table, the one they left there before leaving.

So without any further thought she chucks it all into the sink, not leaving herself time to think twice, the nuts, the eggshells in the trash under the sink, and her fit of anger, her abrupt motions feel like a punch right in the gut, the plastic smell of the trash bag and the more or less rotten food scraps; she grimaces with disgust, throws it all away and closes the cabinet door, runs a moist sponge over the tablecloth, without a word, with broad motions, nervous ones, maybe exasperated. Then she throws the sticky and poorly rinsed sponge in the sink and goes to get two plates, silverware that she grabs by the handle without bothering to make sure there's just one knife and one fork per person, there must be three times too many, so what, two wine glasses that fall and land on their bases by who knows what miracle, because Christine sets them down without any effort to place them in front of the stacked plates—Stutter sets out the silverware she tossed in the center of the table, knife on one side, fork on the other, mechanical, quick—and she, trembling and ashen too, takes the pot from the stove and empties half onto his plate, but for herself hesitates, pausing over her plate a few seconds too long, uncertain, then she makes up her mind, two spoonsful, barely anything, it'll go cold without her touching it, while soon Stutter, with that childish avidity she sometimes sees in Ida, that greedy way of shoveling it in that adults never permit themselves, will attack the food,

But wait, what is this, if there's no bread in the sweetbreads?

Sweetbreads are giblets found in calves or lambs that disappear before they become adults—her own voice, like a hair stuck at the back of the throat, tangled between tongue and palate, sickening, in front of Stutter, dubious like a small child, inspecting the shape of the sweetbreads and morels on his plate, the shiny and creamy look of the sauce, then planting his fork in without hesitation, tearing off portions that are too big, mounds he devours and whose chunks swell up his cheeks, waiting for the slow and laborious mastication of the food, not even aware of his indecorousness, still talking, nose buried in the old soup dish,

Who are the two girls?

and this is more or less the only moment—when he asks this question—where he addresses Christine, sitting up straight, staring at him and sickened by this young man curved over his plate, a little old man hunched too much in his chair, swallowing like a dog utterly absorbed in the act of swallowing; it disgusts her, she who hasn't touched her plate and is just clinging to a beer, ignoring the glass she placed in front of her, yes,

And now?

she drinks as if to drown the words that come back to her, the elbows on the table, the hands in front of her face; she lets her fingers play among themselves, the fingers slide between those of the facing hand, she doesn't notice herself doing it but he sees it from time to time, always at the moment he asks,

Who were those two girls?

and she, who answered the first time, stops answering this question, she just watches him stuff his face and forgets him as soon as he starts chewing the food that seems so ugly to her in this precise moment—brown, flaccid, morbid—the food whose smell has something repulsive to Christine, who just stares at him in front of her clattering with his fork—how long has it been since he's eaten?—struggling in other battles too,

What are those two girls like?

hands covered in stains, red-fingered, long-nailed, as though he doesn't know what to do with them. He grapples with the fork in one hand and a chunk of bread in the other, he breathes too loudly while he chews, he doesn't swallow the food and stubbornly reduces it to crumbs—he breathes like a tired fat man who's run too long, sated, on the verge of explosion or a heart attack, red-faced and dripping with sweat, climbing the ten flights up to his apartment on a night when the elevator has broken down—and Christine can barely bear to listen when he tells her that all of this is Marion's fault, because Denis did everything for her, can't forget who she is, Marion, a kid like her, yes, an *urchin*, good lord yes, it's her fault that Denis... she was the one who made a date with the guy that night in a closed factory, behind the parking lot, and the jenever, the whiskey, who had the booze and who was pouring, do you think? who? nobody wanted to accept this idea but the truth is it's like it was her, with the crowbar,

What?

she asks again,

What, what are you talking about?

but the other forgets he's even telling a story,

Who are the two girls?

and he chews, he finishes chewing, serves himself again from the pot, without even asking he sticks his bit of bread into the pot and tosses the chunk of bread bloated with sauce and morels into his mouth,

Fuck I was hungry, you haven't eaten anything, why haven't you eaten anything?

suddenly aware of Christine's presence, of her distant air and that way she keeps her elbows on the table and her hands as if in prayer, fingers pressed together, the ones on the left hand sliding into the interstices between the fingers on the other hand, slowly, gently, as though he isn't here; he finds this gesture so sweet it's almost guilty, sultry, and this idea bothers him, troubles him, entices him also, he lifts his eyes to Christine's fingers and looks at them carefully, then lowers his eyes, holds his breath, sighs without knowing why, his mother's voice whispering in his ear,

A heart that sighs has not what it desires,

before continuing,

You don't know Marion, nobody knows her and if you all knew her you might even be happy to see us show up, because if you knew the things she's done, I mean, but, hey, do you have another beer?

Yes, she has another beer. She doesn't get up to get him one but just points to the fridge; he gets up and as he does this he doesn't say anything else. That's something for Christine, at least, who realizes she doesn't want to know more—she who for years did everything she could to guess who Bergogne's wife was, now she doesn't want to know anything, now she wants the shadows to remain in shadow, the night to belong to the night, she finds it grotesque to learn what Marion has put such effort into hiding, or rather into making disappear. Christine realizes and wonders how she didn't think of this earlier, how she could have let herself be so blinded by her distrust—a form of jealousy, yes, no doubt she behaved toward Marion as though she had a claim to Patrice's love life, like a mother overprotective of a man who isn't even her son, not even a nephew. And it's so obvious to her, yes, how she's imagined so many possible lives for Marion and understands only now that she doesn't want to know any of them, the reality of any of them, because nobody has that right if that's the decision Marion has made.

It's so simple that she realizes it wouldn't only betray Marion to listen to what the young man says, but it would destroy what her neighbor has tried to build a life on, a life in which she could tear herself away from a form of death, not by hiding, then, but by layering over, saturation, which Christine does every day in her work, yes, you can layer over your life to call it into being, superimpose coats of realities, different lives so that at last only one is visible, nourished by the previous ones and surpassing all of them; she's never imagined this could be true anywhere besides in painting, she who's done this on every canvas she's painted, layering and playing with transparency, layering over until a shape appears that has nothing to do with the ones that, from beneath, have made it possible for this one to appear through superimpositions, glazes, recording the strata and marking the coats that don't let themselves dissolve completely and that rise again, resounding as they fade, nourishing the new image with the depth of their matter and ultimately bowing to it, leaving it all the space, in all the splendor of its appearance.

And now?

this time the words cross the border of her lips,

And now?

this time she wants to be done with it, she gets up,

And now? What and now? What do you want now, what does *now* mean?

and he stays in front of his empty plate, with the traces of bread in sauce that look like broad brushstrokes. He wipes his fingers with a dishrag that he moves to take not by standing up but by sliding his chair with a noise that smacks of effort and the friction of its legs against the tile, pivoting a quarter turn and moving all his weight to tilt the chair and lean it enough—balanced on two feet—he passes his hand under the sink, says nothing, wipes both hands on the square of too-damp fabric that stinks of staleness, unless it's the smell of the dog, he doesn't know and yet,

And now what now? What do you want me to tell you now?

How long this is going to last.

How should I know, you think this all depends on me?

The chair falls back on all four feet, Stutter is surprised for a fraction of a second, stops talking and then,

It depends on Marion.

I'm not talking to you about Marion.

And now Christine is standing against the doorframe. Stutter has to contort himself to see her; he turns, tries to get up, but he's too close to twist around and has to make an effort, and then he blurts out me I was in the hospital, I wasn't there when it happened but it's the same thing, I knew it, we've known her for so long, Marion, everyone knew her, my brothers were in school with her and I can tell you before I even knew who she was I knew she and her girlfriends got into all kinds of trouble, bets, challenges, they wound up with the cops before they were even fifteen, maybe thirteen, yeah, must have been twelve or thirteen the first times, you think I'm making it up go look on the internet, they said it all at the trial, all of it, everyone said it, they even wrote it in the papers, the lawyer, he repeated it with his big words swimming in his black robe—he explains that he's imagining all of this, the lawyer and the black robe, because he wasn't there, but he explains how anyway the judge, the prosecutor, whatever, they were women so obviously they blamed it all on Denis, even if he had to spend hours explaining that it was for Marion that he did what he did, but maybe not clear enough that it was her who asked him to do it, and besides, did he say it, at least to defend himself or to pretend to defend himself a little, who knows, was he still crazy enough about her, blinded by her, dependent on her, to defend her against the evidence and against himself, when it was already clear he was going to rot behind bars for years at least?

Stutter knows only what he was told, he remembers the disgust in Christophe's voice when he came to the hospital to tell him—what he doesn't tell Christine is how this was the first time Christophe went to see him there, the first in a long series when both of them began to get to know each other not as two individuals sharing almost the same story, but as two brothers who've never met might meet face to face and be surprised at their resemblance. He'd only been the instrument of a woman but he'd been sentenced to the max, as though he'd been the instigator, the mastermind—did they really believe a man would go and thrash another man with a crowbar behind an abandoned factory, in a parking lot, in the middle of the night, in the middle of nowhere, over some hash or stolen goods or whatever? as the judge or the prosecutor accused, just to avoid seeing it was Marion that made the date with the guy in that cold and damp square of fucking asphalt between the parking lots and the concrete of the decommissioned factories, and who'd told Denis about it, full tilt, handing him the vodka, the whiskey or the jenever, yes, because Denis had given himself courage by drinking—but do they think it wasn't her that put the damn crowbar in his hands, making him drink, showing him the route? And Stutter throws this all out with a sort of theatrical rancor, too hasty, like a fable learned by heart so long ago that nobody, for having heard it and repeated it, for having said it and said it again in such remote circumstances, so different each time, even wonders where he got all these details about a parking lot where the potholes reflected the branches of dead trees dancing in the November wind, the dismal rain, the mist, the deathly clinging drizzle, it infiltrated everyone's memory to the point that there are no other possible stories but the one to which Stutter and his brothers have held on until now—look, now it's time to settle the score with Marion—

Enough about Marion.

You're not interested in your neighbor?

It's not my business.

What is your business?

My paintings. Only my paintings are my business. And in fact I'm going to go back and look at them and get back to work. I'm sick of wasting my time with you, that's enough now.

And he is no doubt offended, no doubt he's aghast to see her angry at him and looking down on him almost physically, because he's remained seated and she, standing against the door, is occupying and saturating the whole space, so that he's forced to see her from beneath, and to see her this way, even if it's almost nothing, even if it's so little, is enough to make this moment uncomfortable for him, which is why he takes his bottle of beer and empties it in a few gulps, like that, he wants to say, everyone loves to know gossip about other people, little secrets, and these, these aren't so little, your neighbor's secrets, no. He wants to say it but he doesn't say it; he stands up because suddenly the doorframe is empty, Christine hasn't waited for him, she's gone back to her paintings.

She hears behind her that Stutter has just come into the studio—he stops a good distance from her and is no doubt watching her. She doesn't turn around. She's just taken her smock, an old white coat she's had for ages, too slender for the woman she's become, that holds the memory of the other one, so thin, who fit inside it, almost floating—that young woman who painted more ardently and sometimes more foolishly too, thinking it was enough to be sincere to be gifted, to be honest in her approach and stubborn in her resolve, for art to come to her. She doesn't need to turn around to know that behind her the young man is watching her put on her smock, and she doesn't know or doesn't calculate the effect that certain gestures by a woman have on a man, after having coiled her hair into a spiral that she holds with her left hand before fixing it in place with the pencil she took from her work table. She doesn't see herself do it, she makes this same motion every night and doesn't realize that, behind her, Stutter is over-come—the power of the appearance of her neck, a few locks of short hair, the same burning orange as the others, an impossible orange, a few white hairs and gray ones too. She doesn't hear the silence and breath of the young man, but on the other hand she can tell very clearly that he's pacing, and very quickly he starts, or rather continues,

Anyway you don't want to hear about Marion but you really should know, you wanted to know, you haven't stopped asking why we're here, what we want, if you want to know then you have to understand and—

and he stops, perhaps troubled because she doesn't even seem to be paying attention to him anymore, as though she's not only absented herself but also found a way of hiding from him; she's approached the painting of the red woman and she's working on it. He won't approach her quickly, not head on. He'll take a few more steps from right to left, brushing past the work table, perhaps noticing that she's turned Ida's drawings over, or not noticing, noticing nothing but the scent of her perfume that will come and trouble him more, at the very moment she resumes what she'd already started earlier, redoubling her efforts,

And you, poor thing, you wouldn't rather be next door instead of being stuck with the old crazy lady?

What?

You heard me,

all of this without turning around, without even raising her voice, almost with sweetness or compassion, is it a form of compassion, this tone trembling with a light veil of... what? sadness? emotion? resignation, bitterness? She takes a few drops of a very matte blue directly from the tube, myosotis, a blue he doesn't know, with that movement whose excessive slowness is maybe only to allow her to speak without turning around,

Because you think the two girls, the champagne, and you over here...

and this time she doesn't hear how he's moving toward her; all she hears is the buzzing of her own voice resonating in her throat, she feels like she's speaking with earplugs in, living on mute, hearing her voice only as she'd hear it from another room. She's surprised that he doesn't answer, that he doesn't yell like he did earlier, is this what she wants, to make him angry, is this what she wants, to make him mad with rage to see how far he'll go, as though she doesn't know, as though, playing with fire, knowing that it's fire, she thinks she can control the flame and the danger of inferno, will he catch fire and spin out of control like a torch, taking everything in the house with him in a blaze of which in a few hours nothing will remain but ashes, or is he just a paltry little flame to snuff out with a simple breath?

Christine continues, imperturbable and slow,

You don't think your brothers are making a fucking fool of you?

and him not responding, coming to rest behind her and steadily contemplating the nape of her neck, unable to tell if he wants to bite her or hit her, to kiss her or to lick her, to throw any object at her skull that could bash in her head or reduce her to a pulp, or to scream, to flee or to yell at her that she's just a bitch who doesn't know his brothers and she has no right to talk about them, to judge them, to say what she's saying, because his brothers love him and if he's not with them it's because they needed someone trustworthy to

(A heart that sighs has not what it desires, my little darling)

do what they want, and of course there are the two girls and the glasses of champagne and of course he'd like to be at the party with them, of course why isn't he at the party with them, why has he always felt they have this way of dismissing him, of leaving him to the side, of using him as a punching bag too, vague memories in which the other two liked to laugh at him just as so many people have laughed at him—the echo of laughter at his life, at his ridiculous way of carrying himself, every day, and her, now, talking to him without even being bothered to look at him, fiddling with her brushes and scorning him in this lighthearted tone, as cutting as glass,

So you don't see that your brothers are using you?

…

You don't see anything, do you, poor thing?

…

You don't see that they're with the two girls and that you,

Why are you provoking me?

and her not answering, pretending she's absorbed by something else and doesn't hear him,

It's true they're not half bad-looking, the two girls.

You're not bad-looking either.

What?

The time it takes to understand—the voice at the back of her neck—the breath with that odor of sweetbreads and beer and maybe also sweat, fear, anger and whatever else, Christine turning around and not having time to back away, already he's on her—she doesn't recognize him, it's like a shadow, too large, hiding the light, a backlight just in front of her that she didn't have time to see coming, to hear, but she was too far, didn't hear anything—she starts, holds back a shout and then the anger,

Who do you think you are you little shit?

and this gesture she makes without even realizing it, her fingers passing the barrier of the smock because it's not closed, the fingers not hesitating, diving in and coming back out with the box cutter with the rusty blade that rears up—a second, maybe two, long enough for Stutter to smile like an incredulous child and then for everything to change—in the night of his mind,

A heart that sighs

his mother's voice rising up,

has not what it desires.

36

You're still just at the aperitif?

Didn't we say nine o'clock?

Weren't we supposed to come after nine?

Patrice is sitting very far back from the table, such that they can see almost all of him, his legs spread apart, chest puffed out, one arm tensed, its hand closed in a fist on the tablecloth, the other resting on his thigh, rubbing his palm against his pants as though he's itching from who knows what—pruritus or impatience—but above all it's all the tensed neck, the staring face barely hiding the anger he's holding in, yes, it's that most of all that they see, and when they realize he won't answer and will just stare at them as though he's about to bark at them to get out or to shut up, they're surprised, a bit shocked and incredulous. So they press the point, repeating their question because they need to hear someone say they haven't come too early, they need

Wasn't that what we said?

a confirmation that wouldn't cost Patrice a thing, seeing as it's now after nine thirty. But he seems to be regarding what they're saying with scorn or indifference, which they don't understand, no, so they don't let it go,

Wasn't it nine o'clock that we said?

and finally he lets out,

Don't worry, it's fine, it's fine,

as though their insistence was more irritating than their desire to not have made a faux pas by arriving too early.

They're surprised by his reaction, but they also find it curious that he took the time to set the table, and all these decorations, all the time it must have taken him, not the whole afternoon but still—it must have taken him a fair amount of time?—he wanted to do things properly, they can see that, so why ruin everything by dressing so carelessly and being so openly hostile, as though he can't help it and he takes some kind of pleasure in sabotaging all the work he's done, as though he's not aware that women too might like it if their men made a little bit of effort, that Marion like anyone else might notice the set table, the preparations, but that she might have also noticed his taking care of himself? What's the use of doing things properly if it's just to neglect yourself, not taking the time to dress up like he would for a special occasion? He's not being asked to do himself up like a Christmas tree, but it's still a bit of a special occasion after all, yes, that's what it is, he's the one who did everything to make it one, preparing the decorations and the meal, taking the initiative to call them; and here he is not even having bothered to dress in anything besides what he wears every day, a pair of baggy jeans, greenish at the knees because of the hay for his animals, and this half-zip sweater with holes in the elbows and bits of wool making tiny twisted fringes—yes, even if he's at least shaved, couldn't he have made an effort when he took the time to prepare everything else?

But soon all of that will evaporate; in a few minutes neither Nathalie nor Lydie will give it any more thought, too busy examining Marion's reaction once they've given her their present.

You like it?

Yes... Yes, yes, it's great. It's...

Marion takes the watch and turns it over, over again, it's a very classic watch—stainless steel body, three hands, round with a white face, a Pulsar. A watch she might find pretty if she made the effort to see it, rather than staying there looking at it without letting it imprint itself on her retina—a watch she'd no doubt have loved to be given in other circumstances, and that she might have admired in the window of a jewelry store, pausing to note that she'd maybe want a watch like that, just as quickly thinking better of it, why would you need a watch when there's the time on your phone and everyone carries those around like an outgrowth of their brain in their purse? But she hasn't had time to note that she likes the watch, hasn't had time to gather up ideas that no longer mean anything—the time it takes for the two girls to give her the box, for her to tear open the wrapping paper, very careful not to let on how she's suffocating, how she wants to escape the attention of the two brothers who have approached, curious, amused at her discomfort and her weak attempts not to show it—them delighted to see her playing the game, *their game,* the one they prepared with such conviction and such patience that they're savoring its every effect on her, the slightest hesitation, the slightest misstep. Because everything about Marion's reaction is painful; everything is a joy to them, they love seeing how she tries to hold on above the void they've opened under her feet, just waiting for the moment she falls in, makes a mistake—will she fall in or, on the contrary, will she manage to not commit a single blunder, to not falter? Will she hold on and take the time to look after her two co-workers until they leave, to have champagne with them without arousing their suspicions? Will Marion control herself, master herself, will she pretend with her co-workers as well as she'll obey and resign herself to what she's asked to do, will she have the strength to submit to what's imposed on her until the evening is over?

Yeah, you're sure?

You're sure because—

Yes yes, it's...

You like it?

Yes great... it's great. It's really... really, yes...

You seem—

No no really, it's really, I mean it, it's beautiful, it's...

For now they're around the table; they're drinking champagne and lingering over Marion's hands, how she's weighing the watch in her hand, passing it from one hand to the other,

Well go ahead, try it on,

as though she's already decided she won't put it on her wrist,

Well go ahead,

as if she's determined to take some time before having to begin the hugs and the thank yous, because she can't see herself looking her friends in the eye while

Thank you, it's really—

imagining the scene and the hypocrisy to which it'll condemn her when she has to

It's great—

Well go ahead, what are you waiting for?

pretend to be emotional about a watch when she can't even see it between her fingers, can't manage to imprint it on her brain, when she's taking refuge in the observation of each detail, all the glints on the glass, on the hands themselves, that feeling of cold on her skin, and yet she's going to have to say thank you and act as though all the emotion she's feeling right now comes only from this, a present she's been given, as though all the trembling in her and her burning cheeks, the rising desire to cry and this inability to raise her face to her friends, as though all of this is just the emotion from a gift that it hasn't even occurred to her to find pretty.

In a few seconds she won't have a choice, but she wants to delay that moment, and if she raises her eyes it's only to seek Patrice, so they can silently communicate their resignation and the understanding of what they have to do, she knows what she has to do, Denis and Christophe know it perfectly well too, what she'll resign herself to doing—that way of complying and buying time even though she doesn't know what that means—time *bought* from where and to do what with, what to do, waiting for what, in spite of her temptation to tell her friends they might want to go home, with the excuse, why not, that she wants to go to bed because she doesn't feel well, she's had enough, yes, all the emotions because of the project manager, you understand, she wants to be left alone and leave everything until tomorrow, or what other solution is there to make everything stop, to make the two others—not her co-workers but the two men—disappear and return to a distant past that's been dead for more than ten years, about which she won't say anything, she still isn't saying anything, nobody would believe it, and even the idea doesn't withstand the look she gives Patrice, long enough for her to hold off, for one more second, the moment of facing her two friends, repeating to them

Thank you, thank you, yes, it's great...

that simple idiotic sentence belied by her tone, a banal thanks, this phrase or some other suffocating in her throat, ending, exhausted, on its last legs,

Thanks girls, it's great...

Well go ahead, try it on!

and this is where she still is, how long after having opened the package Nathalie handed her slightly solemnly while Lydie laid it on thick with an overstressed note of lightness, no doubt out of a will to hide her discomfort, to mask the apprehension she and Nathalie felt in the face of Marion's reaction to this present they weren't sure about,

If you don't like it you can exchange it,

both of them starting almost too quickly to try to reassure her,

We weren't sure about the color but we thought,

No no it's nice,

they want to know what they think, Christophe, Denis,

It's very pretty, very nice,

and barely do they ask Patrice,

Well go ahead, try it,

Try it on,

What are you waiting for?

We'd thought sort of a rose gold,

The band, Milanese mesh they call it,

Try it on, what are you waiting for?

Marion hears and doesn't look at anyone, she murmurs,

No, no, it's great, I mean it, it's great...

and can't manage to take her eyes off this watch that continues to dance between her fingers like an animal, an autonomous being, alive and cold, distant, indifferent or maybe even hostile.

Marion starts to slip the band around her wrist. She looks for the loop, finds it, the clasp, looks at the time, won't stop staring at the hands, the monotonous time that doesn't rotate except for the thinnest hand, which seems to turn in a void and to turn so fast it looks like it's standing still. Marion won't stop making her wrist dance in front of her and then sighs—an excessive sigh, she takes the watch off with too sharp a movement—where are my, yes, she looks for her cigarettes—here they are—takes the pack and pulls out a smoke.

The girls know that in a few minutes they'll ask the men where they're from, who they are, whether it was Patrice who invited them without telling Marion or if it was Marion who invited them, wondering—if that is the case and they're important enough that she'd invite them to her birthday—why she's never found the time to talk about them, even an offhand reference. What a pity. All the more so because at least Denis and Christophe are nicely dressed.

These two have made the effort to put on a white shirt—and an ironed one—and a jacket, as you would for a special occasion, Nathalie and Lydie think. And forty isn't nothing, the midpoint of life, that's significant. The two girls, though they don't yet dare ask, think Christophe and Denis must have come a long way for this party, and that's why they've never heard of them. Maybe they've been waiting for this party for a long time, maybe they took some time off to spend a few days here? But what do they do for work, do they work with their hands or are they more intellectual, are they civil servants or artisans, city people or rural, so they look for details that could reveal something about them, the way they talk, the way they carry themselves; they wonder where they come from, these two, even if they think it's hard to imagine them being from anywhere too close to here, because in that case they'd know them already, they'd have already met them, that's clear, there would certainly have been another occasion to meet them, they would have already come up in conversation, that's even clearer. So they must come from far away and must not have seen Marion for a long time, maybe brothers, they look for—and think they find—common features, family traits, similarities, not really resemblances but a common intonation, an accent—from up north, maybe? no, from the east?—a way of carrying themselves? of smiling, even though Marion has never talked about her family. But she seems so moved, Marion, so troubled—a strange kind of trouble, true, because she's not *moved* the way you are by a profusion of emotions when you're happy, but *moved* the way you would be when you're overwhelmed by something unexpected, a tide of emotions that come up from who knows where, a tremor that shoots through her and whose power she'd struggle to contain—has the joy of being reunited with, let's say, maybe brothers, been spoiled by Bergogne, because maybe he said he'd rather not see them, or maybe he couldn't stop himself from saying something nasty to her in the face of whatever joy she might feel at the prospect of being reunited with people who were present for her life before him, as though he could be jealous of her two brothers or cousins or—no, they don't know, they don't know anything—not even whether these two could be brothers because, after all, she's never talked about her family or about siblings or about her parents, besides her father, who they know she never knew or who she saw maybe once or twice, or maybe she just knew who he was but he'd refused to acknowledge her at birth.

They'll ask if they're not some kind of present, of surprise, maybe to learn more about them, or to feed the conversation, to show they take an interest in others, that they're trying to get to know them and not remaining withdrawn and aloof. They'll ask all kinds of questions that in reality they're already asking themselves, each of them internally but suspecting that the other is asking herself the same ones, and they both also know they'll wait for the evening to be much further along to ask them, so as not to seem too intrusive or curious; they'll wait until after they've all had dinner and the neighbor has shown up with the cakes. In the meantime they'll tell jokes, Christophe and Denis don't seem like the shy type, funny, even, not people you discuss politics with except maybe to toss off a few nasty comments about all those people at the top who've never rolled up their sleeves and gotten their hands dirty, but without saying what they really think of those people, no, not tonight, tonight is just about the pleasure of lambasting our town fathers and then talk will no doubt turn to work, again,

What kind of work are you in?

or to the latest report heard on TV, or the latest news that's a little bit juicy, soon they'll have that shine of drunkenness in front of their eyes that illuminates things and turns them thrilling for the length of a party, a lubrication that will make any serious topic seem pointless or pointlessly depressing. Lydie and Nathalie will be careful to not drink too much, so as not to say too many silly things, even if they like to talk and won't hold back, oh no, we're here to have fun, but they'll be careful because they still have to get home and because even if the old girl knows the way—they've always called their car *old girl*—there's often a badge lying in wait to ambush them, and apprehension already at the prospect of returning to work tomorrow with a hangover. They'll be careful and they know it, but they also know the resolutions you make before you show up at a party mostly, most often, chip away gradually the more you drink and laugh—they know this perfectly well, that's also how they know a party is good, by the way it invites them to exceed the limits they've set for themselves.

Christophe and Denis are aware of all these shifts rising and settling over Marion's two co-workers; they can feel these roller coasters and these doubts coming and going, flooding back, disappearing and then reappearing, and the two brothers like this mix of trivialities—of the lightness from the champagne bubbles with the element of surprise that they've certainly made the most of here in the hamlet—just as they like to think that decidedly The Three Lone Girls have never been so deserving of their name: the neighbor, the wife, and the child, plus now the husband, clearly, and the two girlfriends. And how joyful it is, in Christophe's mind and especially in Denis's, this mixture of looming revelry and looming terror, oh yes, how much it's already paying off all the time they spent waiting for this evening; how joyous also to see this moment, with all the preparations behind it, the hours of thought, of playing it out in their heads—and it's paying off, yes, when it shows them the long labor of the terror inscribing itself on Marion's face, in Marion's voice, because they don't doubt for a second that she remembers what they're capable of, because she went so far as to marry a guy like this one here, this guy who's still frozen in front of this glass he can't even manage to touch anymore.

Anyway, when the girls give Marion her watch, nobody is surprised that Bergogne hasn't given her anything yet—that present forgotten in the next room, in the kitchen, that he nonetheless took the time to wrap. But for him, as for her, it no longer exists. All of it has collapsed, except that unlike Marion receiving the watch from her friends he's not obliged to pretend to keep up the parody. For Marion there's something else playing out, a watch and the formidable face and the hands rushing, knitting, unknitting, regular and emotionless, everything that's happening, which is to say for her, tonight, as though her whole life fits in this precise instant, dancing between her fingers—a birthday—forty years—and suddenly the watch burns her fingers and she, rather than trying it on like they're still asking her to do because they didn't get a good look the first time—or is it because of their persistence in demanding that she slip it on her wrist?—she can't do it again, can't keep the watch on her wrist, no, she took it off immediately and she made an almost imperceptible gesture of rejection, something impulsive that refuses, she lets go of the watch—a wave of melancholy crashing over her, a surge toward Patrice—it submerges her, she feels tears rising to her eyes that she can't hold in—or that she holds in in spite of everything, finding the strength to not let them leave the rim of her eyelid, restraining them from rolling down her cheek; she's powerless in front of him, all of a sudden she sees his beauty—it's his beauty, because he's unaware of it, because he doesn't know it, that she resents him for most often, for being handsome without knowing it, she who's not so pretty as men think, confusing sexy and beautiful, she who's so tired of all of that; she resents herself because he's here and she's never been able to make him happy, unable to do this, even if at first she thought this marriage could succeed, even without her conviction, because he believed in it so much, for both of them, that she told herself it would be enough for her to believe it halfway.

Now she knows it's not, and this reality, at least, she's ready to look in the face.

There's a warranty, I think it's two years.

You have to send in the form or else you can do it on their website.

They're so annoying with all that internet stuff.

Everything's on the internet, even for a watch you have to—

Yeah, that's how it is.

Do you get a signal here?

Why wouldn't there be a signal? it's not the sticks out here.

And all at once they're off again. The girls answering Denis and Christophe, Christophe chasing them with his smile, leaning, without even realizing he's doing it, toward Nathalie—the prettier of the two, it's true—the redhead—yes, they're off again at once, why the silence is so short, why, if not because behind the silence there's the clear fact of a void so vertiginous they're loath to rush into it, just as they're afraid to speak in a voice that's not even low, just normal, so they raise their voices, they talk louder and louder, but it's true that it's not just because of this fear of the rising silence, as though it were more and more intolerable and dangerous, what would they hear if only everyone stopped talking, what would happen if they closed their eyes and waited, but it's impossible, Marion has stood up to kiss her girlfriends on the cheek and she takes them in her arms and thanks them, the girls are almost worried, shaking with laughter to hide that they're uneasy and maybe shaking, them too, from a kind of stupor seeping in, at not recognizing Marion in the overly hasty way she embraces them, with a density they don't recognize in her—what is this seriousness? Denis just smiling before letting out,

We're delighted you joined us, aren't we, everyone?

and this he says in a loud voice, on the verge of a laugh whose sarcasm or nastiness he doesn't even try to hold in, though he holds it in enough to not let it explode. For a few seconds, barely a few minutes, Christophe has been back in the kitchen. From there he doesn't miss a crumb of what's happening in the dining room, he raises his voice to draw their attention,

It's ready!

as though this is all the others were waiting for, hanging on his every word, and they didn't hear him, as though even from the margins of the house he wants them to think he occupies the entire space, coming from the kitchen back to the dining room with everything planned, as though what's going to happen he's already premeditated, timed, prepared, cooked as lovingly as the sweetbreads.

Except that he's standing, now, frozen in the kitchen doorframe, overcome, unable to move forward, his porcelain dish in his hands and a rag to keep from burning himself—he stays silent, as if fogged in by the smells of the sweetbreads and the morels, when something stiffens on his lips, his eyes riveted to the patio in front of the dining room entrance—does he understand and let out, in the face of what he *sees* behind the door, in the night, appearing like a pale thin streak, rushing, a word, a breath? Christophe doesn't have time to panic, to think, no more than he has time to interrupt the girls

Well anyway we've already eaten,

and the red wine already flowing in their glasses, Denis busy pouring and not realizing, nor Marion, nor Patrice, absent from themselves, both of them too distant, not hidden or departed but just absent from everything and wanting nothing; it takes them perhaps a fraction of a second more than the others to understand what Christophe has seen from the kitchen door, coming from outside: the door opens and into the dining room rushes, face bloody, hands bloody, shouting or letting out something like a shout—this shout that returns in a pant and the words stifled in his mouth—sounds, syllables, suspensions, repetitions, articulations like falling overboard, leaving the whole Bergogne residence as if petrified—like too bright a glare—an explosion—no—nothing explodes or shatters, it's just the door opening, the cold entering— a gust of wind perhaps icier than most—Stutter, the presence of Stutter like a bolt of lightning—the faces turning toward him— freezing—but not only the faces—the bodies—time—space itself closing and tightening like a tiny enclave destined to disappear, soon swallowed up by this stupid body holding out an arm to show the bloody hand,

She,

She,

and the tears in Stutter's voice, the anger and most of all the tears of a fright bigger than he is, he who—the others don't know this yet—doesn't see them, or barely sees them, because he's elsewhere in his thoughts, because it's not just his words and his voice that stumble, not just what he wanted to shout and tell his brothers to explain why he's shown up the way he has, having no more choice, unable to do anything besides fuck up everything, yes, and yet he did everything right, he's sure of it, but how could he have known she'd try to jab him with a shitty box cutter and what choice did he have, feeling the burn of the blade, suddenly no longer controlling himself as much as he should have, and closing his fist, yes, it's true he hit hard, he hit like he's never hit in his life, shouting,

Bitch, bitch, why are you doing that, why are you—

he felt the skull shatter, crack, he felt the woman crumple and her head bang against the tile, he felt it in all his limbs, the blood on his right hand that spattered everything, it starts gushing blood right away, the fist punching and reverberating throughout the whole body—his body, because the woman's body is lying on the ground and it hasn't been conscious for a long time,

She,

She,

and he sticks his blood-covered hand out in front of him, to call everyone to witness and already to justify himself—a kid bawling because he's just been caught in the act, as though the act is nothing, nothing at all, as though by bawling louder he can end up making everyone feel sorry for him because the crazy old neighbor lady forced him to beat her to death.

37

Dead before the fact—because for a few minutes it was a dead woman he heard speaking to him in Christine's studio—that mass, the disheveled hair spread over the tile and the blood flowing, yes, the blood mixing with the hair and suddenly everything in him stopped—his voice or all his voices overlapping to demand she stop provoking him like she had, as though all the sentences she'd uttered, the accusations she'd leveled, he'd keep them inside him, all of them, convinced that the hurtful sentences are the ones you don't heal from, the ones the littlest thing can bring back and blow up, because what Christine's words were saying was the naked truth, the one he'd have done anything to never hear, and that's why he'd had to take it until she stopped

Don't you get it?

humiliating him by

That they don't care about you?

attacking his brothers,

They're having fun and you're here?

and when he saw the blood in the hair, all that blood spreading out, flowering on the ground, and her not moving, her body having let go, arms and legs no longer resisting, limp and utterly harmless, her no longer shouting, no longer making the indignant little cries of an animal getting its throat slit—the cry of the rabbits he saw once on TV—then the anger and the blindness stopped,

Stutter saw the woman in her blood, on the tile, with the lights too bright, stripping death bare and showing him what he'd done, just as they'd show it to the paintings in a few minutes, after he left, very much aware this time of having his hands sticky with blood—his own, hers—aware of it all—as though he's come back after being away too long in the heart of this madness in which he'd managed to curl up for how long—seconds, minutes beating a woman because he thought

Who do you think you are you little shit?

he could kiss her or stroke her neck? her mouth? and giving into his rage because she,

Who do you think you are you little shit?

throwing the burn of the blade in such a derisory motion—not so weak, no, it's a determined and very motivated motion, very direct, and if it doesn't manage, this motion, to stick in the knife like it should have, it's because the knife is rusted, blunt, because it doesn't cut anything besides sheets of paper, because it's not capable of digging into flesh, barely of scratching, of cutting, but this time somehow it does, a long and superficial slash, this burn, the time to be surprised by it, to let out a shout or to hold it in, to set his jaw, to grab the woman's hand and twist it, to push, to crush her palm, her bones, her fingers in his hand releasing from the bottom of his stomach, whistling through his mouth, slowly, like a murmur deep and dirty—bitch—bitch—bitch why are you doing this—why are you doing this and maybe if he hadn't seen the terror in her eyes he wouldn't have struck.

It didn't last so long; she fell quickly, didn't resist long. And then his voice changed; that deep guttural tone turned into a series of shouts, almost shrill, that he himself didn't hear, he was yelling the whole time he was hitting her as though he was hitting her with his voice—and then, when she was on the ground, when he finally understood that she wasn't moving anymore and that blood was flowing out from her hair over the tiles, his first thought was the one in which the amazing pleasure of liberating himself from the need to do good mingled with the certainty of his brothers' disappointment—Denis's anger—Denis's scorn. For a minute he stands in front of the woman on the ground and, gasping, he wants to bend over her, to turn her over so her face is facing his and to make sure the massacre is finished—with that voice that tries to repeat to him that she's not dead, that she can't, she mustn't, just fainted, wounded, yes, he has to help her. But he leans toward her and can't reach out his hands. He bends his legs, he approaches, he extends his arm, reaches out his hand, he wants to but he's wavering so much, he can't turn her over, touch her, take her to turn her over and help her and he just makes this idiotic motion—with his index finger, gently, slowly, yes, he just, as though afraid of burning himself, of being bitten, of caressing her, almost, which is to say stroking her over her hair, a few millimeters away, then, wavering still, he touched her, stroked her hair and sprang to his feet, as if surprised by his own gesture, asking her to get up—to say it was okay—that it would be okay—but the truth is he could see she wouldn't move anymore, and the smell of blood took everything over, his eyes, his head; for a moment it crossed his mind to set fire to the studio, to run out to let the house burn, but over his shoulder he was stopped by the mocking look of the guy he went to school with, behind his window, the wood burning in the farmyard and the heat of the fire forcing him to take all his clothes off and let his skin shine with the color of the flames, one summer night—the fury of the blaze and the flames rising toward the stars of a summer sky to guide the aliens to him, drowning out the cops' siren—the blue of the siren—the paramedics too—the white.

He cried so much that eventually he was able to recover a bit of strength. And no doubt he murmured that all of this had to stop, that she was right and he was going to go tell his brothers to leave everything and go, that they'd been here too long and now it had to end, now he was tired, an exhaustion so big, so desolate—his tears soaking his cheeks red with shame—his hands with blood— what the fuck is he doing here, he asks himself what he's doing here, why is he here, that's what he'd like to understand, now, the time it takes to remember that she hurt him and he sent the box cutter flying off somewhere very far but he's still bleeding—he needs to take care of that—and in the bathroom he runs his hand under cold water, in the sink where he threw the telephone; he has this strange reflex to save the handset by taking it out of the sink before turning on the faucet, placing it on the edge, as though it's important to not break anything, as though he's unable to see the absurdity of his precaution; but it was so long ago he thinks it was another day, in another life, with another person and maybe even in another story—is this his story? He lets the cold water flow over his wound—a cut that's long but not deep—between the thumb and the index finger. He looks for something to treat it with and coils his hand in a towel; the pain fades, he needs something to disinfect it, but he can't find anything, or bandages either, so he drops it; it's bleeding again and he doesn't even realize he's just run his hand over his face, that he's gotten blood all over himself. And already he can see his brothers' appalled reaction and their anger, and maybe that's why he ran so fast, telling himself he'll get there while they're still having drinks and maybe kissing the two girls, and what will they have done with Marion and her husband, with the kid—yes, the kid—he thinks of the kid—but it's because of the painter, he liked the painter, what came over him that he attacked her? he didn't want what happened and it had nothing to do with him, it's not his fault because it would have been enough for him to lock her in her bedroom and wait for all this to be over, and maybe at the end she even would have forgiven him for the dog, but she had to get smart and she had to betray him and he

She,

She,

and he can be seen crossing the studio and the kitchen and opening the door and running and letting out groans between cries and shouts; he can be seen running alongside the house, reaching the neighbors' patio and he barely has time to run before he's arrived on the patio, the French door. He sees the dining room lit up and the table, the decorations, the lights, it's sparkling, it's shining, the girls from the back who don't see him yet and him seeing Denis pouring them wine, Bergogne sitting a bit farther away not interested in anything, Marion frozen like a plaster statue, he runs and grabs the doorknob—the blood sticking—the cold of the handle—Christophe in the doorframe coming from the kitchen—Christophe stopped with his dish in his hands—his brother Christophe staring at him without moving and his jaw dropping to his feet as though he's never seen anything like it before, and here he is coming in, Stutter, into the Bergognes' house, but it's not his fault fuck not my fault if she,

Now what happens goes very quickly, and it's as though only a very long slow-motion shot can make it visible.

First the cold that rushes in and Stutter's voice, broken, rasping.

But maybe before seeing him, before the hand that advances and tries trembling to show its wound, before even his voice—maybe before even hearing it or understanding that they're hearing it, before seeing him come toward them with his face bloody and his hand outstretched to accuse Christine and defend himself already, before that, then, it's to Christophe that everyone turns, including Denis, Marion, and Patrice, who could see Stutter and don't manage to identify him—the image of him that they can't register just as they still refuse to hear his voice and his stumbling words, the tears fumbling in his voice because in spite of everything it's all too timorous, too closed in on itself and not projected toward them, unlike what Christophe is doing, because it's to Christophe that they turn, to Christophe who is quicker than the others in his reaction, even more present in his response than Stutter and the way he shows up, Christophe not standing there rooted to the spot as he was for a few seconds—long enough to understand what he's seen behind the French door and to let the image of his brother arriving imprint itself on him and command him to take action—with the way he ran toward the table and too quickly dropped—releasing it over the table, well before touching the tablecloth—the porcelain dish that doesn't shatter upon contact with the table but practically explodes with a noise so sharp, so cutting, that all eyes are hooked on this old milky white dish, this dish so shallow that everyone could watch the spectacle of the morels, the sweetbreads, and the sauce spreading around the dish, flowing first because the dish tilted, almost spilling everything off one side, some of the sauce trickling first onto the middle of the table, making a compact burning bundle on the tablecloth, then squirting when the dish slammed against the table, spatters spreading like dots in a mad, imprecise constellation, spreading out in a greater circle, and no doubt stained their clothes, maybe the wall, the floor—which nobody notices because what everyone sees is how the dish, as it falls, has taken with it a flute almost full of champagne that tips over—the champagne crackling on the tablecloth, foamy, iridescent white, before being absorbed by the cloth and leaving a spindly shape, like an exaggeratedly stretched-out shadow, then that straw color that darkens the brightness of the tablecloth—the sound of glass breaking—a triangle of glass, very sharp, in the place where the glass makes contact with the table, but it's nothing, a dull sound nobody hears because Christophe's voice is already taking up all the space,

Fuck, Stutter!

Christophe's voice though still only a few seconds have gone by, so few between the moment Christophe saw his brother arriving on the patio and the one where he entered, a few seconds during which what freezes the others is seeing Christophe jump, flinging the dish as though he's just burned himself and yelling,

Fuck, Stutter!

as though this time they're no longer acting, as though the play is finished and it's all over, as though Christophe still has a bit of an advantage by calling the end of the game, releasing the others in the same motion, they who at first don't understand, are lost for words, are almost offended and all but blame him for betraying something they'd all put in place together, yes, this happened together, this shared silence, everyone in agreement on what's holding them together—the same act from the start of the threat to the finish—the knife—Christine—and here they are relieved of the lie by which they'd been constrained as if in too-tight clothes.

This is what surprises them at first, what makes everyone come out of that strange lethargy they'd let themselves slide into without even quite realizing it, including Nathalie and Lydie, who are the first to jump up from their seats—what's gotten into him for him to drop the dish like that, and then, a few seconds later—that guy, who's that guy? oh fuck he's bleeding—the sauce stains—his voice, Christophe's voice and his tone so brutal when he throws himself in front of his brother—long enough for the others to see—to understand this presence—first the voice—then the hand—

Fuck, Stutter!

and now everyone gets up,

What the hell are you doing here?

everyone standing up almost in the same motion—the screech of chairs against the tile—Bergogne's chair falling on its side, bouncing, shouts too—voices realizing it's too late, that something is happening that's already absorbed them, overtaken them, Lydie shrieking so loud, Nathalie clinging to her, the girls not understanding—this guy bursting in with his hand all bloody, screaming and showing his hand repeating not the way you repeat when you want to say something again but because your voice is panicking

She,

She,

and can't hold in this hiccup of words, him with his face that he doesn't even know he's just blotched with his own blood, looking for a phrase and holding out his hand to show it to everyone else, his hand,

Look,

Lydie and Nathalie back up as far as they can,

Shit who is that, Marion? what is this?

Is that blood oh fuck is that blood?

Is he hurt?

What's with all the blood what is this?

What happened to you who are you?

What's going on, what is this?

They can't believe it, don't understand, how much more time will it take for one of them to find the strength to demand that Marion answer her, for now they can see clearly that they're not even being considered, not being heard,

Marion what the fuck is this?

What's going on here?

What the fuck is happening here?

Marion can't respond—Marion has run toward Stutter, raising her head, ready to hit him, so small next to him, she starts punching him, her hands like swarms beating down on his cheeks, quick slaps that she repeats harder and harder, more and more and his eyes flutter in response to her punches,

What did you do to her? What did you do to her?

threatening, not hearing the voices of the two girls now entrenched a few meters back, still recoiling, flattening themselves against the wall, holding each other,

Marion what's going on here?

Marion not listening while Stutter,

She,

She, I, she,

Good lord what is going on here?

Who is this guy?

Why's he bleeding?

You motherfucker what did you do?

and him like a maniac,

She,

a maniac,

Had no choice,

Christophe right next to him,

Fuck, Stutter,

Christophe intervening but still letting Marion hit him—he knows she could easily punch Stutter in the face—he's surprised to see her just slapping him dozens of times, like the buffeting of a child, but that's all it is, he lets her do it, lets her exhaust herself, lets Stutter hide his face with his hands,

I didn't want to, I—

Christophe passing next to him and giving him an insulting slap behind his head, with the tips of his fingers, a smack Stutter wasn't expecting. Suddenly he goes silent. For a second he runs his hand over his mouth with his eyes closed. A second or two. Two seconds maybe, Marion still advancing,

What did you do to her? Answer me,

this time Christophe restrains her,

Drop it.

and barely has Christophe come toward Marion—a movement like a threat, a way not of standing up to protect Stutter but of tipping toward Marion,

You shut your mouth.

This time it's Marion who says it, who stands facing Christophe, nothing is holding her back now, this time it's finished, they can't hold them back anymore and that anger Marion and Patrice had to repress, now she knows they're going to let it explode and all she has to do is start shouting and stop putting up with their presence here and let out everything they've been holding in for too long,

Shut your mouth, asshole,

everything that rises to her mouth—insults she volleys, not shouting but rapping them out furiously, except that across from her Christophe has no intention of being pushed around and he turns threatening—she recognizes him at last, like that day he took advantage of Denis's absence to come a little too close to her, and

351

she rejected him so smugly, with such disdain, that he had as much hatred for her as he did an even greater attraction, but that's where it stopped, their little secret, yes, a secret buried in other secrets, the one that tied Marion to Christophe, the kiss he stole from her before she sent him sprawling, asking him what Denis would think if she ever thought to tell him. It's all of this

You haven't changed either,

that she hears, a declaration of rancor and hatred, it's enough for Christophe to make that movement toward her, this movement enough for Patrice to finally react, no more obstacles now, they're here, all of them, is there even a thought inside Bergogne, no, Bergogne has no thoughts at this moment, everything in him is electrified and it's just like a form of liberation, a sort of emancipating anger that Bergogne takes into himself, he sees himself act without premeditation and, instead of doing what he vaguely considered doing earlier, running into the living room to grab the hunting rifle, a handful of cartridges, no, he just takes one of those carving knives with the sterling silver handles with the ribbon-and-knot pattern, a Minerva head on the hallmark, with that old story heard who knows how many times in his childhood, the Germans in 1940 thanking his grandparents for their hospitality, going so far as to offer to let them share their meal at their own table, even though a few kilometers away the same Germans had ordered a hundred villagers to be burned in the local church—yes, the silverware has seen a thing or two, that permanence of violence that invites itself to the tables of families and nations while playing a charade of courtesy—and now Bergogne has barely grabbed the handle and begun to make a threatening gesture when,

Put that down right now.

the pistol's muzzle on him—where did it come from, where was it hiding—Bergogne didn't have time to see it, Denis perhaps maintaining enough self-control, calculating his motion, reaching into one of his jacket pockets for a pistol that looks so small in his hand it's hard to believe it could be a dangerous weapon—a

Browning? a Colt? a Walther?—a compact mass and suddenly not yet silence but something like a state preceding silence, a shift in the wait that prepares the wait, and Denis, his arm extended and the pistol at the end of it, the black metallic cold making itself at home among them—Denis speaking slowly, clearly,

Stutter, you're going to take the knives and toss them outside.

For Patrice, everything stops at the reality of this extended arm, very stiff, pointing to him or to his hand—the knife it's holding. His movement has stopped, suspended at the beginning of a movement that started with determination and force, a convincing gesture, because the hand closed over the handle with the intention of attacking. But Patrice doesn't need a second's hesitation to know Denis will fire if he has to. In the time it takes to tell himself he didn't think one of these guys had a weapon his fingers are already loosening their grip around the knife, almost imperceptibly letting it slip—but he still has enough strength to not let the knife drop on the table, whether because some prideful resistance is ordering him not to abdicate too quickly by letting go of the knife or because, without realizing it, Bergogne can't move his fingers more than this, unable to react in the face of this surprise—not for a minute did he imagine armed men—because the young man in the tracksuit had his knife in his hands, he'd been able to tell himself they'd stay at this level of amateurism, they wouldn't escalate to what's happening now—the pistol pointed toward him, the barrel trained on him for a few seconds. He wasn't aware of any danger besides the one Christine was in, and still, as though sustained by an incurable optimism, he'd told himself this would all end with the three men leaving and the strange fatigue of appeasement, the tears of relief, reuniting with Christine; he'd thought about the next day, when he'd go see the cops, or about his next argument with Marion because she'd beg him not to go see them, to let it all go, to forget everything, and then about those hours of silence that would come when Marion shut herself up in her refusal to explain who these three guys were and what they wanted, what they wanted revenge for, what score they had to settle with her, because he imagined that at the end of the night nothing would be resolved but the guys would end up leaving as they'd come, leaving no trace of their visit but broken dishes and a very bad memory, a defiance that would surface again when the next huckster showed up in the yard, plus the smell, the blood, the dog, and also the pull between the desire to demand explanations from Marion and the point they'd make to respect her right to silence.

But Bergogne understands that that won't be it. That the three men's determination is stronger than his. He has plenty of time to think, seeing the pistol at the end of Denis's arm, that he's stupid to be surprised and also stupid to have believed it would be enough to stay docile and wait for them to eventually let Christine go. Because he understands now that they won't let anyone go; in this moment, Bergogne thinks the three men have come to kill them and that they won't even have the certainty of knowing why they're being killed. In this moment he thinks he's going to die, that Marion is going to die—but he thinks Ida has to escape, that she has to find a way out—and even if it's not a thought he has time to articulate so clearly, there's that old image from the story, his parents' voice, his grandmother remembering the Germans locking in the people from the neighboring village and setting fire to the church, and that sentence he'd heard about two or three very small children who managed to flee through a hole—but where? what space? he never found out and had trouble imagining it—in one of the church walls, this image crossing his mind and making him understand that Ida has to flee. He suspects she's not sleeping, he knows it, just as he knows she has to flee, he has no doubt about what just ten seconds ago he still thought was impossible—the thought of a massacre—the imminence of his death—the desire to vomit all of a sudden—to tell Marion he doesn't blame her for anything—that he's not worth much and she's right not to love him—Marion and him, both together for in instant in the same clairvoyance, both convinced they're going to meet their end here, now, that everything is going to stop for them, and maybe, for the instant they look at each other, thinking of the urgency of getting Ida out, the time it takes for a face-to-face where everyone else disappears, they tell each other they're doomed; maybe it's this idea they share through the disbelief that passes in turns through their eyes, and also that shared terror for Ida, that spark that unites them, that animates them both, in which their love comes together in the name of their daughter, in the need they suddenly have, both of them, to protect her, but how can they be sure she'll make it out, how can they make sure she can run away?

Okay, we're going to sit down nicely.

And Denis adopts an almost devious tone in saying it, displaying a strange sort of smile, as though he's not unhappy about this unexpected turn of events, as though he maybe even imagined this would happen, that this unexpected turn of events isn't really unexpected for him—how to know?—how in any case could he have counted on Stutter, so fragile, so unstable, allegedly cured even though his parents could still testify to his violence and his unpredictability, as though it's this that pleases Denis, seeing him burst in with his eyes bulging, puffy with tears flowing down the cheeks he bloodied with his hand that's still streaming with blood. He's not unhappy about all this fright, so surprising, it contributes to a sense of orchestration that isn't to be sneezed at. Denis has time, tonight, for what he wants to do: all the surprises, so long as they come from him, so long as they serve him and feed the story he's told himself about the party, about the night, the long and interminable descent to the bottom of a hell whose depths he doesn't yet know, just taking pleasure in measuring how far down it goes.

Come on, let's sit.

Marion doesn't dare do anything now—she passes from one of the three brothers to the next, from Stutter's bloody hands to Denis's face, but she barely deigns to stop at Christophe, she has no desire to linger on him, no, she alternately scrutinizes Stutter and Denis, then Patrice, then the two girls and she,

I'm sorry,

just

I'm sorry,

in a voice that doesn't manage to carry to the other end of the room; but in any case the two girls have no intention of asking anything else, now they're waiting, frozen, panting, not understanding what's happening nor why they're caught up in this business—the violence of the turnabout having brutalized them even more than Stutter's arrival, by Denis's weapon—Denis turning in place, his body still, his arm still very straight, pivoting and repeating an order addressed to everyone,

I said: everybody sit down now.

And then, from the edge of the room, very slowly, they return to the table, not daring to say or ask anything, so white they seem to be about to faint. But no, they don't faint. They walk, pull themselves together, come and sit down, but not for a second do they manage to take their eyes off the weapon, the weapon still not trained on them, no, on the contrary, the arm is moving it around, it aims once at Patrice, once at Marion, then back to Patrice and finally at the two girls, its back-and-forth motion slow and fluid, waiting for everyone to have properly understood,

I said—Marion—come and sit down.

It's very slow, almost mechanical, Marion comes and sits down but not for a second does she take her eyes off Denis—she holds his gaze, she gives in but doesn't give up; at the table she sits straight and starts to smile as she turns toward Christophe and, in a very demonstrative, ample gesture, raises her right arm, snaps two fingers together very loudly as you might call, with a condescending gesture, the waiter in a restaurant,

Clack,

this clacking of fingers addressed to Christophe, whom she doesn't even bother to look at,

Can we drink some wine at least?

Denis smiles, yes, that's his girl,

Certainly,

a motion of the head addressed to Christophe who takes the bottle and serves Marion, the girls, and Patrice too—the sound of the wine flowing into the glasses, their immobility and their heavy silences around the glug-glug the wine makes as it falls from the bottle, yes, it could be fun, for the moment Denis says nothing and then,

Stutter, you're going to take the knives and toss them outside. Right now.

But seeing Stutter approach the table, Denis has a spasm of disgust; he takes a napkin and throws it to him, telling him to wipe his hands and face, you've got blood everywhere, it's disgusting. Stutter catches the napkin, wipes his hands and face so clumsily that the blood only spreads, makes you look like a redskin, says Denis, smiling. Come, come, get a move on, Stutter, you're going to take the knives and toss them outside.

Right now.

Denis notices how his brother rushes to the table to take the knives, everyone watches him do it in the same sticky silence, only Marion holds onto her wine glass and starts to drink, slowly, little sips that she drinks while looking sidelong at what's happening, then, to Stutter:

You've always been a psycho. You're just a psycho. You hear me?

And her voice rises when she calls out to Denis,

Which one told me he'd changed? That he could be trusted? Fucking psycho... Trust you? Nobody changes, you hear me—psycho.

Stutter straightens up now, the knives making a noisy and almost shapeless heap in his hands, he shrugs his shoulders and finishes taking Patrice's knife—who lets it slip from his hands to avoid Stutter touching his fingers, Stutter hurries, eyes lowered, hiding so poorly his desire to go off on Marion and her venomous, bitter voice, and maybe also his childish, timid silence toward the two women—he doesn't dare meet anyone's eyes and his movements are brusque, he passes in front of Denis,

What do I do with them?

Outside.

Christophe opens the door for him, Stutter goes out, takes a few steps, he tosses the knives as though he had burning objects in his hands and wipes his hands on his thighs—his blue tracksuit no longer visible in the night and protecting him so poorly from the cold as a jolt, a spasm, like an electrical discharge, runs through his whole body.

38

And he doesn't see glints of moonlight on the blades of the knives, any more than he sees desire; he sees only the glare of his disappointment because he didn't know how to play the part they'd assigned him, couldn't do it, thinking he was up to it when once again he demonstrated that he wasn't, that he wasn't worthy of this outsized trust they'd placed in him, as though he'd already shown he could be worthy of it, no, and the thoughts blur in his head because he's wondering at the same time how he can be blamed for anything, he who was busy while the other two were drinking champagne and had the company of the two girls to themselves—the words still coming back from the neighbor, that need she had to take out that stupid box cutter and him, well, stop thinking about that, stop thinking period, he wants to not think anymore and all he can do is think about his desire to not think, to not let the images and voices of the others harry him,

You've always been a psycho. You're just a psycho.

first Marion's,

You hear me?

and voices distant or close, recent or not, those of others, his mother's, like a syrupy little tune stuck in the back of his brain, coming back on loop,

(A heart that sighs has not what it desires)

the neighbor piercing in, and his own too, which he hears as though it were someone else's, and still Marion,

Fucking psycho.

the voices under his skull,

Stutter, you're going to take the knives and toss them outside.
Right now.

You've always been a psycho. You're just a psycho.

You hear me?

You've always been

A heart that sighs

A psycho.

Has not what it desires.

You hear me?

Who do you think you are you little shit?

(But who were those two girls?)

You dare tell me it wasn't you?

It's you.

Why did you kill him?

(But who were those two girls?)

Now?

And now what?

(But who were those two girls?)

And now what now?

Now it's the breath of his brother who passes by him at a run, without stopping—a silhouette, a rustling, steps going to the Clio in front of Christine's, yes,

(But who were those two girls?)

the voices still dragging on in him, a few more seconds, like a buzz knocking in his head, barely disrupted by Christophe passing right next to him; Christophe runs to his car and Stutter sees him rush in—he doesn't understand why Christophe has opened the driver's side door when evidently he's looking on the passenger side; Stutter hurries, he has to talk to his brother, has to tell him how sorry he is and above all that he didn't want what happened, he's the first to be mad at himself, there's no point yelling at him or giving him angry looks, no, no need to shoot him angry looks, he'll earn their forgiveness, he promises himself, he promises, he doesn't know how but he'll do anything they ask him to do. He wants so much for them to believe him, they have to know she didn't make it any easier on him, the neighbor, really he couldn't do anything to avoid—but that's enough.

He approaches his brother who's already emerging, he realizes Christophe has gone to get his pistol from the glove compartment—what the fuck are you doing here, Stutter?

Why are you getting that?

Because of your bullshit.

Christophe slams the door and with one motion pushes his brother who's trying to keep him from passing, or rather to restrain him,

It's not my—

Shut up.

The smell coming from the stable, cows, manure, the earth surrounding them, the damp of the stones on the farm, saltpeter, the river flowing down below and the burrowing cold of the falling night around them, in them; Christophe is yelling because they can't leave Denis for too long, they have to go. Christophe moving quickly to go back toward the house—the light on the patio outlines a misshapen rectangle with a yellowish tint, like an image through the frame of the French door, more a photo than a film because nobody seems to be moving inside the dining room. But it doesn't last,

Wait, wait,

Stutter tries to hold his brother back, Stutter clinging to his brother and not really realizing it,

She, it was her, she,

Shut up, you're a pain in the ass, Stutter, you're—and Christophe grabs his brother by the throat and digs his nails into his skin, yelling as he squeezes, that's enough of your bullshit now, your bullshit can't last your whole life, you hear me, how much longer is this bullshit of yours going to last? How much longer are you going to be a pain in my ass? And he pushes his brother so violently that his brother falters, surprised by the abrupt brutality of the motion, and takes a few steps back, he tries to free his neck from his brother's fingers and nails while trying not to keel over, windmilling, arms spread apart to counterbalance his body tilting and still stepping back and finally falling, backward, with the sound of a bag of cement exploding. Christophe isn't paying attention to him, he's gone off toward the house—then slows down, stops. He catches his breath. Inhales, exhales, catches his breath. He pauses, then reconsiders. Then comes back toward Stutter,

Get up, for fuck's sake,

Stutter is crying, sprawled out on the ground.

Jesus Christ, for fuck's sake, get up, I mean it.

Stutter mumbling that he didn't want to, they've always treated him like shit, a worthless nobody good for nothing but to act the stooge for all the stuff they didn't want to do. And his body is shaking and the shivers make him hiccup and gasp, as though he's two seconds from choking; he speaks and the saliva flows back into his throat, the breaths blocked and choppy, he speaks anyway, even though he should take more time to take in air—and Christophe leans toward him, he can't help it, he has to help him get up, all the anger he had toward his brother fades, evaporates, an ill wind chased off by a gust of air swelled with sadness and patience,

It's okay, Stutter. Come on, that's enough... What are you talking about, stop blubbering, you're not a chick, Jesus.

And he leans down and Stutter grabs hold of him, the two brothers get up this way, Stutter crying with a despair so great he can't see anything in front of him, hanging on his brother, both hands gripping his arm, not letting them go, face right next to his brother's chest, nestling in without even realizing he's talking and his breath is returning, the words are returning, straight into his mouth, running through the night air at a speed he doesn't recognize and that his brother doesn't recognize either. Which is why, no doubt, Christophe is unable to say anything, to do anything, he who just a few seconds ago was bursting with impatience at the thought of getting back to Denis in the Bergognes' dining room—Denis alone facing the others, pistol pointed at them, but only a pistol—Christophe knows it won't last, it can't, but all of a sudden he no longer has any idea why they're here, why Denis dragged them into this business—and that other whore Marion who's done him so much harm already will just continue to do more, to Denis, but also to them, to him and Stutter, that slut who he always knew his brother should watch out for,

You're kidding, right?

she who'd sleep with anyone for nothing and who everyone had seen whoring around,

You're kidding?

she who made fun of him when he dared claim to have as much a right to it as anyone else, and who threatened him, twenty-five-year-old brat that she was,

You're kidding, right?

and the humiliation was so strong that he feels it like a phantom limb, amputated long ago, that hurts on nights when the air is too damp, like tonight, just as he recognizes his humiliation in the tears of this little brother who he loves as though he were his father, the way he's never managed to become a father to his own children, terrible with his kids, when the only paternity he truly feels in himself is that of something like a guardian, father to this brother who he's never stopped calling my *little* brother, even though there's nothing little about him, but who's so overpowered by his fragility that he still seems to be practically a child. It's hard for Christophe to hear his brother repeating in the same fevered voice, it's you guys, it's you guys, you hold my head under the water every time, as soon as I try to get out you push me down, for a laugh, to amuse yourselves, and you leave me everything you don't want to do, why the dog why was it me who had to do it even though I didn't want to, you wanted to, it was you, fuck—

and Stutter closing his fists and starting to hit his brother's chest, fuck, why is it me who has to get dirty doing things I don't want to do while you two act like kings, huh? the good life for you drinking your champagne and laughing with girls—I saw it when I came in, you weren't to be bothered, I come in and that whole time you're going to keep the girls for yourselves—

Come on, that's enough, Stutter. That's enough. Stop talking nonsense. Come on, brother, don't worry, it's fine, it's fine, it's okay, it's nothing, we're just having some fun. He takes him in his arms, we're having fun, we'll have fun, I mean it. He holds him and it lasts a long time between them, this embrace, the desire to cry rising up.

I swear to you, we're gonna have a party, come on, it's okay, stop blubbering. Come on, not your fault, not the dog either, you got nothing to feel bad about.

And the girls?

The girls? Don't worry. We'll take care of the girls.

The heat of the house. That whiff as soon as they enter, which stuns them for a few seconds, the time it takes them to get used to it; a short time like the one eyes take to get used to bright light, their noses to smells so different from those outside, organic, powerful and cold, chased off by the reeking stenches—not just the smell of the cigarettes Marion is almost chain-smoking or the effluvia of body heat, fear multiplying that acidic exudation that taints everyone's breath and the women's perfume—but also the heating, the aroma of the sauce from the sweetbreads left over and getting cold, that nauseous mix of the end of the party when it should only just be beginning. But what clashes with the vigorous cold outside is also, when the two brothers come into the house, the speed with which Christophe points his weapon with the demonstrative motions of the kind of guy who might fire at any moment, trying to show he can laugh at the same time, playing clever right away, as though he's unconcerned by this fever throbbing in his wide-open eye—is that red on his cheeks just from the cold outside? or is he less at ease than he claims, does he feel, having barely arrived, the need to appear talkative, playful, calling out to everyone—I'm such an idiot sometimes, I forgot my little toy out in the car, how stupid is that? Anyway, how's everyone? you didn't miss us too much, Stutter and me?

The Bergognes, the girls, as if incredulous and dumbstruck, as much as Stutter, facing them, rooted there, his back against the French door, watching Christophe still trying to act as though there's room to play, because he has a gun, because he's point-ing it at someone else, not a man but a woman, yes, because now it's an obvious fact that amuses him, three men on one side and three women on the other, with Bergogne stuck on the ladies' side though he should really be in the stable with the cows and the mutt's carcass. This thought crosses Christophe's mind, what the hell's the farmer doing? he aims at Bergogne and wants to ask him, as though he could say it's funny, isn't it, this situation, three men and three women and then this sad hick in the middle keeping score. But he holds back and doesn't say it, there are more urgent matters, he has to take care of Stutter, let his brother have some fun too.

Hey, Marion, do you mind pouring Stutter a glass of wine? Or is there any beer?

You heard him, Marion, he'd prefer a beer. You have beer?

Marion not answering, face closed, jaws set tight, keeping her eyes on Denis; Marion turning for a second toward Christophe and Stutter—long enough to strike them down, yes, with a quick murderous look that would hurl lightning bolts if it could, but the look doesn't strike anything down. Denis turns to Marion, smiles at her with a kind of disenchanted sadness, then sits down and, still with a show of calculated and laborious gentleness, too meticulous, almost obsequious, speaks to Marion as though he's murmuring in her ear or speaking to her after making love, in the intimacy of a bedroom, a bed,

Come, Marion, let's talk now, shall we? We have some things to say to each other, I believe? Marion?

Marion?

Christophe has found some beers in the fridge; he comes back with a bottle of Leffe and, shit, of course, no opener, so be it, the old-fashioned way, Marion, your lighter?

Marion doesn't respond, she doesn't even hear him, lets him take her lighter from in front of her—he uses it to open the bottle, the sound of the cap falling on the table, Stutter takes the beer his brother hands him, thanks him with a nod of the head. He drinks, his brother smiles at him as if to say come on, all is forgiven, it's in the past, let's have some fun now, shall we? But he doesn't speak because Denis,

Well, Marion, you don't have anything to say?

She doesn't answer. Silence. Then Christophe comes over to Denis. He leans in, puts his hand in front of his mouth and his brother's ear so nobody can hear; Denis listens solemnly. A few sentences and Denis's face suddenly opening up,

Seems you want to dance, Stutter?

yes, this smile just emerging on his lips, and Stutter not responding, just, very embarrassed, immersing himself again in his beer,

You think you've earned it?

Denis hesitates, or rather pretends to hesitate,

Come on, why not! It's a party, after all! Right, Marion? Stutter needs to have some fun, he's earned it, it's true, he fucked up but he needs to relax and after all it is a party!

So Denis stands up,

What do we do, how does it work with the music here?

he asks Marion, Patrice, everyone remains stunned; Denis sees the computer—a laptop sitting on a chest of drawers, speakers, hey, look at that, they're quite modern here. Denis starts to laugh, your husband's so cool, Marion, he even has a little playlist for a shindig, can we see? And he approaches, nobody quite understands what he's up to and the two girls are holding each other by the eyes as though it's the only way they have to not fall apart or to be certain they're actually experiencing what they're experiencing, the surprise giving way to a mute shock so strong that all reality finally dissolves into a sensation of brutal hyperrealism—the detail of a beauty mark they'd never noticed on the cheek of the other, a crack on a wall, Bergogne's thick mug and that ball of skin near his earlobe, the smallness of the dining room that they'd always imagined bigger, and all at once the hyperrealism disintegrates, breaks down into incomprehensible blocks—like landslides—the void opening up beneath them, and them, letting themselves be devoured out of an excess of disbelief, watching each other as if to find in the other the reflection of their own bewilderment, not counting on Marion who's split off from them, and when the song rings out in the dining room they don't believe it right away, Léo Ferré's voice and Denis at the computer, back turned to all of them,

You remember,

C'est extra,

Marion, the karaoke nights?

Les Moody Blues qui chantent la nuit,

Marion, the karaoke nights!

Comme un satin de blanc marié,

He sings and Ferré's voice comes out of the speakers, he turns the volume up very loud, too loud, it reverberates, it's vibrating in the dining room and Denis turns back toward Stutter,

Come give me a hand, come on, hurry up!

and here they both are telling everyone to back up, they get up and Stutter and Denis put the table against the wall—silverware falls, plates break, the two girls move over as far as they can, they're huddled together, backs to the wall, unable to speak, just as Patrice and Marion are silent, having come together, do they know it, do they see themselves doing it, seeking each other—this need he has to take her hand, to grab her by the arm, even if for a moment she rears back, hesitates, hides her desire to cry and welcomes his hand, biting her lip as if to say again over and over how sorry she is, but he tries to answer that she doesn't have to, even if it's absurd, because it lasts a second, Léo Ferré's slow song, that

C'est extra

thunderous,

C'est extra,

crooning his swaying, unifying sentimentality, this song they all know and that they've loved and to which they've loved, one day or another, one time or another, long ago, in another life; now Denis stands back, upright, in front of the French door, he motions to Christophe, yes, and to Stutter, yes, go ahead now, and Christophe goes to find Nathalie, appears in front of her and nobody hears any of what he says and you can see her recoiling, refusing, stricken with panic, with anger, her head shaking no, hands in front of her, but in reality soon she won't have a choice, in a few seconds Christophe will grab her by the forearm with such force that she won't even think about resisting, pulling her, bringing her toward him, leading her to the middle of the room all while exerting such pressure on her that she can't say no, just throwing panicked looks all around her, she won't cry out, won't say anything, will seek Marion, Marion, come, you have to come, this has to stop, why aren't you doing anything and him continuing to pull her into the middle of the room starting to shout come on, Stutter, come on! as he approaches him, your dance partner good sir! Your dance partner! what are you waiting for! and Stutter will approach Nathalie who is frozen at first, who will recoil when the other tries to take her by the waist, she'll recoil farther, will fight, Nathalie backing up and shouting—a shout of terror because Stutter is covered in blood, all she can see is the blood and this tear-ravaged look of his, the traces of his brother's nails in his neck, hair full of mud, she'll want to run away but also to know whose blood this is on him, and then to not know, Lydie will go toward Marion and will she have the strength to yell, to demand that Marion make it stop, that they be finished with all of it, will Denis watch all of this while smiling and tapping out time,

C'est extra,

that's right, it's extra, it's a treat and it'll be a treat too when they we put on some techno, with a fat bass and a beat with that swagger and swing whose slippery sounds they recognize,

Turn the light

On

Turn the light

Off

Stutter as if liberated and Christophe going to Lydie who'll have already crept along the wall and will try to escape him, but no, he reaches out his arm, she'll push it away, will refuse, will yell and Stutter will want Nathalie to drink from the bottle and he'll take his sticky hand and shove it behind Nathalie's skull to force her to drink, come on,

Turn the light

On

one sip, we'll share, her refusing, soon resisting, the time it takes for Marion to yell that's enough, to shout that's enough even though nobody can hear her because of the

Turn the light

Off,

the time it takes for Patrice to cross the room and fold down the screen so violently the computer falls onto the tile with a dull sound that stops the music, the two brothers,

Hey, we weren't done?

allowing the two girls to push them off and, with a few steps, move aside. And it will be at this moment that Marion, at last,

Okay, that's enough, that's enough,

will let out, with abundant resignation in her voice, and abandon, a few words—what Marion can say. What Marion is finally going to say.

39

At this moment Marion is agreeing to talk so everything will stop—just as she'd like to apologize for all the unpleasantness her friends have just been put through and for that which Patrice, for years, has selflessly absorbed—at this moment she's approaching Denis to talk to him, at this very moment, then, in the house next door, on the tile of the studio floor, here's Christine's breath returning, the feeling returning to her body—the heat and the cold, the pins and needles in her fingers and feet—the cold of the tiles so cold it's almost a burning sensation that awakens her.

At this moment, Christine's thoughts aren't thoughts but rather—or barely—flutterings over her body, vague sensations that begin to take shape in her mind, reminding her that she's laid out and that she's in pain—it's not yet a question of what's causing it or of precisely where the pain is strongest, nor even whether her body is broken entirely or if it can get up, walk, or if there'll be no question of that ever again. No. For now all these questions are locked up by the pain, circumscribed by it; the questions she could ask herself return to a corner of the brain where the pain seems to be absent, they go back to a point Christine can't manage to reach, unless the opposite is true and it's the pain that, in flashes, rises up and reminds Christine that she has a leg, and then another, a foot at the end of each of her legs, a stomach like an island stranded in the middle of an ocean—breasts, arms, eyes, a neck and a head made of a mouth, a nose, ears. It's as though all her limbs have been separated from her, wrenched from her, confined to the space of their pain, not yet connected by the consciousness of constituting a single being. But the cold of the tile will help her: the sickening smell of blood, of beer in her mouth, the desire to vomit will help her. The skull bangs, tightens, crushes; and then, interfering, a more diffuse pain in the nose, sinuses whistling, trouble breathing, nostrils obstructed by thick blood, already clotted, that leaves little room to breathe.

While Christine drifts up toward consciousness, regaining a bit more life with each minute, there will be, at Bergogne's house, as if by the movement of a pendulum, Marion's life becoming more and more fragile; as though, from one house to the other, from one generation to the other, from one woman to the other, one is diminishing as the other regains her strength, neither aware of the other, one thinking the other is dead while the other, coming back to life, has no idea that the first is currently falling apart—not literally, not physically, no, because on the contrary Marion is full of resilience nourished by her anger and her rage, even galvanized, but you can see her inner collapse and it appears so sharply to everyone that now she can no longer hide it from anyone. Nathalie and Lydie are watching her with astonishment, they've already forgotten the victorious, impertinent, unbelievable Marion of this afternoon, the Marion who impressed them so much in front of that imbecile project manager and in front of the boss, and they search behind her ravaged face for any trace of the magnificent Marion who's made them dream so many times whereas now, here, in front of them, this Marion has collapsed—the tears she's no longer holding back but letting out without reserve or concern for being seen, that broken, uncertain voice they'd never have recognized,

Okay…

haggard voice

You've won, you win,

trying to recover,

That's what you wanted...

struggling against itself to come back, breaking off,

To see me like this... here, like this, in front of...

leaving the two girls and Bergogne—all three having thought they knew her—incredulous, shocked at this unfamiliar Marion, as though they're discovering the shamelessness of that part of herself Marion has done everything to hide from them for years, and adding, now that she's revealing herself, the ignominy of duplicity to her vulnerability, because what Marion's two co-workers are seeing, what Patrice is discovering, is her fearful, almost spineless servility—a form of accommodation in the face of fear, a way of accepting its stranglehold that neither her husband nor her girlfriends have ever seen in her, and that they're discovering, surprised not to see her cave before Denis, giving up everything, shedding the garments of herself and the image she so liked *giving* others, for whom she'd reinvented herself several years ago, but mostly stunned by all that, before today, she never allowed to appear of the woman now revealing herself to them.

Now she stands facing Denis, because it's to him alone that she has to talk, in that dejected voice—him triumphant, her recognizing everything about him, his tics, his glittering vanity, his petty and crazy joy tinting his cheeks pink, almost mauve, as though he's about to literally burst with joy, while he pretends to remain as calm as possible. She wants to say, she hears herself say, first almost nothing, breaths she'd take for words, then words forming at last, Fine... yes, that's right, you've won, you've... you win... that's right... and... you always win, right?... No? Isn't that what I'm supposed to think? That Denis always wins... so leave them... let them leave... they haven't done anything to you, the girls, just let them go, that's enough... and Patrice didn't do anything to you either.

She thinks nobody can hear her, because she's unable to raise her voice or hear it herself, as though it's buzzing so loudly around her that she can't be sure she's uttered the slightest word, but also because, without realizing it, she's come so close to Denis that she's speaking with her face raised to him, with the feeling she's addressing him in a voice that's not soft—she can hear the friction, the scraping in her throat—but so low, so very low she thinks only he can hear her; and that's all she wants, all she hopes for, that they don't hear her, that they don't detect in her voice the vibration of her resignation and her surrender. She still has this vague hope that they won't hear her, that the girls won't realize she's not the cool and wicked girl no one can resist, that she's not who they think they know. And now she almost resents them for how naïve they were to think she was so strong, so powerful, she suddenly resents them so much she wants to turn around and attack them both, yes, this impulse, this desire she has to repress to pounce on them and send it all tumbling down, to lay into both of them and yell that since she's lived here obviously nothing and nobody has been able to have the slightest hold over her life or over her, that's how kind people here are, didn't you know?

And how to explain to them that anyway nothing can hurt her because her life has been dead since the day she met Denis, too early in her adolescence, barely out of childhood, because for years she lived in his shadow and in terror—do they have any idea what that is, terror, when the idea of fear makes her *gently* laugh, because with fear there's always the idea that you can make it through, and so long as there's a possible escape it's nothing, nothing, while terror, terror erects the same impregnable wall each night, each night the same hell beginning again—is she going to scream at them and blame them for never having known what it could be like to live with a guy like Denis, who crushes you and erases you from your own head, who steals you two or three trinkets from a store from time to time to pretend to dote on you, coming back with arms full of jewels, of telephones, of clothes stolen who knows where just to make you dizzy because a few nights earlier he went so far that even he was surprised at his fury, almost killing you, not just

abusing you that time, only to imagine a pillow-talk reconciliation that reconciles only him with his need to fuck, but you let it
happen because it's better to play dead than to really die, and too
bad if he rants at you swearing he loves you and promising punish-
ments you can't even imagine if you even think once more about
leaving him, about leaving—leaving? not even in my dreams, I
didn't even do it in my dreams anymore, I didn't dream anymore
I was so scared of running into him there, because he decided it
was my turn to pay for his anger and his own humiliations, even in
my dreams I sink straight to the bottom of the night, every night,
has one of you two ever pissed herself at four in the morning to
hear the man you live with who can't even get his fucking keys in
the lock because he's too drunk, do you know what it's like, that
dread and that rage, the desire to kill him—not only a desire, but
the idea that gets clearer and clearer, the means taking shape, the
heart flinching at the end but not the idea, just the fear of actually
doing it and of missing him, of blowing your shot but nothing
else, never—just because he told you you're going to get a beating
because he decided your pussy stinks of someone else's jizz—his
words, spat on what remains of your illusions or the hope that one
day it'll all work out, because to him you deserve to drag along
on your knees asking forgiveness and admitting that you're just a
whore who'll never do it again; and this whole world that comes
back into her head, she can almost see it on parade as she stares
at Lydie and Nathalie with such anger it looks like she's ready to
kill them—the two women not understanding, what did we say
to her?

Nothing, we didn't say anything to her, we didn't do anything!

but it's true that in the dining room everyone else has heard
her, all of them, say yes, you've won, you always win... and then
as though she can't take it anymore Marion attacks them now,
why are you looking at me like that? She attacks them, the girls,
Lydie, Nathalie, but also Patrice and Christophe, Stutter, Denis,

everyone, what the fuck do you want from me? what did I do? stop, stop waiting, what? what do you think, girls? that you can just snap your fingers to get rid of all the assholes on Earth? that I can... that I can what? Her voice jamming, unable to go any further and exhausted, collapsing, the emotion suddenly engulfing her and the tears overflowing—she waits for something from her husband, she mumbles, I can't do anything, I can't, you have to understand, there's nothing I can do... So, yes, she turns back to Denis, she has enough strength left for that; I don't know what you want, I don't know, fuck, I don't know... I can't do anything for you, you hear me? I can't. You can smile all you want, it won't change anything... so come on, come on, let's go talk... but not here. Come upstairs. Just the two of us. At least it'll be just us two—and we'll settle our scores, we'll fucking settle them.

Yes, go upstairs. Go upstairs, both of them. Is this an idea that sprouted in her so quickly it might seem she's been letting it ripen for a long time? or, on the contrary, that the idea comes to her just at the moment she mentions it, becoming aware of what it can offer her in the way of opportunity and that, realizing this just as quickly, as she says it, she stares at Patrice with a sort of questioning or almost an exaltation in her eyes, as if seeking support, which he answers without hesitation, with an unmistakable look? Because without really knowing why, as though his eyes too have started shining, he wants her to know he agrees with her. That he trusts her. That he understands her as though he *really* understands what she's been thinking, as though not only does he agree with her but the same idea has imposed itself on him, with the same lightning speed as it crossed her mind, even though he doesn't really know what she's been thinking or what she told herself when she repeated to Denis that they'd go talk, yes, but not here, in the dining room, not even in the living room or somewhere in a room on the ground floor, but upstairs, without specifying where, as though there's some obvious place to go and it couldn't happen anywhere else even though upstairs there are only questionable rooms in which to accommodate them: bedrooms, a bathroom.

But maybe she's not thinking of that, maybe it hasn't even crossed her mind. She's thinking only that she'll have to pass by her daughter's room and that she'll take the time to go in, and that she'll have strength enough to insist that she go in alone. Now something changes. The tears stop flowing. Marion collects herself, as you'd take back from someone who took it without asking something that belongs to you. She knows what she has to do, repeats it,

Upstairs, we'll go upstairs.

and so what if

The bedroom so soon?

Christophe can't help himself,

My my, that was a quick reconciliation, wasn't it?

Stutter starts to laugh with Christophe, both of them by the French door, drinking, snickering at length at the insinuation, eyeing the girls with a look that's not even salacious, no, just ponderous, with a kind of awkwardness they don't know how to untangle themselves from, as though trying to play clever has embarrassed them and made them even more ill at ease than it bothered Nathalie and Lydie, and Patrice too, all three right on the other side of the table, standing, squeezed together tightly while Denis and Marion stay a few more seconds on the right, Denis just saying he agrees, if she wants, why not, he can grant that, of course, like a victor he consents to this whim, he doesn't see a trap in it and he's right, there's no trap, just the idea that Marion can go into her daughter's room—which she'll do after they go upstairs, leaving behind the five others, Denis having taken care to leave Stutter his pistol,

Can we trust you this time?

looking him up and down severely—or playfully,

Can we trust you?

provocative,

We can, you're sure?

Stutter not saying a word as he takes the weapon, contemplating the pistol in his hand, as though it's too heavy for him, or as though he's unworthy of being shown this sign of trust again. He stays with this strange feeling that he's maybe being manipulated, and the idea confusedly crosses his mind that his brother is making a game of tripping him up, that he's waiting each time for him to make a mistake, that he doesn't trust him the way he claims to, but trusts that everything will tip over into an accident, a catastrophe, as though in truth that's what he expects from him, which not even he would be able to name, so troubled is he to be given this weapon—and his first reaction is to look for help in Christophe's face.

So, without thinking, he puts the pistol in his pocket—it's so small, this gun—and like everyone else he leers at Denis and Marion as they leave, Denis following Marion toward the stairs up to the bedrooms and the bathroom, Marion not daring to slow down as she passes the girls or even give them a look that would have to be accompanied by apologies, regrets, just as she doesn't dare stop for Patrice, even if he, on the other hand, doesn't take his eyes off her and moves in her direction, takes a step toward her but without daring to touch her, to hold her back, much less to talk to her, and then another step, but this time toward Denis, planting himself in front of him as though he wants to block his passage, to show him he'll always try to insert himself between his wife and him, but the other swerves, their shoulders graze each other, and then one of the two ventures this light pitch of the chest toward the other, an almost imperceptible motion, their shoulders collide, the appointment is made—a flick of the fingers, provocation, bodies stiff, shoulders tensed, struggle restrained—then Denis continues.

Patrice lets them go up, chewing on his anger, crimson, skin shiny with sweat; he swallows saliva and it tastes dirty in his mouth. Once more he wonders what he can do, what's going to happen, and above all he hopes Marion can follow through on what he thinks her idea is: to go see Ida. To talk to Ida. To tell her she has to leave. She'll have to wake her up if she's asleep, murmur to her that she has to run away until the suggestion finds its way into her dreams, into her sleep, or rather wake her up suddenly if she's somehow sleeping, which he doesn't think she is but you never know, everything possible must be done to get her out of here; Marion is climbing the stairs and he's not surprised to see her doing it the way she does, upright, without looking at him or anyone else. He couldn't say whether she's moving with determination or resignation, like a convict walking to the scaffold or like a ringleader about to give the first shout of the coming rebellion; she's in motion, that's all. With him following her and climbing the stairs as though they're both going—yes, this time Bergogne thinks of it as clearly as it's possible for him to accept, the idea shoots through him that they're going up to the bedrooms, and this image opens him up to all the understanding he needs to grasp the moment: at last he thinks he knows who Denis is to her, or who he was, the one she never talked about and who's haunted their entire relationship. He sees them disappear upstairs, he waits for the moment he'll hear them stop in front of Ida's room, he hopes his idea—her idea that he thinks he understood from her posture—hopes she'll be able to carry it out right away, to go into their daughter's room without the other one following her—that's what he's waiting for now, almost holding his breath to make sure not to miss the moment Marion tells Denis to wait for her, that she wants to go see if her daughter is asleep—yes, that's what's going to happen, it has to, and she'll murmur to Ida that she has to run away as fast as she can, with enough conviction to motivate her but not so much that she paralyzes her, frightens her, even though she does need to give her the courage to flee—through the window? The door? How to do it? Come down and slip in among everyone, pass through a window in the living room or why not get to the patio through the door at the back of the living room that they never use and that must still have the key in it, and then run without stopping, don't stop, but without telling her that not stopping means going past Christine's, whatever you do don't go through her door—but how to tell her that without arousing her suspicions? Let her run, yes. Ida has to get out of here. That's all he's thinking about, he's sure it's all Marion is thinking about too; it's the only reason she suggested to Denis that they go upstairs, Patrice can't see any other, not imagining the absurdity of the remark Christophe has just made, but not imagining any more that the first reason she wanted to step away was that she didn't want them to be heard, simply because she wants her humiliation to stop and for everything that for years she's managed to annihilate, to destroy from the past of her life—those zones tucked so far away they could have stayed buried until the end of time without anyone coming to demand them from her—to remain forever forbidden to everyone else, to their knowledge and their judgment.

40

When she hears the steps on the stairs, Ida thinks they're coming to get her, that all of a sudden they've remembered her and they're going to ask her something. She thinks back to the present her father seized from her hands and threw away, of that shameful feeling of having betrayed him because she already had the present in her hands and she almost accepted it, because she wanted to, because he saw how much she wanted it, that desire she's been thinking about for a little while with the feeling of having committed an error that her father will surely hold against her for a long time. This idea is strong, but the steps coming up the stairs are even stronger. She knows the sounds of her parents' steps when they come up, the steps of one or the other if they come up alone, but this time there are two people coming up—is it her parents coming up? why would someone else come to see her up here?

For a little while she's been hearing fragments of voices, but she eventually put headphones on to play a video game and beat up monsters who burst like soap bubbles when you kill them with a stick. She didn't play long, stopped because she wanted to know what was going on downstairs, keeping the headphones on to filter the noises, the voices, to set a kind of padded protection between the world and her that could keep her safe. She didn't get undressed, she just took off her shoes and kept on her socks—which she's been tugging on for a little while, feet together, legs closed, sitting on her bed, thinking that her stupid socks were bothering her, that they hadn't been put on right, the seams pointing all over the place, hugging neither her heels nor the tips of her toes; she pulled them up, adjusted them, massaged her toes, then she studied the painting across from her that Tatie Christine painted for her and that she got for her birthday two years ago—that little girl that could have been her, except her eyes were an unreal salmon pink and her hair sapphire blue, and she had a bottle-green checkered coat like nothing she's ever worn, neither a coat nor anything checkered, and she was standing up straight in a way Ida's never been able to stand up straight, except occasionally under the ruler held by Madame Privat, who noted down her progress in height and weight. Otherwise she'd never have stood as straight as the little girl with blue hair carrying a fawn in her arms who didn't look scared at all and on whose back you could see two rows of marks, like a sort of computer keyboard with big whitish keys dissolving into the chestnut hair. She often dreamed that Tatie Christine would one day give her a painting of the little girl as an adult, who'd have the same blue hair but a different haircut: she would have abandoned the bob for a looser style, long hair falling over her shoulders, and then, above all, in front of her, taking up much of the space of the painting, whose dimensions would also be multiplied by the young girl's age, there would be an enormous white deer—the fawn's white marks would have spread out and taken over the animal's whole coat, the antlers themselves would be white, it exists, why not him, he'd have his head tilted for a confrontation unless it was to take a bow, impossible to know, both of them would be big and now she thinks not of the deer's white antlers but of the deep brown wood of the stairs that cracks under the steps that stop just in front of her door, and, without hesitation, she takes off the headphones and throws them to the foot of the bed, just as she throws herself into her bed, pulling the blanket over herself to hide that she's not in her pajamas, that she's not asleep—she looks at the time on her clock radio but doesn't see the numbers; no, it's a reflex she has, worrying about the time, as she does almost every night when her parents come up to go to bed, because often it's late and they think she's already long asleep, even though she likes to stay up with her lamp lit daydreaming or reading at the edge of her bed, in the timid yellowish flicker of her tiny lamp whose lightbulb spits out a light so weak it only projects its brightness in a very short halo that Ida knows can't be seen from under her door.

But this time it's not like every night, she's not hungry and yet from inside her stomach she can hear noises of pipes groaning, something twisting; she has no desire to swallow anything but water but she's already drunk her whole bottle. She's still very thirsty and didn't dare go out earlier to fill it in the bathroom at the end of the hall, in spite of her dried lips, she was afraid to draw attention, and now here are the steps coming up to her door. She waits with her eyes closed and will pretend to be asleep, but she can't help it, she has to open them again because she recognizes her mother's voice speaking to someone she understands is a man, and isn't her father.

Her door opens: Ida turns toward her mother acting as though her mother has just woken her, pretending her eyes are blurry with sleep. Her mother has closed the door and now she's leaning over her bed. Marion looks at her daughter, Ida looks at Marion, and she thinks she sees, in the darkness of her bedroom, in spite of the brightness of the little lamp, eyes so shiny, could it be that her mother—are those tears? No, she hears the shaking voice, it's like last night, like so often these last few days and these last few weeks, reading the book of *Stories of the Night,* when, as she leaves, her mother always tells her,

Sweetheart, if a dragon bothers you, just knock his teeth out.

Marion comes and murmurs something in her ear that Ida doesn't understand. Right away she wants to ask her mother if the men have left, if they're leaving soon, if the girls are leaving too. She hears in her mother's voice that she's lying when she says that yes, everyone will be leaving soon, in a little bit it'll be just the three of them again, and Christine will come join them. She speaks with a voice so soft and at the same time so shaky that Ida's no longer quite sure whether her mother is speaking to her seriously or trotting out a story in a cajoling voice to lull her to sleep. She doesn't know, doesn't understand; her mother tells her, sweetheart, don't make any noise, whatever you do don't make any noise, but as soon as you can you have to leave here, you have to try, do you know where you can leave from, from the lean-to, you know, from the bathroom window, you jump into the yard without hurting yourself and you run, you don't go to Tatie's because she's sleeping, you don't go to her house, even if the light is on, you don't bother her and you get out of here, you run and you go to Lucas's house or Charline's house. Marion doesn't imagine that in her daughter's mind the implacable logic of childhood is at work, the questions that leave adults by their wayside, because only children have the good sense to drop pebbles behind them to find their way back, and right away Ida thinks that if Christine has gone home to sleep, why, in the neighboring hamlets, wouldn't Lucas's and Charline's parents be sleeping too, and why should she wake them up rather than Tatie Christine, who's just next door?

But Ida doesn't ask this. She says yes, because she can feel through her mother's fingers as she takes both her cheeks in her hands, in the flesh of her fingers, the radiant heat of fear; she can smell in her mother's breath, so close, not just the breath tainted by wine and too many cigarettes, but in the coppery, bitter odor, she doesn't know what it is and doesn't wonder if her mother is sick, no, she just knows something is happening right now whose gravity she can feel isn't the same as it was earlier—and yet she knows that what's happening is terrorizing her, the three men, the dog lying there in his blood, and still she does everything she can not to be scared, to keep her composure, be brave, and when her mother takes her very tightly in her arms, when she lets out in a breath that she loves her more than anything, she doesn't wonder what this *more than anything* means, what it contains, how love can contain *more than anything* and not be the anything itself.

Her mother embraces her, and this idea of fleeing, did her mother ask her to—

Mom?

but her mother doesn't hear her, she's just returned to the door, closed it behind her, very quickly, without turning back toward her, without taking the time, almost as if escaping the bedroom, and Ida is left alone with the flickering yellowish light that so poorly illuminates the portrait of the little girl and the fawn; she has the feeling both of them are telling her the same thing, she thinks of Christine and tells herself she's going to try to go to her house—every time something bad happens, no matter what her mother has to say, because she's a bit jealous of Ida's affection for her neighbor, she always goes to Tatie Christine's.

When Ida slowly opens her bedroom door, she doesn't hear voices or noises, no movement or motion coming from the dining room. Downstairs everyone seems to have given up talking or expecting anything to happen before Marion and Denis return. Unless everyone is trying to go with them as they wait, to follow them by imagining where they're going, what they'll say to each other, because in the intimacy of that silence why not keep watch—what else to do but perk up an ear to make out a few words, a sentence or two maybe, that might give some clues as to what's happening or will soon happen, simply by taking the time to listen? So, when she opens her bedroom door, Ida doesn't hear any noise coming from downstairs. No voices. Even though it doesn't last, because soon, in a few seconds, she'll hear Christophe and Stutter, whom she'll recognize, just as she'll immediately recognize that distinctive tone they have, an accent from a region she knows nothing about and that makes their French sound like a foreign language, even though you can recognize that it's French.

She opens the door very slowly, very careful not to let herself be heard. The staircase isn't far from her door and she could hear, rising toward her, the voices from conversations downstairs. But nothing. Nor does she hear any more from her mother and the man who's with her. She hears just that they've gone into the bathroom, that they've closed the door without shutting it completely behind them—a strange silence that lasts too long, expands, spreads through the whole house, finally broken by the voices downstairs,

You think you know your Marion?

then silence. Steps, cracks—the legs of chairs being moved. Then, much higher,

Shut your mouth,

only her father's voice slicing through,

Shut up,

when he tries to silence the guys who keep going, excitedly and quickly,

You think you know her?

Bergogne just

Shut up,

responding

Shut up, both of you, I mean it,

with his voice full of an anger she recognizes so well, his voice where everything trembles, which reassures Ida so strongly in this moment. But soon she hears nothing but him, and then almost nothing, as though there's nobody downstairs, or as though Bergogne is alone in front of the two men—and again, are both of them there, Ida isn't sure, she can only make out one other voice with her father's—because what she doesn't know, doesn't see, is how the two guys are speaking in lower and lower voices, as though the secrets they want to reveal won't withstand too bright a light or too sharp a burst of sound, as though it requires murmurs and a dimmed room to hear the rustle of the dirty laundry in which they want to embroil everyone, addressing the two women, now seated and ashen, mute, waiting for the brothers—the ladies, they feel, will be more receptive—and staring hopelessly at the weapons the two others are holding, not seeing the irony and not really hearing the guys telling them with a mournful weariness, sorry though they are, but enjoying laying out these disgusting stories about their friend because they want to tell them, these stories, all of them, because they feel they're redressing an injustice and say so several times, Marion lies to everyone, that's how she is, so they have to tell these stories in detail, not just tainting the portrait they're drawing of Marion's youth but also tainting the details, tainting everything about her, everything that touches on her, everything she might have touched in her youth, tainting her so that at last she'll be nothing more than that, a woman tainted by tainted stories each more sordid than the last, the portrait of a slut that they work hard to make dirtier than anything the three others, husband and co-workers, have ever imagined about her.

And no doubt Stutter is only following, repeating what his older brother has been telling him for years; maybe Stutter is only repeating Christophe's words so Christophe will be sure he's one of them, that he's what Denis demands and expects of them. And maybe Stutter is inventing, embroidering, just to make himself look good to his brothers, no matter, he's behind Christophe at every turn, he walks in his footsteps, he underlines what he's saying, pursing his lips, repeating yes, that's right, and to Christophe it doesn't matter much at the moment whether they believe them or not because what counts, for him, is that in the minds of Marion's co-workers and her husband images are taking root of a young girl who nobody could ever trust, a slut with no morals or anything else, a drugged-up slut who had a hell of a time giving up dope and would have had an even worse time giving up stealing if Denis and them hadn't been there—probably because she'd taken a liking to it, to stealing, and because it was her *nature*—which they suggest but without saying it outright, without articulating it, just with shrugs of their shoulders, letting out appalled sighs apparently inadvertently, starting stories and not finishing them, too afflicted, too affected for that, so sick at such baseness that they can't find the words, so better that the others' imaginations do the rest.

Because what matters isn't so much what they say as what they suggest: these images, they're inoculating them into the husband's brain and the friends' brains like a poison that will spread through them and soon take the place of their own memories. What matters is that what they're letting linger without saying it out loud will soon have the same realness, the same degree of certainty, as if they themselves, co-workers and husband, had known Marion when she was young and had seen her wallow in all the different kinds of shit revealed by these images. The brothers know the poison will make its way, that everything that for now the others are denying and fighting, everything they're refusing with all the ardor and love they have for Marion, with all the faith they feel in the idea they've chosen to have of her, Marion's husband and her two co-workers will eventually accept it, submit to it, believe it, and finally see it as though they've never doubted it or as though they themselves witnessed it too.

The two brothers talk and,

Shut up,

weaker and weaker, more and more pitiful,

Shut up,

not yet begging nor entirely discouraged, but already Patrice is letting himself be anesthetized by emotion, what, a polluted dust in the air, his wife, prison? six months in prison? his wife? her friends cheating guys and her involved, an overstrung thief and liar, a scrapper setting fire to an old woman's house out of sheer pleasure and vice—more nastiness, the words flying like a swarm of wasps around his ears,

Shut up,

he repeats, and this time, from upstairs, his daughter doesn't hear him, his voice is a murmur that dies out and turns into an enormous smile of triumph on Christophe's face.

Ida doesn't hear this; in her head, she no longer has any idea or image of what's happening in the dining room.

Now she's left her bedroom, she's standing up in the hallway and softly closing her door. Already, without really knowing why or what she expects from it, she decides to do something perhaps incomprehensible or illogical, but that she sets about doing with a meticulousness that would surprise even her if she were paying attention. She's surprised for a few seconds that her steps and her body aren't ordering her to obey her mother and try to flee the house as fast as possible, or even to look for ways to make that flight happen. And yet it's in her mind, in her entire being: she still hears her mother's voice, her words, her intonation, the fear and the form of unnamable prayer or plea it contains, and the echo of those words reverberating throughout her whole body. And yet what she does is not obey her mother or try to get out of the house; almost involuntarily, but diligently, mechanically, like in those images of sleepwalkers or zombies or, through the superimposition of two images, the doubling of a character who dreams he's leaving his body in certain old films that Ida hasn't seen, Ida does something other than what she was asked to do and knows she should do. She herself admits, with a kind of naïve astonishment, as though she's powerless against it, that it wasn't to obey her mother's order that she left her bed as soon as she was alone in her room, that she put her shoes back on and turned her bedside lamp off before going to the door. No, that's not why she adopted this cautious feline slowness in opening the door and then slipping into the hall. She stayed on the landing for a few seconds, waiting for what, listening to or rather tracking the voices coming up from the dining room, as if trying to understand not so much what the words are saying as what they reveal about the situation.

Now she stays in front of her door without quite knowing what to do, listening and not listening to what's happening downstairs, taking the time she needs to let the voices coming up from the dining room debate, inside her, with the internal but no more silent voice of her mother ordering her to flee, repeating to her over and over, in the secrecy of her brain, what she wants to see her do, but merging with the voice, present and real this time, of her mother at the other end of the hallway, murmuring, trying to cut a path through the silence, a voice Ida can make out in spite of the ones coming up from the ground floor and that other one whose echo can still be heard in her mind. She understands that this voice is a few meters away from her but at first she doesn't understand whether it's speaking by itself or to somebody, maybe to the man whose steps accompanied Marion's when she came upstairs.

She needs all this time to accept the idea that it's not what's happening downstairs that's calling to her, and all this time to understand that it's not just what might be being said in the bathroom that intrigues her, but first and foremost why her mother came to see her, with that voice, so wounded and flickering, so worried, why this fear Ida has never heard in it, as though she's just discovered a new voice within her mother's voice. But the question shifts into something else: suddenly, why this light coming from the bathroom and this water flowing from the faucet—very hard, as though someone has opened the tap all the way? Is it to cover up what they're saying, to thicken what separates it from us, to make the voices more distant, why if she didn't want to be heard didn't her mother and the man just go out in the yard?

It doesn't occur to the little girl that she might be the answer to this question. She just slides along the wall of her bedroom, in the hallway. She walks slowly because she knows all the noises the floorboards make—how many times has she slunk to the bathroom in the middle of the night, or very late in the evening, to fill her water bottle, to pass in front of her parents' room because she heard them arguing, because what worried her more than their fighting then was the fear of being its subject, or rather its catalyst, as though she needed to hear for herself that she wasn't responsible for the shouts of one or the other—and tonight she moves forward avoiding the pitfalls of cracking wood, stepping over one floorboard, making herself light on another, then, little by little, making it to the bathroom, in front of the door, or rather not in front of it but to the side, taking care to stand against the partition opposite the doorknob, hoping to see without being seen, to be sure not to pass in front of the ray of light from the door, but sure to be able to hear everything.

It doesn't take her long. To listen. Even though the words aren't clear at first, masked by the rush of the faucet. Here she is standing against the door and, because she thinks she can't keep standing without losing her balance, without needing to shift in some way from one leg to the other, she needs a support, she can't lean her shoulder against the door without moving the panel and giving away her presence. She decides to stay crouched, feet flat, arms and hands around her knees, neck and head stretched to place her ear closest to the door, hovering but not touching it, staring at the zone of light that comes through the gap in the doorframe where the sounds are coming out—first that of the faucet whose stream is splashing on the enamel of the sink, then, when a hand closes it, the sound of the water escaping down the drain, making a ridiculous glug-glug, then her mother's breath and her mother speaking in a very low voice, with a kind of cautiousness that's not like her, as though there's a desolation in her voice, a devastation forcing her to speak slowly and almost in a whisper, as though she has to apologize or take care not to let anything erupt around her. Ida doesn't understand all the words, not because they're difficult or abstract, unfamiliar to her, but because they're borne with such a worried deference that Ida has the feeling it's not her mother saying them. No, I never set you up. No. Never. And then long passages of silence, saturating the space in the same way as Marion's strange sibylline sentences, interrupted only by the man's voice speaking in short phrases, almost always as though he's reiterating his questions,

Oh really?

and then again the silence spreading between the two of them, imposing its cottony thickness,

Oh really?

No.

You didn't betray me?

No.

Oh really?

then, still, that silence. Or rather something like two silences that have chosen to confront one another and stand face to face, which Ida discovers from behind the door, her hands gripping her knees, her feet still flat and her back curved, her neck stretched to hear her mother's voice again and try to recognize her when she says, I left and I had a right to, you hear me, I had the right, I told you—

Oh really? You had the right?

and then again the silence expanding, this time beyond even a very long time, the way it can sometimes happen that you stop talking and create, within a conversation, a space of retreat where everyone can come find what they need to nourish a new beginning that they mean to be livelier and more nourished than the initial salvo of words, as though those were exhausted or spoiled too quickly. This time it's not the kind of consensual silence where each party finds a benefit, even an insufficient or meager one, but a benefit all the same. No. Ida tries to imagine what's happening behind the door, and it's only at the cost of great effort that she doesn't get up and run into the bathroom to throw herself into her mother's arms, to make everything stop. She bites her lip, maybe, and continues to hold her fingers even tighter against her knees, why is she so scared, why does this silence seem to go on so long— she imagines behind the door and sees in her mind her mother, leaned over the sink, as though she's sick or dead drunk, closing her eyes, not yet having taken the time to take the towel and wipe away all the water she's splashed on her face.

41

Still, the cold water does her good—for a few seconds Marion thinks she's regaining her strength and even a kind of upper hand over herself, and by forcing on him this time she's taking, it's as though she's also gaining, in a way, a kind of upper hand over Denis, who's staring at her with a look she knows all too well and that comes back to her not even from very far away, not even from the past, no, because this look on his face has always been inscribed in her, ready to resurface, as it emerges now, just a few details to mark the number of years that have passed, but otherwise it's still, just as it's recorded in her memory, that same expression of cold anger and determination.

He's sitting on the edge of the bathtub, legs spread apart as though he's opening his thighs shamelessly to show her his cock and balls through his pants, promising them to her like the punishment that's been awaiting her all these years he's been swearing she wouldn't escape because he was within his rights, within what he thought were his rights, which no doubt has nothing to do with the rights and the laws of judges or of cops, not even the rights Marion invented for herself when she got the hell out the way she did, making good on that threat she'd made so many times to disappear without leaving an address as soon as the opportunity presented itself. And he who'd thought she'd never dare go through with it, who was presumptuous enough to believe she wouldn't be able to venture out of his orbit, as though at the center of his system—in which he played the part of the sun, too incandescent for the cold and insignificant planets gravitating around him to try to escape his radiation—he believed it was impossible for anyone to slip free from his hold and the fascination he exerted on whomever he decided. So when Marion took advantage of his incarceration to vanish into thin air, he had taken a blow worse than the sentence and worse than prison itself; it happened to him just as it happens to others, but he, incredulous at first, had shrugged his shoulders and been haughty with Christophe, especially because Christophe had warned him long before it happened, promising him that, as a loving brother and guardian of the common good, he'd keep an eye on Marion for the whole length of his incarceration, because, he'd said, a girl like that, you just know she'll seize the chance one day or another to get out of here, no question, your cutie'll cut and run, he had insisted with a funny kind of smile, pleased with his joke or maybe exhilarated by the idea that it was possible to take the risk of dissatisfying Denis, unless he was, for a second, secretly excited and enthused by this idea that she might have the nerve to escape him. And since Denis didn't say anything, Christophe launched his pun again, between *cut and run* and *cutie*—so proud of having come up with it that he couldn't help but laugh at it himself, which didn't amuse Denis at all, irritated him, he who, in response, patronized his brother by reminding him that in any case Christophe had never been able to stand Marion and it wasn't so clear what he was playing at with her.

After that, Denis will savor it for a long time, years after, the bitterness of what his brother predicted that day, but at first he didn't want to hear what his brother told him, and he simply repeated to himself, bitter and angry at Christophe above all, for days and days, maybe, in that duration dilated by the narrowing space of the cell, he who'd been sentenced to the impotence of confinement, that obviously he had no doubt Christophe would keep an eye on Marion, an eye bright with covetousness and concupiscence, with poorly concealed desire, and frustration, because Denis had always seen—and known since childhood—how the loyalty of his younger brother and the admiration he'd always shown him were also marred by a sourness that could turn into betrayal should the opportunity present itself. Denis had always known it, just as he'd known how to play it, knowing Christophe couldn't escape, any more than he or Stutter could, the roles assigned them by nature or family or life or what you will: the eldest, the younger, and the youngest, until the end of time. Any attempt to escape this would be as vain as it would have been to try to escape from his prison, leaving him no satisfaction now besides imagining how he could best make use, the moment he got out, of Christophe's resentment toward Marion, Stutter's need for love and his madness, the madness of the damaged child; ten years to imagine the day he'd wash away the affront she caused him when she took advantage of his incarceration to flee—because to him, to leave him was to flee.

And alone behind the glass of the visiting room, alone and still incredulous at her flight, Denis had had to admit he'd been wrong to trust her, or rather to trust his own capacity to subject her to his desires, thinking as he had—with certitude, without doubt or worry—that she would be bound to him without even saying it, without even waiting for him, just by reflex, because she owed him everything and she couldn't do anything but love him, be literally and without constraint *attached* to him because, for all the times he hit her or abused her, it was always her, ultimately, who admitted he was right to do it, admitting the mistakes she knew she hadn't made but that she accepted, as though she understood why she might be accused of them.

It was for this reason that he convinced himself she should have spent ten years living a life like the lives of all the other prisoners' wives, and that she should have submitted to a life that revolved around the prison, around the wait and in total fidelity to his family, to his relatives, but also and most of all fidelity to his absence, avoiding going out, avoiding parties, as one grieves a husband who is dead, so to speak, for as long as it takes to serve his sentence.

She should have refused to strut down the street, to drink in the presence of other men or treat herself to trips to shops or bars with her girlfriends, and make prison her life so that everyone around her would see how much she was its victim almost as much as he was, shattered by the penal system, giving up her own life, surrendering it to regular visits to him, bringing him more than just news of the outside, saving euro after euro for his comfort, repudiating anything that might look like a semblance of comfort for her, more dead than he was, wandering at home, in the street, like a shut-in who doesn't know that's what she is, as prisoners' wives wander, as prisoners' relatives and friends wander, all of them sentenced without being convicted, punished for a crime they maybe know nothing about, collateral victims who don't recover from the injustice done to them by their not being taken into account, sentenced to the peripheries of prisons and jails, as she should have gravitated around Denis's cell, tuning her life to his circular and cadenced steps around the prison yard, to his hours in the weight room and his nights of insomnia, waiting for visiting days with the same fear that they'd make her wait around for hours before letting her into the visiting room, and having to put up with the same conversations with prisoners' wives, the litany of griefs of mothers and fathers, the anger, the bile, the resentment and all that misery she'd have absorbed as wives and lovers should absorb with resignation, learning from one another all the tricks to give their husband—for the others all the partners were husbands—a bit of pleasure if not money, fearing each time that overzealous guards would search her so she wouldn't bring her man anything suspicious, all because of a word out of line or a look they judged misplaced.

And instead of that woman he had imagined waiting with the others, taking her place early in the morning in the queue of people congregated in front of the prison gate, in brutal heat or driving rain, no matter the weather and the degree of humiliation they had to accept, he'd had to bring himself to realize she wouldn't be coming and that, for the ten years he'd spend here, the only woman he'd see would be his mother, and her alone.

Now, now he tries to act as though he's relaxed, arms spread out from his body and hands on either side, on the edge of the bathtub. Sometimes he inspects himself in the very large mirror that takes up almost the whole wall above the sink, in which Marion has abundantly splashed herself with water, leaning over the bowl, plunging her hands into the water, soaking her face, stopping and then starting again, as though it's never enough to extricate her completely from what's happening, as though she still can't find her way out of a long bad night. He looks at her in the mirror and she doesn't turn around to talk to him. She watches him in the mirror too, her back to him, endlessly plunging her hands under a trickle of water that she opens and closes with the faucet, not even noticing what she's doing, how she's rubbing her cheeks, her face, her neck, her hair, before straightening up and watching his movements once more in the mirror, not even taking the time to dry her face or hands,

I didn't set you up, I wrote to you, I left a letter before I left.

Never got a letter.

Ask your brother.

Never got it.

I'm sure he knows.

Doesn't change a thing.

And the words spread through the room and race, even dulled, even diminished, to the other side of the bathroom wall. Ida hears them, and even though she doesn't understand everything, she picks up snatches and tries to connect them to one another, her mother,

I never asked you, never asked you to...

Marion's voice,

I never asked you,

No, you just made a date as though you were going to meet him, making sure I knew where and when he'd made the fucking date with you,

No,

You couldn't stand his face anymore,

No,

You wouldn't stop saying you were sick of him,

No,

That you didn't know how to get rid of him,

No,

You want me to tell you what you said?

I never wanted—

Your words, your own words, you want them?

I never asked, never...

Oh really?

Ida reluctant to go back to her room or wondering how she could make it to Tatie's house, but most of all, all of a sudden, she has the feeling that she can't move from here, that she can't go away and leave her parents, as though in some way she thinks they'll never manage without her. She wonders—it passes through her head even though she knows it's not a good idea, more like a ball of rage that rises in her and bursts like a soap bubble—if she shouldn't go into the bathroom and yell at the man to leave. But Ida doesn't do anything, she stays where she is, crouched, biting her knee through the cloth of her pants, clenching her jaw so tight that soon she might yell, she hears her mother's voice through the divider and on the other side of the door,

No... they said...

...

What you did.

I didn't have a choice.

How you did it,

I had no choice, I didn't... Never had a choice.

I had nothing to do with how you did it, nothing,

He was the one who was screaming,

You were the one who did it.

Yes, it was me. He was screaming and I smashed his face in like you wanted me to.

No...

Oh really?

Let them leave.

You think it's your decision?

Let them go.

That's what you think?

…

Marion? You think you're in any position? To ask me anything now? You?

I'll do what you want—

What I want?

Let them go…

Because now you know what I want?

What you want, no, I don't know what you want.

No, Marion. You don't know what I want.

And he goes silent, leaving Marion floundering in an old story where tears burst out, which Ida hears, recognizes, because she's heard her mother cry all alone, though she claims the last time she shed tears they were joke tears, crocodile tears, kids' tears when she was ten, giving the excuse a bit boastfully that after that she never shed a single tear again, not going so far as to say she fell too quickly into real life not to trade in her tears for an immense rage and a need to burn everything down, to tell everyone to fuck off, her mother first and foremost, but also the school and all the rest, that whole world in which her childhood and her youth and her entire life had made her feel like she was sinking into some kind of spongy, disgusting silt. Ida knew this business of never crying or of not knowing how to let go and let the tears come was false, of course, she'd caught her mother many times with tears in her eyes, but she'd never dared tell her.

This time, on the other side of the wall, in the bathroom, nobody says anything, nor even, it would seem, in the dining room.

No more noise comes up to the hallway or to Ida's ears. Then the single voice continuing, it's Marion's almost imperceptible murmur; the voice begins to whisper something, as though to itself. Ida wonders how the words are reaching her—it's at once very close and very distant—but she hears her mother repeat that she never wanted what happened and that she had nothing to do with it and, maybe for a few seconds, not even a minute, Marion really is addressing herself, maybe she's experiencing once more the mad decision to leave, to finally leave Denis and his family, and maybe she still feels, now, the gravity of that decision that had been ripening for several days before she did it—she who'd dreamed about it for years and who, because all of a sudden it was possible, had begun to doubt her ability to do it—yes, she remembers that morning so well—a May 24 about ten years ago, when it was a bit chilly for the season, when it had even been raining and she'd left her house without an umbrella, just as though she was going downstairs to buy cigarettes or bread, the length of a quick round trip with a bag a bit bigger than usual but certainly no suitcases or anything that might arouse the suspicions of Denis's parents who lived on the same street and kept an eye on her as soon as she went past the block of buildings, Denis's friends who all lived in the same housing project and took the same buses and the same trams as her. She'd had to act as though she was just going to take the bus or the tram to run some errands or go see a friend—still knowing they'd surely track her and that they'd start to wonder as soon as they saw her leave the project and cross the invisible barrier of her ordinary routine and the zone allotted her by her life and Denis's, and, casually, she'd taken a bus and walked for a long time until she found herself at a train station, suddenly staring at an arrivals and departures board, then on a platform, and, finally, frightened, very excited too, heart about to burst in her chest: on a train.

She'd done exactly as she'd planned it: take the first train leaving for anywhere—yes, that's what she'd done, boarded a train telling herself not to ask herself any questions, sitting down in a car, waiting for a conductor to come kick her off or stick her with a fine she'd never pay anyway because she didn't have an address; upon arriving at the station in Paris she'd decided not to stay, dreading the dense and shifting crowd in which she decided not to drown, telling herself that sooner or later Christophe would come this far to find her, that he'd look in all the stations, the fleabag motels near the stations, the squats, because he'd know she'd taken a train and that its terminus would probably be Paris—a place to wash up, this station or some other, before winding up on the street. So she'd decided to cross Paris, which she did on foot, letting chance guide her to a station she didn't know, stopping only occasionally, on benches, sometimes on a café patio, taking advantage of what she still had, in a wallet that was always too big, a few ten-euro bills that wouldn't last her the week. That was how she found herself, that May 24, on the boulevard de L'Hôpital, how she waited for hours at the McDonald's next to the Gare d'Austerlitz, sipping Coca-Colas and stuffing her face with cheese bacon burgers and potato wedges with ketchup, and how she took advantage of an unexpected ray of sunshine to bask in the Jardin des Plantes, treating herself with the bit of money she had left to a visit to the menagerie.

Night had come and, before she was even hungry, she had entered the train station, which seemed abandoned and empty, and again she boarded the first train and even took care not to look at its destination or even its stops, deciding as arbitrarily as possible that she would get off at the third stop if there was one, if the conductor hadn't kicked her off already, and that, no matter the city or the godforsaken backwater, that's where she'd remake her life. And at that exact moment she'd felt furious kicks inside her stomach: yes, definitely, good idea, the baby agreed with her.

42

Ida no longer quite knows what she's hearing, she's not even sure she's still listening—or else she wonders whether she's listening more to her body pulling her in all directions, her knees creaking, her back twisting, her neck hurting because it's tilted strangely; she doesn't know whether it's her body making her stand back up or what she's hearing and understanding less and less, sentences, attacks, words, the man's and her mother's, him getting worked up and answering that if he'd been crazy they wouldn't have thrown him where they threw him but in with the nuts at the nuthouse, he doesn't say crazy, he says at the nuthouse, they'd have thrown him into the nuthouse, his voice rises to say he's not like his brother,

What do you think?

and above all that she knows it perfectly well,

You know it perfectly well,

why's she playing at that, Marion, sure she'd prefer it, that'd suit her just fine, her and her shitty little conscience.

This is all Ida understands—deciphers—because afterward everything becomes blurry, her mother's voice trying to make space for itself, to rise up, to struggle, to push away the man's to take the upper hand and release over it—as though by forcing her voice she could help its truth impose itself—cutting words, so powerful they could silence the ones Denis is spitting with a more and more palpable anger that he's controlling less and less, as though this imperturbable determination he's enjoyed showing this whole time is now cracking to reveal chasms, perforations in his voice, and he's finally starting to stammer in his turn, not like his brother, but sliding toward the painful trembling of a voice that cracks, crumbles, and has to start over again to make itself heard. So he starts over again, hurls out very high, very clear, dominating and crushing everything—what did you think, Marion? that I was going to get out of the hoosegow and find myself a little wife to lay my little hatchlings without finding you first?—leaving her unable to react, and taking advantage to lay it on thicker—Are you that fucking stupid or do you take me for a joke?—then, letting a void insert itself between them and letting Marion take advantage of this silence to defend herself, as if smashing his head in with a rock—I don't owe you anything, I don't owe you anything, you don't want to hear it, that you don't exist anymore—and both of them start talking at once, so fast, so loud, or rather the voices have already risen so high that they begin unfurling their anger, their violence, and now their words collide without answering each other, neither of them listening anymore, no more than they see each other, even though Denis has gotten up from the edge of the bathtub and is approaching the sink, and she turns around, they face each other, they're almost touching, her already beginning to push him away,

Don't come near me,

as the words overlap,

Don't come near me I said,

clinging to each other,

Don't touch me,

and Ida no longer understands,

Don't come any closer,

she can feel it unfurling, it's going to breach the seawall, soon, she feels it and wonders what they're talking about because she doesn't understand anything, not what they're saying nor why they're saying it, why their voices are overlapping at that height from which all she perceives is the vertigo into which it's drawing her, and the fear rises in her and turns into anxiety, into panic, she hears it beating in her chest and growling inside her and, from behind the wall, in the wall itself, which is vibrating, in the door separating her from what she's hearing, it goes on, like a torn curtain—the confusion and his voice, snatches rising up that Ida catches, bits of phrase—I feel sorry for you Marion—your fat farmer and your shitty life—your little living room and your girlfriends from your shitty job—and then her mother's voice blurring or going silent to gather strength, or because she's run out of strength even though he hasn't, his voice hateful and inexhaustible crossing the silence next door—this is what you dreamed of? This shitty life down on a rotten farm?

Don't come near me,

Your fat farmer and your shitty life—your little living room and your girlfriends from your shitty job—

Marion doesn't say anything more. Maybe Ida senses something, because she gets up at the exact moment he approaches Marion, trying what exactly as a sign of appeasement, palms raised,

Come on, Marion… Marion. Sorry, I don't want to hurt you, sorry. If I say sorry. I'll take you with me if you want, we can start over if you want, Marion—the silence and then his voice starting over in several tones—Marion?—Marion…

Marion.

Marion.

Marion fucking listen to me.

Silence. Him unable to stand this silence. And maybe the hateful expression she shoots him as her one and only answer; the refusal he receives like a slap because he'd perhaps hoped or thought this whole time that it would be enough for him to reappear for her to fall back under his sway, immediately submissive to him again, as though she'd only found the strength to break free of him because of the distance and, because she'd been freed from his magnetic field by the presence of the prison walls—as though the walls had caused interference—and because they're now face to face with each other, she would, in spite of the ten years and all the space separating them, return to him, submit to his power of attraction as though she has no capacity to resist it, as though there's no doubt whatsoever that she could walk away from her current life without the slightest regret, because he's certain she despises it as much as he pictured it with dismay. That's why he doesn't understand when—go fuck yourself, Denis—go fuck yourself. What do you think? That I'm going to leave with you? I'd rather die. I'd rather die, you hear me. And if he turns threatening, it's not so much because she's thrown the humiliation of a refusal in his face as at seeing his power of domination collapse completely, as though he needed to test it with a face-to-face to be convinced even though everyone around him had never stopped repeating it to him, and even he, from deep in his cell, couldn't do anything but reluctantly admit it, even if it was just to acknowledge it in the context of the facts and the evidence, without truly assimilating it, letting this knowledge exist in a superficial layer of his intelligence while the innermost feeling refused to bend and admit that Marion was lost to him forever.

Now Denis feels a bitterness and a disgust so strong in the face of the ingratitude she showed him by fleeing and leaving him for ten years without a word... yes, ten years like an idiot, rotting away behind the disgusting walls of an overcrowded prison. And all so she could do what, what better, what more, than come bury herself in this rotten hole in the center of France, in the middle of nothing, of fields oozing with pesticide and cancer, boredom, desertification, and resentment? All so he can see her now, her hair still wet, splashed with water to understand what's happening to her, her pretty face barely aged by the years, as though her fucking beauty is as solid against time as she was against him, resisting him as she did so many times when she pushed him to the edge over nothing, in the magnificent and terrible time of their life together, where their life was nothing but a series of explosions and shouts but also of promises, of reconciliations and of fucks so wild he was certain he'd never experience anything like that again. He's so disappointed to find her here, to see her so full of hate for him, that he doesn't comprehend, doesn't want to or can't understand how violent he was, which he doesn't see and has never seen, not even understanding what he forced on her and what kind of nightmare he thrust her life into.

You really think… Marion, you really think I still want anything to fucking do with you? is that what you think? it's nice here, right, that's enough for you? Well you can go ahead and die here, I don't care, I don't give a flying fuck, sweetheart, that's right, because… all those nights smashing up your pretty whore face, you know, in my dreams… yeah, that's right, I had dreams like that, smashing you with the same crowbar as that other asshole. And now I just want to leave you here to rot, that's how much you disgust me… I thought about it so much, your shitty little party, forty years old, sweetheart, with your hick husband, here in your fields, you can go fuck off and die in your fields, and let me tell you, yeah, that's right, it sure warmed me up to think about it, to imagine how I could ruin it for you, your nice little family soirée… Hours and hours, but believe me, believe me, that's not why I'm here, not for that, sweetheart, that's not why I'm here, oh no.

And Ida isn't sure she hears him when he says, she's not sure what he said, because at the same moment she hears Marion's shout,

Get out!

And he explains now how he imagined Marion taking the train, finding herself all alone one night at the train station in a city where she knew nobody, her stomach already heavy—how many months, huh, how far along were you, five, six months?—and that's the only reason I'm here.

The strangest thing is surely that Denis has no doubts about what he's started saying and that Ida, from across the wall, doesn't hear right away. It's strange because he doesn't understand the contradiction in which he's enclosing himself, swearing that if Marion fled while she was pregnant it was because she was doing something besides fleeing, something far more serious and unforgivable, namely abusing the power and the privilege nature had given her to hold in her stomach the life of his child—he who for having taken a life would go rot in prison while she, no less responsible than he, would go carry that life elsewhere, far from him, depriving him of his child and of that life to which he also had a right, his share in the life she decided to deprive him of while he paid the full price of the death he'd inflicted. He had her to thank for this injustice; that was the reason he wanted amends, even more than the collapse Marion's departure had caused. But this strange contradiction underneath everything he's saying, now that he's started speaking as though he's repeating out loud sentences he's recited alone dozens and dozens of times, or sometimes not alone but with this or that cellmate, the same ones resignedly listening to him even though they were itching to tell him to shut up with this story they couldn't bear to hear again, we get it, your old lady left with your kid and you think it's the first time that's happened here, how many of them do you think there are, guys who find themselves bawling over a shadow, but each of them careful not to take him to task for talking, for going over the same story again, and taking note, for themselves, of this conflict in which he'd enclosed himself, when Denis started spewing bile about Marion, telling the sordid details of a little girl abandoned too soon by her dingbat mother, a tale of misery and woe and maybe he'd pitied her the day he met her—but no, no pity, just the most exciting girl he'd ever met, she would've made a dead man hard, this bitch—and they, after hearing it over and over, they'd tried their best to get him to see this contradiction, but no, in the same salvo Denis could keep on tossing out sentences spiked with splinters and thorns that skinned his hiccupping voice, sometimes giving in and stopping abruptly under the sway of emotion, of anger, then, starting again, he could hammer on without seeing the problem that Marion had cheated on him dozens of times and that for a tenner she'd have cheated on anyone the way she cheated on him, and that in spite of it all the worst thing she did when she left him was to leave with the kid she was carrying and not for a minute had he entertained the notion that he could not be its father, because he could claim the two propositions with the same confidence and see no problem therein: the child was his, and Marion had slept with everyone.

Ida, now, is very close to the door; she's this close to opening it, to coming and throwing herself between the man and her mother and she hears her mother, emerging from her silence, answering something she didn't hear; what are they talking about, Ida wonders as she hears her mother scream that she never wanted to see them again, any of them, or to go back there, and that for years she's even had nights of insomnia, that's how afraid she was that the night would bring her back to them, carried by the foggy, bloated, depressing density of dreams, with their sneaky detours and their knack for plunging you straight back into the heart of the hell you'd managed to escape. But no, dreams are there to bring you back to your hell so you can find, with the same dread, the faces you left behind and with all of them the streets, the buildings, everything you fought against. Marion shouts I don't want anything that comes from back there, I don't want anything that comes from you, nothing.

Ida listens: We're not good enough for you? is that it?

Ida listens: I just want you to leave me alone, I just want you to go.

Ida listens: Nothing that comes from there? But that's your home, Marion. Back there. That's your home. It's your home and there's nothing you can do about it. You can do whatever you want, you can put feathers in your ass or adopt their hick accent if that's what you want but you can't do anything about it: back there is where you come from. Everything about you is from back there: your face, your voice, your manners, the way you carry yourself. You can't escape that. You're like me, sweetheart, you're like Stutter, we're all the same and even your daughter... *our daughter,* she's from back there. Doesn't she come from back there, our daughter, our little Ida? Why'd you call her Ida? Why didn't you ask me? Maybe she wants to know where she comes from, don't you think? No? Her family? We'll go ask her what she thinks, shall we? Let's go ask her.

Ida listens to the bodies moving in a grand motion and her mother's shout—slaps, a volley of slaps that Ida couldn't say whether her mother is receiving them or giving them,

You stay away from her, don't you go near—

her mother shouting and all of a sudden Ida bursts into tears and even though she thought a few seconds ago that she was going to go throw herself between the man and her mother,

I don't want my daughter to see you.

here she is doing the opposite, launching herself into the hallway,

She has a father and it'll never be you.

starting to run, shouting,

Don't you go near her, you leave her alone! Leave her alone!

with all her strength,

Marion,

as though all her terror is rising up in her, freezing her, burning her, running down her spinal column with a tingling sensation she's never felt, so she races and hurtles down the stairs—on the other side of the door, Denis and Marion have realized Ida was listening to them. Both of them launch themselves after her. Denis pushes Marion aside with a great movement that flings her against the sink and dashes into the hallway. Marion gets back up, she shouts, she shouts with all her might and she's there, a few meters from him, running behind him in the hallway, going down the stairs now shrieking in the voice of an animal getting its throat slit, but Ida is already downstairs and, in front of a dumbfounded Patrice, in front of the two women and the two guys, Ida no longer knows what she's doing, it's as though her father himself seems foreign and monstrous, like the others, as though everything seems monstrous and hostile, she doesn't know what she's doing, doesn't think, she runs and races toward the door, because, soon, soon she'll be outside, soon she'll be outside, soon she'll be outside, soon she'll be outside.

43

Soon.

But also soon, the gunshots.

Soon death will come knocking at the hamlet just as it comes knocking everywhere, for it is at home everywhere, at home when it wants to be, making itself comfortable in apartments where it's never set foot or even deigned to cast an eye; at home all at once, like a queen without shame and without manners, vaguely obscene, leaving distraught and desolate all who thought for a moment it had forgotten them.

Soon: seven shots ringing out in the emptiness of the night, four of which will hit their target, the others getting lost somewhere in a piece of furniture or a wall.

But before that, even before Ida's run toward the stairs and the dining room, before she's left her bedroom, when she hears her mother coming up the stairs followed by a man she knows isn't Patrice—she knows all the noises here by heart, all the house's intonations and vibrations—just a bit before this, then, in the other house, Christine regains awareness of her body, of her mind. Slowly, in fits and starts. As soon as she moves, the pain strikes a blow, as though there was a lag between the moment Stutter hit her and the moment the pain made itself felt. Christine hasn't yet thought of getting up. She focuses all her effort on opening her eyes, on breathing. She moves, and each time she does the pain orders her to limit her movements, reminding her that for each blow she took there will be another to answer it, less strong, perhaps, but enough for her to feel it like the shock wave of a disaster, just as the aftershocks that follow an earthquake grow less and less powerful until they become imperceptible and so to speak nonexistent.

The time it takes to become aware that she's breathing and that she's opening her eyes, it's already an effort so intense that she has to rest and wait, stop to let an additional degree of consciousness rise in her mind, illuminate it, offer her a spark to face the darkness, until she can finally awaken to the silence around her. The image of Stutter comes back to her with a crispness kindred to invention, as though she can see each blackhead on his nose and the little wrinkles under his eyes, the vertical ridges on his lips, his childish face twisted with rage—and that spark of pleasure she saw, she's sure of it, not yet able to accept the idea of seeing him so satisfied. And then she extends her hands in front of her, fingers spread apart, she tries to prop herself up. She does, she doesn't know how it's possible, but this thing happens: she manages to crawl a few centimeters. Then she stops. Gathers her strength. Waits—yes, no noises, no movements or voices. She finds the strength to start again. She lifts her hips, pulls along her legs, which unfold slowly, knees on the tile; she hurts in a way she didn't know it was possible to hurt, her arms reach out and help her, she does it. Soon she's close enough to a wall to lean against it. She tries to get up. She tenses. Rears. Rises. Almost lets herself fall forward. Against the wall. And too bad if her hands stain the paintings, bring one down with a noise that doesn't even startle her, no, she's focused on her effort, she succeeds in getting back up.

Soon she'll have to leap into the void—with nothing to hold onto—but she's not there yet.

She stands leaning against the wall, the red woman next to her. Now stand up. Now advance. Now straighten up again. Her fingers on her face, the need to touch her cheeks, her mouth, her nose—but she can't—hurts too much—the pain before even touching it—she checks again, she chews in her mouth to be sure she hasn't lost any teeth and can't believe all this blood that's flowed—as soon as she brushes her nose with a movement too sudden, too direct, the pain is so strong it wrings a cry from her—at this moment her legs give out, she's going to fall again and she has to hold on. She can feel herself almost faint again—legs, but also arms, the whole body collapsing on itself, she manages to cling to the stool in front of her work table, she wants to sit down but she won't be able to, so she tenses her legs as straight as possible, stiff as posts, spread very far apart, feet flat, as much as she can to steady her legs and lean on them so they don't move, don't succumb to the shaking and the waves of weakness or the pulsing in her blood that makes her falter. She places both hands on the stool, she tries to keep her arms stiff—she has to use them as rigid supports to take the time to breathe, to think—

Okay, it's fine, it'll be fine. Yes it'll be fine. I need to. I need.

And seeing all her things on the table, her notebooks, her paintbrushes, she sees herself once again taking the box cutter from the pencil box and wonders why she did that—as though she suspected the young man had the upper hand, as though she felt maybe he'd try to—

On the table: Ida's two sheets of paper, turned over. For a second Christine studies them, she hesitates. She wants to, yes, but she hesitates. She doesn't know why she hesitates. She waits a bit longer and then finds the strength to extend her arm, to turn over the two sheets—to look again at Ida's drawings for her mother's birthday with their English flower gardens, the hodgepodge of marks, of colors,

Mom I love you with all my heart this big,

and Christine lets herself be overcome with tears she wouldn't have thought she could still shed ever since she finished crying over love that didn't last, over success that didn't last, over youth that didn't last, over the nastiness around her that did last, of course, and hardened, casting off all restraint; the hardness against which she hadn't measured up, the hardness of indifference and of humiliating words directed at this body and this face which the years were dismantling with perverse precision, the hardness of this art world that trampled over all the efforts she'd made, all the conviction and ardor she'd put into it, that with the same jubilation trampled on years of her work because of a negligence of which she'd been guilty, maybe, and that had served as an excuse to torpedo her and drive her to abandon everything, everything she'd had to pay above and beyond for only to find herself, at the end of her road, with disillusionment and bitterness her only companions, which had lasted, and grown, inside of her. And now she understands how it all fossilized and hardened in her because she didn't know how to look it in the face, how everything calcified in her; and she releases herself from all of this, yes, by crying, tears of which she'd have thought herself incapable, melodramatic tears, an abundance of tears at Ida's disarming and unbearable innocence, cruel in its very sweetness, abominable in its vitality, in its faith in life and in love and in a little girl's unfailing trust in her mother, something breaks her right in this place—pure love slashes through her—Christine can't take it anymore, she's mad with rage, she needs her anger to save her, she needs to be angry at the sight of Ida's drawings and her unbearable declaration of love for her mother—a rage like a knot that's been choking her for years, that she's been holding sealed inside by staying far away from everything, here, from everyone, and maybe from herself too.

So she gathers herself. She tilts her neck, lowers her head resolutely between her shoulders and she shouts—she thinks she's shouting, but nothing comes out of her mouth. It's as though she heard the shout projected before her, outside herself, by her entire being. She's going to regain her footing in the present. Now she's going to leave this nightmare. Come back. Think and react. If Stutter isn't here, it's because he's joined the others at the Bergognes' house. And her brain accelerates. If he's gone that means they're all gone, or maybe if he's gone to join the others then she's no longer a hostage. What happens, then, if he's gone? Are they gone, just like that? No, no. Otherwise Bergogne. Otherwise Patrice would have come here. Someone would have come to find her, if nobody's come that means nobody's been able to come, which means the others haven't left, they're still over there. The telephone, she should call, she has to call—but all these images in front of her, the Bergognes, Ida, the house and the smell of the cakes, the memory of Marion's two co-workers' cars pulling into the yard, their headlights sweeping over the inside of her kitchen and the two guys worried.

She feels her strength coming back, the present taking over her whole mental space, ideas, questions, as though the pieces of the puzzle, of space and time, can articulate themselves among them. If Stutter is gone, maybe they're all gone. Or no, if he's gone to join the others, then is it all over? What happens then, if he's gone? Did just he leave or did all three of them leave? Yes, surely all three of them, why would the other one leave alone and leave his brothers, all three of them must have left, all three of them—but this isn't possible, she thinks, the three brothers have decided to stay longer and who knows what's going on next door, what they've decided, maybe to stay longer, still over there and still holding Bergogne, his wife, and their daughter? She doesn't even think anymore to wonder if there could be reasons behind it, everything seems possible to her now without needing to be motivated by a reason, an idea, a plan as simple as a demand for ransom—but who to demand a ransom from here, of all the ridiculous possibilities that one would be the worst, it almost makes her laugh. That's not it, it's related to Marion. Except now she wouldn't dream of criticizing Marion for anything, but instead she wants to tell them they're going to get through this, the two of them, that they're all going to get through it and it'll be over soon. But then what's happened? Why is she alone here and what's going on over there, just next

door, at the neighbors' house? The telephone. The police. Officer
Filipkowski's number: You call me with the slightest concern.

She remembers it now, what he said to her as he handed her
his card. She remembers his voice, his hand handing her the card:
she should call him, she thinks, she has to call him on his personal
number, his cell phone must be easier to reach than the police station switchboard at night. She has time to regret having called the
police station before, she should have called him first, Filipkowski,
not do what she did, call the police station. But she doesn't know
yet if she can—all these images in front of her, Bergogne, Ida,
the house and the cakes, the cars pulling into the yard, the two
guys worried—what did they do? What's happening next door?
And this question nags at her for a few more seconds, she has to
lean against the wall so she doesn't fall, her body is in so much
pain, she's having trouble breathing, her nose hurts and she doesn't
dare touch it—she goes like this, slowly, clinging to the wall and
advancing one foot in front of the other, she finally enters the
bathroom and doesn't dare turn on the light, as she does every
night without even being aware of her gesture. But this time the
light—the brightness of the lamp, its harshness—frightens her so
much that she's scared to meet the reflection of her face in the mirror. She tries to take the telephone; she goes and finds it without
too much trouble because she remembers Stutter threw it into the
sink. She's surprised to find it not in the bowl but on the edge.
She reaches for it, taking pains not to meet herself in the mirror
above. She picks up the telephone with an unsteady motion, she's
not confident she noted down the officer's number, did she just
take the card on which he'd written his number without taking
the time to enter it in her contacts?

She sees herself fairly clearly putting the card in her wallet,
which, yes, which she put back in her purse, it was inside the police station, this she remembers perfectly, it was yesterday, just as
she remembers Bergogne waiting for her in the parking lot where
the rain had left large puddles in which the reflection of the white

and blue-gray clouds played hide-and-seek with the sun; she sees herself in Bergogne's car placing the purse at her feet rather than keeping it in her lap, yes, she must have put it down—at her feet? or in the back seat? no? had she kept her coat on?—for a few seconds the anxiety of having forgotten her purse in Bergogne's Kangoo, she waits, concentrates even more and then no, no, she didn't leave it, that's not possible because she had her keys in it so obviously she needed it, so no use scaring herself like that. She surely did what she does every time she comes home, leaving her purse on the chair closest to the door, then covering it with her coat. That's what she usually does, why would she do anything different this time? She hesitates, it's that the idea of returning to the kitchen terrorizes her—she doesn't really know why, whether it's just the pain, the crumpling of the body, the time it'll take her to get to her purse, the time it'll take to pick it up, find the card, and call without risking wasting too much time, Stutter could come back, her brothers could come back and decide to finish her off, right there, with a knife, the way they killed her dog, striking her down like a dog, that's it, and this time the idea makes her angry and she decides to absorb the muscle pain, to absorb it into herself and ignore it, even the more acute pain in her nose, and the one clenching her entire face, especially around her eyes, and the one she feels in her hands, with which she could have protected her face for a few minutes and which took some very hard blows, her hands that nonetheless aren't broken, yes, and it's thanks to them that she can cling to one piece of furniture and then another and, like a blind person, gropingly, she returns to the kitchen, looks for the purse, which she sees not sitting on the chair as she expected but on the ground, as though someone had put it there, against the cupboard where she stores her conserves and all kinds of things she has no use for. But the purse is there. Christine looks outside—the night isn't so dark, she can make out the shapes of the hamlet's walls, a few clouds hiding the blue of the night and the stars—but she doesn't wait any longer, she needs a certain amount of time to reach the purse. She leans down and so be it if her body seems to be ripping and she can feel the violence of her blood pulsing inside her, of her headache, and most of all, leaning down, as though the blood is rushing to her nose and into her eyes as it rises back to her face—burning sensations, needles in her flesh—she keeps herself from falling, clutches the purse without even checking whether the card is in it, she's sure it is and realizes how much she doesn't want to stay here, and that's why, without thinking, she takes the risk of confronting the steps and going up—slowly, painfully—to her bedroom, upstairs, because she thinks that only upstairs will she feel safe, knowing she won't be safer than anywhere else, but what matters is the feeling of safety rather than the hypothetical reality of it.

So she goes up, she enters her bedroom and locks herself in. Here she can turn on the light because she won't encounter any mirrors. She can lie down on the bed to let her body relax—she feels so exhausted. Here she is rummaging through her purse and not finding anything, of course she doesn't find anything, even though there's almost nothing in her purse, a wallet and a small paperback and some crosswords and some tissues, and that's about it. When she finally finds it, this card, when she reads the number to herself three or four times, she tries to type the digits on her phone but her bloody fingers are sticky, they're shaking, can't find the keys anymore, they're stiffening. Christine has to collect herself and breathe, calm down. Yes, I'm calming down. She starts again and will start again several times in a row—still telling herself she needs to calm down, you have to calm down calm down now, calm down I told you, and finally she succeeds, she takes the telephone and places it next to her ear and, while she waits for the ring, she hears herself begging in a whisper, she hears herself addressing the captain of the police station like a friend as she asks him to pick up. But the ring continues two, three, four times before a virtual woman's voice asks her to leave her message and her callback number. She's terrified at the prospect of having to leave a message because what message could she leave him that isn't a confused, muddled message, a message that communicates only its own urgency. And yet she has to leave a message—she has time to think he'll call back when everyone is already dead. She doesn't even wait for the beep to start talking and she's already gibbering, scrambling to say that they're in the house and they killed my dog, they killed my dog and you have to come, they're going to kill us, they're going to kill us, they're going to kill my little sweetheart and her voice chokes when she hears herself utter the only words that really grip her, ravage her, they're going to kill my little sweetheart and she can't speak anymore, she's gasping for breath, *they're going to kill my little sweetheart,* this sentence crumpling in her mouth, and she weeps, *my little sweetheart*, it bores into her heart because she herself is surprised to love this child so much, to hear herself say these words of love, so warm and tender, my little sweetheart, and it seems to her that she hears something, yes, she hears someone coming into the house—she's sure of it—she stays frozen, unable to move—the phone in her hand that she can't shut off, she's trembling, alert, yes, she tenses, clutches the phone so tightly, she doesn't know if what she's hearing is coming from the outside of her body or if it's just the blood beating in her veins, her breath too hard in her chest, then she reasons with herself, you have to calm down, now you're going to calm down, I told you calm down. Finally she succeeds, a semblance of calm returns: she listens, it's clear, there's someone in the house.

Someone has just entered the kitchen and has entered at full speed, she doesn't understand what she's hearing just as Ida doesn't understand what she's seeing as she arrives at Christine's house. Ida can't shout or cry anymore but she's shaking and breathing so hard it sounds like she's already run for kilometers when she's just flown down the stairs from her bedroom and then crossed the dining room as the adults looked on and, behind her, she heard Denis's voice yelling at the two others to catch her whatever they do, the shouts of her mother as she tried to prevent Denis from running. Ida ran so fast that the two guys didn't really understand when she burst past them, even though they tried to block her in front of the door. Something happened that prevented them, she didn't quite see what it was, was it her father, did Patrice launch himself in front to create a diversion or was it just the surprise or what, she doesn't know and she ran as fast as she could and she entered Christine's house—sure she'd find her in the studio or maybe still in the bedroom upstairs, not knowing where she'd find her, racing into the studio and stopping on the threshold, in front of this painting taken down from its wall and that's fallen face down, but most of all the blood, all this blood on the floor, an enormous pool of blood and not only that stain but all the others, against the walls, stains on the walls, like stains made with hands, with fingers. Suddenly Ida stops moving. She stays silent. Motionless. Then she steps back. She doesn't know what she can do and though she murmurs Tatie, Tatie, her voice goes dead in her throat. She steps back farther and returns to the kitchen.

And soon: seven shots ringing out in the emptiness of the night, four of which will hit their target, the others getting lost somewhere in a piece of furniture or a wall.

44

In a few seconds, the first gunshot, which will come from Ida's house. She and Christine will jump, will go silent, will remain still for a few minutes that dilate and thicken until they assume the blackness and the almost sticky thickness of a petrol-blue night.

Then another shot.

Then a third, a fourth—the latter very close to the former.

Ida will jump again, as if lifted by the blast or the power of the shots. She'll remain unable to react right away, then she'll have what resembles an idea yet isn't really an idea, more a sort of reflex she'll never know why she had, nor whether it was the right thing to do or not.

For now, Ida returns to the kitchen and goes to the cupboard. As she does she hurries to the drawer on the right and opens it without shaking, confident in her motion and in what she's looking for. She doesn't look long; she knows where it is, in the Samsung box of Christine's phone—what mania possessed Tatie Christine to keep all these boxes? The key is there and Ida grabs it, she takes the time to put the lid back on the box. She holds the key firmly in her palm, folds her fingers over it, her hand now closed tight in a fist, but when she tries to close the drawer, on which she has to lean almost her entire weight, pushing with her whole body, her chest out in front of her, arms and shoulders shoving hard because it's difficult to push it all the way, she realizes she won't be able to do it. She'd have to try several times, which she knows because she's stolen the key two or three times before to show Charline and Lucas the house for sale, to look for treasures that might have been forgotten there. But now she doesn't take the time to close the drawer all the way, it's just too difficult to push so hard and most of all a gunshot comes and shuts down all effort, leaving Ida paralyzed, overwhelmed to the point that she lets out a cry as though it's just hit her.

So she forgets that it's important to close the drawer if she doesn't want to be found, or rather she gives up trying, as though the drawer burned her fingers when she heard the explosion; she exits the house very fast, not worrying about what's behind her, running, and now here she is rushing into the old neighbors' house, because she's sure that there at least nobody will think to come looking for her. And it's true that, for what may seem like a rather long time, nobody has entered this house where for several months no one has lived but a few families of mice and shrews, colonies of spiders and some insects. Upstairs, in all the bedrooms, massive armoires that would have to be stripped to the bone to be transported and taken away, just like the china cabinet in the kitchen that's as old as the house, just like the sideboard reigning over the dining room that's more than a century old, splintering everywhere and straight out of a Rimbaud poem, with its atmosphere of fragrant perfumes and dried flowers; and then, above it, in their wooden frames touched up with gold paint, black-and-white photos of severe and weathered faces, gently retouched to bring into focus faces you'd only recognize from seeing them on ceramic medallions on cemetery steles, next to names that no longer mean anything to anyone. A dead house, one that's still standing even though nobody really seems to care anymore or to be interested in buying it—a few Dutch people and two English couples visited, but no one came back.

It's in this house, where nothing remains but old furniture that's too difficult to move, whose owners will soon resign themselves to getting rid of it for cheap if a secondhand dealer can be bothered to come haul it away, to sell off at a pittance everything left over from the nineteenth and twentieth centuries of life in the countryside, all of it dying away slowly, leaving no trace of its passage but the immense carcasses of the furniture, but also of the walls and soon enough only names on moldy registers that nobody will ever look at again, fossilizing before disappearing from even the memories of the families and the neighbors and, ultimately, from the surface of the world, it's here, then, that Ida has just entered, overcome by the smell of dust and humidity, of cold, by this deathly odor in which the droppings and corpses of mice and flies mingle with multiple pasts, the emptiness of a space resonant like an oversized museum, its air, vibrating, poisoned with dust and beeswax, making Ida gag slightly. But maybe what destabilizes her most is this suffocated, heavy silence, itself loaded with a kind of dust, something like a dust of time, a thickness of words spoken, of noises, of fragmentary bursts, as if overloaded with vibrations. Ida has the feeling that what you can hear is the intimate sound of the night, or maybe it's like the way you'd feel the innermost life of a giant animal who's just swallowed you whole—whale or dinosaur—unless, perhaps, Ida is disoriented only because she's just entered a place that's like a sanctuary dedicated to silence and stillness, she who's just experienced the overly noisy and turbulent agitation of a wild life—as though this counterpoint represents not so much a comfort as a sort of too-radical transformation, as though the refuge she's come here to find turns out to meet her expectation so much that it's almost worrisome, even hostile, because she's barely entered the house when she realizes she can't lock the door—the door having swelled over the winter because of the rain, it'll take a man's strength to shut it. She was already so happy to have opened it, because it was so difficult that she had to go at it with blows of her shoulder, heaving herself against the door with all her might, and Ida is still shaking from having run, with the silence freezing the house and vibrating in her ear like a whistling sound—because of the gunshots, were those really gunshots she heard? Several shots, yes. It's like during a hunt, the gunshots you hear coming from the forest, from across the river, except now it's so much closer… Everything reverberated in the air in this strange and unreal way, as though only one or two shots have been fired and the echo has repeated several times into the night, or maybe more, three or four times, the way a storm can sometimes roll in the air at length before exhausting itself completely. She doesn't know, or rather it's as though all of it is thinning out inside her and she has no more grip on the true duration of things. She sees herself taking the key from Tatie's kitchen, gripping it tight, running faster than ever and leaving everything behind her and entering the house—this house into which she doesn't quite dare advance any farther and in which she stands, now, breathless, swallowing dry heaps of this dust that makes her eyes itch, telling herself she has to move forward, hide, not make any noise, and wait somewhere where she won't be found.

At last she advances, she knows where she's going to go. Upstairs, in one of the bedrooms, Christine has left a whole pile of canvases that she stores here because she no longer knows where to put them in her house. Up there there's an armchair where Ida will be able to sit and wait; she also knows that in the upstairs bedrooms nobody has thought it necessary to close the shutters. Christine comes once or twice a week to open them and air everything out, so maybe it won't be too dark up there, in any case less so than downstairs, because even if there's still electricity in the house better not to use it: yes, that's it, better to go upstairs and not draw attention by turning on any lights. She's very scared of the dark, but less than she is of what's happening in the hamlet. So she has to make it across that impenetrable zone to reach the stairs and follow them up to the relative brightness of the night. Yes, that's what she has to do, and she has to do it as fast as possible, not think about it, because if she waits, if she takes the time to think more, soon she won't be able to move anymore and will be turned, so to speak, into a pillar of salt—petrified the way she was at the pool, out of terror at the idea of having to dive—but now, yes, she has to take the plunge, so she darts across that thick, very dark zone that swallows up part of the dining room and the living room and moves toward the stairs, she can see the tops of the steps and most of all, upstairs, all the way up, the floating grayish marks of relative light—yes, it seems almost illuminated—a lighting of shadows, of paleness, of blues and grays.

Soon Ida is in the big bedroom where the paintings are waiting for her—they're turned to face the wall—and the armchair in which she tells herself she's going to sit. But it's to the window that she moves, not only to see the great space of the night outlined there, the sky taking up the bigger half of the top and, below, the former neighbors' yard, but also maybe to tell herself she's safe here, that here nothing can happen to her. And yet this safety resembles the silence of death, it's almost more worrisome than the anxiety of what she heard and saw at her house or at Christine's—and the images, the blood, the blood immediately returning, the shots, does that mean Tatie is dead and are her parents dead or is she herself going to die tonight? In her mind the blood in the studio comes back, and the dog's, sticky on her hands, and she, who was so sure she'd find Tatie Christine, wonders where she is, why there was nobody at Tatie's, besides that horrible silence and that painting on the ground, those stains on the walls and that puddle on the floor—so could she do something other than sit down and burrow into this armchair from the seventies, which probably hasn't moved for almost fifty years, that's stayed in this room, between a bed and a window, where no event in the world could move it a single centimeter?

Ida isn't going to sit there, in that armchair. She tries to stay calm and she thinks about her mother and her father; her mother's shout behind her when the man started to run. She thinks about the bursts of voices and the light from the bathroom escaping through the cracked-open door—has her mother been lying to her for years and is it possible that her mother is that strange woman who had, supposedly, before her, a life so different from the one she knows, and does that mean that, in some way, it's as though Marion used to be someone other than Marion? As though there is in her mother's body a woman besides her mother who now wants to hurt her? Now she's afraid of the woman living in her mother's body; Ida thinks someone unknown to her is inhabiting that body, she wonders who this stranger is who cries in secret and tells her not to let herself be bothered by dragons, to kill them, to knock their teeth out, whether everything she's heard tonight she really heard, and why her mother has never spoken of these men who came today, why she had to keep all of that to herself in the secrecy of a story that has sprung up monstrous and wild. Ida doesn't understand. She wonders if all of this is a dream or if it's truly reality, she swims in the cottony silence of a too-silent night, and suddenly she understands: a gunshot, followed by another.

The fifth. The sixth.

This time, from here, from this house where the silence itself is a kind of buzzing, the echo of the shot extends deeper, spreads not only into the space of the countryside, as though nothing can stop it from expanding like a gaseous cloud over the fields and the river, toward the houses, well beyond the hamlet, over all of La Bassée and even elsewhere, but also toward the interior of beings and of things, spreading there as easily as it spreads outside. Ida feels the cold of this house that's heated only every now and then so the humidity doesn't proliferate; Ida feels the cold rising in her, she tries to count the number of shots in spite of the confusion into which the echo's repercussion plunges her, as though the explosions are shattering against the walls and against the night sky, as though the clouds are volleying them back, returning them and making them explode again, in empty space this time, and softer, but enough to make it not so easy to count the number of shots. Ida manages to think that people are *really* going to die, which is to say not the way she's been scared until now for her parents and for Christine but realizing that with each gunshot tearing through the silence it is above all a projectile tearing through a body, and, if her mind refuses this idea, Ida still allows herself to be utterly devastated by this revelation of bodies perforated, torn to pieces by the bullets at the moment she hears the bang, the multiple echoes spreading into the sky, over the hamlet and the countryside, making dogs howl for kilometers around, because suddenly she hears them, from far away, the dogs howling and making a kind of chain that stretches how far, so very far, reacting to the bangs, losing itself in the endlessness of space and time—because it also seems the dogs have been howling every night since forever, for centuries, as though the barks you hear are only the echo or the continuation of the barks and warnings of the first dogs raised as lookouts, as though over centuries spent surveying paths, roads, trails, the dogs' dogs, the dogs sired by the dogs' dogs, haven't had time to take the threats lightly, to turn away from them, and they still must to repeat the ancestral warning of a danger or a threat to come—and Ida trembles, maybe from cold, she's alone in this big house whose timber creaks above her head, in the attic, around her, underneath, in the floors and the furniture.

She sits down not in the armchair but under the window, there at least she's enveloped by a sort of halo of light—a pale blue brightness that warms nothing but allows her to see herself, sitting on her bottom and hugging her legs with her arms, holding them tight, trying to slip her head into the hollow that separates the tops of her thighs, her knees, the top of her chest. She's crying, tears, groans, shaking, doing everything she can to stifle her cries and not allow herself to cry—is she aware that her body is stiffening and her eyes can no longer blink, that they're staying stubbornly open and her mouth isn't closed but almost locked, her jaw set so tight that all her facial muscles will hurt for three or four days? This silence billowing out around her, as though it's enveloped everything and is going to last forever, as though this leaden shroud will now settle around her eternally and never again will Ida staring see movement or life—little insect stuck under its glass case, pin planted between its shoulder blades—even if of course the mind is still agile, terror galloping through her brain with the questions it conceives and raises. How to imagine what happened at Christine's and where is Christine, how to imagine that Ida staring hasn't heard anything but the gunshots—to the point that soon she'll tell herself she hasn't heard them, that there were no gunshots because there would have been shouts, because there would have been signs, people running, cars starting, doors slamming, calls for help, windows broken, whereas there's been nothing but this silent and heavy void buzzing in her ears. She tells herself it's not possible, that it's not possible to not hear anything because she knows this house isn't so airtight, that from where she is you can hear the noises from outside and that she'd hear if things were happening. Is she all alone here, or maybe in the whole hamlet and everything around her has evaporated or never existed, is everything a dream, yes, her dream—soon she'll wake up, the sound of her alarm clock will pull her from this nightmare and it'll be time to go to school, that's right, she'll hear her mother in the bathroom brushing her teeth and drying her hair, France Info turned down low on the kitchen radio, the microwave and her hot chocolate almost ready, instead of this ongoing silence, that must be it, instead of her mother's voice and that man's,

But that's your home, back there, Marion. That's your home. Your face, your voice, your manners, the way you carry yourself, you can't escape that... and *our daughter*... Doesn't she come from back there, *our daughter*?

45

Of course, Ida would like for all these voices rising up and filling the silence of the house to finally quiet down, rather than repeating these conversations that seem strange and senseless to her, she who doesn't want to hear what they're saying, so much does she perceive the scale, or rather the enormity, of what they open up beneath her feet, as though she's being told that everything she believes is her life is in reality the life of another little girl, or that, because her mother is inhabited by an unknown Marion, shaped by a life of which nothing is known but the silence with which she tries to cover over it and hide it from the judgments of others, Ida too is someone other than this easygoing little girl who loves her parents and has been badgering them for weeks because she wants a gecko like her friend Lou.

As though, then, all of a sudden, she's been informed that she's someone other than Ida Bergogne, as though it's been revealed to her that maybe her name isn't Ida Bergogne, that she has no name, that she's not the person she sees in the mirror every day and that her hands don't belong to her, nor her eyes, no more than her mouth or her legs. But Marion had always said Ida's name was Ida Bergogne, her father had always said her name was Ida Bergogne, everyone knew she was Ida Bergogne, and in truth nobody ever even wondered what her name was because as the daughter of Patrice and Marion she naturally carried theirs, just as Marion's last name was Bergogne because she'd chosen to separate from her birth name—even though she could have chosen to put the name she got from her mother next to Bergogne's, but she'd chosen to make her mother's name disappear, to disappear with it, to dissolve into her husband's name as a chameleon melts into its surroundings. But it's true that when Ida was born her mother hadn't yet met Bergogne. Ida was so small when their meeting took place that Patrice became her father so easily and so self-evidently it was as though that was what he'd always been. This business of having had another name at birth wasn't a problem, so much so that they'd forgotten when Bergogne adopted her and officially became her father. All of them, Marion and Patrice first, and Ida too, had eventually forgotten, and the idea that her father wasn't her biological father had never really intrigued her, and now she thinks that everything that was hidden from her doesn't just connect to something kept quiet, she thinks of it as a weight they pressed down on her, as though they wanted to let the years amputate her from what's just burst out in her house, and she's overcome with the strange feeling of having been deceived without knowing by whom or why, but deceived, by her mother and even by her father, because neither one of them ever tried to explain it to her. So, hearing her mother's voice,

Ida,

coming from who knows where,

Ida, Ida, answer, answer me,

Ida, not understanding how long the voice has been calling her, and whether it's really calling her, if it's really her mother she's hearing and not the voice of some sort of phantom wandering inside the walls of the empty house, sounding like her mother's,

Ida, I know you're here, it's Mom, it's me, sweetheart,

her mother's voice, more and more precise, the voice seems to her sharper, clearer, suddenly Ida understands that her mother has come to find her here and that she's not being abandoned, and she cries, Ida cries and no longer feels that sensation of having been deceived or duped but a wild gratitude and she trembles and blurts out,

Mom, Mom,

in a trembling voice, and when her mother appears in the doorframe Ida doesn't have time to realize what's happening—what she knows is that her mother is coming and that she leaps into her arms, on her knees, and that she holds her as tight as she can to her chest, her mother crying too and kissing Ida's hair, running her hands through her hair, my baby, my baby I love you so much, I love you, I'll never leave you, I'm here, I'm here, it's going to be okay and Ida wants to believe her, yes, of course it's going to be okay, everything's going to be okay and it takes her a bit longer to realize that her mother has laid down the rifle next to her—the hunting rifle, on the ground, which Ida sees in the night's pale light, on the floor that looks gray and matte, the rifle whose black double barrel has glints of blue—she recoils slightly and doesn't understand, doesn't say anything, doesn't ask questions, she just finds it surprising—she's always been told not to go near the rifle, that it was forbidden to touch it, to go near it—only Patrice is allowed to and now she sees her mother in this house with this rifle and she wonders whether her mother shot the cartridges she heard, she wants to know but doesn't dare ask, why this rifle, why here, on the floor, and suddenly her mother, her mother who a few seconds ago was holding her in her arms, squeezing her so tight and telling her not to worry, it seems to her that her mother has loosened her embrace and that she's... falling... weighing... that she, yes... is crumbling... it seems like she's sagging, soon the weight... her mother... her mother's weight... on her, Ida, Ida who is surprised and

Mom? Mom?

her mother not answering right away,

Mom? Mom what's going on, Mom what's wrong? What's wrong?

and Marion

Nothing, sweetie, nothing

Nothing,

• • •

Mom, are you sleeping? Why are you sleeping?

No I'm not sleeping, it's okay.

No Mom it's not okay, it's like you're sleeping on me, what's—

And Marion tries to get up and she can't; she's having trouble staying awake now, but it's okay, everything's happened so fast, like an image returning to her brain, when she hears Ida just behind the bathroom door, she hears her shout so loud, and Marion, in that moment, realizes that not only did Ida not leave like she wanted her to, like she should have tried to, but she's come to listen to this conversation from which she's understood in a few words everything her mother has labored to not let her hear until now, everything she'd promised herself she'd never tell her or if she did then with the details changed, maybe adapted, and most of all taking the time to explain it to her with words chosen to smooth over the reality, to make it more presentable, less violent and less unfair, maybe, or cruel, telling her each thing, each detail of the story, because she'd have felt her daughter was ready to hear them, if one day it were possible to hear them, and now it was too late and after Ida's shout there was Denis's movement when he pushed Marion to get out ahead of her—she knows what he's decided, the reason he came, she knows it just as she knows she's been waiting for this moment since the day, since even the minute she boarded the train holding her round stomach with both hands under it, in a semicircle, with all the people she encountered during her trip who offered her their seat—had she ever met such kind people in her whole life? would she, without her daughter, have ever managed to meet someone as kind as Patrice and those strangers on the train?

Now Marion thinks of him and sees him again, downstairs in the dining room as she hurtles down behind Denis who's running to catch Ida; she's a few meters from Denis and catches him just as he's about to go down the stairs; she throws herself on him, he topples over, holds onto the railing and she hits him with all her strength, she grabs him by the hair, screams at him to leave her daughter alone, she scratches, shouts, and Denis stops and turns around and tries to punch her in the face but she pushes him, he's about to fall down the stairs but catches himself as he yells at his two brothers to stop Ida from leaving, to restrain her, but the other two don't react quickly enough, and it's Patrice who reacts once Ida has already crossed the room yelling—he who understands because he heard everything, because he's known everything all along, including what he pretended not to know, what he thought he didn't know but deep down he'd understood from the beginning, she suspects, he's always known who she was and maybe he's even the only one to have ever known, the only one to have accepted it, to not have taken that little air of superiority she encountered so many times in men, and in women too, though with the women it was coupled with desire and jealousy or with blissful admiration, no, he desired her for herself, knowing who she was, she's never doubted his love for her, yes, how could she have found anyone better than him for her daughter and for her? how could she have found a better refuge to escape Denis, to escape her past, to escape that life she'd had to drag along, and thanks to him, thanks to the giant shadow of this man, this improbable lover, she'd been able to hide. And him, Patrice, she sees him throwing himself on the two brothers and sees Ida taking advantage of the moment to leave, letting the door slam behind her, she flees and Denis goes out too—he pushed her so violently that she's the one who fell down the stairs, who slid down several steps, holding herself up the best she could but leaving him time to get away and cross the room and exit the house—the door slams, the two brothers are yelling now and Bergogne is trying to restrain them, Marion joins them, she hears the two others ordering them not to move, to stay there, but nobody's listening to them anymore, not even the two girls who are still in a corner at the back of the dining room and sitting on the ground, hands on their head or in front of their face, as though their hands could protect them from the gunshots that are coming.

The first, which rings out in the house: it's Christophe who fires it.

He aims at Patrice and misses—Patrice who's turned away so fast in an about-face and darted toward the living room with huge strides—that's when Christophe fired—the bullet vanishes, he's too worked up and Patrice is moving too fast, even though he's not running, just strides that carry him at full speed from the dining room to the living room, and he no longer hears the voices yelling behind him, Christophe

Hey where do you think you're going?

ordering him,

Get back here!

and Patrice not hearing, because his mind and his movements are all concentrated on what he has to do, grab the rifle from the wall and get the cartridges—which is the longest, which would leave Christophe time to come into the living room if Marion didn't throw herself on him to restrain him,

Stop,

her body facing his, her clinging to him and staring him down, provoking him,

What, motherfucker? What?

and him not responding, he tries to push her off, to not see her, to not look her straight in the eye because God knows what he might see if he got lost in that jungle, her eyes, no, but he loses just as many precious seconds while he's still yelling at Bergogne,

Where you going like that? The fuck are you doing?

and when he finally frees himself and makes it to the living room, Patrice is loading the rifle and that's maybe what Christophe sees—Patrice who's already checked the safety with his weapon pointed downward, who's already pressed the bolt to swing open the double barrel—because on the other side everything happens so fast that Patrice can hear only Christophe's shouts as he approaches, but he does what he has to do, he doesn't see Christophe threatening him with his pistol and telling him he's going to shoot if he doesn't come back right now—but Patrice has already taken two cartridges and loaded them into the double barrel and raised it until you hear

Click—

The break action closed again and now Marion moves out of the way, rushes toward the door where Stutter—

The second shot, almost point-blank.

Christophe takes the discharge from less than two meters away, right in the chest, the body is tossed and crumples against the living room wall, great spatters of blood and the body collapsing—Patrice is oblivious to everything, the explosion made his head spin, deafening him, before tonight he'd never heard a rifle shot in a closed room, nowhere besides in forests and fields has he ever heard the explosion of a rifle shot, and even if he was perfectly familiar with the force of the explosion he realizes he didn't know its sonic violence, even though he doesn't let it stun him for too long, because he lets the anger in him rise another notch, his anger that has nothing to do now but spread, take over all the space of the frustration and the tensions accumulated over the last few hours, and yet even as he trembles he has to stay calm, act as he does on a hunt—methodical, controlled, breathing to channel his emotions so they're all expressed at the precise moment he pulls the trigger, with a movement that manages to unite the arbitrary and his feeling in the moment he fires and the precision of the shot.

He takes three cartridges, loads one into the empty barrel and puts the other two in the back pocket of his jeans and, still not running, he returns to the dining room with his big strides, his enormous body suddenly appearing light and so quick—barely has he noticed the two girls crouched against the wall, almost under the stairs, still paralyzed, when he sees, now, near the French door, Marion and Stutter facing each other and him threatening her and holding her at gunpoint—she's no longer yelling because now Stutter is threatening her with the pistol and she knows he's going to fire, he's dying to do it, his desire is twisting his face and pasting a kind of vain and painful grimace on his face at the moment he sees Patrice appear, and right away he shifts his arm and aims at Patrice.

The third gunshot missing its target completely, Patrice hesitating to fire back because of Marion's presence, that second-long hesitation that the other doesn't make, Stutter—

The fourth gunshot ringing out loud enough to burst their eardrums and the smell of powder in the shrunken space of the dining room, and this momentary buzzing that sets in, whistles and transforms the space around them.

46

The fourth gunshot, then, is fired by Stutter, this time not missing its target: Patrice takes the bullet in the shoulder of the arm he shoots with—he drops the rifle and lets out a cry of pain in a voice even he doesn't recognize, has never heard from himself—and immediately the blood is spreading to his neck, near his ear. He thinks he's been hit in the jaw, that his face has just been torn off because the pain is so red-hot it floods the entire top of his body. Patrice falls, Marion cries out—she cries and her reaction isn't to run to Patrice, because she knows if she runs now Stutter will kill her, yes, she knows this, without having to think about it she knows it, and it's for this reason first, before the hatred and the anger, before the desire to slaughter him because he shot at Patrice, because he killed Christine, because he's Denis's brother, just because she knows he'll kill her if she doesn't do anything or if she runs to Patrice, for this reason, then, she throws herself on Stutter and bites the wrist of the hand in which he's holding the pistol, the hardest she can, until she draws blood, and his cry, his hand opening, the pistol falling, her kicking it so it slides far off somewhere, to the other side of the table,

Whore,

near the two girls who see the weapon but

You're nothing but a whore,

hesitate to pick it up, should they,

Whore,

Marion isn't listening, she's fighting—to the end, she fights, including when Stutter takes out the knife and the blade clicks in front of her, she doesn't have time to see it, doesn't know what's happening, the hand-to-hand is so fast, him throwing himself on her and does she feel the blade tearing the flesh and perforating her stomach, in what spot, tearing into her, burning her, blocking her breathing and her whole body pulls back but she fights, pushes him away with both arms, with a strength she didn't know she had, she pushes him so hard that Stutter is surprised too, thrown off balance and against the wall, this time isolated enough that—

Soon. Another shot—the fifth. The fifth is coming. Then the sixth. All of it very fast, because Patrice has picked up the rifle and he fires it the best he can, in spite of the pain, the blurring vision, the fifth shot misses its target and the cartridge is lost in the wall above Stutter; Patrice adjusts, aims, and shakes, wobbles, aims again and this time he can be satisfied with the effort produced, and when he fires his whole body falls backward, heavy, like an inert mass, a dead weight, and even if he wasn't able to combine the necessary power and precision in spite of it all he managed to get somewhere: he fired so fast, twice in a row, almost in succession, because he realized that Stutter had taken out his knife and that he'd stabbed Marion, that the moment he was alone against the wall would be very short, Bergogne fired so fast that Stutter cried out with a cry that covered Marion's, Marion, Stutter, his shout, and his blood above the thigh, the pain of the gunshot that caved in part of his thigh, he sticks his hands in his blood and his eyes open wide, filled with tears, he shakes, collapses, incredulous, murmuring what, begging what, eyes blurred with tears asking Marion she doesn't know what, whether he's trying to ask for her forgiveness or why they shot at him, or to say he doesn't understand and that his terror now is the thought that they'll finish him off, the fear they'll deal him one last blow, without pity, giving him the gift of a night without end out of disdain and scorn for his life, his life of panic and submission, and he slumps as though it's his life weighing too heavy on his body, which cracks and falls, his life with its back to the wall, a ten-year-old kid leaving Marion and Patrice for a second with no reaction, or with one of disgust, of pity.

Marion lets him cry—she doesn't feel the wound in her stomach, she's thinking about Ida and running as best she can toward Patrice, surprised to discover she has to bend to move forward, but she moves forward, she goes to Patrice, who also has his back against the wall, but on the other side of the room, in the corner of the living room. His legs are stretched out, two cartridges in his hand, and the rifle is next to him. He's having trouble breathing, worried he'll faint; his sweat is mingling with his blood, Marion comes toward him and tries to help him and she shouts to Nathalie,

Girls, Nathalie, Lydie, girls,

and he doesn't know if it's really true,

Patrice,

what he hears when he feels the hands on his face, his wife's voice,

My love,

is it really the heat of her hands he feels on his cheeks, is it really her placing her lips on his, telling him she loves him and him wondering if he's not crazy or already dead, in spite of the pain and the burning in his arm.

And now, now it's time for that other gunshot—the last.

Marion picks up the rifle. Marion takes the cartridges from Patrice's hand and he wonders what she's going to do—Marion's look, so determined, as she takes the rifle—because she knows how to use it, he's aware of that; he remembers his astonishment, back when they met, when he took her hunting and she shot and hit her target several times, quite the huntress, with the patience for it—but the horde of guys and the glasses of mulled wine on the roofs of the cars, the orange vests against the gray green of the foliage and the high grass in the fields, the dirty jokes and the two-bit gags, the stultifying conversations about stories she didn't know anything about or didn't give a shit about, yes, it was quite clear to her that her place wasn't there. That was one thing she learned very early on, to know where and when you're in your place. For a girl, that's the kind of thing it's best to know early on, especially if your mother doesn't take care of you and you have no father, if you wander around all day with your girlfriends and quickly start flirting with theft and sex, when there's nobody but an old friend of your mother's who took a liking to you and takes you in from time to time, because you don't disgust her too much with your smell of dirty squats, your piercings and your two filthy dogs that you'll leave at the SPCA because they're as washed out as you are; you'd like to be able to say one day, to all the prim and proper ladies you meet, that you, you'll never be in your place, and that what you need is a nice fat guy, comfortable as a security blanket, to hide you at his house, without suspecting that you could wind up actually loving him; because now Marion has to stop the fight against herself; now she understands that this place he offered her, she's never really known how to accept it, that it was difficult for her to receive it, this place, because she has to admit she didn't want to love this big comfortable and accommodating man who doesn't match any of what she believed she could or should ex-pect from a man, solely because she'd been unable to imagine that anyone could really love her, *her,* that anyone could make a place for her, and unable to think that a man who could love her was also lovable because he was capable of loving her, and not, as she'd thought, as she'd fought with herself to believe, worthy of hate or scorn because he loved her, as though he had to be a fool to love her, or as though to love her was already to be worthy of her scorn or her indifference.

Now she doesn't know what hurts her more, that fall on the stairs because of Denis, the knife wound in her stomach, or this heat rising inside her, a numbness, the sounds dying out or growing distant or dilating, or whether it's seeing everything she failed at with her husband by refusing the love he offered her—all this because she'd known so little of love that it frightened her and repelled her when it came to her—just as Patrice, now that she's leaving the house with the rifle, wonders if he shouldn't shout at her to stay, if he shouldn't beg her to stay; he knows what she wants to do, she has to do it if she's going to have a chance at being through with these stories to which he'll never have any access but Ida's presence, because Ida is a pure presence in which worlds coexist that know nothing of each other, that reject each other— slabs of the past and swathes of the future in which Patrice doesn't even see himself, because he's not sure of anything, but sure, in spite of everything, when he sees Marion's two co-workers coming toward him, when one of them calls the police and the other the fire department, that something is ending tonight, something that concerns not only Marion and her past but that concerns him too. And maybe, as he revisits this day, as he thinks back to his hand shaving that beard that didn't suit him—the desire, the good and fine desire to make her happy—he'd like to tell Marion,

Hey, I forgot your present in the kitchen,

to tell her,

You know, I feel so lonely sometimes,

to tell her,

I'm just an old wretch who sees whores, in town, because he's lucky enough to go into town. And his sexual frustration makes him ashamed, perhaps, but he knows the violence that lays waste to him, that would be so much worse if there weren't the release of sex and hunting from time to time to convince him that life can go on this way without blowing it all up—without blowing himself away, himself and his life, a bullet in the head like one of his old friends who worked at the factory—oh yes, how he hides from himself his desire to put a bullet in his head each day—and not just because his work is difficult—he'd like to tell her how each day she and Ida save his life, without even knowing it. And then all he wants to keep, even in the silence of his loneliness, the pain of living through it, his work that he's always loved with a passion and his hamlet and his animals and of course the three lone girls of his house, three girls and three ages like the love of three women, so much love for one lonely man, like him, yes, Christine and Marion and Ida—Ida more than anything.

He'd like to say all of this. He says it to himself, and that's already something.

Because Marion has left.

Marion advances with the rifle and very quickly has to stop, the wound hurts more and more. She puts her hand on it and soon it's covered in blood—blood, she knows blood, she's never been afraid of it, not worth freaking out about. So she advances and enters Christine's house, she doesn't pay attention to the kitchen because above all she's looking for her neighbor, sure she's going to find her dead somewhere in the studio, or higher up, in her bedroom. But when she gets to the studio and she sees the blood-stains, she doesn't understand what's happening. It occurs to her that maybe no, Christine hasn't been killed, that she hasn't—and then why is she coming back to the kitchen, why does she have to come back through here, or maybe it's that finally this detail has taken its place in her mind: the open drawer, the cupboard with its open drawer, yes, why all of a sudden does she think this is what's strange, she doesn't think of Christine or of Ida, she won-ders where that son of a bitch Denis is, she tells herself he wasn't able to catch Ida but she knows he's somewhere, she knows he's going to come back, he's not going to just do nothing, and yet she finds herself in front of the open drawer and sees that the Samsung box isn't quite in its place, that the box has been opened and sud-denly she's scrambling, she lets the rifle fall to her feet, the collision with the tiles which she doesn't hear, she doesn't hear anything, doesn't see anything but the telephone box that she opens and fuck the key to the house next door isn't there and she understands that Ida hasn't gone far, that she didn't listen, that she didn't run away down the road but went to hide in the house for sale—she can't hold back a cry, and what if Denis followed her, what if Denis saw her, where is he, she wonders where he could be because he's disappeared completely. Marion tells herself she has to stop him, not suspecting that he, from where he is, is watching to see who's coming in and out of Marion's house, and Christine's house too.

Because his first reflex, Denis's, was to go look for Ida not at the neighbor's house but in the stable. All he found there was the not yet entirely cold carcass of the German shepherd. Yes, his rage. He gives the carcass a rageful kick, he kicks the dead dog's body with all his might; it flies up and lands with a dull noise. Denis—nice Denis, as they used to call him when he was very little, because everyone thought Denis was a name only nice boys had, all that kindness he'd ended up pantomiming throughout his childhood, aping in his adolescence, and spitting on endlessly in his adult life—as though there's no score to settle but that of the supposed niceness to which his name was meant to bind him, no, all that's over now.

He leaves the stable after making sure Ida's not here, and suddenly, in the yard, he becomes aware that he left Stutter his weapon. He doesn't like not having a weapon. He wants a weapon. He heard the gunshots, he doesn't know what's happened. Crossing the yard, he has no thought but to go to his car and get the crowbar he put in the trunk; now he's armed and he feels ready, in the darkness, when he sees Marion coming out of Christine's house—yes, it's her, with a rifle in her hands. She's holding herself strangely tilted, almost bent. He thinks she's wounded and rather than run toward her he lets her run, wondering where she's going: and he realizes where she's leading him. He can tell she's in a bad way and, now, he arrives slowly in front of Christine's house; he doesn't enter, looks through the kitchen door, then yes, finally he does enter and takes the same path Marion did, that Ida did, he sees the traces of blood and the disorder of the house. He doesn't hear anything, no noises, he doesn't try to find out more and retraces his steps into the kitchen. There are spatters of blood on the ground, drops that are recent, very recent. He follows them and can't help but smile. He understands, yes, he exits the house and he's out front, more drops, there are some, just like that, drops sinking into the night—Denis takes his cell phone and turns on the flashlight; the beam casts its spectral whiteness on the ground, the halo accentuating the irregularities, marking the shadows in black on the ground—the holes, the bumps, the stones sticking out, the cracked cement, the tufts of grass—and the blood, the drops of blood tracing something like a line toward the empty house that soon rises up before him.

He has to push the door and doesn't make a great effort to do so: it's not totally closed. He projects the white light onto the doorknob—more blood, blood still on the knob, he touches the blood with his fingers and stops to lick them,

I think it's not looking so good, my little Marion, not looking so good is it my little scoundrel?

and in the house the flashlight from his phone still spatters the ground with its cold white light, and he's still following the trail of blood, the drops seem to him to be getting fatter, or else they're dripping more continuously, could be, he doesn't know. He walks simply following the path indicated to him and, as he should, he thinks of Hop-o'-My-Thumb,

Marion? What's happened to you, Marion?

then he says nothing, he keeps advancing. He takes a few steps into the entryway, into the dining room, and he stops. With a motion of his wrist he moves the light from his phone and follows the line of blood drops. He sees that they lead upstairs, he advances slowly, suspicious—she has a rifle—he's not that foolish, won't let himself be taken like that. He suspects that upstairs she's waiting for him, maybe she's preparing to attack even though he suspects she's with Ida. So he advances very slowly and turns off the light on his phone—he takes the rail of the stairway with one hand and with the other holds his crowbar firmly. He starts climbing the steps—very slowly—he advances, making as little noise as possible, and that's why Marion and Ida start when they hear him—his voice coming up to them, taking a tone that's too calm, too sweet,

Marion? Marion? Why'd you leave? Why'd you deprive my daughter of her father? You think you had the right to do that? You think you can just do that? No, Marion, you can't just do that, not even you.

And, in the bedroom, Marion are Ida are huddled against one another. Marion has her hand over Ida's mouth to muzzle her, they can't make any noise—not the slightest, she knows her own breath is too heavy—now she tries to pick up the rifle but to do so she has to break away from her daughter—she has to pick up the rifle—I'm going to pick up the rifle and she makes the sign to Ida to tell her to keep quiet—index finger over the mouth—she picks up the rifle—

Marion? Why didn't you say anything to Ida? You could have told her her father isn't that old tomcat, no? Ida? Can you hear me? I'm your daddy. Ida. I'm the one who's your daddy.

And the voice is ever sweeter and softer and slower as it approaches, making itself more precise; Marion does everything she can to concentrate and she takes the cartridges from her pocket. She knows—takes off the safety—presses the bolt that swings open the double barrel—she's clumsy with the movement and the end of the barrel touches the floor with a sharp noise—Ida moves away from her mother—Marion stopping everything—no longer moving—she feels the heat rising inside her and burning her brain, blurring her vision—her breath—and then she feels her mouth so dry all of a sudden and she wonders if what she's hearing in the distance is the siren of the fire department or that of the police—she can make out the noise but it's very far away—she gathers herself up and lets the two empty cartridges fall—

Plop, plop—

On the floor.

I know you're waiting for me, Ida, I know it, I would've liked for all three of us to take a trip together, but you see, your mother would rather it be just the two of us, your mother would prefer to stay here, you see?

And soon he has to slow down because he's about to reach the threshold. He tries to understand how the floor is laid out—soon he can see enough to understand and to see the doors—he sees very quickly which one is open and he's sure they're here. He feels it, he knows it. He can make out Ida crying very clearly and terror spreads in vibrations through the little girl's body, and he can't help but smile, and meanwhile he hears Marion, Marion letting out a sort of animal groan, her fingers shaking as they let go of the cartridges that fall, roll on the ground, she bends down to pick them up, something ripping in her chest but she reaches out her hand, finds them, takes them, her fingers close over them, it's impossibly hard to hold the rifle, she's cold, then too hot, at last she places the cartridges—one by one, hands trembling, fingers searching, managing only by immense effort and, when she brings the barrel back up and she closes the action, hearing the click that means the rifle is ready, it's she who crumbles, who can't take any more, and in the hallway Denis's steps can be heard more sharply now, Ida is crying, she's shaking her mother whom the night sky is illuminating in the gray and silvery specks of a light that's almost negative and Ida—

Ida? I'm your daddy. Ida?

Outside the sirens of the police cars and the firefighters and the voice,

Ida?

Ida hearing the voice so close, and the sirens of the firemen and the police as a silhouette takes shape in the doorframe, Denis entering the room and seeing, under the window frame, Marion's almost inanimate body, her hoarse, heavy breathing, her chest heaving, her hands trying to catch hold of something and, behind her, standing, Ida's eyes and the madness of Ida staring, the space of a breath, a burst, without Denis having time to do anything, the little girl drawn up—Ida pulling the trigger and letting the gunshot explode in a roar that cracks the walls of the old house, a fracas of stones and a smell of sulfur that will stretch over the farms and the fields, all the way to the river and the state road—the spot from which you could see the hamlet of the three lone girls, should you ever decide to pay attention.

The translator gratefully acknowledges the kind and patient assistance of Nicolas Richard, Daniel Medin, and the author, as well as the teams at Fitzcarraldo Editions and Transit Books.

LAURENT MAUVIGNIER was born in Tours in 1967. He is the author of several novels in French and is the winner of four literary prizes, including the Prix Wepler.

DANIEL LEVIN BECKER is the author of *Many Subtle Channels* and *What's Good*, the translator of books including Georges Perec's *La Boutique Obscure* and Eduardo Berti's *An Ideal Presence*, and the youngest member of the Oulipo.

Transit Books is a nonprofit publisher of international and American literature, based in Oakland, California. Founded in 2015, Transit Books is committed to the discovery and promotion of enduring works that carry readers across borders and communities. Visit us online to learn more about our forthcoming titles, events, and opportunities to support our mission.

TRANSITBOOKS.ORG